Sonju

A novel

What people are saying about Sonju:

One of feminism's many challenges is to express it in fiction without yielding to the temptation to oversimplify or overdramatize its evolution within individual women, and within those women's social and cultural milieus. When those milieus are unfamiliar to most readers, the difficulties can be compounded. *Sonju* does a masterful job of guiding the reader through all of this....

Sonju rings with truth and realism. The reader never questions the harshness of the culture nor her commitment to it. The reader admires the small but steady steps she and Korea make together. This story is truly one of a kind, unforgettable, and deeply satisfying.

—Kathryn Berck, author of *The Hostage, The Suppliant, The Hunter,* and *The Good Kinsmen*

Wondra Chang delights us with a story of family, love and the search for happiness. Here is a journey filled with romance, tragedy, and intrigue, a journey worth taking. Enjoy.

—Jose Antonio Rodriguez, author of *This American Autopsy*

Chang gifts us with an epic pulsing with life, fevered with longing, brimming with hope, and coursing with humanity. It's the kind of writing and storytelling that will settle into your heart, your soul, your very bones.

—Brian Petkash, author of *Mistakes by the Lake*

Sonju

A novel

by Wondra Chang

Lake Dallas, Texas

For my parents
Chang Rahk Chin and Yoon Yusoon

Part One

Seoul, 1946

At the sight of the two tall Americans in military uniforms walking ahead of her toward the Korean Central Administration Building, Sonju's heart beat a little faster. A month after America dropped atomic bombs over Hiroshima and Nagasaki, one of her Japanese classmates in high school came to her house to say goodbye and they had cried together. That was well over a year ago. Sonju took another glance at the broad backs of the Americans before she turned left to cross the cobblestoned boulevard. She tightened her grip on the thinking-stone in her gloved hand and hurried, swallowing the dry November air that scraped her throat, puffing white smoke with each breath. The eighth house from the corner, a newly whitewashed traditional house, Misu had told her. After a fourth knock, the varnished wooden gate opened halfway and a young maid's cocked head appeared.

"I'm your mistress's friend," Sonju said.

The maid opened the gate to let her in, and Sonju marched into the courtyard and on toward the living quarters. The maid dashed by Sonju, craned her neck toward the living room and announced in an urgent tone, "You have a visitor, Ma'am."

Misu opened the frosted glass door and her face lit up like the first flower in spring. "Ah, it's you." She hooked her arm into Sonju's and walked toward a room, her long satin dress whispering with each step she took. In Misu's marriage room, everything was new and shiny—freshly varnished paper floor, a double wardrobe against one wall, next to it neatly stacked floor pillows, and on another wall, three works of blue-and-white porcelain pottery displayed on a low credenza. One of them cradled Misu's thinking-stone like a prized jewel. Sonju smiled and touched the stone in her pocket. Kungu, Misu, and Sonju each had picked a small flat stone at a church garden when they were still in elementary school and called them "thinking-stones."

Sonju took off her coat and gloves. As she lowered herself to a floor pillow, she glanced at the embroidered flowers on Misu's pink skirt, then briefly dropped her gaze to her own grey wool dirndl skirt. "You're glowing, Misu. Marriage suits you well."

Misu's small cherry lips turned up and her thin eyes twinkled. She quit smiling and studied Sonju's face. "Something's wrong. Tell me."

After a slow sip of hot roasted barley tea, Sonju said, "This morning, my mother announced that my sister is promised in marriage. The wedding is in April. She said her daughters will not marry out of order." She ran her fingers over the pillow's piping until it turned a corner. "I'm not ready yet."

"When will you be ready? You're almost twenty."

"You're keeping track of my years too?" Sonju winced inwardly at her own shrill voice and this time said in a softer tone, "I want to marry Kungu." Then she asked, "What do I do?"

Misu's brows jumped up. "Marry Kungu?" She sighed as if weary, and said, "We should have stopped seeing him when we started middle school. There is a good reason why boys and girls are separated at that age."

Sonju wanted to say something just as condescending, but said, "But we didn't. The three of us swore lifelong friendship on the thinking-stones. I told you I wasn't going to quit my friendship with Kungu just because I reached the age of twelve."

"We were lucky we didn't get caught with him. But marriage?" Misu shook her head. "Surely, you have better sense."

Better sense? Sonju took a long breath and said to herself, patience, patience. "I also told you if you had been born into a family like his, I would still be your best friend."

Sonju watched Misu chew on her lower lip for a while and said, "Misu, it's my life to live, not my mother's, not anyone else's. The choice should be mine. Unlike our parents, we received a modern education, not that staid Confucian philosophy. For years, we talked about living a modern life."

"You and Kungu did."

It was a mistake to come. Crushed, Sonju tried again.

"Kungu and I understand each other. There are things we want to do. We will be equal partners in marriage having equal voice. How can I give him up?"

Misu's head moved side to side. "Your parents will never approve."

Sonju had resisted her mother's push for marriage for almost two years already. "One more year is all I need," she said. "By that time Kungu will have graduated and secured employment. We can get married then. Even if I have to elope." It wasn't as though she hadn't thought about leaving home for a year, but where would she go? How would she support herself?

Misu said, "You *can't* elope. What would that do to your family?"

Sonju wanted to argue what not marrying Kungu would do to *her*, but said, "I came here to see if you can help me come up with an idea to dissuade my mother." She rose to leave. Sonju had no choice now but to plead with her mother.

Early the next morning, Sonju knelt on the floor across from her mother in her traditional Korean clothes with her hair pulled in a tight knot held at the nape with a lavender jade hairpin. She looked at her impeccably dressed mother and marveled at how alike they looked with big features on square faces, yet so different in their temperaments and outlooks.

Her mother was studying a ledger at her low table sitting tall, mouth firmly closed, her gaze straight on the ledger, and not stirring. Sonju's heart thumped at the thought of what she was about to ask this steely, disciplined woman who was so contained that not a drop of blood would rise on her skin at the prick of a needle.

When she was five, Sonju discovered that not all mothers were like hers. She had gone to Misu's house and saw Misu's mother combing her daughter's hair, all the while talking in a soft, tender voice. After she was done, she cupped Misu's face and smiled. Back at home, a comb in her hand, Sonju had asked her mother to comb her hair. Her mother stared at the comb, then at her with a look of scorn. That was the moment her five-year-old heart crumbled. She lowered her head and retreated to her room like a scolded dog. She decided then not to ever need her mother. Now she had to plead with this same mother to wait one more year.

"Forgive me, Mother. I need to tell you something."

Her mother slowly raised her head, lifted her chin, and glanced down at Sonju.

After a quiet big breath, then again, and once more, Sonju swallowed hard and took one more deep breath. "I want to wait a year, then marry a Seoul National University student I know." Her own voice roared in her ears. Did she say those words correctly? She took another big, quiet breath. Like an animal confronted by a predator, Sonju kept her body still and waited for her mother to pounce.

After a long silence, her mother asked, "How do you know this man?"

"I have known him since I was seven."

"Why haven't you told me about him?"

"Because I knew you would not approve."

"Why would I not approve?"

"He is fatherless and poor."

Her mother kept her eyes on her. Sonju knew what that meant. She would have to say more. Her stomach coiled with each stifled breath. "He and his mother live at his uncle's house." Her mother continued to stare. Sonju buckled. "His uncle is a merchant."

"Then you know you cannot marry this man. From now on, you will not leave the house unaccompanied."

Sonju leaned forward. "I will not be happy with anyone else. He will graduate in a year. He will be successful. You will see. Let me wait, Mother. Please."

"Have you shamed our family?"

"No, Mother."

Instantly, she knew she had made a mistake. "Yes" would

4

have forced her mother to reconsider. Her future with so much promise was now wiped out. Her body went limp and her fingers had no grip left.

Her mother slammed the ledger closed. "We are done with this conversation."

Sonju shivered at her mother's last words as if a slab of ice had been thrown at her. Soon the heat of seething anger surged up to her neck. I hate her, she said to herself as she retreated to her room. If only she had said yes. It could have changed her life.

Her mother began to meet with marriage brokers, and after only six days, had a prospect—an engineering student at Seoul National. "You have a viewing in four days," her mother came into her room and told her, "His family is well established in Choongnam Province."

"Why are you rushing so?"

"The sooner the better, the farther away the better."

Sonju realized her mother meant to banish her. A torrent of sobs broke out. She cried into her hands, her arms pressed to her chest and writhing. The next minute, she heard her mother rise and leave the room. A whoosh of cold air rushed in and slapped her back. In spite of telling herself all those years that she didn't need her mother, her wrenching reaction told her otherwise. She was powerless. She cried in shame until she was exhausted.

The following morning her father called her to the men's quarters and said, "The engineering student is a good prospect for you. The marriage broker told your mother that he comes from a progressive family. You should be happy with him."

Her father had spoken.

Back in her room, she sat leaning on the wall and stared blankly with not even a fingertip moving. Beyond her window, one bright orange persimmon hung on a leafless branch. A brown bird flew over and perched. The persimmon fell.

Sonju knew what fate waited for her. It was the same for all women once they married—submission to a husband and his family. Submission—she was familiar with it. During fifth grade, in front of the whole class, her Japanese teacher had struck her open palms with a bamboo stick for speaking Korean instead of Japanese. Two quick strikes, sharp and hot. When she tried closing her hands, her fingers curled only halfway. She bit down on her lip and willed herself not to show tears. On the way to her seat, she saw her Korean classmates lower their eyes as she passed by. A lump came up in her throat. Back in her chair, she sat tall with steady eyes on the teacher and her chin out in defiance. Below her desk, her hand furiously rubbed the thinking-stone in her pocket, and she felt every angry nerve of the rising welts on her palms. She wanted to remember that pain. She wanted to remember that anger. That semester and going forward, she outperformed all the Japanese students in her class in every subject taught.

Disproving the Japanese superiority was easier than finding a way to defy her mother. But thinking back, she had, in fact, defied her mother for many years without her mother knowing: there was a walled church garden with a long wooden bench under a tree. She and Misu had found it one afternoon after school when they drifted away some distance from home. The place was quiet with rarely anyone passing through other than a smiling yellow-haired priest. The brick-paved ground was always swept up, and every season, different flowers bloomed and lush green plants crowded under evergreen shrubs. One day, a boy showed up. He came almost every day so the three became friends. He was one year older and helped Sonju and Misu with their homework. They played games and chatted before going home. That was the happiest part of her day.

On the day of Sonju's viewing, her mother entered her room, ignored Sonju's puffy eyes, and made her change into a traditional Korean dress. She said, "You will marry this man. His family owns extensive farmland and all the sons received university educations."

After her mother left her room, Sonju tried not to cry. She started counting instead while she paced and occasionally tripped on her long skirt. Before she reached four thousand, her mother called for her.

Sonju entered her mother's room and sat with her heavy, puffy eyes downcast. She felt the student's mother watch her every move. The woman told her to turn her face this way and that as if to study some merchandise. Afterwards, she nodded in approval toward Sonju's mother.

Back in her room, Sonju sat in the corner farthest from the door and rocked back and forth. How would she live without Kungu in her life? All her future dreams and plans included Kungu. She closed her eyes and saw his face when he was eight and every smile and every gesture since that time. She saw his long fingers, broad forehead and generous mouth, and his eyes that conveyed his thoughts and feelings without words. She could hear his calm voice, his slow release of the first word in a sentence, and his soft laughter. She loved him so.

Her dreams and plans had started long before. One day, she saw her Japanese classmates look at an open page of a magazine and giggle. When she asked if she might look at it, one of them told her to get a copy herself and pointed to the further right. She found a cramped used bookstore three blocks away from school where a small middle-aged man greeted her in poor Japanese. She grabbed a magazine with a photograph of a gathering of American people. In the foreground was a smiling boy looking at a girl adoringly. The following page showed pictures of boys and girls dancing. They looked carefree and happy. She told herself her future could be like that.

On the sixth day after the viewing, her parents announced her marriage date, February twenty-fifth, two days before she would turn twenty. She retreated to the corner of her room and whimpered like a beaten animal. She locked herself in her room and refused to join her sister and brother at mealtime, so a maid placed a tray of food at her door.

She recalled her first awakening of love for a boy. She was

fifteen. She was with Kungu sitting on the church bench. She pointed to an article in a Japanese magazine and waited until he finished it. "Did you read the part that Americans choose their own marriage partners?" He nodded. "What an idea!" she said, grinning. "In that case, I choose you, Kungu, as my marriage partner." Then he surprised her by saying, "I choose you, Sonju, as my marriage partner." Then they looked at each other and blushed. On the way home that day, she bit down a smile hugging herself to contain her joy. As days, weeks, and months passed, her imagination soared. On one particular night, she watched the moonlight through her window and imagined herself standing in its low glow in a lush garden somewhere. Kungu moved toward her with the scent of a gentle breeze of early summer air. She went to him. There, where the white flower petals glistened like silver, he gazed into her eyes and embraced her. Every night, she visited the same images again and again, folding her arms in an embrace while imagining Kungu's arms around her.

She woke from her reverie when her younger brother's high-pitched voice rang from the courtyard, "So, Mother, my sister's husband's family grows rice trees?"

Husband? Sonju sat straight up and heard her mother snort and say, "Rice doesn't come from trees. It is a grass. You have eaten rice three meals a day your whole life and you didn't know where it comes from." Sonju squeezed the thinking-stone and watched her knuckles turn white.

Maari, 1947

As the train came to a stop, its metal wheels screeched as if they resented having to halt. Sonju steadied her headdress with one hand, and with the other, lifted her shiny ceremonial coat and dress above her shoes. She took a step down. A whiff of heat from the engine and the acrid smell of burned coal surged up and prompted her to pause and turn her head. Her mother nudged her and said, "This is a short stop."

The moment Sonju's feet touched the ground, two men in crisp traditional garb carrying a bridal palanquin on their shoulders sauntered toward her and squatted a few meters from her. On the palanquin were painted writhing dragons with their open mouths and red tongues that appeared to leap out of the swirls of red, green, blue, and gold paint. Good luck? More like menace, Sonju scoffed silently.

She saw a dozen village women in long Korean dresses close around her, and before she had a chance to take a deep breath, strong arms on each side of her steered her through the palanquin's narrow door. Seated in the cramped box, Sonju straightened her voluminous dress, and thought how incredible all this seemed. In Seoul, a rented shiny black sedan instead of a painted box would have carried a bride. It all seemed a farcical play of the old Korea, but it was happening to her in real time.

Upon a woman's signal with her raised hand, the head palanquin carrier barked, "One … Two …" At three, the palanquin lifted and soon rocked and tilted with each step the men took down the steep slope. Sonju pushed her toes to the floor with all her might so as not to lurch forward. She remembered to keep her head modestly dipped, her face composed, and not to look anyone in the face, not even the laughing and bouncing young village children following alongside the palanquin.

To her left, on the uneven sloping ground, Sonju spotted patches of iced snow that the sun could not reach to defeat the winter's last stand. Nearby and far off into the distance, she could see nothing but stark, lifeless farmland. No rows of shops, no markets, no office buildings, no paved roads. Was this what her parents wanted for their daughter? Couldn't they see it was all a mistake? She remembered then that they were putting her away out of reach of Kungu. She tightened her jaw.

People's muffled voices came from the wedding procession trailing behind, and once in a while her mother's sharp Seoul accent stood out. Sonju stared at her clasped hands. A month ago, her sister accompanied her to the used bookstore, her safe place to meet Kungu since high school. She had hoped to see him and say good-bye, but after half an hour, asked the owner to pass her note to him. Even now the image of Kungu with her note in his hand caused her throat to close up.

After jolting and tilting for a while, the palanquin came to a wide dirt road below, then jostled uphill until it reached a large outer courtyard on a high plateau. At the end of the courtyard was a house with a series of papered doors and a long, narrow covered porch. As the palanquin proceeded toward the house, the wafting odor of meat, poultry, fish, vegetables, and steamed rice grew steadily stronger.

"The bride is here!" a boy yelled and darted in through the open gates of dark wood. Several people peeked out before the palanquin passed through the double gates and entered the inner courtyard. All around, people filled the courtyard like beansprouts growing in a bowl. They pushed, shoved, bobbed their heads, and talked in hushed voices in the slow dragging dialect of the central south: "A modern woman from Seoul, from yangban class, I hear."

"An aristocrat, eh?"

"I hope she's not a snooty city woman like you know who."

"Do you think she is pretty?"

"She looks pretty in an unusual sort of way, I would say. Big eyes, dark eyebrows, thick lashes."

"A straight high nose, wide mouth, and square jaw."

"You know what they say. A woman with a high nose has a difficult fate."

"Hush! This is her wedding day."

As soon as the palanquin stopped in the middle of the courtyard, two women in matching blue silk dresses broke out of the crowd and helped Sonju descend. Sonju raised her shaky hands in the formal bridal pose—her right hand over her left, palms down, her right thumb barely touching her forehead. After the three of them took their shoes off, the two women guided her to the anteroom where more people stood waiting. The crowd parted as Sonju and the two women proceeded to the middle of a large living room. She couldn't see much except the tips of her embroidered wedding slippers below her long red satin skirt. The women positioned Sonju at the front of the wedding table, and one of them told her to lower her hands to her waist. Her eyes still lowered, she found herself standing next to the groom in front of the roomful of old people in traditional clothing. They were sitting in a row, cross-legged and watching.

A booming voice rose from the opposite side of the groom, "The wedding ceremony will commence. The bride will bow twice to the groom and the groom once to the bride."

She lowered herself to the floor in a formal bow, and as she rose, took a quick glimpse of the groom in a deep purple ceremonial robe and a black headdress. He was boyish-looking, clean and well-shaven with a short nose and a pointed chin. He was stocky and not much taller than she was. He was a stranger.

As instructed by the voice, she and the groom stood side-by-side and bowed to his parents, to her parents, and to other relatives in the first row. Next, the voice had the two women come forward. "Now, the bride will bow to her first sister-in-law, the widow of the eldest son. And then to her second sister-in-law, the wife of the oldest surviving son of Second House."

As she knelt to bow, Sonju glanced at her first sister-in-law whose sallow face seemed to have never been acquainted with a smile. She was a thin, tall woman in her mid-thirties with her hair done in a married woman's style—a sleekly combed head with a tight bun at the nape of her neck. All the village women Sonju had glimpsed so far were wearing their hair in the same severe way other than her second sister-in-law who had chin-length bobbed hair.

When the bowing was over, Sonju became a member of the Moon family. From this moment on, in this village, she would be called Her Husband's Wife, Daughter-in-Law, Sister-in-Law, and eventually, Her Child's Mother, but never Yu Sonju. She had become merely a person related to someone else with no identity of her own.

Her eyes were ready to moisten when she sensed movements around her. People were getting up and sitting back down. Tables were set and food was brought in. Plates and bowls were placed in front of each person at the table. Chopsticks clicked and spoons clanged. A few women urged her to eat, but being the bride, Sonju was mostly left alone. Lulled by the jumbled voices and laughter together with ripening odors of people, food, and alcohol, her thoughts drifted to how her life would be different than she had planned and how she would be kept out of all the happenings in Seoul.

Some hours must have passed because the daylight began to wane. There were exchanges of parting words and bowing heads when Sonju's parents rose to leave. Sonju stood in the anteroom and watched as her mother glanced at her, then while turning, touched her hair pin. Her mother soon passed by the garden and disappeared through the double gates. Sonju thought this was how her parents planned to discard her, like an unwanted baggage dropped at the foot of people she had never met. The indignity of it! Her anger superseded any feelings of fear, pain, or sorrow of separation.

She bit her lower lip hard and returned to her seat in the room where the guests were talking among themselves. She lowered her gaze to the valleys and mountains of the shiny satin folds of her ample skirt and thought of the easy days of play and friendships with Misu and Kungu. During her middle school, she once asked Kungu if he had ever lied to his mother. He replied, "No, she tells me to have the courage to be always truthful and to be guided by my conscience, then

12

one day I would know that I lived a good life." Gazing at the boy who would not lie, Sonju had made a promise to herself not to lie again. She wanted to be worthy of his friendship. And here she was. Her marriage was a hoax. She would have to lie if asked why she married into this family, much below her class and a distance away from Seoul. She became angry at her mother again for putting her in a situation where she would have to lie.

A tap on her shoulder startled her. Sonju hadn't noticed that dusk had settled and the room was emptying out.

"You must be exhausted." Second Sister smiled and helped Sonju stand. Sonju followed Second Sister and was led to a room where under a low light from a bulb hanging from the ceiling lay a white cotton *yo* mattress on the floor. A folded, deep red silk blanket covered the lower half of it, and two pillows lay side by side at the head of the *yo*. Sonju turned her head away from the bedding to the opposite end of the long room where, against the wall, sat a large wardrobe and two identical wedding chests that her mother had sent a week before.

Second Sister assisted her in removing the headdress and the robe, and when Sonju thanked her, her voice, not having spoken all day, was stuck somewhere in the back of her mouth and sounded like someone else's. Then she hesitated, swallowed, and looking at Second Sister, asked, "What now?"

After a quick glance at Sonju, Second Sister said with a smile, "Your husband will be in shortly." She pointed at a floor pillow. "You can wait here."

Sonju slowly sank onto a pillow next to the red blanket. All the marriage talks, yet her mother had never told her what to expect on the wedding night. Glancing at the *yo* then at Second Sister, she asked again with a slight quiver in her voice, "What now?"

Second Sister's brows jumped up for a split second, then came a delayed smile. "According to the custom, on the first night, your husband will undress you. You will bleed, a sign that you are a virgin and the marriage was consummated."

Why would she bleed? She just had her menses two weeks

ago. Did the wedding in this village involve a ritual of cutting? Her breathing quickened. Before Sonju had a chance to ask, Second Sister said, "I laid an extra sheet on the *yo* for you. You want to save the stained sheet. Mother-in-Law may ask about it." She held Sonju's hand for a moment. "Your hands are shaking. I would stay here as long as you need me to but I think your husband is waiting." She turned and walked to the door.

Sonju dug her fingernails into her palms to stop the shaking and breathed in, held the breath, breathed out. Second Sister rested her hands on the doorknob, lingered, then left the room after a backward glance.

Shortly after, there was the sound of a man clearing his throat at the door. In his light blue baggy pants tied at the ankles, the groom walked in without the robe and the headdress he wore earlier. On his deep blue vest over the light blue shirt hung four amber buttons, which swung and caught the light from the lightbulb every time he moved. He took off his vest and gave her an awkward smile before he turned off the light. He sat on the *yo* and pulled her toward him. His grip was strong, and for a second, she was frightened. He proceeded to loosen the sashes of her bridal blouse and skirt and then another layer of blouse and skirt. She was left with only her underclothes. While he was doing the same with his clothes, Sonju turned clutching her underclothes. He laid her down, then stumbled in the dark to tug off the sash of her remaining clothes. She recoiled from his touch and clasped her clothes to her chest.

He whispered, "Here, move this way." He drew her to his chest, his hand roving on her underclothes again.

She pushed his hand away. "Please, don't."

"This is what married people do," he said. "Just ... stay still."

He undid the sash of her undershirt and pushed it up. She pulled it down. His breath hot and humid as he shuffled and untangled both of their clothes, then pushed her underskirt up to her waist and pulled her underpants off. She drew her knees up, but he pushed them down. He then got on top of her, fumbled, and opened her thighs with his hand. His flesh touched hers. She felt pressure, and a sharp pain. She swallowed a quick gulp of air as her hands grabbed the *yo*.

He rocked, grunted, rocked, grunted on and on, then moaned and stopped moving. Finally, he rolled off of her. A thick liquid flowed on her thighs and on the sheet. So much blood. He must have broken her inside. And the smell of the man lying so close to her, a smell so bitter and unfamiliar—she couldn't stand it. She wiped herself with the sheet and moved to the edge of the *yo*, and with haste put her pants back on. She turned on her side away from him and wept quietly because she hadn't been able to stop him, because she couldn't stop her mother.

They were silent for half an hour or more. Neither of them moved. Then his hand gripped her shoulder and turned her body flat on the *yo*. He got on top of her again. She lay passively with her body tense and her hands in fists. The pressure came. "It hurts!" she sprang up, screaming between her teeth.

She sat and sensed him move closer with his extended hand. She moved away, straightened her underclothes, and tied the sashes in several knots. She waited until he stopped stirring before she lay back at the edge of the *yo* with her back to her husband, feeling throbbing pain between her legs. She closed her eyes, saw Kungu under the moonlight in the garden and smelled his scent that always evoked the warm early summer air. Her husband started to snore. She felt his presence at her arm's length and wondered if she lacked a moral bearing for thinking of another man while lying with her husband. But what else did she have now that was still hers alone?

Bath House

Sonju woke the next morning, still clutching her underclothes. She sat up away from the *yo*, and pulling up both knees, winced at the throbbing pain between her legs. The blanket rustled. She looked back over her shoulder and met her husband's appraising eyes.

"You are up early." He sat up, stretching his arms and smiling as if nothing happened between them. When he planted his hand on the *yo* to get up, she turned her head, and feeling his stare on her back, held the front of her undergarments tightly in her fist. She listened to him dress.

Before leaving the room, he said, "Dear, after I wash up, I'll be at the men's quarters to have breakfast with my father. When you are dressed and ready, we will bow to my parents together."

An endearment uttered so soon, they were practically strangers … and last night—she closed her eyes in disgust. As soon as the door closed behind him, she lifted the blanket. Staring at her was a large patch of dried red stain with brownish edge on the stark white sheet, a mark that she was broken and could never return to what she was. She folded the bedding and put it away in the wardrobe and wondered if her nights from then on would be as dreadful as the first night.

A few minutes later, a maid brought a basin of warm water and a wash cloth. After she cleansed herself, she changed into a blue satin skirt and a high-waisted yellow satin blouse. She opened the papered doors and stepped outside onto the veranda. In front of her was a brown garden along a walkway and beyond the garden a low rise. Somewhere nearby out of her view, Second Sister was telling a maid to keep the children out of the house. Back in the marriage room, Sonju sat waiting for someone to tell her what to do next. She gazed at the papered doors and windows through which morning light filtered in and made the newly papered floor gleam yellow with varnish. Freshly applied wallpaper with light pink flowers seemed overly hopeful.

A maid brought a small breakfast table. Sonju had some beef and turnip soup with rice.

Soon after Sonju finished, Second Sister walked in smiling and asked, "How are you this morning?" This small pretty woman with immaculate skin and delicate features seemed always to be smiling.

Sonju clasped her hands on her lap and said, "I am fine. Thank you."

"Your husband and his parents finished their breakfast. I will take you to the men's quarters if you are ready. You will bow to his parents every morning with your husband. It's expected."

"Every morning?"

"Until your husband returns to school."

In the men's quarters, Sonju found her parents-in-law sitting side by side to receive her. This was her first time seeing them up close, and she saw that her husband had his mother's short nose and pointed chin and his father's smooth cheekbones and large eyes, though his smiling eyes that lit up were his own.

After Sonju's bow, Father-in-Law said, "It is such a joy to have you. I know it will be a difficult adjustment for you coming from a big city to a farming village. Your sisters-in-law will help you settle in."

Mother-in-Law said, "Follow what they do and learn how this household runs. Until your husband graduates and starts working, you will remain here."

Sonju must have looked baffled because her husband turned to her. "I will try to come home every weekend," he said as if his coming home were a favor to her. His eyes still on Sonju, he told his parents, "We'll leave you now. Guests will be coming."

In their marriage room, he flashed a smile and grabbed her arm, pulling her toward him. She quickly turned and freed herself and walked back a few steps.

He chuckled as though her reaction amused him and stared at her with those smiling eyes. "I like the way you look and the way you walk."

She didn't care. She just wished him to leave her alone. She walked out through the veranda down to the inner courtyard and came to the large galley kitchen where both sisters-in-law were cooking. They didn't notice her standing at the open kitchen door. "Is there something I can do until the guests start coming?" Sonju asked.

Second Sister turned and smiled. Waving her hand, she said, "Oh, no. You are the bride. You don't work in the kitchen the day after the wedding. Clan women and sharecroppers' wives will come to help. Guests will be here soon. They will come throughout the day. I wish Jinwon were here. She could have shown you around the house but she is at Big House."

"Who is Jinwon?" Sonju asked.

Second Sister pointed at First Sister with her chin. "Her daughter."

As if she didn't hear her mentioned, First Sister with a blank look on her sallow face spooned steaming rice from an iron kettle into a big serving bowl.

On her way back to the veranda, Sonju saw Second Sister's husband step down from the anteroom wearing Western clothes—a sweater under his casual jacket and wool pants—the same way many men with a modern education did. He was quite a bit taller than her husband with his father's facial features. He said a morning greeting and bowed to her deferentially, then leisurely walked into the direction of the men's quarters.

Back in her marriage room, she wondered what her husband's family expected of her. She had never done kitchen work before, but she could tell that she would be in the kitchen like her sisters-in-law. She didn't mind really. It would be something to do and an escape from her husband whose hands seemed eager to grab her. Her thought was interrupted when a maid whispered at the door that she was expected in the living room.

A steady flow of people came throughout the day. Bowing, more bowing. Maids set the table, guests left, maids cleared the table and set it again. Sonju sat with her hands together on her raised knee, her eyes downcast, and spoke a few polite obligatory words when she was referred to. Her husband on the other hand went on and on. "Yes, I will work for the government after graduation. As you know, my wife is from Seoul and I hope to get a job there. I will be involved in designing roads and bridges."

One of the guests nodded. "Yes, we need more roads and bridges. Look how our lives have changed since the Han River bridge was built and the railroads were laid."

To which another guest said, "The Japanese used them to steal our resources."

Father-in-Law said, "They took our farmland and took our rice to feed their people."

Brother-in-Law said, "They also took our very valuable artifacts."

"Not only that," a guest said extending his arm and shaking his index finger, "those leaders they tortured and killed were our national treasures."

Another guest said, "They didn't put our people in top positions." He turned to Brother-in-Law and said, "Look what happened to you. As soon as they left, you were promoted to vice president of your bank."

Sonju knew this to be true. The Japanese took care of their own. They lived entirely separate lives from the Koreans. Sonju's Japanese classmate, the one who came to see her before she and her family returned to Japan, had been always respectful toward Koreans and never called Koreans *chosenjins*, but still, she had never invited Sonju to her house. Then Sonju recalled her saying that she was born in Korea. Sonju now thought that, like her Japanese friend, she was an alien in her own country.

The guests were still talking. One said, "Japan left, only for our country to be divided into North and South. We didn't ask the Soviet Union and America to do that. It's *our* country."

As their conversation veered to the matters of family relations and farming, Sonju thought it was right that the nation was grateful to America. Korea would reunite one day, but without Japan's surrender, how long would Korea have been under Japanese rule, always being treated as an inferior people?

If only Korea had embraced America's more tolerant ways, she sighed quietly.

By early evening, the guests had left and family members had dispersed. The maids had cleared the tables. When Sonju finished stacking the pillows in a corner of the living room, a maid led two young children toward the anteroom. The little girl caught Sonju's eyes and tugged at the boy's arm.

Sonju walked down to the inner courtyard to meet them. From the kitchen, Second Sister rushed toward the children. "Bow to your new aunt." After they bowed with their heads down almost to their waists, the boy held his mother's hand, and twisting his body and hiding in the folds of her skirt, peeked at Sonju.

Sonju bent down to his height and asked, "What is your name?"

"Moon Chuljin."

"How old are you?"

"Four."

Sonju turned to the little girl. "What is your name?"

"Moon Jina." She spread two little fingers. Sonju smiled with a nod. In the distance, a train whistled. As if to catch the sound, off to the back of the house the boy ran with his sister toddling after him.

Second Sister said, "Your husband will leave on Sunday to return to school. Things will slow down then."

Shouldn't he have told her about him leaving on Sunday? Beyond Second Sister's shoulder, she saw a tall adolescent girl coming in through the gates. The girl had a lively face with sharp features. Her nose was straight and narrow, her intense eyes close together, her lips thin.

The girl came up to Sonju, bowed dipping her head. "How are you, Little Aunt?" She then turned to Second Sister. "I'm going back to Big House after I eat."

So, this was Jinwon, First Sister's daughter. A bold girl. Instead of asking for permission, this girl declared what she planned to do.

When Sonju's husband came into their room at night, took off his outer clothing, and sat next to her on the *yo*, she said, "I learned today you are returning to school on Sunday. Would you tell me things that concern me so I don't have to learn them from someone else?"

He turned off the light and lay on the *yo*. "You know I have to return to school. As I said, I'll try to come home every weekend."

What just happened? She opened her mouth to repeat her request, but he pulled her down next to him. Soon his stifling breath and eager body covered her. From a distance, she heard a series of mournful howls, some animal in pain. She squeezed her eyes shut and waited for it all to stop. When his sweaty body rolled off of her, she turned on her side. The howling faded into the distance. She listened to her husband's soft snoring, then moved to the edge of the *yo* where the cotton surface was cool. She closed her eyes and saw Kungu, his lean figure approaching toward her, his face lighting up with a smile. She smiled back.

The third day of her marriage went the same way as the day before with guests coming and going. On the fourth day, after the last guest left, Second Sister, wiping her hands on an apron, came to Sonju's room and said, "My children are in bed. Your husband is with Father-in-Law. We can bathe and talk in the bath house."

Sonju almost declined. Baring all to a person she hardly knew made her uneasy. Not even her sister had seen her without clothes. But she needed someone to talk to. So, in the warm, humid bathhouse, they avoided looking at each other as they disrobed, and proceeded in silence to soap and rinse themselves outside the bathtub. Afterwards, each covered her breasts with her hand and arm, and slid into the hot water that rose up to their shoulders.

After they exchanged a few awkward smiles, Second Sister asked, "I like your hair. Is it naturally wavy?"

"Yes. Every new teacher accused me of violating school rules." She was also accused of being vain to have it waved. "By the way," Sonju said, "is First Sister joining us?"

"No. When I ask, she just shakes her head, so I don't ask her anymore. She isn't much of a talker. She doesn't get jokes either. By the time I finish explaining, the joke isn't funny anymore."

Second Sister had more to say about First Sister. Their father-in-law sent First Sister to a girls' boarding school a few months after her wedding to finish out her high school education. She came back after a year, the same year her husband graduated from Seoul National. She had Jinwon a year after she returned. His job required travelling on a government project, and from one of the inns he stayed, he contracted tuberculosis and later died.

"How long was she married?" Sonju asked.

"Four years. When I married, she had been widowed for six years."

"What will happen to her, a widow at such a young age?"

Second Sister got out of the tub. Sonju followed, forgetting to shield her exposed body with her hands. "She will raise her daughter and live out her life here," she said.

While they took turns scrubbing each other's backs with a damp cloth, Sonju thought the same could happen to her if she were to become a widow. A reckoning. Something shifted inside her. It wasn't fear that she felt but a shapeless resolve, a resettling.

Sonju returned to her room and found her husband sleeping on one side of the *yo* with one leg out of the blanket. She observed the man her fate was tied to. Perhaps, like his father, he would value education for women.

Upon waking in the morning, he said, "You slept very well last night. I think you're adjusting nicely."

"I took a bath with Second Sister. It was relaxing. I learned that First Sister went to a boarding school after getting married." she smiled. "I wanted to go to university."

"You're fine without a university education," he said with a dismissive tone. "You have more education than most women. And you studied at Ewha."

"It's not the matter of being fine or not. That's what I wanted."

"You sound like Second Sister. She too says she had wanted to go to a university." He looked at her, and with a smirk, said, "You're married now."

She turned away from him to take a few deep breaths. As soon as he left the room, Sonju walked out to the veranda holding the blanket. She thrashed it, shook it hard, and repeated until her arms hurt and her anger dissipated somewhat. After putting away the *yo* and the blanket, she took out her thinking-stone from one of her chests. She rubbed the smooth surface, and rolling it, thought about Kungu.

A few minutes later, Second Sister came to her room smiling and asked if she had any clothes for the maids to wash. Sonju handed over some clothes and said, "You and I have something in common. My husband told me you wanted to go to university. Do you still think about it?"

Second Sister dropped her head. The silence that followed was so long that Sonju regretted asking. Second Sister slowly lifted her face, then looked at Sonju with glazed eyes. "It doesn't do any good to think about it. I had won a scholarship to study embroidery designs in Japan. I wanted to create art." A sad smile appeared on her face before she said, "I haven't embroidered since marriage. I always get interrupted."

Sonju leaned forward. "I'll be helping you around the house. Maybe one day we can embroider together. I'm not that good. You can teach me."

A maid announced at the door that the guests had arrived. They rose and held hands, looked into each other's eyes, then with reluctance, let their hands fall. Second Sister hurried to the kitchen and Sonju to the living room to look like a proper bride to the guests.

When there was a break between the guests, Sonju and her husband retreated to their room. During one of those breaks, he said, "You carry yourself well. I can tell the guests are impressed by you. They should be, considering the family you come from." And he made sure to bring up her family in every conversation, she noticed. She gave him a thin smile. Would she ever see something in him that she could like? She pondered for a moment and thought perhaps she wasn't being fair to him. She didn't know him well yet.

That night on the *yo*, her husband grabbed her hand. "Come sit," he said. "I won't see you for a week."

The minute she sat, he pulled her closer to him and rubbed her thighs over her clothing. She gazed at him. Not a bad face. A likable face actually. He was her husband. In time, they would understand each other better, and she might feel differently then. She must try to make her marriage the best it could be for both of them. With that in mind, she asked, "Will I be an equal partner in our marriage?"

His head jerked. Then with a chuckle, he asked, "Is that what girls from Ewha think?"

She hid her annoyance and disappointment at having to explain her point and said, "I believe a woman having an equal voice is good for a marriage."

"You're my wife. That's who you are."

She sat up straight, and with new alertness, said, "And you're my husband. Without being equal, I will always be less. No one likes to be less."

Instead of responding, he tried to lay her back on the *yo*. She shook his hand off, got up and walked out to the veranda to cool off. Ever since she was a child, her ambition was to one day do something for others that would elevate their lives in a meaningful, enduring way. She believed she could and knew the importance of fighting for who she was. Over the past four days, however, she felt herself being carelessly taken down by her husband. She could already tell this marriage would take a lot of effort.

The Hill

All was quiet on the veranda after her husband left for Seoul the following evening. In the grey remnants of sunlight, Sonju paced the length of the veranda back and forth. For the past six days, she had been caged in his house with his people in a place where she knew no one. Before the wedding, marriage was just a vague idea. She now realized that she would have to be alert so as not to be swallowed up by him and his people.

The next morning, not knowing what to do with herself, she put on one of the Western dresses she brought with her and went to the kitchen to get lost in busy, mundane chores. She stood by the open door of the kitchen and asked Second Sister to allow her to help in the kitchen.

Instead of looking at her, Second Sister took a quick glance at Sonju's dress and continued to prepare a breakfast. After she placed a spoon and a pair of chopsticks on a tray, she turned to Sonju and smiled. "I know what you can do. You can serve breakfast to Father-in-Law. He'll like that." She shot a quick glance again at Sonju's dress that came down below midcalf. Sonju must admit that every village woman she saw had on a traditional long skirt and long-sleeved top. In the past, she had worn a traditional dress only for special occasions to see the family elders. She knew it would be a challenge for her to keep the long skirt off her feet during everyday activities.

The next day upon entering the kitchen, Sonju noticed Second Sister wearing a Western dress over woolen stockings. She must have had the dress all along but hadn't dared to wear it. Sonju was amused and took it as a possibility that she could bring some changes in that household. To test that hunch, she asked with a casual air, "I would like to see the village. Is tomorrow a good day?"

Second Sister added a bowl of rice and warmed liquor on the tray. "Let's wait until Mother-in-Law tells us."

Sonju hid a smile knowing that Mother-in-Law would hear about her wanting to be out and know that her new daughter-in-law, only six days married, was asserting herself. That, at least, was something.

Other than serving Father-in-Law, Sonju had nothing to do except greeting a visitor or two or having a quick lunch with Second Sister in her room. During one of those lunches, she learned that of the three maids, one took care of the children at all times and the other two washed vegetables and fruit and dishes in addition to washing clothes and keeping the entire house clean. They had four servants who lived in the rooms facing the outer courtyard. Three of them worked in the fields along with sharecroppers. The fourth, the old servant, stayed around the house to run errands for the family and to take care of the upkeep of the house. There was a small kitchen at the end of the servants' quarters where the maids cooked for themselves and for the servants. This arrangement wasn't all that different from what Sonju was used to. Her family had only two servants and two maids at the house because the field work was done outside of Seoul.

Second Sister said, "First Sister and I do most of the cooking and mending clothes."

"I am not accustomed to doing either but I will learn," Sonju said, wondering what they did other than work. If she had known that she couldn't get books here, she would have brought some with her.

Finally, on the tenth day of her marriage, Second Sister said that Mother-in-Law gave permission for Sonju to visit the clan elders that morning. "We have to dress in traditional clothes when we go out," Second Sister said, "until the villagers get used to seeing us in Western clothes at home."

After breakfast, accompanied by Second Sister, Sonju stepped out of the house for the first time. In the middle of the outer courtyard, she paused to breathe in the air that carried a scent of cool earth that was pleasing to her. At the edge of the courtyard, a red dirt road snaked along a knoll, on top of which stood the skeletons of tall trees, and above those stretched an endless sky. She had believed her future would be wide open like that. Her eyes became blurry, but she quickly tilted her head back. "Look at that sky. So immense. I think I could become a poet." She kept blinking. When her eyes dried, she straightened her head.

"I don't see poetry in this sky, but I'm glad you do." There was a smile in Second Sister's voice.

They walked down the steep slope to the right and followed a long mud brick fence. Second Sister said, "First, we'll visit Big House Master, the head of the clan. He sat next to Father-in-Law at your wedding." She went on to explain that their father-in-law's grandfather had three sons. Big House Master comes from the first son, their father-in-law from the second, hence Second House Master, and Little House Master from the third. About thirty years before, Big House Master left the farmland under their father-in-law's care and moved to Seoul to oversee the clan boys' education. Three years ago, after Sonju's husband passed the entrance examination to Seoul National, Big House Master returned to Maari.

After making a left turn again, they came to imposing double gates. Once inside the gates, they followed a stone path winding through a garden. The entire compound was terraced upwards with a house and a garden on each level. They took wide stone steps to the upper level.

A maid saw them walk up, and after a bow, hurried to the main house and announced, "Ladies from the Second House are here."

Big House Lady came out to the anteroom, greeted them with a wide grin, and promptly led them down to the main level to the men's quarters where Big House Master was sitting in front of a low table, the folds on his face revealing gentle living and a good temperament. Behind him hung a large scroll of poems in thick brush strokes. Every item in that sparse room showed understated grace—nothing fussy, shiny, or competing. The visit ended with him welcoming her to the clan.

Sonju and Second Sister visited seven more families and skipped the minor clan houses. The next day was reserved for a walk to the interior of the village, Second Sister said.

When they neared the outer courtyard of the Second House, Sonju asked, "When do I stop being a new bride?"

"When Mother-in-Law lets you leave the house on your own."

The next day, Sonju and Second Sister started on the same narrow red dirt road but turned left this time and passed a cluster of small mudbrick houses with thatched roofs, then farther up the road a community well where several women were washing clothes.

In the midway along a well-trodden path, Sonju and Second Sister stopped near a gently sloping area where about two dozen low mounds lay. On the eastern side stood old pine trees, their trunks and branches bent toward the eroded graves. Second Sister said, "These graves belong to our clan's ancestors. They came here to settle over four hundred years ago."

Sonju's own ancestors were buried on the outskirts of Seoul, but here, with the dead so close to the living, she mused that there must be a few good stories about ghosts in long hemp robes rising from the graves at night.

They resumed their walk and came to a plateau, where about ten meters below, several one-story modern structures squatted along a wide athletic field.

Second Sister pointed at the site. "Big House Master had this elementary school built. Most of the teachers are our distant relatives either by blood or through marriage."

"Are there female teachers?" Sonju asked, her voice light and a half octave high.

"Yes, two. But they're not from here."

Someone was playing an organ at the school. Sonju looked in the direction of the music. She said, "I would have liked to teach but my parents believe only women from needy families work. I still want to teach one day."

Second Sister turned halfway and moved her arm in a wide arc. "The village stretches far out there even beyond the hills you see. Most of the villagers are our relatives. The closer they live to Big House, the closer the blood ties are. Everyone in this village knows everyone else, even the ones not related to us, so when a stranger comes, people get stirred up."

Sonju kept quiet and hooked dangling strands of curly hair behind her ear. Second Sister glanced at Sonju. "Your wanting to teach ... we bury those ideas when we marry," she said looking away, "at least here." They turned and trudged home without a word.

On their right, at the northern edge of the plateau, the ground fell straight down to several parcels of farmland, each demarcated by narrow dirt paths. On one parcel, a peasant in ragged clothes was tilling the soil, his skin leathered by the harshness of the sunlight of many summers, and his obedient cow pulling the plow. From the chimneys of scattered thatch houses at the end of the farmland, smoke curled up in lazy ascent, then scattered away into mid-sky leaving a trace of burnt straw odor in the air. Sonju's breathing slowed. She could picture herself living in one of those houses that had no fence to confine her, no gate to shut her in, and no one to answer to. Here was a place she could return to let her mind wander wherever it wanted to go.

That evening, at the sound of the train, she went to the kitchen and placed food and tea for two on a small table and carried it to her room. She waited. The family had already eaten dinner.

Her husband came into their room and asked her how she had been. She looked at him. His face, his smell, even his voice, were so oddly unfamiliar. He dropped his satchel on the floor and sat at the table. He wiped his face and hands with warm wet cloth she had set out on a tray. They had a quiet dinner together. Afterwards, she placed the table outside the door for the maid to pick up.

She was the first to speak, "Yesterday, Second Sister and I visited the clan elders and today we went to the interior of the village. There are some big ideas here—school for all children …" He grabbed a book from his satchel and began to turn its pages. "I was talking to you," she said.

"Hmph!" His eyes still on a page, he asked, "Do I have to respond every time you talk?"

"Yes. You wouldn't like it if I ignored you."

"But I talk about important things."

"I was talking about important things—sharing my experiences and thoughts with you." His eyes were still fixed on a page.

He didn't have to be short. I didn't say anything objectionable, she muttered to herself. "I may find what you say unimportant to me at times," she said, "but I'll regard it as important because you do." She then scooted over to her wedding chest and took out an English-Korean dictionary with curled corners from many years of use and one of five *Life* magazines she had packed in the wedding chest. She flipped the pages. Her mother had forced her into this marriage and look how it is turning out, she muttered to herself again.

"Can you read English?"

It took a moment for her to register her husband's question. "What? Can I read English?" Without taking her eyes off the page she was not reading, she said, "A little, with the help of a dictionary. I mostly look at the pictures."

The next day, he told his niece, "Jinwon, your aunt here can help you with your English." Jinwon stared at him with a blank face. Sonju wanted to hide. Why did he have to brag? She hurried to the kitchen.

When he was home again the following Saturday, she found herself avoiding him by going to the kitchen for this or that, and when he left, she was relieved. She continued to serve Father-in-Law his breakfast each morning, which appeared to be an unspoken favor. First Sister never served any members of the family or guests and mostly remained in the kitchen or in her room tucked away, not seen, not heard.

One late afternoon, the female clan elders were visiting in the living room. Sonju was serving tea and snacks when they made comments to Second Sister's four-year-old boy about having a new aunt. The boy started showing off and bounced around pointing at Sonju. "Yu Sonju. Yu Sonju. Her name is Yu Sonju."

When Mother-in-Law scolded him for calling her name, Sonju said, "I told him my name." Second Sister must have heard her son being scolded and rushed in from the kitchen. She tried to distract her son, but he wouldn't stop until Mother-in-Law grabbed him and spanked him, landing two loud slaps on his bottom. "You are a rude boy," she said. "You know very well you're not to call grownups by their names." Chuljin cried, and a maid led him out of the gate.

After the elders had left, Second Sister followed Sonju to her room, saying, "I'm sorry about my son's behavior."

Sonju smiled. "Actually, it was nice to be reminded of the days I was called by my name."

"You miss home, don't you?" Second Sister asked with a sympathetic look. "I have visited my family only once. My father was sent to prison for disagreeing with a local Japanese official." She dipped her head briefly before she continued, "It's not likely I will see my family any time soon. Never have I seen Mother-in-Law leave to visit her family. First Sister? She has never left Maari." She paused with an unconvincing smile and said, "But what married woman visits her natal home often or has visitors even?"

In her room, Sonju thought it might be just as well that she wouldn't be allowed to visit her family. They had already abandoned her, hadn't they? Sonju hated her mother all over again. Then came the image of her mother touching her hair pin during certain moments, and her heart softened.

Sonju was fifteen when at her grandfather's sixtieth birthday celebration, a woman pulled her into a small room in the back of the house and said, "Come. In this crowd, no one will notice us missing. I am your aunt." Sonju had never heard that she had an aunt. "My mother's sister?" she asked. The woman closed the door behind her and said, "Yes. Sit with me. You look so much like your mother. She and I used to be close." Sonju studied this woman with gentle eyes and soft voice. She wasn't regal like her mother, but she was gracious. Her aunt said, "When your mother was seventeen, she was to marry into a family close to the Imperial House. A month before the wedding, word that I was barren reached the man's family. Her betrothed, being the last of the line, needed a woman who was likely to produce many heirs." As she said this, a veil of sadness softly came down on her weak smile. She continued, "Even though Japan had annexed Korea fourteen years earlier, the royal connection mattered. More than it does now. The rejection devastated our family and humiliated your mother. For days, she hardly ate. She kept one engagement gift, the lavender jade hair pin."

Ever since that time, Sonju thought she understood her mother's decision to keep the hairpin. It was a reminder of her injured pride that strengthened her determination to have her daughters achieve what she could not. Sonju had often been sorry that she chose at times to see her mother in an uncharitable light, so she decided to try to think kindly toward her mother. But when she found her marriage difficult, especially after a trying conversation with her husband, she blamed her mother.

The first days of spring arrived with the smell of the dark damp soil after a quiet drizzle. A day or two later, shy heads of greens pushed up in the garden and on the rise. Soon afterwards, buds emerged on the cherry tree branches, and on them, tiny grey birds with red breasts chirped back and forth. It was spring, the season that had always awakened the restless excitement in her.

She took a deep breath and told her mother-in-law she would be at the hill near the school. Before Mother-in-Law's narrowed eyes landed on her, she dashed out the gate, and by doing so, declared herself no longer a bride. At the hill, she looked down where a patchwork of parceled land lay like a quilted blanket, and beyond, sat silent mud brick houses with thatched roofs. Standing there she spent half an hour or more by conjuring up images of Kungu's lean figure, his unhurried gestures, and the expressions on his face when he was telling her about something, when he smiled, when he looked her into her eyes. She was happy to find this refuge, a place where she could be alone in her own thoughts without worrying about being interrupted.

Two days later, she returned to the hill after lunch and again three days after that, and then every few days, each time anticipating to be reproached by her mother-in-law, but instead the family became used to it.

Mother-in-Law's Grief

"Here you are," Second Sister's cheerful voice flew in seemingly out of nowhere. "I don't know why I never thought to come here before," she said and sat drawing her knees up and pulling down her skirt, looking as though she was settling down for a long visit. "So," she turned to Sonju with a conspiratorial smile and asked, "what do you think about this village life?"

Sonju needed to tread carefully. She was still new in this family. "Hmm. I don't know yet," she replied.

"It's very different from Seoul, isn't it? I grew up on a farm outside the city, so this is not much different for me." After a moment's hesitation, Second Sister asked, "Why did you marry into this family? You must have had many proposals from families of higher standing in Seoul."

This question was not unexpected, so Sonju had a ready answer. "I kept putting off marriage. Then a suitor for my younger sister came along. An April wedding was agreed, so I had to get married earlier than I would have liked." She told herself she said enough. Not to give Second Sister time to come up with another question, she asked without a pause, "How did you come to marry your husband?"

"A matchmaker approached my father. After the viewing, my father said this was the best match he could hope for. I didn't dare tell him I wanted to go a university. On my wedding day, I felt like a cow being pulled by the nose."

Sonju's married-woman routine began early the following morning. It was the day for the workers to till and flood the fields. Before the workers came to eat breakfast, the two maids helped the Second House women in the kitchen. Sonju did the chopping, cutting, mincing, and slicing—the simplest tasks but still challenging for her.

A group of workers arrived. They ate on the rice straw mat in the inner courtyard and promptly left afterwards. Lunch and dinner were sent to the fields. All day long, Sonju had no time to rest, no time to think. She slept well that night without being troubled by the thoughts of her husband or their marriage.

As kitchen work became familiar to her, she stole time between meals to flip through *Life* and looked up a few English words in the dictionary to maintain her studying habit. She still wanted to teach one day.

When her husband came home that weekend, he still seemed a stranger to her. She knew so little about him. Perhaps there were things she could learn about him that she could like, something she could respect him for. She asked, "What is your goal in life?"

"To go as high as I can in my career," he replied almost automatically as though that was the most obvious answer.

"How do you do that?"

"Get to know the right people, those who can help me get there."

Trying to elevate the conversation, she asked, "Is success in career your only goal?"

"What else is there?" He looked at Sonju, baffled by her question.

That was it? Kungu had chosen to study business to become a banker to help poor people negotiate bank loans to start small businesses. Instead of learning anything favorable about her husband, she found him to be selfish and lacking sophisticated thoughts for a man studying at Seoul National. She said very little to him after that, but he didn't seem to notice her disappointment.

Once in a while, though, she caught him staring at her. "I adore you," he said to her. "Look at her. Isn't she perfect?" he said to others. To clan men, he bragged about her family's influence. Poor husband. That influence had been shrinking since the Japanese occupation in 1910. The next time he said he adored her, she looked at him, searching for flattering words to say to him and saw his eyes glint with a smile. She said, "I like your eyes when you smile."

During the week in her husband's absence, she thought that perhaps they would have a different kind of dialogue once he graduated and got a job in a city where they could buy books and magazines and educate themselves. They would have more to talk about. He might even become more thoughtful.

In the courtyard, Second Sister was telling a maid to take the children somewhere to play. Shortly afterward, she came to the veranda and sat. "You have a pensive look on your face. It's difficult to come to a family such as this, isn't it?" She extended her arm out as she said, "I want to leave this place and move to a city one day. To anywhere as long as I can live with just my husband and our children." She dropped her arm on her lap and released a big lung-emptying sigh. "I know it's not going to happen. Mother-in-Law told me a woman's body and soul belong to the husband's family once she is married." She shook her head. "Everything belongs to the husband—children, property, decisions—everything."

Sonju drew her knees closer to her chest. "Sometimes I think if I were born low, I could have worked until my nails disappeared to have my own money and live the way I choose to. What an idea. Right? Live the way I choose to."

Second Sister twisted her delicate lips and said, "Not even men can choose what kind of life they want to have. They have to do what their parents say."

"But men still have privileges and much more freedom than women do."

"Very true," Second Sister said, nodding.

Sonju listened to Second Sister tell a story about Sonju's husband dozing off during study when he was a middle schooler and waking up when a whip landed on him only to find Big House Master staring down at him and about how the clan was fierce in everything they did, and that education made it possible for the clan's new generation to marry well and to advance in society. "They believe in good genes too. You will hear them say, 'One wrong woman ruins three generations.' You and I met their requirements." Second Sister laughed, but her laugh didn't sound cheerful.

Since that talk, Sonju pictured herself growing old among her husband's family and becoming another Second Sister, or worse, First Sister. Sonju observed that in spite of her pretty smiles and polite words in public, Second Sister was quite lively and animated especially when she complained about being trapped in this household. On the other hand, First Sister was cocooned in her silence, standing in the same spot in the kitchen doing the same task day in and day out. Sonju wondered whether First Sister was always that way or if life had altered her. Regardless, First Sister should be treated with the respect due to being the wife of the first son, but she wasn't. One couldn't tell her from the servants or peasants. This slow moving, gloomy woman went about the day wearing a long, drab, muslin Korean dress, speaking rarely and being rarely spoken to.

Once in a while, Sonju would catch First Sister stealing glances at her, and when their eyes met, this awkward woman would turn her head. Every time that happened, Sonju felt vague unease at the difference between them in the way they were treated.

One day, after finishing the evening chores earlier than usual, Sonju took First Sister's hand and led her to the veranda. "First Sister, sit with me. I don't know much about you. Tell me about your husband. What was he like?"

First Sister rubbed down her muslin skirt a few times, and dipped her head. "… Umm, there isn't much to tell." She glanced at Sonju. Sonju nodded, urging her to continue. "I didn't come to know him that well," First Sister said. "Right after the marriage … Father-in-Law sent me to a boarding school in Seoul for a year."

"What was it like after you returned?"

"Umm … my husband traveled for his work. When he came home, his parents … There wasn't much time for me. That was my married life. Yes, it was." She rocked back and forth, her eyes drifting sideways toward the juniper fence at the end of the garden on the left. "It might have been different for me … umm, had I borne a son. I would've held a place in the family. Instead … I'm called a husband killer. That's my fate. Yes, it is."

Sonju gasped. A husband killer! This woman with the dull countenance of resignation and halting speech, beaten down, not belonging anywhere, rocking, and always looking down or away—and someone called her a husband killer. Sonju first felt rage, then bleak helplessness and sorrow. She stared down at the wooden planks of the veranda so overwhelmed by her emotions that she didn't notice First Sister quietly leaving.

The next day, Second Sister confirmed that it was Mother-in-Law who called First Sister a husband killer. "I heard it just once, but once you hear it, it stays with you."

Sonju didn't feel like talking to anyone after that. She avoided looking at First Sister because she would have felt even more helpless. Things got worse for her when one day she witnessed something odd and disturbing between First Sister and her daughter: Jinwon passed by her mother in the living room but neither she nor her mother acknowledged each other. Then several days later, it happened again. So, the next time Sonju was alone with Second Sister, she asked, "First Sister and Jinwon act like they are invisible to each other. Have they always been like that?"

Without taking her eyes off the heap of garlic she was mashing on a cutting board with the blunt end of a knife handle, Second Sister said, "When I married, Jinwon was eight years old. Even then, she hung around her grandparents most of the time. They doted on her, the only child of their first son." Scraping the garlic into a small bowl, she said, "I've never seen Jinwon go to her mother for anything."

That still didn't explain their strange behavior. Sonju argued, "They sleep in the same room. They must talk to each other."

Second Sister turned to Sonju. "Once in a while, I hear them talk but their conversation is very brief—a short question and an answer. I once saw First Sister giving Jinwon a small plate of rice cakes she had saved. Jinwon took them and walked away without saying a word."

Warm April sun filtered into Sonju's room through the papered windows and doors and made her mellow. She sat against the wall resting her hands on her raised knee and thought about her sister who was now two days married to a medical student who came from a highly-esteemed family. Her mother had at least one daughter who married well, she mused smiling. The warmth in the room made her sluggish and sleepy. She was eyeing a pillow to rest her head for a nap when Jinwon appeared with a gush of energy. "Little Auntie, come with me," she said with impatient haste.

"Where are we going?" Sonju didn't hide her irritation in her voice. She would rather not see or talk to Jinwon or Mother-in-Law for a while. They were both cruel.

"You'll see," Jinwon grabbed Sonju's hand, pulled her up off the floor and led her to one of the servant's rooms.

"Why are we …?" Before Sonju finished the sentence, they entered a room where Mother-in-Law was sitting on a small bench in front of a loom weaving fabric. Sonju was in no mood to talk to her Mother-in-Law. "I am sorry, Mother-in-Law. I interrupted you," she said and tried to leave, but Jinwon held onto her arm.

After she added one more row to the fabric, Mother-in-Law stopped. "This is my hobby room." She turned to Jinwon, and with a gruff voice, asked, "What do you want?"

Jinwon ignored her grandmother, picked up two pillows, and placed them on the floor. She sat on one and pointed the other to Sonju. "Grandma, we're going to tell Little Auntie about our family. Start with how Second Uncle got to marry his wife, please. I like that story."

Mother-in-Law snorted at Jinwon, then turned her eyes to Sonju. "My oldest son had died some years before, but my

39

second son, even though he was getting on in years, kept putting off marriage. Finally, my second son agreed with one condition. He wanted a woman from a long distance away." She turned to Sonju. "You have seen your father-in-law's deformed hand. My son believed deformities came from intermarrying." Sonju had seen Father-in-Law's left hand with no fingers and had assumed an accident. If only her parents had known of this major blemish in their daughter's new family.

Mother-in-Law continued, "My husband and I traveled to many places to search for a suitable woman. Every time we came home, I would show my second son the pictures of the young women I viewed but he would tell me not to rush. We were getting tired of traveling so much, and the farm needed our attention. Someone told us about this young woman not far from here whose family had originally come from North Korea."

Jinwon nodded to Sonju as if to say, "This is the part."

"I showed my son her photograph in her high school uniform. To my surprise, he put it in his coat pocket." Mother-in-Law smiled, seemingly lost in memory.

With a grin Jinwon said, "Second Auntie says her husband used to carry that picture in his wallet. She showed it to me. She thinks the story is funny." Sonju thought it rather sweet. Jinwon turned to her grandmother. "Now, Grandma, tell us about your marriage and how poor your family was."

Mother-in-Law smiled showing all her teeth. "We were poor. Very poor. On my wedding day, I could see my face in the breakfast bowl. My mother used a lot of water to stretch a spoonful of barley into a meal. My brothers worked on empty stomachs on other people's farms.

"We all heard about the young man in the Moon clan who couldn't marry a woman from his class because of his deformed hand. His family was looking for a healthy maiden from a healthy stock. My parents said his deformity didn't matter because he wasn't going to work with his hands anyway. I was relieved that my family and I wouldn't be hungry again."

Jinwon waved her hand to stop her grandmother. "Now, tell us about your name."

"My husband taught me how to read and write. It wasn't difficult at all to learn. I was already good with numbers."

"Next," Jinwon said, rolling her hand in a prompting gesture.

"Before marriage, I was called Pretty. My parents never bothered to give me a legal name because I was a girl."

After a quick glance at Sonju, Jinwon said, "Grandma, tell Little Auntie why you needed a name."

"My husband told me that if I didn't have a name, it's like I didn't ever live, and that I must have a name so that our children and our children's children and their children would know their lineage." With a wide grin, Mother-in-Law said, "He named me Chusun. That is my legal name." Mother-in-Law seemed proud of having a legal name as if it were a thing of honor. Sonju was touched by it.

Jinwon exclaimed in mock disbelief. "She had no name! Can you believe that, Little Auntie?" Then her head turned to her grandmother. "And besides, Grandma, your name sounds like a man's. That's what happens when you let a man name a girl."

Mother-in-Law gave Jinwon a scornful look and turned back to Sonju. "My Mother-in-Law died soon after I married, so I became the lady of the house. I got along with the clan's female kin and handled many family affairs and chores." She leaned an arm on the loom, her smile slow and widening. "You should have seen your father-in-law when our first son was born. He was so proud of the baby boy with no deformities."

"That's my father, that baby." Jinwon said to Sonju.

Sonju gave Jinwon a nod. Second Sister had told her some time ago that some of Mother-in-Law's children died young. Now she wondered if those early deaths had anything to do with birth defects. "How many children did you give birth to?" she asked.

"Seven. Three died young. One died at birth, another choked on steamed sweet potato when she was three, and the third one was found dead one morning. He was two months old." She nodded several times to herself. "Then my first son ..." She stopped and stared into the distance for a long moment, then turning back to Sonju, said, "He did everything early—walking, talking, reading. He was the smartest boy in the clan. He went to the best schools in Seoul starting in kindergarten, then Seoul National and then promotion after promotion at his work." She seemed to come alive by the memory. The corners of her mouth rose, her eyes were dreamy. Then a cloud came over her face. "The day my son died, my exceptional son—he was only twenty-six—my world changed." She choked back a sob, and her body slumped. She recovered, but the lines on her face seemed more pronounced as if pulled down by the weight of her loss.

After seeing the death so grieved, Sonju could now understand her Mother-in-Law's anger thrown at the widowed daughter-in-law however misdirected that might be. Mother-in-Law continued, "My second son became the oldest living son. He had never been a very healthy boy. He often fell ill after some hard, physical activities."

In tender voice, Sonju said, "He seems healthy now."

"That's the worst thing, a child dying before the parent. It is so unnatural. And I have experienced it four times over."

Sonju took Mother-in-Law's veined hands and stroked them. "Leave me." Mother-in-Law said in a thin voice.

Jinwon got up to leave. "I'm going to Big House. I hope I find some clan boys there."

Sonju returned to her room, thinking about tears Mother-in-Law would shed alone. Her heart ached. She must be good to her mother-in-law, she said to herself.

Rice Planting, Fall Harvest

Not long after Sonju returned to her room, Second Sister came in smiling and sat down. "I saw you and Jinwon going into Mother-in-Law's hobby room. What did you talk about?" She asked as though she had the right to know everything that happened in the family.

Sonju's heart was still heavy. She dreaded a talk that would certainly excite Second Sister who often criticized Mother-in-Law when they were alone. She said, "Jinwon coaxed her grandmother to educate me about the family. Mother-in-Law told me she didn't have a legal name."

"I've heard that. Because she was born a girl. Yet," Second Sister shot her index finger up in the air. Sonju braced herself for Second Sister's speech to turn feverish. Second Sister said, "She tells Chuljin right in front of his sister that he is special because he is a boy and that he'll be the head of the family one day. Do you know why we women are still treated the way we are? Because of mothers-in-law like ours."

Sonju had to take a deep breath. How did her neutral comment turn into yet another opportunity for Second Sister to vent her grievances against Mother-in-Law? Sonju pulled her lips in.

Second Sister reshuffled her skirt, then her words came again, "I'm *not* going to force my children into marriage. I'm *not* going to force my son and his wife to live with me and my husband. And I'm *not* going to enslave my daughter-in-law." Her face flushed as she thrust her index finger up into the air every time she emphasized the word, "not."

Sonju waited until Second Sister's face had gained her normal peachy complexion to ask, "Mother-in-Law said your husband was a frail youth. Is that true?"

"Yes. Even though he looks healthy, he isn't all that sturdy. After the wedding, Mother-in-Law wouldn't allow us to bed together for a month. She said, 'He has a pretty wife and he will overexert himself and get sick.' She kept me up nights teaching me how to play cards until my husband fell asleep. I was so tired that I often dozed off while playing. Nothing happened between my husband and me for a month. In a way, I was glad. By the time we consummated, we were familiar."

Sonju imagined if her husband were not endowed with great physical health, she too might have had a month to get to know him better and learn what to expect before they consummated. She sometimes thought that her wedding night's experience colored her perception about intimacy. She had once tried imagining Kungu in bed with her while under her husband's weight, but only ended up feeling contempt for herself for the wrong of it.

On the day of the rice planting, the Second House women and maids woke up at dawn to cook. Soon the workers swarmed into the inner courtyard and sat on the straw mats and crowded around the tables waiting for breakfast. Maids carried food to the tables one tray after another. Just before noon, lunch was carried to the fields. The same busy work repeated for three more days. On the fourth day, three village women came to the kitchen and placed food in large baskets to carry to the fields. With the baskets on their heads, they were ready to leave.

"I want to follow them," Sonju said.

Second Sister gawked at her and chuckled. "A field trip?"

"Yes. Let me carry something."

Sonju carried water jugs, and trailing behind the women, walked beyond the underpass of the railroad toward the rice fields. The women chattered among themselves and laughed.

"What are you laughing about?" Sonju asked.

"We were saying that you talk so fast with that Seoul accent, we missed half of what you said."

"Do you want me to speak slowly?"

"No. We're getting used to you now."

Sonju looked up at their baskets full of bowls and food. "How do you balance a basket on your head?"

"We have carried things on our heads since we were children," one of the women said. "But, Second House Lady, why do you want to go to the fields?"

"I want to see the rice planting. My family has overseers to manage the family's farmland on the outskirts of Seoul, so I never saw our farm. My younger brother thought rice came from a tree."

The women grabbed their baskets, exploding with laughter. "Rice from a tree," they repeated it and laughed until they reached the fields. Sonju laughed along until a chorus from the distance brought her attention to the men and women stooped in rows in the flooded muddy fields, singing. They were planting rice in concert with the rhythm of the song, their faces steady on the seedlings, their legs bare all the way to the knees, water up to their ankles.

Sonju and the women placed the food, water, and liquor on rice straw mats on a raised platform under a lone shade tree at the edge of the fields. More food came. At the end of the song, the workers stopped planting and came to the mat, carrying the smell of sweat and wet soil. They rubbed mud on their legs to scrape off the blood-gorged leeches. They wiped the blood droplets from their legs with their muddy hands. Before they sat down to eat, the women poured water on the workers' hands.

Sonju watched the workers return to their planting after lunch. Next year those men and women would still be sharecroppers and field workers doing the same back-breaking work in the same fields for the people like herself who didn't bend and dirty their hands. Yet she didn't detect any of the bitterness in their sun-soaked faces that she would have felt. There was dignity in that, an attribute she lacked.

When she returned to the kitchen with empty jugs, Second Sister asked, "So what did you see?"

Sonju replied, "There's something beautiful about a person hard at work."

"My husband will appreciate your take on it. You two must have a kindred spirit. Not me." Extending her arm outward, Second Sister said, "I would get far away from here if I could." Perhaps Second Sister was right about the kindred spirit. She thought she could learn to understand Brother-in-Law better than she did her husband. He was a quiet and thoughtful man who chose his words carefully. She once saw him take down a set of Koryo-period celadon pottery from the attic above the kitchen, place it on a table and study it, turning each piece slowly with a satisfied smile the whole time. Sonju liked that about him, his ability to appreciate beauty.

When her husband came home, she was excited that she had something to tell him. "I went to the fields to watch the workers plant rice. Do you know? They sing while planting."

He averted his eyes from her. "Why do you mingle with them? It's not ..."

Deflated, she tried to justify herself and resenting the need to have to. "Your brother goes to the field and talks to the sharecroppers and farm workers. He tells your father about how many workers they will need this year and how much yield they expect and at what price they think they can sell the rice. I find all of that interesting."

"My brother goes to the fields because that's his duty," he said tersely, and added, "not yours." Just like that, he shut her down. She wondered what was safe to talk about with him but she wasn't going to censor herself just to appease a man, even her husband, and neither would this be her last time to go to the field.

Less than two months after rice planting, the monsoon rains poured and brought sweltering heat and humidity. Everyone in the family was forced to stay home. They moved around as little as possible and remained inside under mosquito nets and ate simple food.

When the rain finally abated after a solid month of daily

downpour, Jinwon took off saying, "I'm going to Big House to do my summer break homework."

"Homework?" Second Sister snickered. "She hates to read. A card game is more likely. She and the clan boys play for money. I heard she wins almost every time."

Sonju was fanning the napping children. "Interesting girl," she said. "She does what we cannot do, coming and going any time anywhere."

"She is spoiled," Second Sister said.

Sonju wondered if Second Sister's opinion of Second House family would be different if she were allowed to leave the village.

On a hot and sluggish Sunday morning in August, Sonju was passing by the living room on the way to the kitchen, but paused when Jinwon suddenly declared to the family with a sly smile, "I have a brilliant idea. I think I'll sell candies." Jinwon turned to Sonju's husband. "Little Uncle, bring some candies for me next time you come." Wrinkling her nose in a scowl and waving her hand, she said, "The people here only know of cheap, colored candies. I'll have a servant make a wooden tray that I can hang around my neck so I can sell candies door to door to our clan."

Second Sister was watching and listening from the work area. Mother-in-Law shook her finger at Jinwon. "You will do no such thing. We are not merchants." She left the room mumbling. Sonju's husband smiled and watched his brother pull out his wallet. With money in her hand, Jinwon took off.

Sonju went to the work area and squatted next to Second Sister who was pouring water over soybeans that had started to sprout in a glazed pot. She asked, "What does Jinwon do with the money?"

"It's a mystery to me. She will get another brilliant idea when the money runs out."

"And money from winning card games?"

"I know she buys dried squid and roasted peanuts at the village store."

"We have a store?"

"The hunchback, you saw him the other day talking to Mother-in-Law, didn't you? He owns a small store near the school gate. He sells snacks, candles, matches—that sort of thing." Second Sister covered the clay pot with a burlap cloth and stood up.

Sonju rose too. "Maybe she buys for everybody she plays with."

"Not likely. She's not a generous person."

On the way to the kitchen, Sonju whispered, "Just think where we would be now if we had Jinwon's ingenuity and force of personality to get what we wanted." She just wished Jinwon would be more thoughtful for her mother.

September arrived with much awaited coolness in the air. For over a week now, Mother-in-Law had been muttering loudly enough for Sonju to hear, "It's been over six months, more than enough time to conceive a child." She soon began her ritual of burning incense and praying to Buddha first thing in the morning.

Every time she heard the soft tick-tock of Mother-in-Law's wooden prayer bell, Sonju's heart shrank. For the past few months, she had been wondering if she were barren like her aunt. Now that Mother-in-Law was speaking the words, the possibility of infertility seemed more real to her. Until recently she had thought that a child might bring a change to the misaligned state of her marriage, but now she wanted a child for her own to love and to guide. But what if she couldn't conceive? Like what happened to her aunt, would her parents-in-law arrange a mistress for her husband to have his children?

She escaped to the hill. Down below from where she stood, the barley in the fields undulated like music and whistled when the wind changed its direction. There she imagined a very different life, the life she could have had. Once away from the hill though, she felt guilty for imagining so much less about her husband and their life together. She at times thought she focused too much on her disappointments and tried to let them go, but they all came back at every new disappointment. Like the time she flipped through his engineering books when he wasn't around and found them utterly indecipherable, and having read no books since her marriage, she had asked him to buy some for her. She made the same request a few times. Eventually she stopped asking.

The week before, she had asked him what he talked about with his father. "Oh, about my studies and my future goals and about the discussions that came up in classes," he said. "I would like to hear that too," she said. "Hmph! What a useless curiosity!" he said and turned away.

The next time he mentioned his classes, she asked if there were any women in his class. He said, "No. After graduation, we will all go to the construction site and deal with the contractors and workers. They are all men." Then he proceeded to tell her how well his professors regarded him. His lips moved in a curious way in a smile and his eyes shimmered as he said, "I'll get strong recommendations from them when I graduate."

She could tell that he was extremely proud of himself. She looked at his boyish face and said, "I'm sure you will. People like you."

"I'm hoping for a post in Seoul," he said. "It's a quicker way to move up."

She might return to Seoul soon despite her parents' desire to keep her far away. She grinned. They couldn't do anything about it because she was now married and was no longer under their care.

The workers cut the stalks with sickles, stacked them, and transferred them to rice straw mats in the outer courtyard. Afterwards, they separated the grains from the stalks with threshers. Then they spread the grains to dry, hulled them, had them polished, packed the white rice in rice rope sacks and stacked them in the storage building. Most of them would be sold.

The moon was getting fatter each day, which meant *Chuseok* holiday was approaching to give thanks for this year's harvest. Half a dozen village women came to help the Second House women prepare for the feast. Several worked into the night under the light of the moon.

On the morning of the feast, the same village women with their children in tow showed up early to help. Then the clan members from the city came for the holiday and stopped by. The house was noisy and saturated with mingled smells—the raw scent of freshly picked fruits and vegetables; the scent of nutty smell of rice cakes steaming; and meat, fish, and poultry sizzling. The spirits of the ancestors were served first before the family had the feast in the living room and the sharecroppers and their children ate in the anteroom. Pinned between two women, a sharecropper's little boy quickly shoved two pieces of rice cake into his pocket, then glanced around. Sonju looked away.

The next morning, the family walked to the burial mountain. A servant carried the food, drink, and a reed mat on an A-frame back carrier. Sonju, Second Sister, and First Sister carried the extra food.

In front of Father-in-Law's parents' graves, the servant spread the mat, and the three daughters-in-law laid out food and drink on the marble offering table. After the family bowed to the dead ancestors three times, they walked down to the first son's grave. While the parents-in-law watched, the rest of the family bowed, then stood for a moment in silence. Sonju turned and saw Mother-in-Law wipe her eyes on her sleeve and smile down at Chuljin, the future head of the Second House family.

After lunch, the children romped in the yellowed grass or hid behind the bushes to relieve themselves. Father-in-Law pointed at empty grave sites midway up the hill and told his second son that he wanted those sites for his wife and himself. Sonju's husband complained to his brother about the poor maintenance of the family burial site, so Brother-in-Law went down to the caretaker's house and returned shortly, putting his wallet back in his pocket.

Without anyone noticing, First Sister was back at her husband's grave and was pulling the weeds that had grown tall. Sonju walked down and squatted near her. Some weeds came up easily but others she had to fight. The stubborn roots of the dry, rough weeds surrendered only after clinging dearly to clumps of dirt and leaving scratches on her hand. The core of all living things, the will, should persist to the absolute end like that, and she too should have stood up to her mother to the end, she told herself, and swallowed her regret before moving on to the next weed.

First Sister's Outing, 1947 Fall

The following Monday, maids were already at the work area pumping water and sorting dirty laundry when Sonju went to the kitchen. Only Second Sister was there. "Where is First Sister this morning?" Sonju asked. "The kitchen looks empty without her."

"She is catching the 7:45 train with a village woman to go to the city market."

"First Sister? To the market?" Sonju grabbed a ladle and stirred the beef soup that had started to boil. "And why does she need a chaperone?"

"She has not been out of Maari since she returned from the boarding school. And besides, it's a proper safeguard for a widow."

With a ladle still in her hand, Sonju stepped toward the open door, craned her neck to check the clock in the living room—7:20. Just then, First Sister came out of her room in a soft green top and skirt that Sonju had never seen her wear.

"First Sister is pacing the living room," Sonju said to Second Sister as she put the ladle down on the counter. "And here comes the village woman."

As soon as First Sister and the woman passed the well toward the gates, Sonju turned to Second Sister, "Why all of a sudden?"

"I told my husband you felt bad for First Sister. He saw you and her pulling the weeds at his brother's grave." Second Sister filled a small bowl with steaming rice and placed it on a tray. "Sometimes it takes fresh eyes to see how bad things are. He and his father arranged this outing for her." I would have liked to go to a city market too, Sonju thought.

When First Sister returned home that evening, Sonju asked her, "Did you enjoy your outing? Tell me what you did in the city."

A flicker of a smile passed over First Sister's face, the first smile Sonju had ever seen on her. "Umm, we went to the market, had lunch at a restaurant, then stopped by a fabric shop … We went to a public bath for a scrub. Yes, that's what we did."

Sonju could almost taste the smell and hear the sounds of the markets she used to frequent in Seoul. "I'm glad you had an exciting day. Why don't you rest? Second Sister and I can manage the kitchen."

First Sister hesitated. "Umm, Mother-in-Law …"

"I'll tell her I pushed you out of the kitchen if she asks."

On the way to her room, First Sister hesitated a few times and looked backward at Sonju with a tight, anxious expression. It broke Sonju's heart.

That Saturday night, Sonju told her husband about First Sister's outing. "It's good she had a chance to get out, don't you think? She had not stepped out of Maari for fourteen years."

"Hmph," he grumbled. "Nothing good will come of it."

She glared at him. "You would rather she be kept locked up in this village? What joy does she have here?"

He stared at her. Her voice must have been sharp. Before he could say anything, she left the room, went to the garden by the kitchen and leaned on the cool plastered wall of the bath house. She and her husband upset each other so often. They were not meant to be a couple. The waning moon and scattered stars above seemed to nod in agreement.

On the first Tuesday of November, four hundred heads of Napa cabbages were delivered to the house. The Second House women and the two maids first brined them and for the next two days, they stuffed the brined cabbage, leaf by leaf, with a mixture of sweet rice paste, hot pepper powder, fermented baby shrimp sauce, minced garlic and ginger, and thin strips of white radishes. Then the stuffed cabbages went into tall, fat glazed earthenware pots. The servants buried the pots in the ground near the kitchen to keep the kimchi cold all through winter until spring.

Two days later, Second Sister's morning sickness began,

and she told Mother-in-Law about her pregnancy. Every clan woman came to congratulate Mother-in-Law. The early morning prayers didn't stop as Sonju hoped.

Second Sister was miserable with nausea and vomiting. Sonju pleaded with Second Sister to stay in her room and let her and First Sister take care of the kitchen, but Second Sister declined and said, "I'll get looks from Mother-in-Law. You don't become a lady of leisure until both parents-in-law die."

The day after First Sister made her fifth trip to the market with the chaperone, Sonju was on her way to visit Big House Lady when she saw First Sister's chaperone in the outer courtyard chatting and giggling with another village woman. They were pointing at Second House. The village woman saw Sonju and nudged the chaperone. Their conversation abruptly stopped, and with a stilted smile, they greeted Sonju. They must have been talking about First Sister. Sonju cut her visit short.

Second Sister was at the well and saw Sonju. "That was quick," she said.

"Yes. I have something to take care of." Sonju didn't see First Sister in the kitchen. There was only one other place she could be. In the corner of her room, First Sister was stacking neatly folded clothes. She was startled to see Sonju walking in. Sonju sat, and not wanting to alarm First Sister, spoke in a steady voice, "First Sister, on the way to the Big House, I came across your chaperone talking to another village woman. From the way they acted, I was sure they were gossiping about you. Do you know why they might do that?"

With fear in her widened eyes, First Sister regarded Sonju briefly and gave her a small nod before she said in a trembling voice that she met a man at the market and they made plans to elope. Her face contorted, she began to cry, rocking, trying to stop her torrential sobs with the back of her hand. After she gained her composure, she looked up at Sonju. "I have to take this chance. It's a chance to leave, you see?" She covered her face in her hands and sobbed again. Then she gazed down and said in a resigned voice, "I must have been evil … in my previous life …

54

to deserve this miserable life. Yes, I must have. I was living only because I didn't die."

First Sister's last words pierced Sonju's bosom with immeasurable sadness. She covered her face and quietly cried along with First Sister. She must help First Sister make this desperate escape, she decided, and wiped her face on her sleeve. "Where is your man and where would you settle?"

"Umm, if I can still elope ..." First Sister rocked again. "He is staying at a lodging near the market. We planned to settle in a small fishing village in Jeolla Province."

"I'll try to help you," Sonju said, leaving First Sister who started crying again, and went directly to Father-in-Law.

When Sonju told him about First Sister, he stared at Sonju speechless. She said, "Father-in-Law, this man may show up to take her, and things may get messy if you try to stop him. It will taint the family's reputation. The chaperone has already started gossiping. Please let her go before she elopes."

Father-in-Law looked away. Neither son was home. He thanked her for telling him, then said, "Keep her in her room until her departure tonight."

As Sonju left the men's quarters, she heard Father-in-Law calling for the old servant. She returned to First Sister's room and told her to be ready to leave that night and remain in her room until someone came to get her. First Sister covered her mouth, and through her liquid eyes, smiled gratefully at Sonju. Returning her gaze, Sonju said, "Have a good life to make up for the lost years."

When Sonju entered the kitchen, Second Sister asked, "I saw you go to First Sister's room and then to the men's quarters. What's that all about?"

When Sonju told her, Second Sister gasped in shock. "She found a man to elope with? It's so ... I don't know what I'm trying to say." Looking at the bowl she was holding, she mumbled, "... so out of character for her."

"First Sister will remain in her room until she leaves," Sonju said. "No one other than Jinwon will be allowed in that room. We'll have a maid take First Sister's dinner to her room."

After a minute or so, Second Sister put the bowl down on the counter and said, "I don't know what to expect, you know, with First Sister gone. What will Mother-in-Law do?"

Sonju didn't respond to Second Sister. Things were moving fast. First Sister was leaving. Nothing must go wrong.

On the *yo* mattress that night, Sonju lay still, unable to sleep. She heard soft footsteps. She rose to peek through a tear in the papered window of her room and watched the dark shapes of First Sister, the chaperone, and a male servant walk toward the gates. She blinked to clear the mist in her eyes, felt the corner of her mouth move up, and wrung her hands all at the same time. What would it be like to leave? Just leave and start new? Imagine! Sonju kept her eyes on the hushed figures until she heard the creak of the gate closing.

For days, Sonju revisited First Sister's words, her smile through a pool of tears, her rocking, the three figures disappearing out of the gates in the dark. For days, she kept an eye on Jinwon and wished she would do something—smash something, cry, or scream. What did the mother and daughter say to each other on their last night together?

Sonju didn't have to tell her husband about First Sister when he came home that Saturday. Before dinner, her husband said, "My father told me you were involved in First Sister's leaving." She couldn't tell how he took it. She decided that the less she said, the better it would be. "Yes," she said, and no more. He didn't make any other comments about it. People in the village tsk-tsked but soon forgot and went on with their lives.

About two weeks later, out of the blue, the Second House family heard Jinwon singing at her highest notes, a sound that seemed to rip her throat apart on the way out. She still hadn't uttered a word about her mother. It must be her way of dealing with her loss, Sonju supposed. How complicated Jinwon's feelings must be, especially because she had consistently ignored her mother. But she was still a child, and it was her mother she lost. Sonju's feelings for this adolescent, now practically an orphan, turned tender.

There was little change in the Second House after First Sister left, yet the atmosphere was somehow different. Contrary to what Second Sister had anticipated, Mother-in-Law acted the same toward her as before. Sonju was busier with one less pair of hands in the kitchen. It didn't help that Second Sister continued to suffer morning sickness and poor appetite, saying once again, "All my teeth are loose. It was like this during the entire pregnancy both times before. And that's not all. Chuljin and Jina were both breech babies and my water broke well ahead of the delivery."

What she heard sounded so serious that Sonju began to think something might go wrong with the pregnancy, or worse, with Second Sister. The family would need extra kitchen help very soon. She rolled an invisible thinking stone.

Second Sister was losing weight no matter how much she forced herself to eat. She couldn't hold down food. Then in December, Sonju's husband said with that sulky look of his, "I had hoped for a post in Seoul, but I start a job in Pusan in February."

She tried to lift his mood. "Isn't that still good? It's the second largest city."

"It may delay my advancement." Without looking at her he said, "I paid a visit to your father. I thought he would want us in Seoul."

"What did you say to him?"

"I said I would appreciate his help in procuring a post for me in Seoul."

"What did he say?"

"He didn't seem eager. He said you took great pride in hard work. What did he mean by that?" He looked at her this time.

"I don't know." But she could guess. Her husband disappointed him by attempting to use his influence. Or perhaps her father knew that his wife would consider it too soon for Sonju to return to Seoul. They might never want her to live in Seoul where Kungu was. Even though she knew they couldn't stop her from moving to Seoul if her husband secured a job there on his own, heat climbed to her face. She hid her anger and held her husband's hand. "You'll be successful without his help."

She knew he was trying to find his way in the world as she was in her own way. She would follow him to Pusan and help him achieve what he wanted. What he wanted was not complicated—to become a high-level bureaucrat as he had said many times. Most of the large private companies were run by family members where he would have no chance of moving up high as he could in the government. She came to understand over time that he had a need to prove himself worthier than his brother. What else could he want or even hope for? Not a decision-making privilege in his family, certainly not the family farmland. That night she held her husband close to her chest and felt his heart beating.

The next day, after she saw her husband off, Sonju returned to the kitchen and prepared a tray of roasted barley tea, a cup, and sweet rice cakes to take to her room. She had come to savor the time alone after an uneasy weekend with her husband. So, she was annoyed when Jinwon appeared in the kitchen, took one look at the tray, and placed another cup on it. Sonju walked toward her room without a word and heard Jinwon follow two steps behind her like a little child, this child who lost her mother only a month ago. Sonju's irritation melted away.

"What shall we talk about?" Sonju set the tray down on the floor between them.

Jinwon picked up a cake. She ate like a hungry chipmunk and said, "About my great grandfather ..." She poured tea in a cup and gulped it down. "See, long after his sickly wife had died, he went to inspect the cotton field and saw a young widow." She ate another cake. "He had a small house built and turned over the household responsibilities to my grandparents. After that, he sent his servants to the widow's house. They covered her with a burlap sack and brought her to his new house to be his second wife."

Sonju poured tea in her cup and took a sip. "He had her kidnapped? Why didn't he ask her to marry him?"

"To save face for her. See, the idea is that she was a virtuous woman and had no choice but to marry her captor." Jinwon grinned.

"Oh, I see." Sonju ate one and pushed the remaining cake toward Jinwon. Jinwon picked it up and finished it in two bites. "How do you know all this?" Sonju asked.

"People talk." Jinwon guzzled her tea. "My grandfather had a sister who was born with her spine all fused. She lived her whole life in a squatting position like this." Jinwon lifted herself from the floor and walked with her knees bent sharply and arms swinging out. Of course, Jinwon hadn't witnessed this, but still. Sonju held her breath for a moment. First, Father-in-Law's deformed hand and now this. Jinwon sat back down. "My grandfather married her off to a poor man and gave him farmland. She died during childbirth."

In her dream that night, Sonju was nursing a baby, but it changed form. A child with frog's legs with four toes each and hind legs with human baby feet. It turned its sweet face, stared at her with clear eyes as if it were looking into her soul. Then it called out, "Mama, Mama," all the while scratching her breast with three sharp claws attached to its tiny front leg. Droplets of blood formed on the three red lines on her breast. Sonju grabbed the claws. She woke up clutching the *yo*.

The vivid image of the baby's claw stayed with Sonju throughout the day and wouldn't leave, causing fear to crouch in the deep hollow of her belly. Then the next day, the sun shone on new snow that had fallen overnight. She wished she had words for what she saw—mounds and mounds of whiteness under the bright sun, not much else to weary her eyes and no sound to disturb her ears. She forgot about the nightmare. She forgot about the last three breathless months dealing with one thing after another. She took in all the white scenery her eyes could hold and filled her lungs with pristine air. It felt like happiness.

The following week, her husband surprised her with a

Life magazine that was only two months old. The secondhand bookstores must be getting them directly from the Americans in Seoul. She was relishing her excitement at his thoughtful gesture when Second Sister entered her room and dropped a basketful of mending in front of her. Some clothes bounced up and settled back in the basket. Second Sister sank onto a pillow. "I'm doomed to get old here."

Sonju picked a pair of pants from the basket and threaded a needle. "Why do you say that?"

"My husband turned down a transfer to Seoul. Again." Second Sister's lips twisted. "He wants to stay close to his parents, you know, his duty to his parents as the first son and all that." She picked up a sock, and with fury, threw it back into the basket and sputtered, "I'm tired of living under my in-laws. First Sister left. You'll leave, soon. And I'll be here to face Mother-in-Law all alone."

Perhaps she should stay, Sonju thought, but once her husband started his job in Pusan, she wanted to join him and help him succeed in his career. She didn't offer to stay and felt like an unsympathetic, selfish person. They focused on mending in silence for two minutes, maybe five. Jinwon sang *O Sole Mio* somewhere nearby. Sonju said, "I like that song." No words came out of Second Sister. Their mending continued in silence. Sonju felt guilty but her husband would need her too. When the mending was done, Second Sister picked up the basket and left the room.

For several days, Sonju said little to Second Sister, afraid she might upset her for not offering to stay at least until Second Sister had her baby. Instead, she focused on moving to Pusan in February to join her husband. Sometimes she worried. It had been over nine months, and still no stir in her belly.

First Election, 1948 May

Every morning out of Mother-in-Law's room, the prayer bell sounded and the smell of burning incense wafted. Sonju thought about her childless aunt more and more.

In February, a week before Sonju's husband graduated, Mother-in-Law called Sonju to her room early in the morning and said, "Your sister-in-law is likely to have complications with her pregnancy, so you will remain here in Maari. Your husband agrees."

Sonju passed her room and continued to the veranda. The snapping cold morning air seeped into her bones. She gathered her breath, blew out the air and watched the white cloud disperse then disappear. She would have willingly agreed to stay if asked, but why didn't her husband discuss it with her first? More than anyone, he should understand how hurtful it was to be excluded from family decisions. Would all her years with him be like this? She closed her eyes. Someone once valued her and loved her. Perhaps that should be enough. That was more than most women had.

She entered her room and was closing the door behind her when Second Sister came in. She looked upset. "I didn't ask Mother-in-Law to keep you here," she said.

"Of course, I will stay," Sonju said.

"Mother-in-Law could have hired another maid after First Sister left. I know what she is doing."

"What do you mean?"

"You'll be here a long time." With those words, Second Sister left.

Second Sister didn't smile for a few days. Sonju didn't bother to ask her to clarify what she meant about Mother-in-Law's intent nor did she bother to confront her husband when he came home. The same had happened before.

After a week in Pusan, her husband came home with a

swagger in his walk, now that he was financially independent. He even said he would give her some money every month. That night she lay facing her husband, and moving closer, asked, "What is your work like?"

"Right now, I'm being trained as a junior engineer. I study the plan, go to construction sites with my supervisor, inspect the materials, and watch how he deals with contractors."

"It sounds like an interesting job. I would like to work one day." As soon as she said it, she knew it was a mistake.

He said, "You will have your work. Have children and raise them."

Oh, those cutting remarks. Fine. She edged away from him. "What happens if I can't have children? Would your parents arrange a mistress for you? It betrays my idea of marriage, but if they do, I will go back to Seoul and find work." He turned and pulled the blanket to his neck.

It was Sonju's second May in Maari, yet there was no sign of life in her belly. Her worry was constant. The sound of Mother-in-Law's prayer bell seemed louder each time, and Sonju couldn't help conjuring up the images of her infertile aunt living with her husband and his mistress and their children under the same roof.

"Tock, tock, tock," Sonju was mimicking the sound of the prayer bell when the old servant poked his head into the kitchen and said that a politician had arrived with his assistants and they were gathering villagers near the train station. He asked if he could go there for free liquor. As soon as both Sonju and Second Sister nodded, he took off. While scooping steaming rice into a bowl, Sonju heard a few muffled words of the speech coming over a microphone from the distance. Half an hour later, the happy servant returned, his face red from drinking, his breath reeking of cheap rice liquor. He handed two leaflets to Sonju, each with a large grainy black-and-white photograph. Sonju looked at the pictures and asked the servant, "Which one spoke?"

"I don't know."

On the day of the very first general election in the nation's history to elect people's representatives for the new republic, Sonju hurried to get breakfast ready so that she could go to the satellite district office to vote. She looked at the leaflets again and asked Second Sister, "I know who I'm voting for, but how do you think the election will go here?"

Second Sister touched her large gourd belly with one hand, and with the other, swirled the boiling soup with a ladle. "The politician who bought the liquor ..." She put down the ladle on the counter. "My water just broke."

A large puddle began to form on the kitchen floor. "Come! Watch the soup." Sonju yelled out to the maid at the well. "Be careful. There's water on the floor." She ushered Second Sister toward her room and on the way announced loudly to the closed door. "Mother-in-Law, the baby is coming!"

Another maid rushed to Second Sister's room, spread the *yo* on the floor and left. Second Sister pointed at the wardrobe and said, "Diapers." Sonju took a dozen from a neat stack. The maid brought a basin of warm water.

Two hours later, Second Sister's labor started. A telegram was sent to Brother-in-Law. The village doctor and his nurse came. After six hours of labor, Second Sister, her hair soaked, her face red from pushing, and knuckles white from holding onto Sonju's arms, delivered a baby. When told she had a girl, Second Sister squeezed her eyes shut and groaned. The nurse slapped the baby's bottom until a loud cry was issued.

Second Sister held her baby all cleansed and swathed in a cotton wrap. "The easiest of my three deliveries. Not a breech baby this time." Mother-in-Law came into the room, lifted the wrap, looked under it, turned around, and left the room.

Sonju saw water collecting in Second Sister's eyes, and thought, with all the complaints about Mother-in-Law's special treatment of boys and all the talk about what she would not do to her own daughter-in-law, Second Sister was a hopelessly passive person. She wished Second Sister would wipe her tears, at least.

Brother-in-Law came into the room. He thanked Sonju and smiled at his wife. Sonju realized that she was wrong about no change coming to Korea. Here, Brother-in-Law came into his wife's birthing room to check on his wife and watched the baby jerk her arms, kick her legs, and yawn. "A healthy baby," he told his wife.

Second Sister looked up from the *yo* mattress at her husband and sighed. "Another girl."

He smiled at her. "That's fine."

After Brother-in-Law left the room, Sonju said, "Let me hold the baby." How light the baby was! She smelled the baby and cooed to it. "You are the first to be born in this family after the end of Japanese occupation. And you were born on an important date," she told her. "1948 May 10, the very first general election for the National Assembly. Three years after the Japanese left, our country is finally going to be an independent republic. So, what is your future plan?"

That evening, Sonju saw a rice straw rope hanging above the double gates to announce the birth. Charcoal sticks protruded in regular intervals in the rope's twists to ward off evil spirits. When Second Sister's labor had started, in anticipation of a baby boy, Mother-in-Law had had a servant insert a dried red pepper in the loop in between the charcoal sticks. After the delivery, she had all the red peppers taken out from the rope before hanging it. The rope was taken down three days after it went up. After the customary one month with the baby in her room, Second Sister returned to the kitchen to resume her regular kitchen work.

The baby was robust, and her cry was loud and frequent. The grandparents complained. Second Sister twisted her lips and said, "They wouldn't complain if it were a boy."

It was three months before the baby calmed down. Only then did Jinwon come into Second Sister's room for a second look at the baby. Sonju moved to make room for her to sit close to the baby. "Jinwon, look how much the baby has grown already," she said.

Jinwon studied the baby, then turned to Second Sister. "I heard babies change, but after three months, she is still ugly. Don't tell people she is yours."

Second Sister had a crooked smile, appearing insulted by that comment, but surprisingly she said, "But look how her eyes sparkle." Sonju knew then that this child her parents named Jinjin would grow up knowing that she was special in spite of her grandmother's disdain for her being just a girl.

By September, eighteen months into her marriage, Sonju was sure she was pregnant. She tired easily. Her breasts felt heavier. Her nipples turned darker and were tender to the touch. In less than ten minutes of being told, Mother-in-Law waddled out the gate, her arms and large hips swinging. By that evening, everybody in the clan seemed to know of Sonju's pregnancy, and many clan women came to wish for a healthy baby boy.

A few days later, Sonju entered Mother-in-Law's hobby room and waited until Mother-in-Law finished the last line of interlaced yarn and turned to her. She said, "I came to ask you about your sister-in-law. How bad was her deformity?"

Mother-in-Law peered into Sonju's eyes. "Your sisters-in-law have healthy children without any deformities."

"I still want to know."

"My sister-in-law was fourteen years old when I married into the family. She had a short neck and back and walked with her knees bent, standing about a meter tall. Other than that, she seemed fine. She grew into a healthy spirited young woman. She even got married. At seventeen. I worried about her but she wanted to be married." She made small nods, her eyes seeming to recede into memory. "My father-in-law and my husband arranged her marriage to a young man who had a widowed mother. They bought him farmland in his village. The young couple seemed to get along. Within a year she died of complications from childbirth. She was six months along. Can you imagine, a baby in such a short body?" With a nod

65

and a sliver of a smile, she said, "Her husband was good to her. I believe she was happy."

"What was wrong with your Mother-in-Law? You said she died shortly after you married."

"I don't know. I heard she was sick most of her married life."

Sonju returned to her room, grabbed the thinking-stone from her bridal chest and rolled it furiously to shake off the images of the baby with frog arms in her dream, the way Jinwon walked low to the floor with her knees bent, and the young woman's pregnant belly.

The question of "what if" remained with her for a while. She now imagined what her child might be like and what kind of parent she would be.

It was mid-October, a month after she told her Mother-in-Law about her pregnancy. She heard an unfamiliar voice coming from the courtyard. A young woman's voice said she needed work. She said she was childless and had been thrown out of her Mother-in-Law's house after her husband's death.

Mother-in-Law must have considered her daughters-in-law—one pregnant and the other with an infant. She hired the woman and gave her a servant's room next to the gates. This young woman proved to be a hard worker and a good cook. She also knew how to throw a nice inviting smile and swing her round young hips in a seductive way.

With the new maid working out well, Sonju thought she would be able to join her husband in Pusan after her baby came. One night as she turned to lie down to sleep, she saw something move in the courtyard. Three days before, during their hide-and-seek game, Second Sister's two older children had made several holes on the papered window and one was big enough for Sonju to see outside without squinting. Under the dusky blue light of the waning moon, Father-in-Law took careful steps, passing leafless peony shrubs and the maple tree near the well, toward the servant's quarters. He came out about a half hour later and stole toward the main house. This occurred every night. Sonju tried to fight off her disappointment in him. What would Mother-in-Law do if she found out?

On the eighth night, Father-in-Law was out again and turned the corner toward the servant's quarters and disappeared. Then she saw Mother-in-Law following, carrying a chamber pot with both hands, going the same way. A few minutes later, short, startled shrieks tore the night's still air, then silence. Shortly afterwards, Mother-in-Law emerged and walked back to the main house without the chamber pot. Father-in-Law ran to the well and poured water on his head and face. He shook his head like a wet dog, drew his crossed arms to his chest, and shivering, walked toward the room to his wife.

The next morning when Sonju walked into the kitchen, Second Sister and the maids were asking among themselves: what happened to the woman, where did she go on this chilly November day? Sonju knew then the woman had left. She grabbed a large bowl and stepped out to the garden next to the kitchen, took two heads of kimchi from a pot buried in the ground. When she returned, one maid was saying, "Maybe she was lying about the whole thing, being a widow and all that. She was too happy to be a widow. The way she acted, she could have been someone's mistress thrown out by the wife."

"She did have a seductive streak in her," Second Sister said, and turned to Sonju. "I forgot to tell you. After Father-in-Law finishes his breakfast, we're going to a clan home to make a *yo* mattress."

Sonju watched the two maids leave the kitchen and was relieved the gossip came to an end. "A *yo* for whom?" Sonju asked, cutting the kimchi into bite sizes.

"One of the clan daughters is getting married in a month. It's a tradition for the clan women to make the nuptial *yo* for the clan's daughters."

On the way to the *yo* making, Second Sister said, "The hostess's husband has a habit of leaving home for days. Every-one knows he has another woman somewhere. He always has a woman somewhere. He is gone again so women can talk freely in his house without men around."

By the time Sonju and Second Sister arrived at the *yo* making, the clan women were spreading cotton in layers on a large white muslin cloth. Big House Lady slid sideways on her hips to make room for Sonju.

"Isn't Second House Lady coming?" one of the women asked Second Sister who situated herself between two women and was presently arranging her calf-length dirndl skirt to cover her legs. Sonju noticed that Second Sister was always polite and obedient and smiling in the presence of elders, even at the house. The elders often praised her for those qualities.

A woman next to her answered instead, "Why should she? Unlike Big House Lady here, she has not one but two daughters-in-law to take her place." Big House Lady smiled and didn't make any comments.

The cotton batting was thick. The women covered it with muslin cloth and started stitching the edges.

Cocking her head toward the hostess, a woman with a mole on her chin asked the hostess, "Where is your husband this time?"

"I don't know, but I can tell you he is having fun."

A woman with tanned skin smirked. "Is he any good?" Sonju's face turned hot. The women were so bold.

"I don't know," the hostess said, her voice flat and detached. "It's been such a long time. The women must think he is good. Some people saw him in the cities carrying on with young ones." The hostess sighed and said, "I don't grieve over that anymore. He will always chase women."

Sonju vowed that this would not be her fate and that she would not tolerate such behavior in her husband. As it was, she was finding it hard to see her father-in-law the same way as before even though her mother-in-law seemed fine after getting even with her husband.

A woman with unusually large drooping ears like Buddha's said, "At least your husband leaves you alone. Mine complains about my looks, covers my face with my skirt, and does it like chickens do. Quickly." Everyone laughed. Sonju could tell this wasn't the first time they'd heard this. It was so sad and infuriating that she could almost cry.

The one with a mole expelled a loud sigh before she asked no one in particular, "Do you ever wonder what we live for?"

Sonju wouldn't have known how to answer if that question had been directed at her. She would raise children and guide them, but what else? She had once thought she would do good for the country but was it possible now? She heard the hostess snap at the woman. "Why do you ask such a question? That kind of question gets you nothing but trouble. You know the answer. You're born, serve men folk, get married, serve your husband's family. Raise children, marry them off, then become a mother-in-law with a firm hand so your daughter-in-law learns her place and won't treat you badly in your old age. That's what we live for." No one argued.

They placed the muslin covered batting on the white cotton fabric, laid the satin cover on top, and began stitching them together, leaving a crisp white border around the bright pink satin. The woman with tanned skin turned to Sonju. "You're from Seoul. Do all women live the way we do?"

All eyes were on Sonju. She looked at each woman before she spoke. "There are women who go to university and work outside the home. Not all women live the way you describe." Some women nodded. All quiet again. The *yo* was finished.

Big House Lady folded it into thirds and laid it in the center of the room. "This is a gift of hope and dreams from the clan women to the bride-to-be." Everyone stared at it. "My dreams have long ago ceased, even in my imagination," Buddha Ears said after a sigh.

On the way home, Sonju asked Second Sister, "Why was Big House Lady snubbed?"

"Because she has two sons, but neither lives here with their parents. They rarely visit. Our Mother-in-Law won't let that happen."

They walked home without further words, each in her own thoughts about their mother-in-law. When Sonju saw

Mother-in-Law, she told her about the holes on the papered windows and asked her to have her windows newly papered. She didn't want to see other people's private affairs. It took only three days for the old servant to scrape the yellowed paper off the frame and apply bright white rice paper with glue. In a few hours, the paper dried as taut as a face of a shameless youth.

Sonju's Baby, 1949 Spring

On the day the first buds appeared on the cherry tree in the back garden, Sonju had her baby with Second Sister by her side. "I have waited for you for a long time," Sonju said, gazing at her daughter and tracing the ten small fingers and ten toes intact with tiny nails. From her silky hair to her soft, down-covered body, her baby was perfect—a miraculous thing.

Sonju was pleased to see her husband enter the room. It must be an accepted practice now among the educated men. She smiled at him. He returned her smile and sat by the *yo* grinning at the baby. He gently rubbed the baby's hand with his index finger. When the baby grabbed his finger, he beamed brightly, looking astonished by it. He watched her let go of his finger and yawn. This was the very first time Sonju witnessed genuine joy in her husband and became dreamy about all the happy days ahead for her family of three. That was when he fixed his eyes on her and said, "Now you have a child to care for," as if he had waited just to tell her so. What kind of a man took such a moment to make his point? At that instant, she truly despised him, the smallness of his mind, his veiled vindictiveness. She said, "Yes. A child to love and to teach."

Not long after he left the room to see the doctor out, Mother-in-Law entered. "I heard your delivery was smooth. You will have a son next time." Still standing, she discharged a long, loud sigh.

Sonju looked up from the *yo*. "Mother-in-Law, a child was born. I want juniper sprigs in the twist of the rope to announce the birth of a baby girl. She will have all the acknowledgement boys get." Mother-in-Law stared at Sonju for a second or two and left the room.

Second Sister moved closer to Sonju. "You're brave. Do you think she'll do it?"

"Wait a few minutes and peek out the window. See if the servant is inserting juniper sprigs."

Second Sister kept checking every few minutes. The sixth time, after a short burst of a giggle, she said, "Yes, he is!"

That night on the *yo* under the ceiling light, Sonju's husband watched the baby squirm and whispered, "The baby looks like you."

Her marriage might turn out well, she thought, in spite of his insensitive remark earlier. "She has your nose and chin. She is perfect," she told him and watched the baby lying between them. "Let's call her Jinju. After me," she said. "I want to give her something of mine."

"Yes, of course."

"Thank you." She couldn't stop smiling.

The following day, Sonju took out the thinking-stone and rubbed it one last time. She vowed to stop thinking of Kungu. She vowed to devote her life to her husband and her baby. She turned and watched her sleeping baby illuminated by the afternoon light that filtered through the paper windows. Her heart lit up. Even though Second Sister implied that frequent visits and correspondence with the birth family were frowned upon, Sonju wanted to announce her daughter's birth to her family. Her sister would pass the news to their mother.

1949 March 30

Dear Sister,

Your niece, Jinju, was born two days ago on March 28. I will give her freedom to explore possibilities and watch what she does with her life. I am so happy being a mother. You must know this joy being a mother yourself.

I send regards to our family.

A week later Jinwon came to Sonju's room. "Are you getting tired of eating seaweed soup every day? I don't believe the soup helps a new mother produce more milk. It didn't work for Second Auntie." She glanced at the baby and smirked. "Oh, by the way, your baby isn't as pretty as Jina but she passes."

Sonju laughed and turned to her baby. "I have a grand design for you, Jinju."

One late afternoon in May, Mother-in-Law called Sonju and Second Sister to her room. "Bring the rice cakes with you, the ones Big House Lady sent us. Leave the children with the maids."

Second Sister carried a tray of the rice cakes and Sonju a tray of hot barley tea. Picking up a piece of cake, Mother-in-Law turned to Second Sister. "How is Chuljin doing at school?"

Second Sister smiled. "He has been to school only two months but he likes it so far, especially recess."

Mother-in-Law didn't smile. "Keep an eye on his grades. He will be the head of the family one day. He has to go to Seoul National University."

"Yes, Mother-in-Law."

After a sip of tea, Sonju said, "Jinju will start school in Seoul. After university, she can get a doctoral degree if she wants to." Second Sister's eyes darted between Sonju and Mother-in-Law.

"What would your husband say?" Mother-in-Law asked.

"He will agree. If he is not in Seoul by that time, I'll still move to educate the children there as Big House Master had done."

Mother-in-Law asked, "When would Jinju get married?"

"When she is ready. Hopefully one day, she will help people advance in life. Have you heard of Dr. Im Young Shin? She studied in Japan and in America. After she returned home, she had a school built, which is now Chung Ahng Teachers' College for Women. The college has produced many good teachers. Dr. Im is about your age." Sonju noticed Mother-in-Law had leaned in and was listening intently to her. "You see, women can do great things. Don't you want that for your granddaughters?"

Mother-in-Law sat up straight and uttered, "Hmph," then turned her head as if to hide her shame of losing herself in the story.

Second Sister lowered her head as though afraid she might

be brought into the conversation. Sonju imagined congratulating herself for planting a new idea in her mother-in-law's mind. She smiled.

In June, the government enacted the Land Reform Law to redistribute the nation's farmland. Second House family would lose the farmland not worked on by hired hands or servants. Except for Sonju's husband, the family grumbled about the new law. As far as Sonju's thought went, people were either rich with vast land holdings or poor with no hope of owning anything. With the reform, some sharecroppers might become small landowners and their children might be able to get education. Sonju was beginning to feel better about the new nation.

In July and August, as with the past monsoons, the family lived inside a mosquito net, watching the beating rain and then listening to the mosquitos' thin whine. In September, cool air began to blow and the skies turned blue. It had been more than two and a half years since Sonju left Seoul. What would it be like to return to that constantly pulsing, tantalizing, and demanding city? She missed the energy of it and the pace of it. But then, there were endearing things in the village like wild flowers along the dirt paths, cicadas singing their hearts out in the acacia trees, domestic animals that stayed close to people, birds that left and returned like old friends, and even the cool, decaying smell of the dead roots and leaves on the hill tinged with the faint odor of animal waste that she had become used to. Maari, where seasons were a living, breathing force that demanded heeding, where she had shared the same rain and sun with her in-laws who fussed, loved, laughed, hated, and cried as if to affirm they were alive. It seemed odd to her that she couldn't recall hearing her own mother laugh or cry.

That November, Sonju had been away from her family for almost three years. Second House family felt more like her family now, and she no longer had a deep desire to join her husband in Pusan. He had been promoted already without her help. Besides, neither her husband nor her mother-in-law brought up the topic of Sonju leaving Maari to join her husband. Everyone seemed to have gotten used to the way things were.

When the maple leaves turned bright red, Sonju recalled the image of First Sister disappearing out of the gates and wondered about First Sister's new life in the small fishing village way down south. Then the first snow for the year began to fall one evening in December covering everything layer by layer. By the following morning, the world had transformed. Everything around, even the spiky branches, were hidden under thick white fluffy domes, and she thought it the most beautiful sight to behold.

The sun melted the snow in two days making the ground muddy everywhere. Then the temperature suddenly dropped and froze the mud. Jinwon came in limping soon after she left the house to meet a friend returning from shopping. She complained to her grandfather, "I slipped on the ice and hurt my leg on the way to the train station. Look." She walked around in front of her grandfather with an exaggerated limp and yelp. "You should build a bridge from the chestnut tree to the train station so that we don't have to walk *down* the hill and *climb* back up to the station. A bridge about a hundred meters long will do."

Her grandfather watched Jinwon limping a while, and with an amused look, said, "I can have the servants tie a thick rope between the chestnut tree and the station. You don't even have to walk. You can slide down the rope." Jinwon glared at her grandfather and limped to her room. She didn't mention a bridge again. Soon the temperature turned again, and water dripped from the eaves as the midday sun melted the ice on the roof.

Sonju smiled at the image of Jinwon riding a rope bridge as she walked down the slope with Jinju strapped on her back to visit Big House Lady. She was fond of the lady who was always gracious to everyone, befitting the wife of the Big House Master, the head of the clan. She was passing by the Big House guest quarters and what she heard made her stop.

A group of boys were arguing: "College-educated people should cast two votes because uneducated people don't know what their votes mean." "Oh, no, *no!* That will create a class system. This is a democracy. What do you think that means?" "Don't you think we have a class system already? Do you think a classless society is even possible? I think you're a little pinko."

At that instant, Jinwon's voice erupted. "That's a dangerous thing to say. There's a national hysteria about communism, do I have to remind you? I don't want any of you go to jail." Jinwon who read nothing other than maybe glancing through her textbooks—how and where did she get that information? Sonju wondered.

After a brief silence, a dampened voice spoke, "That's true. The school said to report when we hear a slip of North Korean accent, an unfamiliar word, or see any strange behavior."

"We can't trust anyone," Jinwon said. "Anyone can frame us as communists. Friends report friends, even family members and relatives."

"I heard many intellectuals chose to go to the North."

"Shhhh ..." They were all quiet again.

Sonju felt sad for her ignorance of what was going on in the country. In Seoul, she used to read newspapers daily. After Korea was liberated from Japan's colonial rule and was divided into the Communist North and the Capitalist South, and even before Syngman Rhee was elected president by the assembly last August, his rhetoric about the communist threat had been loud. Now he seemed to be fomenting fear in people against North Korea. She wished to receive news about the nation, but no one in the village seemed to feel the need to know what was happening outside of Maari. Second Sister had told her sometime back that electricity only became available in Maari within the past ten years and that most villagers in the interior still used candles or oil lamps for light at night. There was no radio transmission either. She sighed and turned her head back to look at her daughter, who reached out her chubby arms and touched Sonju's nose and mouth with her little fingers. Sonju laughed feeling grounded again.

At the first scent of spring, Sonju was on the hill near the school with Jinju on her back pondering how she should evolve beyond being a mother, a wife and a daughter-in-law. There must be something she could do even in this insulated village. She wished she hadn't sworn to never touch her thinking-stone again. It might have helped.

On the way home, she came upon a man walking with a boxy camera and a tripod. She thought she would have Jinju and her cousins photographed so that even if they later grew up in a city, they would remember their lives in Maari, their birthplace. He said he would return in three days with the developed pictures. Pushing the gate open, Sonju called out, "Second Sister, I have a photographer with me." She bowed to the man and motioned him to enter.

While the photographer was setting up the camera, Second Sister and Sonju combed the children's hair and straightened their clothes. Sonju stood holding Jinju on her arm, and Second Sister behind her three children. The children giggled at the strange sight of the photographer's tripod and black cloth over his head and the camera. After a few minutes of adjusting the lens and directing the group pose, he called out, "One, two, three." The moment the flash went off, Jinju pinched Sonju's neck with a start while Second Sister's children squealed and laughed.

Sonju showed her husband the pictures of everyone, her holding Jinju, Jinju alone, and Jinju with her cousins. The following week, he brought home a maroon-colored album with gold trim and helped her insert the photographs into it. She imagined adding pictures of Jinju next year, Jinju at middle school and high school, then in college.

Jinju in the meantime enjoyed the attentions of her girl

cousins, especially Jina's. Jina was a nurturing child. She would come around, putting flowers she picked in Jinju's hand or on her hair and exclaimed how pretty Jinju looked with a flower. One day, from the men's quarters, Father-in-Law had been watching Jina picking clover leaves in the garden while reciting a children's story about a rabbit in the moon. When he asked what she was going to do with the clover leaves, Jina replied, "Feed the rabbit, of course."

"If I build you a cage," he said, "would you take care of a rabbit?" Surprised at this unexpected offer, Jina opened a smile that was almost too big for her small face.

The next day, he had the old servant cut wood and wire to the correct measurements. In front of Jina, he hammered the wood with his good hand while holding it with his deformed left hand. With some struggle, he attached the wire to the wood frame. That moment changed Sonju's feelings toward her father-in-law and her tender affection for him returned.

That afternoon, a servant brought a white rabbit with red eyes. Every day, Jina searched for clover leaves in the gardens and watched the rabbit nibble them. She cleaned the cage daily as she promised to her grandfather.

Jinwon, now sixteen years old, sought out clan girls her age whom she had ignored until then, saying girls bored her. She led the girls to Sonju's veranda, telling them her grandmother couldn't hear them there. She didn't care if Sonju could hear them. There, Jinwon and the girls giggled and chatted about every clean-cut young man who came to visit someone in the village.

On this particular day, Jinwon couldn't gather the girls, so she joined Sonju and Second Sister on the veranda, where again Second Sister spoke about her desperate desire to move away from Maari.

"Second Auntie," Jinwon said, "I have a solution for you." Both Sonju and Second Sister waited. Jinwon always had ideas. "If your husband took a mistress to take care of his parents, you and your children could go live with him and he can come here once in a while to check on his parents and his mistress. That way, he isn't abandoning his elderly parents and the family wouldn't lose face." Sonju gasped, then quickly sealed her mouth when she saw Second Sister looking down on the wooden planks, seeming to be considering this wrong-headed idea. After a minute or so, Second Sister rose and left without a word.

Nothing was said about it until Sunday evening. Second Sister was tidying the kitchen when she told Sonju, "I presented Jinwon's idea to my husband but he decided against it because there would be a conflict between my children and those born by the mistress. He told me he could not pass such a burden on to the children."

Sonju said nothing. The idea of it was wrong in so many ways.

War, 1950 June

That Sunday morning was like any other Sunday morning. Everyone in the house slept in. Sonju awoke to loud, frenzied words coming from the inner courtyard and fast moving toward the anteroom. "A war! A war! North Koreans are coming!" a male voice repeated.

Sonju bolted up. "What?" Her husband kicked off the blanket, got up, and dashed to the living room, almost slipping in his haste. Sonju followed. Within a minute, everyone converged in the anteroom.

A Big House servant, out of breath and moving his arms wildly, shouted, "They attacked us early this morning!"

Father-in-Law asked calmly, "Tell me. Where did the news come from?"

"A telegram from Seoul. From my master's elder son. My master sent me here."

Second Sister came over to Sonju and whispered. "A war? I don't believe it."

When she was living in Seoul, Sonju knew from reading the newspapers that there were guerrilla skirmishes ever since 1945 when the line was drawn along the 38th parallel but they had never amounted to much. The nation was more tuned into Syngman Rhee's constant anti-communist rhetoric and his opposition to divided Korea. It was public knowledge that he wanted to lead one unified Korea, but so did Kim Ilsung of the North. So, it shouldn't have been a surprise to anyone that a war would happen. But it was. A war! Seoul was only forty-eight kilometers away from the North. Her lips quivered. She pressed her mouth with her balled hand.

Brother-in-Law went to the Big House to read the telegram himself. When he returned, he told the family that the telegram was dated 1950 June 25 and it read that at four in the morning, North Korean troops had indeed invaded South Korea.

So, it was real. Jinju was staring back and forth at her mother and her father. Even the one-year-old child seemed to know something was happening. Sonju strapped Jinju on her back and went to the kitchen. It wouldn't take long for the North Korean troops to reach Seoul. A day or two if they were not stopped. She had never witnessed a war because Japan fought elsewhere, not on Korean soil, but she knew what a war looked like. She had seen photographs of the Second World War in *Life* magazine. All her relatives lived in Seoul. Where would her family go to get out of enemy's way? What about Kungu and his mother? Did they have a safe place to go?

Second Sister was asking, "What do we do? My younger brother is an officer. He will be in the war. My family may not even have heard the news." She scrunched her face and said in an anguished voice, "If only I could go see them now."

All afternoon and evening, everyone in the house, even the children, talked little, and when they did talk, their voices were tight and subdued. Sonju was, at times, lost in thought and when she caught herself, she noticed others in the house moving with unusual rigidity with hesitant steps. Their unfocused, anxious eyes glanced around, not looking at anything in particular.

That night on the *yo*, Sonju clung to her husband, glad that he was home and not in Pusan. "How long would you and your brother stay?"

"It depends on how things go."

"Would you please go to the train station tomorrow morning and find out if the station master has any information about the war?" she asked. "And what the people on the train say to him?"

The next day, he went to the station and learned that the enemy force was advancing toward Seoul. A day after that, he relayed that the South Korean army bombed the Han River Bridge in Seoul early in the morning to stop the North from advancing farther. The following day, on June 28, three days after the invasion, he told her Seoul had fallen.

"Seoul fell? Seoul fell. My family ..." Sonju could feel her heart pound. All kinds of thoughts and images of her family caught in the mayhem and destruction flashed in her mind. She grabbed Jinju from a maid and held her close to her bosom hiding her eyes from her daughter not to show her fear, and paced the room.

Her husband left her to join his father and brother at the men's quarters, and shortly afterwards, she saw her mother-in-law's hefty hips swinging toward the men's quarters as well. Frantic, she strapped Jinju on her back, and crossing the inner courtyard, heard a crash coming from the kitchen. Jinju whimpered, grasping at Sonju's hair.

While picking up shattered porcelain pieces, Second Sister was talking to herself about the enemy passing by her father's house if the North was not stopped soon. Sonju was occupied with her own thoughts too. Seoul had fallen. What did it mean? Did the enemy destroy all the buildings and houses? Did they kill everyone in sight? A picture rose in her mind as real as if she could touch it—thick lines of enemy soldiers advancing street by street, house by house, fighting. And her frightened family scurrying around, even caught in a crossfire. She saw Second Sister pick up a pot, carry it around the kitchen, and lay it down in another spot.

That afternoon, Father-in-Law had everyone assemble in the inner courtyard. "The war may come this way. It could be soon." He turned to field hands, servants, and maids. "Leave tomorrow morning. And, each of you, take as much rice as you can carry to your family. I will let you know when it is safe for you to return." To the old servant who didn't have a family and was over fifty, he said, "You will remain here with me and my wife. The enemy soldiers won't bother old people."

To Sonju and Second Sister he said, "Take your children to my daughter's house in Daejon. I had a telegram sent to her. She can accommodate all of you. You will be safer there than here since it is further south. Surely the war will end before it reaches Daejon." He turned to his sons. "You will start for Pusan the day after tomorrow just in case the government starts drafting men.

"You haven't mentioned me," Jinwon said.

"You will go to your grandmother's family home." Jinwon dropped her jaw and shot her eyelids up at her grandfather, but seeing his stern eyes, she went to her room and slammed the door shut.

The field hands and maids left the next morning, each carrying rice and clothing. Sonju's husband, Brother-in-Law, and the old servant dug holes along the junipers and sunk six large, glazed clay pots. In them, they stored linens, silver, antiques, and grain. They sealed the lids and concealed them with dirt then transplanted flowering plants on top and covered the soil with old leaves. That evening after Jinju fell asleep, Sonju helped her husband pack, sniffling and wiping her tears.

Early the next morning, they watched the train nearing the station. Sonju's husband put the suitcases down on the ground to pick up Jinju. "Say bye-bye to Daddy." Sonju felt her tears gather in her eyes. When Brother-in-Law stepped up to the crowded train and waved at his family, Sonju's husband handed Jinju to Sonju, picked up his suitcases, and boarded the packed car. Once on the train, he and his brother put their heads out the window and waved. The train moved. Sonju, Second Sister, and the children waved until the train shrank to the size of a toy.

In the early afternoon, handing her bags to the servant, Jinwon said, "Grandma, I've never met those people. What am I going to do there?"

"*Those people* are my brother's family. You will be safe there. If his house were big enough, your aunts and cousins would be going there too."

"You said it's a small, small, remote village with hills and mountains. Do tigers come out there?"

"Don't be ridiculous. Besides, you would have a better chance with them than with enemy soldiers with guns."

Jinwon, her lower lip sticking out, left with the servant, dragging her feet and glancing back.

The next day, in the mid-morning, Sonju, Second Sister, and their four children went to the station. As the train pulled up, they saw people already jammed in the cars, spilling out onto the steps, and clinging to the roofs. Sonju and Second Sister held their children close, squeezed up the steps of the train into the car, and threaded through packed bodies and bags. Then circling their children, they pushed out to make room for the children to breathe while inching toward their seats, only to find they were occupied by the people with standing-room-only tickets. They refused to yield. The other passengers shouted, "Give them the seats. They have the tickets." The squatters ignored them and looked to the open window. A passenger said, "What nerve. So you'll have these young children squished while you're sitting on their seats?" Then one burly man standing next to the bench said, "If you don't get up now, I'll pick you up one by one and throw you out the window." The squatters got up, stealing glances at the threatening man. Sonju and Second Sister squeezed onto one bench, with the two youngest children on their laps, and Chuljin and Jina between them.

The train left the station and sped by the adjoining town without stopping. It was passing along a bridge over a river when a woman shrieked. "Look, look! It's a baby falling." Gasps and cries came from the passengers. "What happened?" "A baby fell." "Where?" Some people stretched their necks to look out. "From the roof of the car, right above us." "I didn't see." "I saw." Unceasing screams and wails from above.

Sonju pulled Jinju to her chest and felt Jinju's heart beating wildly against her. She fought not to dwell on the images of the baby falling or its mother's wailing. The train chugged on. Jina cried. Chuljin made faces at his sister. Second Sister tried to quiet them. Her third child, Jinjin, only two years old, unfazed by the surroundings, stared at her older siblings. Sonju put her arm around her five-year-old niece. "Jina, would you like me to tell you a story?"

Jina nodded, still crying.

"There was once a poor lady who raised three daughters. All her daughters married and moved away. She grew old and weak. She walked a long way to a large house with a tile roof. 'My eldest, please take me in. I have not eaten all day.'" Jina's crying trailed off. "The oldest daughter said, 'I don't know you. Go away!' So, the old lady walked a distance to her second ..." By that time, Jina fell asleep, trails of tears still wet on her cheeks.

Across from them, three women in Western clothes sat calmly with their erect postures and their folded hands on their laps. They gave the air of being walled off from fear, temper, horror, and the rising heat in the car. One of the women in a finely woven linen dress, the oldest of the three, perhaps in her late twenties, glanced at Jina's sleeping face, and leaning forward, said to Sonju, "She must have been exhausted from her own fright. From your accent, I assume you are from Seoul."

"I have family and friends there. I heard the bridge was bombed. Did everyone get out?"

"We had to pay a fortune to cross the Han River by boat this morning. The rower said he saw many floating bodies of civilians and soldiers who died while crossing the bridge during that bombing." The woman asked, "Where does your family live?"

"North side, near the presidential complex." The youngest of the three gasped and quickly covered her mouth with her hand, perhaps a helper, from the look of her hand.

With alarm, Sonju asked, "Was that area bombed?"

The woman's voice was calm. "We don't know. We live in the West Gate District."

Sonju took a deep breath. The enemy might have razed the entire area where her parents lived. "Where are you evacuating to?"

"To Daejon. We will stay at a home of a friend of a friend. And you?"

"We have family in Daejon."

"What school did you graduate from?" the woman asked.

"Ewha."

The woman's whole face lit up. "Me, too. What year?"

"1945"

"I am six years ahead of you so that's why you don't look familiar." Sonju returned a smile to this handsome, friendly woman who exuded an air of confidence. The woman continued,

"I don't know how long this war will last but when it's over, please visit us." After a glance at her companions then at Sonju, she said, "We work together. Let me write down my name and address." What kind of work, Sonju wondered then decided it didn't matter and put the note in her skirt pocket.

When they reached Daejon, Sonju said goodbye to the women as they stepped off the train. People poured out, pushing and shoving into the already chaotic station. Evacuees milling around, shouts from left and right. "This way!" "What did you do with the bag?" Jumbled words, loud yelling, mothers calling for children, children crying for their mothers.

Bumping and being bumped on, Sonju and family waded through the crowd, constantly checking on each other for fear of being separated. They were thrust into the train plaza, where people dispersed in all directions, opening up room to breathe. "There," Second Sister said with her chin pointing to a space near a concrete wall. After putting her luggage down, she tied Jinjin on her back in a sling, then held Chuljin with one hand and her luggage with the other. Sonju secured Jinju on her back, gripped Jina's hand, and picked up her own luggage with her free hand.

Chuljin squawked, "Mommy, let go! You are holding too tight." Second Sister yanked his squirming hand. "Hush. I don't want to lose you." She turned to Sonju, and looking unsure, said, "I have visited Sister-in-Law's house only once." What would they do if they were lost? Sonju wondered and felt anxious.

After walking a wide boulevard, turning one corner, then another, and marching on, they came to a large two-story building with a sign that read *Kim Yunggi Internal Medicine*. At the end of the building was a gate that led to a house behind the medical clinic. Second Sister announced, "Hello. We are here."

Sister-in-Law came running to meet them. "I'm so glad you made it. Come in. How are my parents?"

"They're fine. They are with the old servant." Second Sister said while a maid came from the kitchen to collect their luggage.

Sonju undid the sling and let Jinju down. "Our husbands left for Pusan yesterday morning."

Sister-in-Law looked at the four children in rumpled clothes, and turning toward the house, shouted, "Children, your aunts and cousins are here. Come out and greet them."

Sister-in-Law's children, all six of them, came out to the anteroom, lined up, gave a short quick bow to Second Sister and Sonju, and promptly disappeared into the rooms, acting as though they couldn't be bothered. How long would they have to stay in Daejon? Sonju wondered and walked to the room where Sister-in-Law pointed.

The Battle of Daejon, 1950 July

Fourteen family members and two maids crowded Sister-in-Law's five-bedroom house. Meals were served in two different parts of the living room, separated by gender.

Sister-in-Law and her husband didn't own a radio, and Sonju thought they must be old-fashioned or tight with money, but then it might not have mattered. The radio stations might not be operating anyway. Newspapers were not delivered any longer, Sister-in-Law said when Sonju asked about it. Sonju was anxious to hear the news of the war. Finally, on the third day of the evacuation, Sister-in-Law's husband sat cross-legged and cleared his throat. "One of the refugees from Seoul brought his old mother who had dysentery. He told me the president and his administration set up the government in Pusan two days after the war broke out. I didn't know."

Leaning forward, Sonju asked, "What else did you hear?"

"American troops from Japan landed in Pusan on July 1st, then moved north to stop the enemy from advancing farther south."

Second Sister turned to Sonju. "Maybe we can go home very soon."

Ignoring Second Sister, Sonju asked again, "Where are the North Koreans?"

"I don't know," Sister-in-Law's husband said.

In early July, he told the family, "Today I learned that North Korean troops won a battle in Osan two days ago. The battle is moving south."

Sonju's shoulders dropped and she watched Second Sister's hands fly to her chest. She asked, "How far is Osan from here?"

"Eighty kilometers," he said.

At the water pump, Sonju said to Second Sister, "We

would've been better off staying in Maari. The fighting will come here. This is a major city and a connecting point to Taegu."

"What do we do now?" Second Sister's face crumbled. "I wonder how our husbands are doing in Pusan. We should have gone there. We should go there *now*."

Sister-in-Law was on her way to the kitchen and must have overheard them. In an unusually sharp voice she said, "You can't leave now. How do you possibly do that with all the children? And leave my husband's practice? You are better off here."

She was right, Sonju realized. Every day Sister-in-Law's husband came home smelling iodine and exhausted from treating people with infections, dysentery, typhoid, smallpox, diphtheria, and tuberculosis. Some of his patients stayed in the patients' rooms upstairs of the clinic for a few days or longer and once in a while from the work area, Sonju could hear a series of retching coughs and painful moaning sounds. It was worse yet when a patient died and waves of wailings traveled through the house. They couldn't leave now. If they did, they might catch something on the way with so many contagious diseases that seemed to be going around. At least here, they had a doctor in the house.

All throughout the day, Sonju strained her ears to listen for any battle sounds coming near. The war had to end soon. Every day now they were eating rice with thin soup of dried pollack, and on the side, pickled daikon radishes. If they had stayed in Maari, they would be eating plenty of fresh vegetables, all the rice they could eat, and chicken or pork.

Sonju decided to take a chance on getting better food. Carrying Jinju on her back, she ventured into a street market where a few merchants displayed whatever they had to sell on their little wooden wagons. Some sold used items like clothes, pots and pans. Probably they once belonged to refugees. She couldn't find fresh vegetables anywhere. She bought four bags of dried radish strips instead. By chance, she overheard people say how some South Korean soldiers gunned down a large number of North Korean sympathizers and dumped them into mass graves. Sonju gasped at the shocking brutality of it. The world was going mad. She hurried home. She didn't go to the market again.

About two weeks into their evacuation, they were in the courtyard and heard a barrage of gunshots piercing the air, and the sound of one explosion after another coming from some distance, reverberating through the house. Sonju's heart jumped then pounded. Her breaths came out in bursts. She grabbed Jinju in a tight hold and while running, ducking, and wincing, she saw Chuljin and Jina running to their mother screaming. They all fumbled toward their room. At every frenzied staccato sound of gunfire and every loud explosion, they scrambled and huddled together in a corner of their room, pressing their ears and shutting their eyes. Jina and Jinju, and even Jinjin cried and flinched every time there was an explosion somewhere near.

Sonju had to calm the children somehow. "Children, let's sing," she said and started singing, "Twinkle, twinkle little star—" Second Sister sang along and the children followed, swallowing their sobs.

At every gunshot and explosion, their bodies lurched and shrank in a tighter pile. "Twinkle, twinkle—" Sonju urged on. They might die, she thought.

It went on in this way for days. In between the battle sounds, two maids brought food to their room on trays, and they ate exchanging nervous glances. Then during quiet moments, Sonju pictured the faces of her family, her parents-in-law, Kungu, and Misu. She wondered how many of them she would see again.

"Twinkle, twinkle—" Children sang on their own now, more loudly during the battle noises. As the explosions came one after another, shaking the earth and everything on it, they stopped singing and nestled in a pile near the wall. Second Sister said with a broken voice, "My younger brother might be fighting here."

Kungu might be too. He might die. Sonju felt as though all the blood would squeeze out of her heart. She wrapped her daughter in her arms. How could anyone survive this?

Second Sister was wringing her hands. "They must have

come through my father's village." She wrapped her head with her arms and said under her breath, "I can't stand it. I can't stand it."

Loud whizzing sounds raced across the air followed by roars of massive explosion. The house shuddered. They could all die here, Sonju thought. Her chest tightened. It was hard to breathe. Next to her, Second Sister, her head still wrapped with her arms, heaved a loud sigh and bolted up. "I can't do this," she said and sprang out of the room. Sonju ran after her. Second Sister dashed to the gate and disappeared into the dark night. Sonju heard Second Sister's two oldest children behind her, crying for their mother.

Sister-in-Law appeared at the anteroom, rushed to the children and enfolded them. "What happened?"

Sonju shot out her words, "Jinju and Jinjin are alone in the room. Would you watch the children? I'll look for Second Sister." She ran out into the night.

At first, she didn't see anyone. Her heart pounded so hard that she had to stop running and bend over to catch her breath. Gunshots rang. There were explosions lighting the street in front of her. She caught a glimpse of a lump farther down the street. "Second Sister!" Her heart pounded hard again. She ran toward the hunched figure. "Second Sister!" Second Sister was crouching by the side of the road, her arms tightly around her head, not moving. Sonju got down on her knees and shook her. "Second Sister, you're all right. Let's go home."

Second Sister lifted her head, her hands feeling Sonju's arms like a blind person. She slowly rose to her feet, leaning on Sonju. Her arm wrapped around Second Sister's waist, Sonju led her hobbling sister-in-Law toward home in the dark. The battle noise came sporadically now, but it was still happening, the deafening blast of it intensifying Second Sister's thick stink of fright. It had taken only a split second for Second Sister to leap into madness. Sonju thought it could have happened to her too.

The next morning, Second Sister was quiet and withdrawn,

oblivious of her children's anxious glances at her. After two days, she began to talk a little, saying something about her father.

A week after the bombardment, only occasional gunshots rang from the distance far south of Daejon. The family subsisted on thin rice porridge and pickled radish, and Sonju began to notice that not just the adults but also the children were becoming thin. Out of need, she went to the market again. Along the way, she saw the destruction. Houses and buildings were destroyed, and rubble lay every which way. She could still smell the burnt wood and concrete dust. The market had shrunk to only a few stalls. She was lucky to find the last scrawny chicken in a cage. Upon payment, the seller twisted off its neck. When she came home with the limp bird, she told the maid to make soup in a large kettle until meat came off the bones and save the bones for soup for the next day.

On August 1st, a clan man brought word from Father-in-Law for Sonju and Second Sister to stay in Daejon until the war was over.

Days passed. Rice dwindled. Weeks passed. No word from their husbands.

Near the end of September, Sister-in-Law's husband reported, "Our side won in the south! The enemy couldn't take Pusan and is retreating. Up north, the UN forces landed at Inchon and captured Kimpo Airfield, so the enemy is stuck in the south with their supplies cut off."

A week later, Sister-in-Law's husband sprinted to the living room, shouting, "Seoul was liberated four days ago, on the 27th!"

Even before those words fully settled in Sonju's head, Second Sister pulled her into their room. "We're leaving tomorrow. Let's pack."

"We should wait," Sonju said, watching Second Sister walk around the room picking up her things and packing them. "Enemy soldiers are moving north. They will pass through Maari. Who knows what they would do, desperate as they are."

"We'll be safe. The enemy won't ride trains in their retreat."

"Father-in-Law said to wait until the war is over. It's not over yet."

Tears welled up in Second Sister's eyes. "I'm going. With my children. We're running out of food here. At least we have food in Maari. I must have news of my father." She was crying by the time she finished her words.

Sonju recalled the night Second Sister lost her mind. For the first time, Sonju regarded Second Sister as a selfish person. She said, "I can't let you leave alone with three children in tow." Sonju packed her things to leave the following day.

When she told Sister in Law of their decision to leave and thanked her profusely for taking them into her house and sharing food, Sister-in-Law looked worried, reminding her that the war wasn't over.

After three months, Sonju's party left Daejon. On the way to the train station, before she saw what it was, Sonju smelled the stench of fresh kill like the smell of a waste bucket in a butcher shop.

Second Sister crinkled her nose. "What is that smell?"

When they turned the corner, Sonju saw to their right on a wide patch of ground a group of tattered bodies of men and women all lined up, hands bound and faces down, not moving. Dark blood stains on the ground, streaks of blood from the heads to the necks with some parts blown away, and bloodied spots on their civilian clothes. She almost gagged, her nausea working itself up, and wondered if they were also in danger. Instinctively, she and Second Sister turned the children sharply around to keep them from seeing. But of course, they saw. Chuljin and Jina were old enough to know what they glimpsed. That's why they didn't ask questions. They now knew death, how violent it could be. Holding hands, they all ran toward the train station. Sonju wanted to scream. Her head was about to explode in anger. They shouldn't have left. Father-in-law sent word to them not to return until the war was over. The limp bodies reduced to animal flesh, reeking animal stench so sticky it seeped into her pores, into her nose—she smelled it no matter how fast or how far they ran. She didn't realize she was crying.

Sonju and Second Sister spoke little to each other during the train ride. One stop before Maari, the train halted, and without any explanation, the conductor told the passengers to get off.

Sonju's party joined a long line of people walking on the raised narrow dirt paths between rice fields. Chuljin complained of blisters on his toes. Jina whined about her tired feet. Second Sister let down two-year old Jinjin, tied five-year-old Jina on her back, and carried her luggage in one hand and held Chuljin's hand in the other. Jinjin, Second Sister's youngest child, two years old, held Sonju's free hand and toddled without one single complaint. She was a tough girl, born on the election day, not saying much but always observing. Sonju squeezed Jinjin's little hand and turned her head over her shoulder for a glimpse of Jinju on her back. They followed the procession of women carrying bundles of their belongings on their heads and men carrying heavy things on their backs. Near the railroad Sonju saw a large crater. How many had died in that explosion? she wondered. How many had died all over the country?

Further along stretched harvested farmland far into the base of tall hills in the distance. The air was clear all around. Sonju could breathe now. Her heart leapt when she saw in the distance the familiar shade tree under which Second House farm workers had eaten lunch. They hurried through the underpass of the railroad toward the clan houses. As they neared the house on the hill, Sonju looked up and saw the roof peeking above the juniper fence. The chestnut tree at the edge of the Second House property still stood with its lower limb bent at a familiar angle. "We're home, children." Sonju quickened her pace.

Chuljin and Jina clapped their hands and ran up the hill to the outer courtyard pumping their little legs and huffing. Chuljin pushed the gate open, raced to the courtyard, shouting, "Grandma! Grandpa!" From the kitchen, Mother-in-Law came running, flashing a teeth-showing smile and glinting eyes, embraced Chuljin and Jina as they plunged into her arms. Father-in-Law stroked the children's heads one by one. Second Sister and Sonju bowed to their parents-in-law.

"How have you been?" Sonju asked, still out of breath from walking fast up the steep slope to the house.

"Nothing bad happened to us," Father-in-Law said. "We didn't expect you yet, but I am glad you made it home safely."

Second Sister's two older children chattered about the guns and explosions to their grandparents, but not about the dead bodies they saw. Their grandmother reminded them about the rabbit, and they took off to the back to check on their pet. With the children out of sight and hearing, Second Sister asked, "Did the fighting come here, too?"

"Yes, it passed very quickly." Mother-in-Law didn't elaborate, but seemed anxious to avoid the topic.

Dragging her luggage to her room, Second Sister muttered in a despairing tone, "Then the battle must have come to my father's village as well."

After Father-in-Law returned to the men's quarters, Sonju remained with Mother-in-Law and asked, "Is Jinwon back?"

"She is at Big House." Mother-in-Law lowered her voice. "The Little House's two sons went to the North. They are communists. Your husband never told you that, did he?"

"No. Only that they studied very hard," Sonju said, "He said they barely spoke to him in spite of sharing the house for two years."

"Even after they graduated from the university, they rarely came to see their parents." Mother-in-Law clucked her tongue. "Now their parents can't face people. If you see them, don't mention their sons." She then walked to the servant's quarters and ordered a servant to kill three chickens for dinner.

Mother-in-Law cared for Jinju and Jinjin—a necessary task in the absence of maids—while Sonju and Second Sister prepared a meal. She watched her grandchildren devour the food and sniffled. "Look at them eating like beggars," she said.

After the kitchen work was done, Sonju carried a bucket of hot water to her room and washed Jinju and herself with wet cloth, then laid the *yo* on the floor. Jinju fell asleep right away and started to snore.

Only a day later, in the inner courtyard, Second Sister was telling Chuljin he'd better get his books out and study because he was going back to school as soon as it opened. He whined. His five-year-old sister Jina said, "I will go. I can count numbers up to one hundred and I read better than he does."

Chuljin pushed her down, and she wailed.

"Shhh! Jinjin is sleeping." Their mother hissed. Sonju picked up Jina off the ground to keep her away from her brother. Second Sister grabbed Chuljin and ordered him to go study and sent Jina to her rabbit in the back of the house.

Just then, a clan woman walked in. "I heard Second House ladies arrived. I came to welcome you home."

"Yes, yesterday. Thank you," Sonju said and led her to the anteroom. Mother-in-Law joined them.

The woman looked at Sonju and Second Sister, and said, "While you were gone, Yankee soldiers came looking for North Korean soldiers and searched houses." Mother-in-Law nodded at Second Sister's questioning look. The woman continued. "Our young women were scared. I heard they hid in the windowless room at the Little House. They let their hair down and painted their teeth black with charcoal soot to look like toothless old women."

"Was anyone raped?" Sonju asked.

Before the woman could answer, Mother-in-Law said, "No. The soldiers went through here quickly."

"I'm glad you're back." A loud voice came from the gates, and all four women turned.

The hunchback approached the anteroom with his particular gait with his head and arms forward. "I'm not going to sit." He stopped and smiled at Sonju and Second Sister. "Your parents-in-law worried so much when they learned about the major battle in Daejon." He swiped the air with his hand. "War is a horrible thing, just horrible. Many Yankees died here. There were bodies scattered on the rise along the creek. It was a terrible sight. It happened so fast." He shook his head. "Some village boys went from body to body looking for rings and watches. I saw one boy wearing watches from his wrists all the way to his elbows on both arms. Shame, shame."

Sonju again saw the images of the strewn corpses in Daejon. The stench rose in her nostrils. She exhaled and held her breath. She could still smell it, the same odor in her nightmares.

"What happened to all those bodies?" Second Sister asked with a side glance at Sonju.

"Some Yankees came in trucks and took them away. I have to go now."

After the hunchback left, the woman said, "A few young village men turned red. They said that under communism everybody shares and there are no rich, privileged people like us. They wanted to lynch Big House Master."

"Big House Master? And what happened?" Sonju asked.

"The villagers chased them back to their houses, some beating them with their bare fists. The men weren't seen again. I guess they left to join the communists."

The woman continued with the village news until Mother-in-Law turned to her and said, "I need to go to Big House. I will walk out with you."

Before going to her room, Second Sister said, "I thought that woman would never stop talking."

Sonju went to her room and started sorting out clothes to wash. Once in a while she watched her sleeping daughter. It saddened her that even long after her daughter had forgotten the battle sounds, the experience of fear might color her in some way. It saddened her too that the village was no longer a quiet, insulated place. It used to be simple. It used to be innocent. But now unaccustomed unease had settled here not knowing what or whom they could depend on or trust.

She heard Mother-in-Law tell Second Sister, "With all the excitement, I forgot. I have a letter for you from your family." Sonju dropped the clothes and went to the living room. "Any letters for me?" Mother-in-Law shook her head. Second Sister went to her room, a letter held to her chest, smiling ear to ear. Sonju dropped her head, returned to her room, and put aside the dirty clothes in a pile.

Within moments came a piercing scream, then a heart-tearing wail.

Sonju rushed to Second Sister's room, swung the door open and found Second Sister weeping, her upper body collapsed to the floor, her shoulders heaving, the letter still in her hand.

"What happened?"

Second Sister sat up and lifted her wet face. Some hair strands were stuck to her cheeks. "They killed my father."

Sonju sucked in the air. "Who killed your father?"

"Two communist sympathizers. My family knows them."

Someone gasped. Sonju turned. Mother-in-Law was standing at the door looking at Second Sister. "Was your brother there, too?"

"Not my older brother. My younger brother came home a month later and after learning of our father's death, he dragged the two killers to our father's grave and shot them dead. He is back with his troops." She covered her face and sobbed.

Sonju sat very still. This was the first casualty in the family. Something thick and heavy pressed her chest.

"I have to go to my father's grave." Second Sister sobbed again.

"Go see your mother. Go with the old servant," Mother-in-Law said.

The children gathered at the door. "What's wrong, Mommy?" Jina cried.

Sonju took the children to her room. "A bad thing happened to your grandfather, your Mommy's father, so she is very sad."

"A bad thing?" Jina asked.

"Yes. Your mother will tell you about it later."

That night, the servant returned and reported that Second Sister arrived at her birth home safely.

Husband's Return, 1951 Spring

Over the next few days, Second House maids and servants drifted back. Even though life went on as before, the war had not come to an end. The future was uncertain especially for those families whose men were still fighting near the 38th parallel. Finally, a letter from Brother-in-Law arrived thirteen days from the date marked in which he wrote that it was their third letter and that he and his brother would return home when safe.

Mother-in-Law said harvesting was done with fewer men on hand with women taking up more burden than before and *Chuseok* feast was rather somber with no family members to celebrate with. Sonju just realized *Chuseok* wasn't even mentioned in Daejon.

Second Sister hadn't yet returned from her birth home, the two younger children were napping, Jinwon was at Big House, Mother-in-Law in her room, and the maids had retreated to the servant's quarters. Sonju leaned against the wall in the anteroom with the afternoon sun obliquely pouring down on her. Chuljin and Jina had been running back and forth between the inner courtyard and the back of the house talking and laughing. Sonju could still hear their chatter and thought they had been in the backyard for some time now. Then she heard a plane flying low, and without thinking, she lurched, ready to run for the children. She stopped when the hunchback burst into the courtyard and said with an agitated urgency, "Stranded enemy soldiers are terrorizing people on their way back north. They may come this way."

Mother-in-Law came out to the anteroom. "Were they spotted near here? How do you know this?"

"My brother-in-law from Gongju. He told me they should be close to Maari. He said these soldiers take food and kidnap people, and shoot them in the head. I have to go. I have to warn others."

In the near absence of young active men, very little news flowed into the village. The villagers now relied on the hunchback to receive any new information about the war. As Sonju's husband had done at the beginning of the war, the hunchback went to the train station and talked to the station manager and the train passengers.

Promptly afterwards, Father-in-Law went to discuss the matter with Big House Master and returned to tell his wife and Sonju that their servants would walk daily to nearby villages and towns to the south and west to find out the whereabouts of the North Korean soldiers.

Four days later, Father-in-Law said to Sonju, "A group of enemy soldiers were sighted in a village south of here. It's not safe for young people to stay. Our maids and servants will return to their families. You take Jinwon and the younger children and go to my wife's brother's home. Leave Chuljin and Jina with us."

The following morning, seeing Sonju's party getting ready to leave, Chuljin and Jina hung onto Sonju's legs and cried, "Please take us, please."

In their upturned eyes, Sonju read the same anticipation of fear she saw during the days in Daejon. She bent down. "It won't be long before we're back, you'll see."

"No! It will be a long, long time with artillery and gunshots again." Chuljin twisted his little body and cried, shaking Sonju's leg while his sister clutched on to Sonju, crying, "Mommy, Mommy, I want my Mommy."

Mother-in-Law pulled them from Sonju. "They will be back in five days, maybe sooner."

Still crying, the children finally let go of Sonju, their faces wet and slimy.

Sonju turned away, wiping her tears on her sleeve.

The old servant carried bags of clothes and a sack of rice on his A-frame carrier. Sonju carried Jinju on her back and held Jinjin's hand. Jinwon carried nothing. All along the way until they arrived in the remote village in the early afternoon, Jinwon kept repeating how bored she was going to be. Tired of her complaints, Sonju asked, "Would you rather take a risk of getting raped?" Instead of a reply, Jinwon kicked a gravel.

In that village of less than four dozen houses, time seemed to stretch and drag. They didn't know the people and didn't dare to go into the woods. Having little to entertain themselves with, Jinwon and the children took frequent naps. The hours between mornings and nights were unbearably long.

Her husband was safe, but Kungu … Sonju closed her eyes and rubbed her forehead, trying to rid herself of the morbid thoughts. She felt her skirt being tugged.

Jinwon sat up and said, "I've been thinking …" She drew her clasped hands up to her chest as in prayer. "A dark blue, shimmering velvet skirt. That's what I want before I die." She looked serious when she said this.

Sonju stared at her, heartbroken that this lively young woman had thought about the possibility of dying just when she was beginning to glimpse into her future. There were things she herself would regret if death were to happen to her, she thought. "You're fortunate that what you want is something you can have."

"You want something you can't have?" Jinwon asked.

"Let's get you a velvet skirt," Sonju said.

Too excited about getting her velvet skirt, Jinwon didn't question Sonju as she would have in other times. Instead, she beamed a young, hopeful smile. It was a lovely sight to behold, a simple desire filled with so much pleasure.

Jinwon said, "You would like to hear this, Little Auntie. I heard Grandma say to Grandfather that you told her one of the Second House girls may become a great leader one day, like Queen Sunduk."

"Did she seem convinced?"

"No, but she talked about it," Jinwon said with an impish smile and raised brows.

They had been at the village six days when the old servant arrived. "Your father-in-law wants you to come home. He said the danger has passed."

The walk back home seemed much shorter. As soon as they

arrived in Maari, Jinwon left for Big House after a quick bow to her grandparents. Chuljin and Jina squealed and ran to Sonju.

Pulling Sonju's skirt, Jina said, "Auntie, North Korean soldiers came, and, and, and, walked around looking everywhere. Grandpa looked scared, so I was scared. They told Grandma to cook for them."

"I wasn't scared." Chuljin grinned with pride.

Ignoring her brother, Jina said, "One had a gun, a *real* gun. I was so scared. He could shoot us any time he felt like it with that gun." Then with a whimper, she said, "Auntie, they took my rabbit. They put it in a sack. Grandpa said he'll get me another one." Her eyes brimming with tears, she wrapped her arms around Sonju's legs.

Sonju stroked Jina's head and glanced at Mother-in-Law, who nodded and fixed her eyes on Sonju, a sign that she couldn't talk then.

Jina lifted her head, tear streaks still on her face. "After they ate, Grandpa gave them chickens, rice, and my rabbit. Grandma said they were going back home."

Mother-in-Law turned to the children and told them to go to the backyard to play. She waited until they were out of sight and said to Sonju, "Your father-in-law did not give them her rabbit. They came two days after you left. This was a group of five. I had the children with me in the kitchen when they walked to the back of the house. Your father-in-law saw them eyeing the chickens and the rabbit. He told the captain they could take as many chickens as they wanted but not the rabbit. The captain grabbed the rabbit out of the cage and wrung its neck and had the enlisted men do the same with the chickens."

"Did they harm anyone in the village?"

"No. I don't know why they picked our house. Three of them were young boys of fifteen and sixteen. One said he was working on a farm when he was ordered to report to the army. Those boys were very polite. They likely will be captured before they make it up north." She clucked her tongue.

Sonju hated what the war did to people, what people did

to people during the time of war. How would they reconcile themselves in gentler times with who they were during the war? How many would be ruined because of their memories of violence? Her gloom lifted when one by one the maids and the field hands returned. One of the field hands had been drafted to the Army.

The first week of November, Sonju and Mother-in-Law made two hundred heads of kimchi, half of what they had made in previous years. The following week, Second Sister appeared at the gate, her cheeks sunken and eyes hollow, looking ten years older. After bowing to the parents-in-law, she went to her room and shut the door.

Sonju waited half an hour before she went to Second Sister's room, sat next to her and asked, "How did your visit go?"

"I feel like an orphan," Second Sister said flatly without looking at Sonju.

Sonju didn't know what to say to comfort her.

When Second Sister drew her knees up and put her head down on them, Sonju left the grief-soaked room and went to the veranda. She couldn't imagine grieving as much as Second Sister did if her own father had died. Perhaps because ever since she was a child, there was in her a sense of familial alienation against which or because of which she had always fought to hold onto a sense of herself. Without that, she thought, she would have lost her way. Now she wasn't sure if she could still fight the same fight in her marriage. She looked up at the grey sky. It was going to be a chilly, somber season.

Then, in spite of the slapping cold wind, Big House Lady came and asked Mother-in-Law, "Did you hear? The North Koreans were pushed all the way to the Amnok River."

"To the Chinese border? We are winning then. My sons will return soon."

That was in November, five months after the war broke out. A month later, the Second House family was still waiting.

The first weekend in January, the hunchback came and told Sonju and Mother-in-Law, "The North Korean Army took

Seoul again with the help of Chinese troops. Our allies retreated south of the Han River."

Now that the enemy was strengthened, how far south would they advance? Exasperated, Sonju turned to Mother-in-Law and asked, "Do we evacuate again?"

"I don't know. We will see what your father-in-law says."

No one in the village evacuated, but the hunchback said that every day southbound trains passed filled with refugees. The train conductor told him that many of these fleeing refugees were North Koreans, most of them Christians fearing North Korea becoming a vassal state of Communist China which was known to persecute Christians.

One day when the sun was out all day and the melted snow on the roof dribbled down along the eves, Jinwon came to Sonju's room and said, "None of my friends are home, so I am stuck in this house. It's so gloomy here. I can't stand it."

Sonju felt the same way. Second Sister still caged herself in her room and mourned, which dampened the mood of the entire house. Sonju said, "I miss talking to Second Sister. I wanted to tell her about your velvet skirt. How did you put it? A shimmering, dark blue velvet skirt before you died?" She cocked her head to the side looking at Jinju. "You haven't uttered a word about it for five months. You either forgot about it or you're very sure you'll live."

"I didn't forget."

Sonju smiled. "This is the perfect time to wear it, isn't it? Let's go to the market and make a day of it. Before the war, my husband gave me part of his salary."

The following evening, Sonju told Mother-in-Law, "Tomorrow morning, Jinwon and I will go to the market. Some time ago, I promised her I would get her a velvet skirt."

If Mother-in-Law were to protest the frivolity of a velvet skirt in the time of war, Sonju was going to stand her ground but she didn't have to. Mother-in-Law didn't react.

Sonju and Jinwon bought the velvet material and left it with a dressmaker. Afterwards, they had lunch at a restaurant and went to a bookstore, where Sonju found books of short stories by Oscar Wilde, O. Henry, and Guy de Maupassant. The store owner promised he would have *Arabian Nights* by Friday of the following week. Their leisurely walk from one store to another looking and chatting gave Sonju a feeling that things were almost normal.

Next morning, she gathered the children in her room and read *The Happy Prince*. Chuljin complained that it was silly and boring. "A statue cannot talk," he said and left, muttering that he didn't believe any of the story. Jinju seemed confused about the fuss Chuljin was making. Second Sister's two daughters, Jina and Jinjin sat, eagerly waiting for the words to flow from Sonju's mouth. One story a day, Sonju told them. After the children dispersed, she was flipping through the pages of another book when an idea came to her. She could read the books to the clan women perhaps once or twice a week and have a discussion afterwards. She was sorry she didn't think of it before. She would need more books. She shared her idea about a reading discussion with a few clan women.

The following Friday, Sonju and Jinwon returned to the market and picked up Jinwon's velvet skirt. Sonju bought two books in addition to the one she had ordered. Shortly after they arrived home, Jinwon pranced in her new skirt but had the good sense not to go beyond the house to flaunt it.

A few days later, the *yo*-making hostess's two daughters offered their home for the reading. The first time, four people came—the Philanderer's two daughters, their mother and aunt. Three days later, two more joined—the woman with Buddha ears and the dark-skinned woman from the *yo*-making. After reading and the book discussion, the women gossiped about the village people. The third time they met, what the women said about the stories surprised Sonju and surprised them too— their excitement at a world they had not known, the wonder of it—the wonder probably not so different from what Sonju had experienced when she first saw the photographs of Western people in a magazine. Sonju was imagining with others again and helping enrich the lives of those women who were not likely to have this kind of experience otherwise. This gave Sonju a sense of fulfillment she had craved.

The day after the fourth meeting, Buddha Ears came to Sonju. "I heard it's easy to learn to read and write. Can you teach me so that I can read stories on my own one day?"

"Yes, of course. We can start now if you have time."

Sonju felt gratified by this woman's willingness to learn something new, especially because this was the woman who had said during the *yo* making that she no longer dreamed even in her imagination. She drew a grid on a piece of paper and filled in the consonants across the top grid boxes and vowels down the vertical grid boxes, sounding out a consonant and a vowel together to form a character. After practice, Buddha Ears left with the alphabet chart, a stack of blank paper, and several pencils to practice at home. Sonju promised she would give her a handwritten copy of *The Last Leaf* so that she could practice reading on her own. Before copying the story, she lay down on the floor and lifted her legs and arms up in the air and kicked in her excitement.

By the time spring arrived, two more women had joined the reading group, the birds had returned, and the fields had been tilled, but Second Sister still locked herself in her room and wept. Sonju spent more and more time with the children, all four of them.

The hunchback came in mid-March and announced that the allies had pushed the enemy forces back to the 38th parallel and Seoul was liberated again. After hearing that news, every afternoon and evening when the northbound train whistled, Sonju expected her husband and his brother to come through the gates. She checked the blossoms on the cherry tree every day and saw the first open blossom with Jinju the day she turned two.

One afternoon a few days later, Sonju found six-year-old Jina sitting quietly alone on the veranda leaning back with her palms planted on the wooden planks and her legs stretched out. Her school bag was nearby. She had come to the veranda straight from school. Jina looked up at Sonju. "I like to watch the plants grow. May I stay here?" She had helped her grandfather plant new plants in the gardens when the soil was damp after a spring shower.

"Of course." Sonju lowered herself next to Jina.

"You and Mommy used to do grown-up talk here," Jina said without looking at Sonju.

"Yes, but you can stay," Sonju said. Poor child, her mother aloof and silent. "Your impatiens plants are getting bigger," she said.

Jina opened her fingers wide and studied them. "I hope those flowers are red. I want to stain my nails with the petals," she said, but her voice was flat and her expression blank.

Sonju remembered the feeling of crushing rejection when her own mother refused to comb her hair when she was five. She moved closer and wrapped her arms around Jina. "When they bloom, would you stain Jinju's nails too? And mine?"

All four children were playing in the back of the house, invigorated by the warmth of the mid-April sun. Sonju listened to them chatter and argue and wished Second Sister would join her on the veranda with a bright smile. She still found Jina gloomy at times and when she argued with her brother, it was with bitterness and intensity. It was getting late, and she thought she should collect the children soon. Then she heard, "We are home!"

Sonju ran toward the voice. Mother-in-Law lost her shoe on the way to the courtyard but before she had a chance to grab her sons' hands, Father-in-Law led his two sons to the men's quarters. The sons turned and bowed quickly to their mother before they disappeared into the men's quarters with their father. Mother-in-Law looked down, muttering something between her downturned lips, trudged back, and pushed her foot into the shoe.

Sonju went to the backyard and told Second Sister's

children, "Your father has come home." Then to Jinju, "Your daddy, too. We'll greet them when they finish talking with your grandfather."

Clapping and giggling, the children followed her to the anteroom. They sat on the ledge, side by side like sparrows on a powerline, and waited. After a while, they became bored and restless. Chuljin and Jina were shoving each other. Jinjin asked where her father was, and Jinju was busy staring at Chuljin then at Jina. Even though Sonju talked about her daddy often, Jinju would have to get to know her father after nine months of absence.

Fifteen minutes or so must have passed when Brother-in-Law, his head hung low, came out of the room.

His children shouted, "Daddy!"

He lifted his head and came over. He then gathered his three children and went to his room.

Sonju studied her husband's leaner face as he walked up to her and said, "Welcome home."

"It's terrible news about Second Sister's father," He said, picking up Jinju. "I need a bath."

Sonju had the maids heat water in the bathhouse, and when dinner was ready, she had them take trays of food to Second Sister's room. After she took a tray to her Father-in-Law, she sat by Jinju at the table in the living room where Mother-in-Law seated herself next to her son, and putting pieces of meat in his rice bowl, asked, "How was it in Pusan? Did you have enough to eat?"

"Pusan was not directly attacked. For six weeks, the UN troops fought battles along Masan, Taegu, and Pohang. The American forces blew up the Nakdong River bridges to stop the enemies. Hundreds of refugees died crossing the river to get to Taegu. After the enemy lost and retreated, we were on our way home. We turned back when Seoul was taken again in January. We left when the refugees from Seoul left."

"I am so glad you are home." Mother-in-Law put more meat in his bowl.

After a bath and more talk with his mother, Sonju's husband

came to the bedroom, watched his sleeping daughter for a while, and lay on the *yo*. Sonju pulled him close. "We missed you." Without words, he proceeded to undress her, then his hungry rush took over, same as before.

Looking well-rested the next morning, he said, "I'll visit the clan elders after I finish breakfast with my father."

"Before you go, you need to know something."

"What is it?"

"Little House sons voluntarily went to the North. Don't mention them to the Little House family. Your mother asked me if they ever indicated to you their communist inklings."

"No. Why would they?"

"I feel bad for the Little House family." The war wasn't over and the returning soldiers could retaliate on them in revenge.

He told her that one of his colleagues who went to the university with him left for the North. He had no idea that his classmate had Marxist ideas. This man left his wife and two children behind. Sonju said, "What a tragedy." Her husband said two of his colleagues joined the army even though they didn't have to since they were government employees. She wondered if her husband had ever thought about sacrificing himself for a cause as his two colleagues had done.

After six days at home, her husband and his brother returned to their work. That evening, Second Sister came to Sonju. "Thank you for taking care of my children and the kitchen."

"I missed you," Sonju said.

Second Sister closed her eyes briefly then said, "I will accept life as it is."

In early May, Sonju received a letter from her sister.

1951 April 22

Dear Sister,
I hope you are home safe. So many times, I wished you

lived in Seoul. I wish that even more so now at the thought that the war could have gone much worse.

We returned to Seoul as soon as it was freed in March, the fourth such liberation. I visited our parents and brother and found them safe. During their evacuation to the family house of one of their servants, the men's quarters and most of the servant's quarters were destroyed. My family also evacuated to my husband's relative's house in the country. No relative of ours suffered any casualties, but our cousin Duson volunteered and is still fighting along the 38th parallel.

Seoul is devastated as you can imagine. There are reports of talks to end the war, but we will live with the remains of the war for a long time.

I wish I could see you. I hope you and your family are safe.

Sonju felt relieved that her parents and brother were safe. She folded the letter at the creases and thought of Kungu. Was he safe? Was he alive? Unlike her husband, he would have volunteered to fight for the country.

Sonju's Grievances, 1951

Sonju's husband came home on the weekends as he did before, and they soon settled into the same pre-war pattern—his habitual dismissal of her, her simmering anger toward him. In July, he was promoted again, his second promotion. It had been only three and a half years since he started working, and he now had five junior engineers under him.

With a dazzling smile in his eyes, he said, "My superior's brother-in-law is a close friend of the head of the Interior Ministry. If he transfers to Seoul, he wants me there with him."

"I'm so happy for you and for our family," she said. "Perhaps we will be in Seoul when Jinju starts school."

His transfer to Seoul could happen in a few years. She reckoned her mother-in-law might try to keep her from leaving, and he would likely go along with his mother, so on Monday, she entered Mother-in-Law's hobby room and said, "Mother-in-Law, the other day, you heard my husband talking about the possibility of him being posted in Seoul. I don't know if that will happen or when that will be, but I will move to Seoul when Jinju starts school whether he has a job there or not."

Mother-in-Law stared at her, scratched her arm, and with a resigned voice said, "If you move ... even though you may think I am old-fashioned and stubborn, I have heard what you said about women who accomplished great things." After a shift of her bulky hips, she asked, "How would your sister-in-law get along without you?"

Sonju stood her ground. "You can hire another maid. Any maid can do what I do."

Mother-in-Law lowered her eyes, and after a long silence, she asked, "If you move, how often would I see my son or you?"

A sudden understanding hit Sonju like an unexpected storm. Mother-in-Law's fear of losing another son, this time to a city far away, distance that might grow in her son's heart as it had happened to the Big House sons. Sonju took Mother-in-Law's hands and stroked them. The loose skin moved passively over the bones. If it weren't for Jinju's education, she wouldn't mind staying, she thought, gazing at her mother-in-law. Her daughter's pointy chin and clear intelligent eyes came from her grandmother, and Sonju was glad for that.

With a warm smile, Mother-in-Law said, "Besides, how am I going to pass my days without hearing your talk about great women? They are like new adventures to me."

Those words felt to Sonju like an acknowledgment of her relevance to her mother-in-law, an acknowledgment she had needed from her own mother. She was overwhelmed with gratitude. She cupped her mother-in-law's hands in her own, and with the same warm smile, said, "I am very fond of you, Mother-in-Law."

Children's chatter was coming in through the gate. As she was leaving, Sonju told Mother-in-Law, "Jinju is not yet three. You and I have at least two more years together."

Sonju was still relishing her mother-in-law's words when some days later she heard arguments coming from the inner courtyard.

One man said, "Your daughter-in-law from Seoul is corrupting our women."

Sonju's ears perked up. Too bad there were no more holes on the papered window. Otherwise, she would have looked out through the holes.

The man continued, "My wife talks back to me now. She said your daughter-in-law told the women if there's nothing to eat but one egg, boil it and give half to the husband and the other half to herself."

She heard her father-in-law laugh and say, "My daughter-in-law said that?" He laughed again.

Mother-in-Law said, "So, you would rather have the whole egg while your wife goes hungry? Is that what you are saying?"

Sonju couldn't believe what she was hearing. Her in-laws were standing up for her. No one in her birth family had done that for her before.

Another man said, "Your daughter-in-law read a story about a husband and wife giving a gift to each other, and my wife asked for one."

Mother-in-Law spoke again, "Set aside the best part of meat, chicken, or fish for your wife, especially in front of your children so they learn to appreciate their mother. Your wife has been eating gristle, chicken feet, and fish tails while you enjoyed the best parts."

The first man said, "Second House Master, say something. Your daughter-in-law brainwashed your wife, too."

Father-in-Law cleared his throat. "Big House Master had the school built to educate all of the village children. I sent my first daughter-in-law to a boarding school. My third daughter-in-law is an educated woman with a fine mind. It seems to me that she is doing what Big House Master and I have done. Go home. No more talk about this."

The men left, still muttering.

Sonju released a puff of air, "Ha!"

The next day, Buddha Ears came to a reading with both wrists bruised. The next time, Sonju glimpsed under the edge of sleeves fresh new bruises extending beyond Buddha Ears' wrists. When the reading session was over, she walked with Buddha Ears, and after they turned the corner by the mud brick fence where no one was around, she gently pulled Buddha Ears' skirt. When she asked about the bruises, Buddha Ears said her husband didn't want her to learn to read and get fancy ideas. At the next meeting, Buddha Ears had one arm in a crude sling made of a cotton scarf. She told the women she fell at the well, but lowered her eyes when they met Sonju's.

Sonju could sense that the abuse was getting more serious each time. What next? After reading to the women, Sonju told them there was something she had to take care of and asked them to continue with their discussion until she returned.

Buddha Ears' husband saw her walk through the open gate into his courtyard. His eyes shone with hate. His mouth twisted, ready to shout something. Sonju walked up to him, glaring.

"You broke your wife's arm," she said and saw from the corner of her eye Buddha Ears' maid dashing out the gate.

Buddha Ears' husband punctured the air with his index finger pointing at her, his face red with fury, spittle flying as he yelled "You, you. How dare you talk like that to a man?"

She snickered. "What kind of man abuses his wife because she is learning to read?"

He walked back and forth with his fists clenched, loud breathing coming from his nose and mouth audible from where Sonju stood. He stopped pacing, raised his balled fist, and got closer to her. Sonju didn't move. Instead, she stared at his fist until it slowly began to loosen.

The gate squeaked and Sonju's father-in-law walked toward them with the maid several steps behind. Buddha Ears' husband looked at Sonju's father-in-law, and dropped his hand. His mouth fluttered ready to speak.

Father-in-Law said, "I understand that you have been abusing your wife. I spent money worth a plot of farmland to educate my daughter and my first daughter-in-law. Your wife is receiving a free education. Now, you make sure you take your wife to the doctor tomorrow morning. I will visit you again to check on your wife's progress."

Red faced, the man bowed to Father-in-Law.

Sonju returned to the waiting women.

The Philanderer's wife said, "We discussed the reading already. We were gossiping. Is everything well?"

"Yes. Everything is taken care of," Sonju said. "I see that you can run this reading group by yourselves."

"We still want to hear your opinion and all the other things you tell us," Buddha Ears said with a big grin. In spite of her husband's ongoing abuse, she hadn't missed one meeting. Sonju almost choked with tender feelings. She felt anger and sadness too, but most of all, admiration for Buddha Ears' eagerness to learn.

The following morning, when Sonju carried a breakfast tray to the men's quarters, Father-in-Law said, "Don't take matters into your own hands."

Her heart was crushed like a scolded child who had disappointed her most admired person in the world. But she couldn't just watch and do nothing when she was partly responsible for Buddha Ears' situation.

By the afternoon of the following day, everyone in the village seemed to know what she had done. Men openly talked about her among themselves in her presence. A few men walked around her as if she were a leper.

When Sonju passed by three women standing under the chestnut tree, one of them said, "Look at her. Who does she think she is?" The kindest remark came from a woman: "You rattled some people, only because a woman had done it."

That Sunday, her husband returned from his visit with the clan men and said, "I heard what happened. Why do you stir things up? Why can't you just let things be?"

His words came across to her like a provocation even though they were basically the same words as her father-in-law's. It was a peek into her own bias against her husband, yet she couldn't help herself. "Because things are not right."

"So, is it your job to make things right?"

"I taught his wife how to read and write. I felt responsible."

"What would have happened if my father hadn't shown up in time before the man broke your arm too?"

"He wouldn't have. I'm your wife." It was possible that he was genuinely concerned about her. With a certain degree of remorse, she watched him snort and turn away.

One woman quit the reading group as a result of her action. Buddha Ears never mentioned it and the other women didn't bring it up. Sonju was relieved not to see further signs of abuse on Buddha Ears.

Over time, the village noise died down. Sonju was preparing for the next reading group when Jinju toddled into the room and handed her a half-eaten rice cake. "Thank you for sharing. Mmm, it tastes good. Next time, share it with Daddy. He would like that."

"I know." Jinju's favorite words.

"Do you know what Daddy does when he is away?"

Jinju's hair swung from side to side.

"Daddy does important work. He makes plans for roads and bridges so people can go to places easier. They will be the best roads and bridges."

Jinju repeated, "Best roads and bridges." They both clapped their hands and said it one more time.

When her husband came home Saturday, Jinju sat on his lap and clapped her hands. "Best roads and bridges. Daddy, you will make the best roads and bridges."

Sonju smiled when he glanced at her. "I told her what you do at work." She couldn't tell if he was flattered, and wondered if his daughter's words would inspire him to do his best work for the public.

When she was sure of her pregnancy, she entered Mother-in-Law's room and sat next to her, and held her old veiny hands. She said, "I want you to be the first to know. I am pregnant."

"That is the best news. When is the baby due?"

"Mid-March." This time, Sonju hoped for a boy just to see her mother-in-law's joy.

The unbearable heat still persisted into the late evening. Her daughter was sleeping with slightly parted lips. She fanned Jinju's little face and imagined her life filled with children.

That Saturday, when she told her husband about her pregnancy, he said with a smile as big as the moon, "another child!"

"I want to have at least three children," she said, "an odd number so they will always have a majority when they argue among themselves."

"Another child." He nodded with a look of dreaminess she had never seen in her husband before. She thought if she bore a baby boy, she would like to name him after her husband. With a bubbly voice she said, "Now that another child is on the way, do you think there will be changes in our marriage, a turning point?"

"What's wrong with our marriage?" he asked, mockingly.

She was crushed. Their conversation had started out so well. "I don't want to be a mere appendage to you. I don't want our children to see me as such. I have my own thoughts and ideas so I want you to hear me. I want to have a voice."

"What voice? Are you a politician?" He smirked.

She bit her lip at his slight. "No, I'm a person just like you. Are my opinions not worthy of your consideration?"

"How can you think that? I tell you I adore you."

"I don't know what you mean when you say that."

With a sly smile, he said, "I like that you're different. I even like the way you speak."

"But not what I say."

"No. Don't challenge me. I'm your husband."

She could feel her face flush. "Don't dismiss me. I'm your wife, your equal." She narrowed her eyes and said, "We are bound together for life and it's up to us to make our marriage satisfying for both of us."

"Why do you say that? I'm not complaining."

Four months into her pregnancy, Sonju felt sticky wetness in her underwear. There was bright red blood. More flowed. Stabbing pain in her lower back, then sharp cramps in her abdomen. Her pelvis squeezed and her hip bones were trying to pull away from it. And the pain worsened. Then it stopped and started again. Two hours later, she passed the fetus and all the pain ceased. She transferred the fetus to a layered cotton scarf. Holding it, she saw facial features, and arms and legs, and fingers and toes. It tried very hard to be her baby. Not yet a child, yet it was her child. She went to the corner of her room and wept.

She felt grief, but there was something more than grief. Her life the way she lived it was slipping by with no trace of sound like the silent fetus in her hand. Her unformed child's soul must have entered her. Something felt different, something new. She wanted to cling to someone. She couldn't understand why.

Second Sister suggested burning the fetus.

"No. Please bury it in the midway of the rise."

While Second Sister buried her child, Sonju rocked back and forth in her room behind closed doors.

The next day and the day after, she sat on the veranda staring at the small disturbed spot on the rise and felt profound disappointment in the hollowness of her belly. What made her body so hostile to a newly forming life?

She was still haunted by the image of the fetus—the child that left her body—when her husband came home. He failed to see any change in her, but she needed him, needed someone. "I lost our child. I see it when I close my eyes. Why did it quit me? I beg you, please be good to me. Tell me things. About us."

Her husband stared at her with his mouth half open. Then he said, "There will be another child."

"But this child …" She wept and wept.

Sonju's unborn child sometimes appeared in her dreams, mute and unsmiling but fully formed. After the dream, she remained curled up on the *yo* and whispered, "Stay with me, Child." She felt her life would go astray without it. Looking at Jinju, she glimpsed the Child. She told no one about her recurring dream and was grateful her mother-in-law didn't say anything about the miscarriage.

She couldn't see her marriage changing in the future but didn't know what to do about it. In spite of the chill air, she sat on the veranda to gaze at the rise for a long stretch of time several times a day. Strangely, she felt calm during those moments.

Two weeks after the miscarriage, she took her husband's coat and pants to the veranda to give them a good shake before ironing them. A pink note fluttered down to the wooden plank. A quick glance made the blood drain from her face. For a short second, she saw nothing but blackness, then she wobbled into the room.

"How long has this been going on?" Her voice shook as badly as the note in her hand.

He peered at it, then smirked. "It's nothing."

Those dismissive words. "It's not nothing to me. Stop if you care about our marriage." Her anger rose, but she hoped he would gracefully save himself. All he had to do was to promise to stop. That was all she wanted. Instead, he said, "It has nothing to do with our marriage. You are my wife, my inside woman."

"Your chattel, you mean." She cried.

"I tell you, these women don't mean anything to me."

"These women!" She felt sick. "How many?"

He shook his head. An irritated smirk shaped his lips. "All men do it."

Full of contempt, she shrilled, "Not all men! *Your* particular kind of man."

"Only your particular kind of woman would make such a fuss about it."

Her heart went cold. Her marriage was done. No more trying, no more disappointments. She said in a low, chilling voice, "Don't expect any more children from me." It was odd that she actually felt relieved at that moment.

The next time her husband returned home, she hardly spoke to him. When he tried to touch her at night, she hissed at him, "I meant what I said." She turned away from him, pulling the blanket and wrapping herself tightly in it.

After he left for Pusan, Second Sister peeked in at Sonju's door. "May I come in?" She stepped in, studying Sonju. "You're awfully quiet. Your husband told me you were cross and he didn't know what to do. He adores you."

Hot fury like a trapped fire erupted in Sonju. "Adores me? It's just words! Did he tell you why I'm furious with him?" She didn't wait for Second Sister to respond. "I'll tell you why."

Second Sister's eyelids jumped up, and her upper body made a slight retreat.

"I found a little pink note with a hand-drawn rose. It read *Seven o'clock. Can't wait.*"

Second Sister covered her mouth with her hand and watched her with rounded eyes. Sonju said, "When I confronted him, he

119

said that's what men do." Second Sister looked down, then back at Sonju.

Sonju went on like a train going high speed. "I asked him to stop, but he accused me of making a big fuss out of nothing." She heard a small choking sound coming from Second Sister's covered mouth. "I told him not to expect any more children from me." As Second Sister dropped her hand and gasped, Sonju continued, "'What can you do about that? You're stuck with me,' I told him."

Sonju's face was hot and her mouth dry, but she wasn't done. Her anger wouldn't let her be done. While she paused to wet her lips, Second Sister said meekly, "I always thought he was so sweet … the way he talks about you."

"He says things that make him look good. That's all it is." Sonju noticed Second Sister fidget with her fingers. In a calmer voice she said, "I'm sorry to burden you with my grievances. It's not fair to you."

Second Sister moved closer. "To whom would you say such things?"

"Thank you. This marriage was never meant to be."

Second Sister stared at Sonju before leaving.

Alone in her room, Sonju listed in her mind all the ways she had tried to make her marriage work. No matter what she had tried, though, she always felt beaten down in the end. Her marriage had consumed her to the point of exhaustion. She needed encouragement. She dug through the layers of folded clothes in her wedding chest. When her fingertips met the smooth surface of the thinking stone, a flutter of delight passed through her heart. She held the stone tightly, cupping her hand with the other. With her cupped hands on her chest she said, "Kungu, I want to smell the scent of warm early summer air you always carry. I really need to hear your calm, reassuring voice again. I need you to look me in my eye and tell me I will be all right." Then she realized that Kungu might not have survived the war. Why hadn't she fought for him?

The Unraveling, 1951 Fall

The fragile union between Sonju and her husband was unraveling, and she didn't care. He pretended nothing was wrong between them, uttering endearments and going about his usual routine. When he entered a room, she left that room or grabbed whatever book that was nearby and sat as far as possible from him to read.

On a late October day, Mother-in-Law handed her a letter from her sister, and Sonju immediately thought something bad must have happened to her family. Why else would she receive a letter all of a sudden? She opened it. Her sister wrote that she was with child again, and their mother had taken ill. She relayed that their father requested Sonju to come to care for their mother.

Just in case her mother's illness was contagious, Sonju left Jinju in the care of Second Sister. On the train, she felt unsettled, this being her first separation from Jinju, and her first trip back to Seoul since her marriage. She sat staring out the window and considered what had become of her, crushed by the behavior of one ordinary man. During the nearly five years of their marriage, all the exchanges between them—disappointments that squandered occasional glimpses of happiness, his careless remarks and her bitter words—all deposited layer upon layer deep within her. What now? And what in the future?

Submerged in her thoughts, she hadn't noticed the train stops along the way, only coming to herself when all the passengers rose from their seats and pulled down their luggage. She took hers, and when the train stopped with the final squeal and sigh, she stepped off and looked up at the station's familiar dome. After the long steps up and onto the stone floor of the Seoul Train Station, then out onto the cobblestone plaza, she stood a moment to take in the city. She was not surprised to find the city decimated. It was the hub of South Korea after all, where the major government agencies, transportation, mass communication, schools, and commerce were located. On one of the major streets near the plaza, a few tall buildings remained untouched, but some stood with their windows blown out, only a shell of the building remaining, others were flattened to rubble. On the street that ran along the plaza, tree trunks stood burnt black, their branches dark metal spikes. Amid the ruins, however, there were reminders of the city she used to know— pedestrians, street vendors, black smoke from old buses, hissing wires overhead from the streetcar.

She waited for a taxi for almost ten minutes, and finally climbed into a Jeep that used to be an American military vehicle. On the way to her parents' house, she recognized the buildings only by the barely standing columns and parts of the walls that jutted up, which appeared haunted by their own devastated forms. Some familiar storefronts remained intact, but they looked shabby and meagre. Interspersed, new construction was underway with bags of concrete piled up on the sidewalks.

Along the streets men carried huge piles of unfamiliar American refuse on A-frame carriers strapped to their backs; men old and young, some maimed, begged for money on the sidewalks; merchants and customers haggled over prices; a young American soldier looking lost in a foreign city turned his head left and right in the midst of pedestrians walking briskly in every direction.

The taxi approached her quiet neighborhood, leaving behind the dust and fumes, and arrived at her parents' house. As soon as the maid opened the gate, the smell of brewed Chinese medicine wafted from the kitchen. The maid bowed, led Sonju to her mother's room and announced, "She is here."

Sonju found her mother sitting on her *yo*, propped up by pillows. Her face was haggard but her countenance was still imperious. Her mother looked at her husband sitting near her and smiled, then turned her face to Sonju. "I was fine until ten days ago when we finished rebuilding the damaged parts of the house. That's when I got sick for the first time, and your father felt the need to have you take care of me. I am much better now. You did not have to come."

Just then, her brother, no longer a boy, strode into the room. The last time Sonju had seen him, he had been a chatty, senseless youth with an uneven high-pitched voice. She looked at him with a wide grin. "You have grown into a man. Which school and what are you studying?"

Her brother ran his hand across his shaved cheek as though all his manhood rested on that narrow patch of his face and said in a deep voice, "I am a freshman at Korea University studying law."

She asked him why he chose that major, and he said he was aiming for Supreme Court. She didn't bother to ask him why he wanted to be on the supreme court because she already knew the answer—the highest glory for himself and nothing else. He reminded her of her husband. "You will raise our family's esteem, and Mother will be very pleased," she said turning to her mother. She and her mother exchanged a quick intense stare. Sonju was pleased with herself to say those loaded words. She then proceeded to tell her family about Jinju and her life in the village. Perfunctory conversations followed with long interspersed pauses. Sonju didn't expect her family to ask about her marriage, and they didn't.

The next morning, she stayed with her mother for a while, then after lunch, walked toward the used bookstore where she used to meet Kungu. She didn't have to get close to see that the whole area had been flattened. Did the bookstore owner survive? She had known him all through her high school years and two more years after that. She felt as though she had lost a friend.

She turned and walked to the church garden, her childhood refuge where she felt a sense of belonging with Kungu and Misu by her side. Even though the church front was destroyed, the bench still stubbornly claimed its old place. She saw scattered little stones on the ground and she could almost see and hear the three young friends lost in play. Her heart had been so light then and her ideas about her future boundless.

After a sweeping glance around the enclosed garden, she left and went to her sister's house.

Her graceful sister in her haste to rush toward her almost fell. They grabbed each other's hands smiling and tittering. Sonju caressed her sister's bump and asked, "Where is my nephew?"

Sonju quietly went to the room her sister pointed to and opened the door to peek at the sleeping boy. She wished she had brought Jinju with her.

Her sister led her to a room with tatami floors, and they sat down when a maid brought a tray of tea.

Sonju lifted the cup and said, "Your child must take after his father."

"And yours?"

"Jinju looks like me except for her nose, chin and hair. She has straight hair. I would have brought her if I had known Mother was better," Sonju said and looked around. "You have a nice house."

"It was built for a Japanese family. This used to be some mid-level government official's home. It has built-in closets and an indoor bathroom." Rubbing her round middle, she said, "You have to tell me about your farm life. I still can't imagine you living in the country."

"My farm life ... Let's see. It's different. I don't work in the fields if that's what you are thinking. It's a big household with the clan people coming and going all the time. People there are very warm. They take care of each other. When someone is sick, the whole village knows. When someone has a baby, they all know. When a stranger comes, they all know." Sonju laughed a little. "They cry, they laugh. They are real and natural."

With a knowing smile, her sister said, "Unlike our family."

It was an enlightening moment for Sonju. She stared at her sister in her tasteful Western-style knit dress in muted brown holding her cup with both hands and bringing it slowly to her mouth. Her sister looked so much like their father with the same oval-shaped face with features that were ordinary but pleasant. Her compliant sister, kind-hearted and patient, but not known to have her own opinions, had her own thoughts about their stringent upbringing that stifled any spontaneous expression.

Her sister asked, "How is Jinju, my niece I haven't met yet?"

Sonju smiled at the thought of her daughter. "She makes me smile. She gives me these tight satisfying hugs with that small body of hers. She is not yet three, yet she has such deep affection."

"And your husband?"

At the mention of her husband, Sonju felt her jaw stiffen and hands fold. Her sister was watching her. After a long exhale, she said, "He still works in Pusan."

"Is there some trouble in your marriage?" her sister asked cautiously.

Sonju sighed and replied, "It happens to many women."

"Another woman?" Her sister asked with some hesitation.

"More than one."

"Oh." Her sister uttered and looked down.

There was a short silence before her sister talked about her mundane domestic life, an easier and safer topic. Sonju was disappointed that her sister returned to her family's reticence about personal matters.

The following day, she found Misu in the living room surrounded by her three children. Upon seeing Sonju, she grabbed Sonju's hand and almost jumped up and down laughing before she saw her brood watching. She turned and told them, "Children, bow to my best friend and then go to the park with the maid." She pointed at each child as they bent their little heads in a bow and said, "Four, three, two years old."

Watching the children toddle out, Sonju said, "Very obedient like you."

"Yes, I'm lucky. When did you come to Seoul? You should've written me." Misu pulled Sonju down to the floor as she sat.

"I came two days ago," Sonju said. "My mother has been ill. She is much better now. How are you?"

"I missed you. How long has it been? Almost five years?" Misu got up to get the tea tray and poured a cup for Sonju and one for herself. "My mid-morning tea. It's still hot." Sonju nodded and took a cup.

Misu said, "I want to hear all about your country life."

"You would envy its clean air. In a way, though, it's easier to breathe in Seoul."

Misu crinkled her nose. "Easier? You might not have said that after the city was bombarded by the artillery fire. Even now, my maid has to wipe the grey powder from all the pulverized concrete and stones twice a day. But I shouldn't complain. So many died during the battle." Misu tugged Sonju's skirt. "You are far away. What are you thinking?"

Sonju took a deep breath and looked at her friend. "My husband has strayed. We're no longer intimate. My choice."

Misu's lips parted and closed, not quite forming a word.

Sonju closed her eyes briefly. "I think about Kungu a lot. Sometimes the thought that I mattered to someone sustains me."

"You loved him so much."

"I still do."

Misu gulped. "Your husband doesn't know that, does he?"

"He doesn't care to know what I think."

Misu looked down, then glancing up, said, "I ... I don't know what ..."

"How does your marriage work?" Sonju asked.

Misu smiled. "My husband is very good to me. I feel fortunate. I'm not all that particular like you. You're the dreamy one." She paused, her smile gone. "I don't know what I would do if my husband were unfaithful to me. I'm so sorry."

"My husband's indiscretions might be bearable if he were willing to stop, if there was something in him that I could respect, or if he had ideas, some thoughtful concerns about the world around him. Kungu had those."

"He did." Misu took a sip and set her cup down. She tapped her hand on Sonju's arm with a sudden twinkle in her eyes, and said, "I just remembered. About two months ago, I came across him on the street."

He survived the war! Sonju's heart leapt. "And?"

"We didn't talk long. He asked about you. He works at the Chungmu-ro branch of the People's Bank."

While Misu talked about her children, Sonju waited with all the patience she could muster for the proper time to leave.

On the way back, giddy with excitement, she almost took a wrong turn. She wanted to shout, "He's alive! I'll be able to see him."

That night, Sonju went over the words she would say to Kungu: How did you survive the war? How has your life been? Your mother? I missed you so much.

When morning came, Sonju walked into the large light-filled bank with its grey marble floors and white plastered walls. At the sight of Kungu, her heart stopped for a second or two, then began to pulsate madly. He was looking at the papers on his desk. His colleague was standing next to his desk with a stack of papers in his hand. She couldn't take her eyes off of Kungu, off of that face that was so well-known to her.

He was saying something, and as he lifted his face toward his colleague, his head made a quick turn. His face froze. Staring, he rose slowly as if unaware of his confused colleague and walked toward her, still holding her gaze.

She smelled that familiar, endearing scent of him when he stood in front of her. "Hi." Her voice barely audible. "Hi." His nod barely visible. They stood staring at each other. A man walked by them toward the back and broke their locked eyes. They moved to stand by the wall.

Kungu asked, "How are you? How did you find me?"

"Misu told me yesterday that you work here. My mother was sick, and I came to take care of her."

"How long are you staying?"

"I leave the day after tomorrow."

"Can I see you before you leave?"

"Tomorrow, not today. My parents are expecting me home soon."

"I get off at noon tomorrow. Ducksu Palace at 12:30?"

"12:30 at the gate."

She didn't recall how she returned to her parent's house. All she remembered was her heart lurching with happiness as she walked out of the bank building.

Her mother was drinking the brewed Chinese medicine when Sonju entered the room. Now that his wife was gaining strength, her father had returned to his routine of having his meals at the men's quarters and spending most of his day there receiving friends, associates, and his overseers. There wasn't much for Sonju to do to care for her mother other than to help her mother lie down on the *yo* or sit back up. They didn't need her for that. Sonju began to think that her father must have wanted to see her. Even though she didn't see or talk to him much when she was growing up, he was the gentler of her parents, although his word was always the final one.

Her mother presently wanted to lie down again, and after she saw her mother close her eyes, she returned to her room without seeing her brother. The maid told her he was studying.

The evening passed slowly, but Sonju needed it to pass quickly. Come night, come.

In the morning, she looked in on her mother and watched her finish the last drop of Chinese brew. Back in her room again, she wished the time would leap forward.

Sonju walked side by side with Kungu on the palace grounds. She had so much to say to him, yet no words came. It must have been the same with him too. They walked and came to a quiet place where naked trees lined the narrow passage along a wall of tall evergreen hedges.

"I have thought about you often," he said.

She didn't know what to say first in spite of all the words she was going to remember to tell him. She merely nodded, staring at him through blurry eyes. How could she release all the words at once, to say how often she thought of him, how much she missed him, how much she loved him still? But then, he knew. She didn't have to say them. She managed to ask, "How have you been?"

He smiled. "I need more than a day to tell you."

"You had wanted to buy a house of your own. How did it work out?"

"My mother and I bought a little house near my work. She passed away rather suddenly of pneumonia shortly after we moved in, right before the war." He turned and rested his eyes on hers. He didn't say anything, but his eyes conveyed more than words could say.

"I went to the church garden," Sonju said.

"I go there sometimes," he said.

They walked slowly, following the path.

Sonju said, "I often wished your mother were mine. I'm sorry not to have met her."

They occasionally stopped walking to look at each other. She told him about her life—her daughter, her parents-in-law, the school built by Big House Master. He spoke of his mother's dedication to his father when he became ill, and after his father's death, to his education. He was recently promoted at the bank. He was able to help about a dozen people to become business owners so far. He then looked where the tips of the bare branches pointed up to the sky and said, "I missed you so much."

The train screeched and stopped at Maari. As she stepped out of the train, Sonju briefly saw her husband getting on two cars down. He didn't see her. She didn't call to him. She wasn't bothered by her own indifference.

When she approached the inner courtyard, Jinju came running, shrieking in delight. She squeezed her daughter until Jinju peered up at her and said, "Mommy, you can let go now." Her daughter seemed grown all of a sudden in her five-day absence.

For days afterwards, during her quiet moments alone, Sonju thought of Kungu and smiled and cried. Their time together was so brief and the moment of their parting so hard. They both turned their backs and wept. She had thought all she wanted was to hold him in her eyes to know he was alive. But that wasn't enough. She was desperate to see him again one more time. The following Saturday she sent a letter to Kungu and told her husband she would go to Seoul again. He didn't object. It didn't matter anyway whether he did or not. He probably knew that too. As far as she was concerned, he no longer had a hold on her, and there wasn't much he could do about it without losing face.

A week later on Saturday, she faced a stern-looking woman in her mid-forties at the gate of Kungu's modest traditional house with a tile roof. The maid took one look at Sonju and averted her eyes, then carried Sonju's luggage to the living room. She then walked out of the gate with an angry clink of the lock. The maid must have been upset at having to wait for her before she could leave, Sonju mused.

The first thing Sonju noticed in the living room was a bookcase filled with European and Russian novels. Kungu had always liked Russian novels. She took one out and had read the first 21 pages of *The Idiot* by Dostoevsky when Kungu came in through the gate.

When he saw Sonju, he said, "I could get used to you being in my home."

After he changed, he brought a lunch table from the kitchen, saying his maid always prepared a meal before going home. During their first meal together, he talked about the books he had collected, which books he was moved by and impressed with. She told him about the reading group she had started with the village women. They talked on about many things the way they used to.

After lunch, they moved to his room and sat leaning against the wall. He held her hand and smiled. Their first touch—there was something shocking and magical about it. She had longed for it since she was fifteen. She told him about her imagination of him embracing her under the moonlight. He laughed and enfolded her in his arms and asked, "Like this?" She put her arms around him and leaned on his shoulder. She said, "During the war, I thought you might have died. I died thousands of times thinking I failed you. When I pleaded with my mother to let me wait until you graduated, I should have told her I bedded with you already. It was too late when I thought of it."

He tightened his arm around her waist and said, "We are together now."

She lifted her face to look him in the eye and pleaded, "Kungu, I want this. Just once. To have no regrets."

He was quiet for a moment, and said, "We may regret."

"I won't. Would you?"

They sought each other unhurriedly as though they had unending time. She felt something new. She closed her eyes and her body trembled at the intense, almost unbearable pleasure. Body and mind, they were as good as married, and she would have no regrets. They embraced and rolled, laughing and laughing. They pulled each other up and leaned side by side on the pillow against the wall, his arm around her. Combing her hair with his long, lean fingers, he said, "During the war, the thought that I may never see you again occurred to me."

She listened to the steady beating of his heart and drank his scent. "Did you fight in the war?"

Kungu paused a while. He was never one to speak in haste. He always took his time. "It's a long story," he said. "My uncle was an anti-communist activist, so he reported the leftists and communist sympathizers to the authorities. When the North occupied Seoul, his family went into hiding."

"You didn't?" She stroked his face, feeling on her finger tips his smooth forehead, the rise of his nose, the curve of his lips, the angle of his jaw.

"I should have. One day, three North Korean soldiers came to my house and forced me into their army. One man from each family, they said. And they knew about my uncle."

She sat up and looked at him, puzzled. "You fought for the North?" She had never heard of such a thing, not even from the hunchback or her brother-in-law in Daejon.

"Many did. During training, the North Korean soldiers said they would take the conscripts to North Korea after the war. That was scarier to me than the fighting, because that meant I would never see you again."

"Where did you fight?" her voice rang out.

"There was a battle against the American troops at Osan on July 5th. After winning there, the North kept moving south to Daejon."

"I was in Daejon. I thought you might be there. I never imagined you fighting for the enemy side though. The battle was intense there." She was scared all over again at the mere thought of Kungu in the thick of that relentless fighting.

"It was more intense and longer further south around Pusan." He held her waist tighter as though he needed an anchor. "When the North lost the battle, we the conscripts discussed deserting. The situation was chaotic. Not only were there the isolated North Korean soldiers—some of them in civilian clothes—roaming around the area trying to rejoin their forces but also in the mix were communist sympathizers, deserters, and refugees.

"You didn't always know who was who. The North Korean soldiers set buildings and houses on fire, tortured and killed civilians. The South Korean soldiers hunted down the North Koreans and their sympathizers and tortured and killed them in revenge. There were bodies on the streets, their hands bound and shot in the head."

She was still haunted by the sight of gruesome corpses on the way to the train station on her last day in Daejon in September only a year before. She could still smell the blood at the oddest moments when she wasn't even thinking about the war.

Kungu seemed submerged in his memory. He loosened his arm and spoke in his measured calm voice, "One night, four of us stole peasant clothes hanging on a line. We changed into them and took a rural road to the east. We burned our uniforms for heat. At dawn, we drew suspicion, young men traveling as a group, so we parted ways. I took country roads and told people along the way that I was a refugee from Seoul trying to return home. They probably knew I was a deserter because of my age, but they didn't question me. I carried other refugees' bags or carried their young children on my back. Some of them shared their food with me. One night, when I couldn't stand the hunger any longer, I went to an empty field and dug up a lopped off turnip. I didn't care if my fingers froze. Sometimes, I drank boiled tree bark for sustenance.

"I don't remember reaching my house. The way my aunt tells it, one day a skeletal ghost with huge sunken eyes and cheeks appeared at the gate. When she let him in, he collapsed on the floor. She took a closer look and recognized me. I remember eating and lying down. When I woke up, my uncle said that I had slept for twenty-seven hours. My aunt had a bath ready. I took a long one."

"Why was your uncle's family in your house?"

"Their entire house was destroyed during the war. They stayed here while rebuilding their house and moved out shortly after my return. My aunt hired a maid for me, the same one you met. She thought I needed one."

His gaze fell on the floor a moment before he said, "In the middle of the fierce fighting, I thought that might be the day I die. Then I saw you in my mind and I wanted to see you again even if it were just for a second." He turned his face and smiled at her. "Now here you are. I am glad I'm alive."

"Fighting with the enemies against your own countrymen," Sonju said. "How conflicted you must have been! You really could have died. Just the thought of it scares me all over again." She clasped his hand and stared at his long fingers. She would miss him ever so much, but no regrets.

1952 February

Back in Maari, Sonju's life took on a different tone. She smiled more and faced her husband without anger.

"Just one time," she had told herself, but in mid-February, she went to Kungu again. This time, she told him all the details of her marriage. She told him about the child she miscarried and how she sat on the veranda looking at the spot it was buried, and how she still saw it in her dreams now and then. She then wept.

He listened keenly. After wiping her tears, he folded his hands around hers. "I'm so sorry about your loss. I had always hoped your husband and his family would be good to you."

"His family *is* good to me. At times, I wish my husband would ask for a divorce. He can use my refusal to be intimate with him as a reason but he is too proud. How the public regards him is everything to him."

"If he ever does ask, come to me."

She nodded and said, "This is our last time." The ache in her chest wouldn't let up at the thought of never seeing him again, but it must be this way. If she left her marriage, Jinju would have to remain with the Second House family just as Jinwon had. That wasn't an option for her. She leaned her head on his shoulder and wept. "When it's time for me to leave, you stay in the room. Don't say anything. Please do that for me."

The next morning, she bought a ticket to Maari at the train station and sat on the long wooden bench next to an old man with a thin grey beard. Her eyes puffy and heavy from crying, she stared up at the high windows and felt the diffused light on her face. She abruptly rose, walked out of the station, and caught a taxi.

Kungu opened the gate. His eyes grew wide. "What happened?"

"I'm going to ask for a divorce. I know how to get custody of Jinju." She glanced at his confused face yielding to a smile.

"I'd better go. To catch the next train." She hurried to the waiting taxi.

When Sonju arrived at Second House Sunday evening, her husband had already left for Pusan. She would wait for next Saturday to tell him.

When Second Sister asked why she went to Seoul so often, Sonju said she had some things to take care of. Second Sister stared at her but didn't insist further.

While waiting for Saturday to come, Sonju considered the enormity of what she had to do. Her heart jumped and bumped.

When her husband came home, this time smelling of perfume, she felt rather sorry for him. He went to the men's quarters to talk with his father, then to Big House. After dinner, Sonju played with Jinju for a while and read a story to her. When she saw her nodding off, she laid her on her *yo* and waited for her husband. Half an hour later, he came into the room and changed into his night clothes.

After he sat on his *yo* and was ready to lie down, Sonju said, "We have to talk. Our marriage hasn't been satisfactory for either of us. It has become unbearable to me. I want a divorce."

"Huh?"

"I want a divorce."

He straightened his back, and after a long stare, he said, "In marriage, even if you're unhappy, you endure it and make the best of it. A divorce? Absolutely not. It's ridiculous."

"I had an affair."

"What?"

"When I went to Seoul, I reconnected with the man I have known since childhood."

"You have a lover?"

"Yes."

His face reddened and his eyes turned hard. He spat out, "You slept with another man. I can't keep you."

She kept her steady eyes on him. "I'm not asking you to."

His face redder, he turned and flailed his arm, but collected himself and said, "I don't know anyone who is divorced. What would people say? Wait a minute. Let me think." He squeezed his temples with his fingers, his breathing becoming coarse. He dropped his hands and squeezed them into fists. His face still flushed, he hit his thigh with a fist, then took a few deep breaths. Afterwards, he lifted his chin and closed his eyes.

She waited.

He opened his eyes and seemed resigned. "We'll divorce as quietly as possible. I'll tell my parents that you had yourself checked by doctors when you went to Seoul and you can't have any more children. I'll tell them I want a male child and you have agreed to an amicable divorce." He dropped his head and said, "I'll tell my father next week. I need some time to sort through things."

"I'm taking Jinju with me."

He lifted his head, then his face blazed. "I'm *not* going to let another man raise my daughter!"

"Then I'll tell people I'm divorcing you because you caused my miscarriage and infertility. I told Second Sister about your multiple affairs. What would people say when they find out that your wife left for another man? If you let me take Jinju, you can see her as often as you like."

He stared at her with an incredulous look. "You will lie to keep Jinju?"

"I'll do worse if I have to. You were ready to lie about me to your parents, weren't you?"

He blinked, sighed loudly, then looked at her. His voice trembled as he asked, "Was I such a disappointment to you?"

She turned. His question so childlike and clueless that she felt tender pity toward him.

The following Saturday, Brother-in-Law had been with his father since he arrived home. From the kitchen, Sonju watched her husband come home and enter the men's quarters to greet his father, his usual routine. Half an hour later, her husband walked out of the men's quarters with his head hung low. Brother-in-Law bowed to her but no smile, no words of greeting. Her husband must have told them both about the divorce.

In less than five minutes, Father-in-Law sent for her.

"You called for me." She knelt in front of him ready to hear her father-in-law's words against the divorce. She looked at him with a resolve not to waiver.

His face was glum. He cleared his throat. "I have received a letter that you stayed at a man's house twice."

For a second, she was utterly confused. A letter? She couldn't breathe.

He continued, "You will leave in two days. You will have absolutely no contact with Jinju until she finishes high school. Your contact will confuse her, and she will have problems bonding with her new mother."

She let out a scream, "No! She is my child. I can't live without her! I can't! Please let me take her. She is my child."

Father-in-Law's mouth was firmly closed.

A woman's cry, all muffled. Her own cry. Father-in-Law's face was out of focus. Touching her own hot, wet face, she pleaded between halting nasal sobs, "Please let me take her."

"We will take care of all the necessary legal procedures for the divorce. Your father will be informed." Turning his face from her, he said, "I have nothing more to say."

Jinju must not see her crying, she told herself. She hurried to the back garden, whimpering and tripping. She leaned on the prickly juniper fence, and covering her face sobbed into her hands. Her life without Jinju. It felt like a chunk of her was about to tear off. Her daughter. How would she live without her daughter? Her mind was blank, and she couldn't think of any means to take Jinju with her. Her exhausted sobs dribbled out. Perhaps an hour passed. The earth swallowed the sun. Then a few faint stars appeared and trembled.

When Sonju went to her room shivering, her husband was on his *yo*, quiet and still. She lay on her *yo* next to her sleeping daughter. She felt Jinju's little chest rise and fall, and heard an occasional puff of soft breath. Her life without this puff of breath next to her. Her own breath quickened and her heart squeezed. She sat up beating on her chest to get the pain out of it. She was dizzy. She was losing herself. Breathe in, hold, hold, hold, breathe out. Again. She would have to pull herself together. Breathe in, hold, breathe out. One day, Jinju would want an explanation.

The night hours were long. Feral cats shrieked. The wind whooshed. Windows rattled. Sonju wept silently under the blanket until dawn.

A maid brought a basin of warm water. All of her meals would be served the same way so the family wouldn't have to face her for her benefit just as it was done to First Sister. After her husband left the room, she walked out to the veranda and out of the gates. At the train station's office, she sent a telegram to Kungu.

That afternoon, a messenger brought a telegram from her father. She was not to return to her parents' house. She wasn't planning to, but her heart hardened nonetheless.

As she gathered her daughter in her arms, her tears came. Hiding her tears, she said, "You'll stay with Mommy all day today, won't you?"

"We'll go to the hill?"

"No, it's too cold outside. We'll stay in the room. We can hold each other tight. We can play 'I can see' game."

"All day?"

"Yes. This is how we play. I'll go first." She closed her eyes. "I can see Jinju. Her hair comes to her neck with bangs. She tilts her head back when she laughs. When she eats a candy, she holds her sticky fingers in the air away from her clothes. She hugs me really tight." She opened her eyes and hugged Jinju. "Now, you go."

Jinju closed her eyes, then opened them a slit, then quickly closed again. "Mommy is real pretty. She is tall, taller than Second Auntie and has curly hair that comes to here." With her eyes still closed, she touched her fingers midway on her neck. "She smiles at me big. She smells good. She hugs me a lot. And she tells me stories."

Would her daughter remember her five, ten, fifteen years from now?

In the evening, a telegram from Kungu arrived. He would wait for her. She rubbed the thinking-stone before putting it on top of the layers of clothing in her luggage. She took photographs of Jinju from the photo album and placed them under Jinju's outgrown dress at the bottom of the luggage.

Father-in-Law called her to the men's quarters. He said, "I heard your family doesn't want you back. I hope this money will help you." He handed her a bulging envelope.

Sonju raised her face and saw that his eyes were soft and full of concern. She gave him a kneel-down formal bow, the last as his daughter-in-law.

In the early morning darkness, she went out to the veranda and sat facing the midway of the rise where her unborn child was buried. She returned to the room, hugged her sleeping daughter one last time before leaving, and took the first train to Seoul. In the midst of the train chugging, a baby crying, a man's eager pleading, a woman laughing, Sonju could still hear her own long animal-like cry begging for her daughter.

Part Two

Kungu, 1952

Sonju reached Kungu's house in mid-morning Monday. His maid picked up her luggage at the gate and led her to the guest room. She then walked out without a word but returned with a table of rice, tofu and beef soup, and with a side dish of kimchi, sautéed anchovies, and seasoned seaweed squares. Before Sonju could thank her, the maid had already turned and left the room.

Sonju nibbled at the food, then placed the table outside the door. After two sleepless nights in Maari, a fog of drowsiness rolled in, her breathing becoming slow and weak, her body rubbery. Struggling to keep her eyes open, she laid the *yo* on the floor and slid under the blanket. Nightmares of one familiar face morphing into another, accusing fingers, her retreating to a corner. She screamed, but no sound came out. She woke up confused, fell asleep again, only to waffle between sleep and wakefulness and wading through eerie dreams.

At the sound of a door opening, Sonju tried to rise from the *yo*, but only managed to barely open her eyes to see Kungu hang his overcoat, jacket and tie on the wall and roll up his shirt sleeves.

Coming toward her, he asked, "Did I wake you? I should've been quieter." He helped her up to sit and lowered himself next to her wrapping his arm around her and said, "The maid prepared dinner for us. Do you feel like eating now?"

After dinner, they sat on pillows leaning against the wall, each staring at the floor. One or two minutes had passed that way when he took her hands and squeezed them a few times. He then said, "Why don't we put your things in our room? I made a space for them in the wardrobe and the bureau." He carried her luggage to his bedroom.

She hung her clothes and put away her empty luggage in the wardrobe.

He said, "After your visits, I found your hair on the floor and on my clothing. It was a nice reminder of you. Such a small thing, yet it was a great comfort to me. And now you're here to stay."

At those words, tears broke loose and flowed on Sonju's cheeks. She had been thinking about the daughter she left behind ever since she left Maari. He wiped her tears with his shirt sleeve as he used to as a boy and looked into her eyes. She told him about the letter and losing custody of Jinju. "I could've had Jinju with me if not for the letter. It was all agreed," she said choking with sobs. "Who had me followed? Brother-in-Law? Second Sister asked me why I went to Seoul so often. Would he have done it? If not him, then who? Why would anyone want to ruin my life? How can I live without Jinju?" She sobbed all over again. She lived without Kungu for five years. That was hard, and now she would have to live without Jinju for much longer.

She passed the night cuddling up to Kungu thinking about what Jinju might have done upon waking and not finding her mother there. She could hear her cry, see her frantic search for her mother. She couldn't sleep until the early morning hours only to wake up two hours later.

In the morning, Kungu saw her puffy eyes, and a pained look came over his face. Before he left for work, he pleaded with her to be sure to eat something.

Not long after he left, Sonju heard the sound of the gate opening and closing. She listened to the maid's busy steps and water slushing and pouring, which reminded her of the Second House maids washing at the well. She opened the bureau drawer, lifted Jinju's neatly folded pale-yellow dress, brought it up to her cheek and inhaled her daughter's scent. How was she to bear her daughter's absence each day for fifteen years? It had been only one day. She had to do something to hurry the hours until Kungu came home. She went to the living room, took *The Idiot* from the bookshelf, put it back after reading the same dozen pages she had read before, then took another, doing the same, not remembering what she had read. After the maid left for the day, she took wet rags and repeatedly wiped the floors and the windowsills until sweat dripped and stung her eyes.

That evening, she told Kungu, "I need to do something. Why don't we let the maid go? I can handle this house on my own."

He put his hand on her shoulder and said, "I don't want you to do without a maid. She works only Monday through Friday eight to three and Saturday nine to twelve. She needs this job." He smiled and cocked his head for her response. She nodded.

"By the way," he said, "would you come to my bank tomorrow with your registered stamp? Let's open an account in your name. I'll put some money in it."

"I'm not without money. I told you I have money from my father-in-law."

"So, you'll have more. I've seen my mother struggle to save. She always said a woman must have money of her own."

The next morning, she opened an account in her name for the first time in her life.

Sonju had been living with Kungu for three weeks. After he left for work, she stared at the scraggly plants and shrubs in the garden along the fence and thought she could redo the garden. At the storage shed, she found a regular shovel and a rusty hand shovel. She asked the maid for the direction to the neighborhood market.

She didn't have to go far to encounter looks and whispers from women she had never met—merchants and shoppers elbowing one another, stealing glances at her, and whispering among themselves. What were they saying about her? She kept walking avoiding their eyes and ignoring their whispers and gestures. At the end of the market street, she found a garden shop. After her purchase, she hurried home.

In less than an hour, a young man delivered the shrubs and plants to the house. Sonju arranged them in the garden, viewed them from different angles. She dug, scooped, planted, filled, packed, and watered. Black dirt lodged under her nails, blisters formed on both hands, and her shoulders ached, but her gloomy thoughts remained at bay. She would take blisters and body aches gladly not to slip into sobbing and pathetic stupor.

When Kungu came home, she showed him the shrubs and plants, naming each one and told him what the garden would look like in two or three years. She realized she was excited. During tea after dinner, she told him what had happened at the market, and he said, "It must be hard for you, but try to remember that those people are not important in your life."

He was right. They were not important to her. Besides, she had faced the hostile villagers in Maari before. She could manage this, she said to herself. "Tomorrow, I'll buy stationery to write to Jinju," she told him.

His face brightened. "That's a good idea. She will know one day how much you thought of her during your separation."

She went back to the market the next morning. She bought paper, a pen, and a rectangular box covered with silk fabric with images of chrysanthemums and rocks. When she returned, she sat at the low table in the bedroom and began:

1952 March 21

My daughter Jinju,

You are all I think about. This sudden change … I don't know how to manage it. Forgive me for leaving you. When you are grown, I will explain what happened to your Daddy and me, why I had to leave.

I always thought I would share your joys, disappointments, and frustrations. I thought I would go through all that with you. Most of all, I thought you would know that I love you no matter how you are and what your choices may be.

I don't know how I will stand not seeing you. Please remember me. I love you. I wish I had said those words to you every day.

After she wrote the letter and put it away in the box, her thoughts wandered to possible calamities that might await her daughter and Kungu. Other children might taunt her for her mother being divorced. The gossip might reach Kungu's superiors.

That evening she asked Kungu, "If your superior found out about us, would you lose your job?"

"No. I'll tell the truth. He knows me well."

She thought, he had lived by that ever since a boy.

His hand gently squeezed hers. "There's a positive aspect to your estrangement from your parents. You have no one to answer to."

"That thought didn't occur to me. Since I'm out of the norm and put aside, I don't have to be acceptable to anyone, do I?" She was momentarily elated. "I'm freer now," she said, yet she didn't feel free. "But Jinju. Children can be cruel, and she is so young."

Kungu wrapped his arm around her. "Some children are. Her family will protect her."

Sonju thought of her father-in-law and mother-in-law. They would protect her.

In spite of her incessant thoughts of Jinju, Sonju's life settled into a regular rhythm and gentle touches. Every morning, she tied Kungu's tie, a ritual she needed to perform for her comfort. Yet the persistent, recurring thoughts remained—what it must have been like for Jinju to find out that her mother wasn't coming back and how it was explained to her. Forgive me, forgive me.

It was particularly painful for Sonju on her daughter's birthday wondering if Second Sister did something special for her daughter. She wrote a long letter to her daughter. She felt moody and unsettled that day.

On Monday, Sonju was at the market picking a fresh bundle of wild vegetables when a young woman's voice called out, "Sonju!" A thud in her chest. She turned.

Okja, an old classmate, approached her with a wide smile. "What a surprise to see you. Are you visiting?"

Sonju hesitated. "No, I live here."

"Then we are neighbors. We need to visit. I'll bring my children to meet your daughter."

Her friend Misu must have told their classmates about Jinju. Sonju said calmly, "I don't have my daughter with me. I'm divorced."

"Divor …" The classmate shifted her purse from one hand to the other, looking flustered. "I need to go." She turned and walked off.

Sonju clutched her empty shopping bag. Now all her classmates would know about her divorce and her daughter. Her girl cousin would find out and tell all her relatives. Their whispers will turn into questions, and her proud mother would dip her head in shame. It broke her heart. She ran, and upon arriving at Kungu's house, went straight to her room and wrote a letter to Jinju asking for her forgiveness.

The next day, Kungu presented her with a box of fancy stationery and said, "You had a tough time yesterday."

One late morning in May, after passing about two dozen stores lined up on both sides along the street, she stopped near the entrance of a small bank where a middle-aged woman set up buckets of fresh flowers. In one of the buckets, pink peony petals were about to burst out of their crowded layers.

She was walking home holding three stems of peonies when she noticed the same classmate she had encountered before coming straight at her. Two meters away from her, the classmate said, "I hear you're living with a lover. People talk."

Sonju stared at the accuser and didn't drop her eyes.

"An adulteress, that's what you are. Leaving a child for a lover," the classmate said, her voice rising. "Don't you have any shame? You tainted the good name of our school."

While being harangued, Sonju tried to figure out a way to leave the scene. She didn't want to go around the classmate. Doing so seemed cowardly. "Think what you will. Move out of the way,"

Sonju said, and clutching the peonies to her chest, walked right ahead as Okja, her mouth gaped open, stepped aside.

Back home, she placed the flowers in a vase on the bureau and wrote another letter to Jinju.

Someone knocked at the gate. Sonju opened the glass door of the living room as the maid went to the gate. Lately the maid had been talking more to her with softer gestures and at times even smiling.

"Who is it?" The maid asked.

"We are her family."

Sonju's heart jumped. She took a deep breath. At her nodding, the maid opened the gate cautiously.

Her mother, with her mouth pinched shut, walked toward Sonju a few steps ahead of her younger daughter. This wouldn't be a sit-down-and-have-tea visit. Standing in the living room facing her mother, Sonju met her mother's fiery eyes and waited for the downpour of accusatory words.

And it poured. "Your father is in poor health from the shock of your shameful act. He doesn't receive guests. He hardly talks," her mother said with force in her words and heavy breathing between sentences.

Why did they come? Sonju wondered. They had disowned her.

Her mother pulled out an envelope from her purse. "Your divorce papers came. I don't want them in my house." She slapped it down on the bureau. Sonju glanced at it, then watched her mother become more agitated. Her mother's contorted face hardened, and her lips trembled. Her mother at that moment was almost unrecognizable. She walked a step closer to Sonju. "Many women smarter than you follow the conventions." Her mother's voice quavered, becoming louder. "What you have done, what you are doing is worse than death!"

"Mother! Mother!" Sonju's sister called.

Her mother's nostrils flared as she expelled air. This was the woman who used to tell her daughters to always restrain. Her mother's words provoked bitterness in her afresh. She felt her anger rising. Her mother had no right to force that marriage on her and drop her off to strangers like an unwanted baggage and not take any responsibility for her action. Sonju said, "You shouldn't have forced me into that marriage. I paid for your mistake." Before her words turned harsher, she turned around, entered her bedroom, and closed the door behind her. She heard them leave. Her hands shook.

After collecting herself, she wrote to her friend Misu, explaining everything—her affair, divorce, and life with Kungu. She asked Misu to meet her at White Crane near Kungu's house.

A week later, Misu walked into the dimly lit tearoom dressed in a well-tailored pink suit.

"I'm glad you came," Sonju said.

"My husband doesn't know about you," Misu said. "If he did, he would have forbidden me from seeing you."

Forbid her? Was Misu trying to tell her what sacrifice it was to show up for a fallen friend? She wanted to throw a sarcastic retort to Misu, she really did, but instead she said, "Thank you for coming."

"I feel somehow guilty. I'm partly responsible for your situation. When I told you where Kungu works, I didn't know it would lead to an affair."

Did Misu come to relieve her own guilt? And that scolding tone. Sonju said, "I'm not holding you responsible for my divorce. It was my choice to have an affair. If you decide not to see me, I'll understand."

After fixing her eyes on Sonju's for a moment, Misu rose and walked out into the sunlight.

In the smoke-filled room, Sonju remained in her seat, looking at the empty chair when a young waitress came for her order.

Several days later, she received a letter from Misu.

1952 May 22

Dear Sonju,
 I thought about our conversation and felt bad about

leaving you abruptly. You once asked me what I would do if I were not happy in my marriage. I thought about that question but don't have an answer. I guess I would have talked to you, and you would have listened.

You were always different from me, but we were friends then, we are friends now.

Misu

Sonju wanted a friendship gladly given, not obligated. She sensed that a fracture had run across their friendship. In spite of that, she immediately sat down and wrote:

1952 May 26

Dear Misu,

I was moved by your letter. Thank you. I want us to be friends for a long time regardless of where our lives take us.

Sonju

She hadn't heard from Misu in reply and wasn't sure if there was anything left to their friendship. She didn't know whether to cry or get angry. She felt lost and didn't know what to do with her unsettled mind. Her thoughts turned to her daughter, and she ached in the flesh. She missed her so. Then one day during tea, Kungu asked if she regretted their affair. She told him, "I bedded with you because I didn't want to live with a regret. As far as Jinju goes, she was to come with me. Until the letter." Who wrote that letter? she asked herself again.

In early June, Sonju's mother and sister appeared at the gate again. They sat for tea. Her mother started weeping. Her sister sighed and gazed at their mother with such sadness and pity that Sonju couldn't bear to look at either of them. It unsettled her deeply to witness her mother weeping. This was the same mother who had always seemed impervious even when she was sick.

Her mother stopped weeping and said to Sonju, "Your father is not improving."

Exasperated, Sonju asked, "What do you want from me? If I plead for your forgiveness and give you an assurance that I will repent, would that change anything between the family and me? I will still be the divorced daughter who shamed the family, still won't be invited to the home, and you will not accept Kungu."

Her mother stared at her for a long time without words and left with her younger daughter before finishing the tea. Why did their visit always end in the same way with nothing resolved? Would her father's health improve if she said the words they wanted to hear? She knew she was hard and cold for not asking forgiveness, which made her feel worse.

A few days after her mother's visit, Kungu said, "I think a change of scenery would be good for both of us. Let's go to the countryside."

On Sunday when the sun was high, they took a bus to a remote country place south of Seoul and walked where cosmos bloomed along the edges of a narrow dirt path, their colors varying from white to magenta. She studied those simple, open-faced flowers, the lacy leaves, and tall thin stems swaying gently in the breeze. She said, "Look at these frail plants, attended to by no one. Yet, they manage to stand tall and bloom fully in their own sense of glory. There's a lesson in this."

He smiled and squeezed her hand, the other hand shielding his eyes from the sun. "Life seems perfect at this moment," he said.

Under the shadow of his hand, Sonju saw happiness in his eyes and felt deeply contented for the first time in her life.

Three days later, Kungu returned from a visit with his uncle's family. Sonju never accompanied him. He had said they hadn't asked about her. She knew he wasn't happy about it, but he was grateful to them for taking him and his mother in after his father had passed away.

"I don't like visiting them." He squeezed his temple between his thumb and the forefinger, and said, "Every time my aunt sees me, she talks about her second son. She says he was either captured by North Korean soldiers or was brainwashed by the communists and chose to go to the North."

Sonju remembered how she worried about Kungu not knowing whether he died or lived. "It must be hard on them not knowing."

"I feel bad for them. I came home but their son didn't. My stomach reacts violently when my aunt talks about her missing son. I don't want to be reminded of it. After each visit, it takes me a while to get the fog out of my head."

"Fog? What do you mean?" This was the first time he mentioned it.

"I cannot think clearly. I'm forgetful at times. There are things I don't remember about the war."

He had headaches too. She said, "It's only been a little over a year since you came home. You were forced to fight with the enemy. You almost starved. Your aunt could be right. He might have gone to the North. It's not unheard of." She held him until his muscles relaxed.

Kungu visited his uncle less and less often. Sonju worried that his uncle's family might blame her for it. She worried about his fog too, but after a while, those worries dissipated, and she forgot about them.

On the first day of monsoon rain, Kungu was sitting in front of old newspapers that he had spread on the floor, applying a coat of polish to his shoes.

Sonju said, "Remember we talked about how we can bring changes to this country? I have always wanted to teach, but what school will hire a divorced woman? I want to study but no university will accept a twenty-five-year-old woman."

Kungu picked up his shined shoes and gathered the shoe polish and brush in the paper. "You can still study on your own. There are textbooks," he said.

At that suggestion, Sonju started frequenting bookstores and bought books on art, architecture, and philosophy in either

Korean or Japanese translation. She devoured them. She bought used college textbooks. She realized that she missed out a great deal by not going to a university. There were things in the textbooks that she couldn't comprehend. She would look for a book that explained the way she could understand.

1952 November

The air was crisp on that ordinary November day. At dusk, a loud banging came from the gate. Kungu and Sonju were drinking tea in the living room. They set their cups down. The banging continued, rattling the metal lock. Kungu went to the gate while Sonju watched through the half-open glass door.

"Who is it?" he asked, his hand on the lock.

"Taegil," a man's voice yelled out.

Kungu hesitated a moment before opening the gate.

A rough-looking fellow in a brown sweater stepped in, strands of his overgrown hair almost touching his eyes. "Hey buddy!" His voice was loud. "A promising banker, I hear."

Kungu pushed the gate halfway, turned slightly and hesitated again, then turned back to the man. "Why are you here?"

"What kind of greeting is that to a war buddy? Have you forgotten me?" He nudged Kungu with his forearm with a toothy grin. "It's me, Taegil. We fought together." He strutted into the courtyard.

Kungu walked alongside the man, keeping a distance between them. "How did you find me?"

Halfway to the living room, the man stopped when he noticed Sonju watching him. Kungu stopped too. The man sharply pivoted and lifted his arms in a shooting stance. "Pow!" He jerked his head backward as if he were shot.

Kungu froze, his face suddenly pale, gaze blank. Sonju immediately sensed something ominous. Her heart stopped.

The man cocked his head, thrusting his face into Kungu's. "Aren't you well?"

Kungu stood still as if he didn't hear the man. Sonju rushed to the man and pointed to the gate. "You should leave."

"But I'm his war buddy," the man protested as he backed away and out of the gate. She slammed the gate shut and locked it.

Kungu was still standing in the same spot. Her chest hammering, she put her arm around his waist and led him to the bedroom. He sank to the floor and stared straight ahead. Even when she sat in front of him studying his face, his blank eyes still stared through her at the same spot as if she were invisible.

"What is it?" She asked. "Kungu, look at me."

"Ohhh ..." He closed his eyes and moaned. "Forgive me."

"What is it? Tell me." She grabbed his shoulders and shook them. "Look at me!"

His eyelids lifted slowly, and hardly moving his lips, he talked to himself, "I see it. Why didn't I before?"

Sonju shook him again. "What do you see?"

"Something happened during the war ... I did something."

"What did you do?"

He didn't answer. His eyes were far away.

She shook him. "Tell me. What did you do?"

He took a deep breath and looked at Sonju. He started talking but sounded more like talking to himself. "Taegil and I fought side by side near Waegwan all day. It was getting dark. I couldn't see well. Explosions like lightning, then dark again. Gunshots from everywhere, artillery fire, grenades. A bullet passed by my ear. I didn't expect the enemy so close. Right then, another explosion bright as daylight. I saw a figure. He saw me, too. I pulled the trigger. It happened so fast, yet it seemed like hours, everything moving slowly, and him falling backward."

"That's war. You were almost shot. Kill your enemy, that's what soldiers do in time of war."

"I recognized him. Why did I shoot him? Why?"

Hiding her fright, she searched his eyes. "Who did you recognize?"

"It ... it was my cousin I killed. I see it clearly now."

For a moment, all she saw was darkness. She heard him mumble, "Taegil must have known. He said I talked in my sleep."

"Did he tell you what you said?"

"No, he just gave me an odd smile. It stuck with me," Kungu choked down a cough a few times. "I must have blocked ..."

156

Her heart was drumming. She tried to keep her voice calm. "We'll sort this out together."

Remain calm, carry on a normal routine, she told herself. "Do you want more tea?"

His nod barely showed.

She brought tea to the room, and they sipped slowly staring into space. Must say something ordinary to break the silence, she told herself again, but when their eyes met, she only managed a faint smile and a squeeze of his hand.

He patted her hand and put it aside. "I feel a headache coming. We're out of aspirin. I'll get some. Do you need anything from the drug store?" He said, sounding casual.

"No, but I'll go," she said, still worried.

"No, you stay here. Fresh night air would be good for me."

The drug store was only a ten-minute walk. Half an hour passed, but Kungu didn't come. Sonju washed the cups in the kitchen, returned to the living room, and listened for the gate opening. At nine-thirty, Sonju went to the bedroom, laid the *yo* on the floor, and paced. He was all right, wasn't he? Nine-fifty. It seemed an eternity.

He finally came home at ten-twelve with aspirin and a paper bag.

"I bought the aspirin and took it at the drug store. On the way home, I stopped by the roasted chestnut stand and waited for a fresh batch." He handed her a brown bag. "Your favorite." He smiled.

"Thank you. It's still hot. How is your headache?"

"It's going away."

"I'm glad. Let me get a bowl for the chestnuts."

When she returned with a bowl, he seemed fine. He had bought chestnuts for her.

Sitting next to her with a small paring knife, he peeled the charred shells. Black soot and brown fuzz collected under his fingernails.

She ate the naked yellow nuts Kungu handed her. "They're so good. Thank you."

He kept shelling and she kept eating. He ate one and teased her. "You ate all but one."

He was all right, she thought. Back to his normal self. He even joked and smiled. "You kept giving them to me." Sonju returned the smile. Things were well again.

Sonju woke up to the subdued early light coming through the windows. She nudged Kungu. "Wake up. You'll be late for work."

There was no response. She sat up and shook him. "Kungu, wake up." He was still. She shook him again. Her heart dropped.

She placed her ear to his nose and touched his neck to check for a pulse. His skin was cool. "No!" she screamed. She put her ear close to his nose again. "No!" Smoothing his hair, she cried, "Wake up, Kungu. Get up!" She lay close to wrap her arm around him, his body so still. When her cheek touched his, she got a chill. "Kungu, tell me this isn't true. This can't be." She sat up, stared at him, and cried. She lay next to him, held his cool hand, and talked to him to his ear, "You could have talked to me. We could have pulled through this together." She sat up again and wept.

She didn't hear the gate open and close but heard quick footsteps outside her door.

The maid barged into the room without knocking. "What's wrong? I heard you ..." She looked at Sonju, then at Kungu, and fell to her knees, weeping.

Sonju shook Kungu, crying, "Tell me how I am to live without you."

"Don't stir the body. Let him be in peace." The maid pulled Sonju's arms away. "We have to notify the master's uncle and the bank." Standing up she said, "I'll go," and pointed at Sonju's pajamas. "People will come."

Kungu's uncle and aunt came within half an hour.

"He was fine last night," Sonju explained. "He was fine." She wiped her tears on her sleeve. "Last night, he bought some roasted chestnuts. And he peeled them for me. I still have the peels." As if to prove to herself how perfectly fine he had seemed, she went to the kitchen to retrieve the shells. There she found a water glass and three paper squares with traces of white powder on them. With shaking hands, she tucked the papers into her skirt pocket, brought the bowl of chestnut shells, and showed it to Kungu's uncle and aunt.

The aunt glanced at the shells, then turning to Kungu, wept. "Look at you. You're so young. You were like a son to me."

Sonju gazed at the black crescent tips of Kungu's fingernails. She kept repeating in her head, "I should have stayed up, should have watched him closer."

The maid came in to say that a man from the bank was here.

"Let him in," The uncle said.

The man came into the room, bowed to Sonju, then to Kungu's uncle and aunt. "I am Kim Chonil. I am so sorry." Kim Chonil. Just two days ago, Kungu had talked about inviting him for dinner next week perhaps, their first try at entertaining.

The uncle said to the man, "I am Kungu's uncle. Thank you for coming."

"Kungu was a good friend of mine, a classmate at the university."

The uncle said the funeral would be in three days and the man left after saying he and others from the bank would attend the funeral.

Shortly after that, Kungu's uncle rose saying he would be back. His wife told Sonju they would take care of the funeral and followed him out. After the uncle and aunt left, the maid went to the kitchen.

Sonju sat, looking at Kungu's peaceful, gentle face, lips slightly open. She lay next to him with her arm on his chest, holding his unresponsive hand. She said quietly, "Kungu, you cannot die. We just started our lives together."

The maid came in with a tray of food. "You have to eat something." She gently pulled Sonju up to a sitting position and brought a spoonful of broth to her lips.

That afternoon, Kungu's uncle returned in mourner's attire of stiff hemp cloth over his wool suit. "We're moving Kungu's body to my house today."

"No." Sonju covered Kungu with her upper body, held him with both arms, and clung to him.

Two men walked in with a coffin.

The maid pulled up Sonju away from Kungu's body and held Sonju from the back. She whispered to her, "You know people can't come here where you live."

Sonju lunged forward when she saw through her blurry eyes the two men lift Kungu, but the maid's hold was firm. The men placed Kungu in the wooden box, closed the lid, and picked it up. Sonju tried to move toward the coffin, but the maid pulled her back and held her until all three men left the room.

The gate opened and shut with a clatter.

"I'll lock the gate," the maid said leaving the room.

Sonju lay on the *yo*, gazing at Kungu's spot. "I came to you. Why did you die? I'm all alone, don't you see?"

The maid returned to the room and said, "Earlier, my master's uncle told me to stay with you tonight and tomorrow."

"He took Kungu away," Sonju said with bitterness. "He doesn't want his people to see me."

The maid covered her face with her hands and wept.

Sonju was quiet but tears kept coming. Soon she drifted into sleep and awoke in the darkest hour of the night. Kungu couldn't be dead. Just the night before, she felt his warm body next to her, heard him say, "I love you."

When she woke up again, the light was on and the maid was sitting next to the *yo*. She looked at the clock. "Three o'clock. What are you doing up at this hour?"

"I wanted to make sure you're all right."

"That's what I should've done, make sure he was all right. After that man came, he was not right. I thought he was, but he wasn't."

"What man?"

Without thinking, she said, "This man came yesterday evening. He called himself Kungu's war buddy. When he made a gesture of shooting, Kungu's face turned pale. After the man left, Kungu told me something happened during the war. A bullet almost hit him, and he pulled the trigger. It was his cousin he shot. It all came to him when the man made the shooting gesture." She was feverish. "I thought everything was fine after we talked."

She bolted up. She shouldn't have said all that to this woman, to anyone. She searched the maid's eyes. "No one can know about this. He died in his sleep, understand? This is the only thing I can do for him now." Sonju didn't want Kungu's life to be shamed and his death questioned.

"No one will know," the maid said.

Sonju had no one left who would stay beside her.

1952 November 16

My Daughter Jinju,
   The man I loved died suddenly two days ago. I don't know what to make of it. I can't believe he is gone.
   I wish you were here with me. I think I would be all right if I could be with you.

She whimpered and moaned, couldn't continue the letter.

The day after the funeral, the maid said, "It doesn't seem right to me that you couldn't be there."

The clanging of pots came from the kitchen, the splatter of water falling from the pump, the splash of washing and rinsing in the work area. Noises, noises were everywhere, so loud. Stop! No sound, please. She wanted to be alone. She wanted to shout ugly, angry words.

The maid brought a tray of tea. As she turned to go, Sonju reached out and touched the maid's arm. "Thank you for what you've done for me these last few days. I don't know how I would have been without your help. Now I must do on my own. I won't need your service after today."

"I understand, Ma'am."

The maid must have thought she couldn't afford her service. No matter. She needed physical work, needed to cry and throw things.

With just herself roaming in the house all day, there was no sound of life. "Why did you have to die, Kungu?" She asked the empty air again and again. "You said you were glad you were alive." Their union was so brief, they had only nine months together. "I hate my mother. I hate my father. Go to hell, Taegil." After repeating the same words four or five times, it seemed pointless. She stopped. She grabbed a damp rag and cleaned the whole house. Anger was watching her. She threw the rag again and again. She plopped down and cried. After her crying died down, she sat still taking in absolute silence as loud as a trumpet blowing in every crevice and in every molecule in the house. Everything was still, unmoving, even time.

At dusk, she lay on the *yo* and held his spare pajamas tightly in her arms, extended her arm and swept the *yo* surface with her hand. Such an indifferent white surface.

There had been signs, she realized now. Those confused looks on Kungu's face, unfocused eyes, more frequent headaches. She shouldn't have dismissed them. A week before he died, he had told her he had transferred most of his money into her account. He must have had a premonition. He had wanted her to move on.

On her sixth day alone, the maid came. "How are you doing?" she asked, lowering herself onto the floor.

"Thank you for asking. I'm doing better." Sonju wondered why the maid had returned. Does she want something of Kungu's, a keepsake?

An awkward smile crossed the maid's face. She fidgeted, her hands knitting and unknitting, creasing her forehead. She parted her lips, ready to talk, only to close them. She cleared her throat. "I have to tell you something sinful I've done." She dropped her head. "I'm the one who wrote the letter to your father-in-law about you and my master. I did that because my master, you know, he had a good future ahead of him. And he was such a decent man too. Never brought a woman to the house. After you started coming, neighbors started gossiping."

The letter! Fire started in Sonju's belly and filled her chest. She wanted to lunge at the woman. Without that cursed letter, she could have had Jinju with her right now. Her hands in balls and her jaws tightened, she trembled, not knowing what to do with them. She wanted to beat the woman with her fisted hands.

With downcast eyes, the maid continued, "From your letter, I figured you were a married woman because you have a Seoul accent but a country address."

How clever of you, Sonju thought with venom in her eyes. The maid fidgeted again with her hands, then her eyes still lowered, said, "I was so furious that you were ruining my master's future. But after you came to live with him, I realized you're a nice lady and my master was so happy. I heard you mention your daughter and many times, I saw tears in your eyes. I asked myself, 'Who am I to be so judgmental and get into other people's business?'" She grabbed a corner of her skirt and wiped her eyes with it. "My guilt was eating my stomach, so I confessed to my master. He said my letter brought you to him. And now my master's gone and you're alone without anyone because of me. Damn me." The maid hit her chest with her fist, then slumped down almost flat on the floor, crying.

Sonju glared at the woman, shaking. She wanted to pound on that woman's back and shout, Give me back my daughter! Then she became afraid of her impulses to let loose of her fury and actually beat the woman and she might not be able to stop. She unfurled her hands and dropped her shoulders. After a few slow deep breaths, she took another look at the woman's slumped body. Kungu had already forgiven this wretched woman. He wouldn't have wanted Sonju to hurt her. She watched the weeping woman's back and saw that he had his maid's loyalty and eagerness to protect him. Besides, this woman didn't have to confess, yet she did. Sonju respected that. She asked, "Would you work for me as you did for your master?"

The maid lifted herself and wiped her tears. "Of course, Ma'am."

There were days Sonju didn't cry. She thought of the days of cosmos flowers, the black stains under Kungu's fingernails, and all the days in between. She often gazed out blankly or stared down at a lonely cup on the tray.

For several days in early December, the sky brooded, dropping its grey to the ground. The maid had gone grocery shopping. Sonju was in the bedroom folding Kungu's laundered clothes and piling them up on the floor in neat stacks when she heard a loud banging and an argument at the gate.

Sonju went to the living room and looked out. The grocery bag was leaning on the fence near the maid who had her back against the gate trying to push it shut. Someone was muttering something behind the gate.

Looking at Sonju, the maid said urgently, "There's a man wanting to talk to the master. He followed me to the gate, said his name is Taegil. He smells of alcohol."

At Sonju's nodding, the maid let go of the gate, and Taegil tumbled in swaying and staggering.

"Buddy, Kungu, come out. You don't want to see me? I scared you last time, didn't I?" He swung his arm and almost lost his footing. "Get me a job, buddy," he said. "Come out. Shall I go see your uncle instead? How would that work out for you? Heh heh."

Sonju marched to the storage shed at the end of the courtyard, grabbed a shovel, and walked calmly toward Taegil. Then she swung the shovel against his leg with all her strength. The flat of the blade hit his leg. He cried out and fell, grabbing his leg, and thrust one arm over his face.

"You snake!" Sonju screamed at him. "Kungu died. You can't blackmail a dead person, can you?" She didn't sound like herself, her snarling voice rough. Sonju raised the shovel. For a split second, she thought she could kill the man, then saw naked fear in his wide-open eyes. His elbow still pinned on the ground, he tried to block his face with his forearm, and with his free hand, he attempted to grab the shovel, all the while slithering this way and that toward the gate. With the shovel raised above his knee, Sonju kicked him again and again until he was out of the gate. She slammed the gate shut and locked it, turned and stared at the maid. They both grinned. The maid took the shovel from Sonju's hand and returned it to the storage shed. She would never tell a soul about her murderous thought. She was scared of herself, of what she could do.

Taegil's incident shook her up. After a long bus ride and a long walk, she came to a small gravestone standing in front of a mound, the grave unremarkable from all the rest other than the recently dug red dirt on the surface. She sat facing Kungu, felt the December chill of the soil through the wool scarf under her folded legs. All she could think was Kungu in the cold wooden box, his body in hemp clothes, his arms and legs aligned and bound to keep his form for the next life. No! She wanted him in this life. She needed him in this life.

Two months after the funeral, Kungu's uncle wrote to say a buyer for the house would take possession in one month. Sonju wanted to scream and bang on the wall. What more would be taken away from her? Kungu's presence was still in his house. She could hear all the little noises of their life together, Kungu's and hers—the patter of going from one room to another, the newspaper flipping, a teaspoon hitting the saucer, quiet talks and laughter. After the move, what of Kungu would remain?

She had no choice but to visit real estate offices fighting the cutting blades of the freezing January breeze. With nine days left to move, Sonju packed her clothes, then walked to the bookshelf in the living room and emptied Kungu's books, his treasured collection, into four boxes. In another box, she packed the books she had studied. Then, she kept the bedroom dark and slept twelve, thirteen hours a day.

For five days, the maid would come in and say, "You need to eat more," but Sonju would just wave her away.

On the sixth day, Sonju saw tears on the maid's sagging cheeks and felt tenderness for the woman who grieved with her and chose to care for her. "We have to move in three days," the maid said.

Sonju got up and went to the living room. Wind was whipping outside. Clothes on the line chained together and stiff as corpses did a dance of the macabre, swinging side to side, up and down. She no longer wanted to be in that house.

Life Alone, 1953

In a small, rented house, Sonju stood near the living room window that was covered with a thin layer of moisture. With a page from the newspaper, she wiped a small circle to look out. The maid was moving about with great vigor as if on a mission to stay busy. After pumping water to the tank, she squatted in the work area near the kitchen, rinsed clothes and twisted them like taffy. She pressed her hand on her knee to push herself up, then hung the clothes on the line.

Sonju took a low table to her bedroom, picked up a pencil and straightened the paper. She had not written to Misu about Kungu's passing. But instead of writing, she put the pencil down and rested her chin on a cupped hand. She must do something to earn a living, but she had no references. Besides, no respectable employment would be available to her. Then came a sudden recollection. She dashed to the bureau drawer, grabbed a cotton bag, and poured the contents on the table—buttons, old coins, short sashes, a few safety pins, torn-out newspaper articles, and a little piece of paper with a name and address on it.

Saturday afternoon, the taxi dropped her off at a large house with a thick stucco fence. A full-faced young woman with a glowing complexion opened the gate, blinked, cocked her head, then gave Sonju a bright smile. "I remember you! Let me tell Lady Cho you're here."

"I recognize you too," Sonju said.

Even before reaching the living room, the helper announced, her voice lilting, "The lady we met on the train is here." Then she added, "during the evacuation."

The glass doors opened. A well-dressed young woman with plump lips stepped down into the courtyard and stretched her arms out in a welcoming gesture. "How good you came!" Turning to the helper, she said, "Yunghee, tell Lady Cho we have a special guest."

Sonju followed the women into a large living room with a varnished papered floor. Yunghee hurried to the back. Next to the low wooden furniture on one side of the room sat a bronze sculpture of an amorphous female figure, and on the other two walls hung oil paintings, watercolors, and charcoal sketches.

Walking in from the back of the house, Lady Cho saw Sonju and stepped toward her. Yunghee, who had been jiggling with excitement, bounced out of the room when Lady Cho gave her a brief glance.

"So good to see you," Lady Cho said with a warm smile. "You remembered us."

Sonju said, "It has been almost three years. I thought you might not remember me."

"How can we not remember you? You made an impression on us, the way you handled the children in all that chaos. You seemed in perfect possession of yourself. We talked about you now and then." She stopped smiling, and with a look of concern, asked, "But what happened to you? You look so thin."

Sonju looked down at her loosely hanging coat and dress.

"Please sit down and warm yourself," Lady Cho said.

After they sat, Lady Cho turned. "You met Miss Im on the train."

People in Seoul must have adopted a Western word, Miss, Sonju thought and said, "Yes, I remember. I am Yu Sonju."

"I am Im Nari," Miss Im said.

They smiled at each other.

There was a pause, and Sonju felt an urgency to break the silence. "Since I saw you last, my life has changed drastically."

Lady Cho asked, "Did your husband die during the war?"

"No." Sonju gazed at the piped edge of the satin pillow she was sitting on.

"You don't have to say anything," Lady Cho said. "First drink some tea, and we will eat together."

Yunghee brought a tea tray and quickly left. Small talk passed about the imported jasmine tea they were drinking. They said other foreign goods such as dry powdered milk and

Western clothes donated by the Americans were also available in the black market. During their conversation, Yunghee came in again and set a table between them. With nimble efficiency, she was in and out carrying trays of food, and after she transferred the food from the last tray, she left the room closing the door behind her. Lady Cho, Miss Im and Sonju sat around the table eating even though it was too early for dinner.

Lady Cho asked Sonju, "How did you fare during the evacuation?"

"The six of us, two adults and four children, stayed at my sister-in-law's house for three months. Where in Daejon did you stay?"

"We stayed southeast of Daejon. Battles were fought all along the small villages near us. We didn't return until late March after Seoul was liberated."

Lady Cho and Miss Im told her about the scarcity of food and the atrocities committed by both sides—all the things they already knew, just different locations. Sonju told them about the difficulty getting news, the desperation of people, and the diseases her brother-in-law treated.

Sonju didn't realize she had been steadily putting food in her mouth until she was full. "Everything is delicious," she said.

Lady Cho went to the door, and opening it, called out. "Yunghee, have the cook come in to greet my friend."

Sonju lifted her eyes to Lady Cho.

"You and I went to the same school. We are friends," Lady Cho said as if their friendship were a natural thing to assume.

Grateful to be referred to as a friend, Sonju dipped her head slightly at Lady Cho who was now back on her pillow.

Within minutes, a middle-aged woman with a broad face and build came in and bowed to Sonju. She bowed again when Sonju complimented the food. As the cook was leaving, Lady Cho told her, "Send Gija in to greet Lady Yu."

Lady Yu? But then, what would they call her otherwise? She certainly wasn't a Miss, Sonju mused.

Miss Im said, "Gija has been with us less than a month. The person before her left us to get married."

Presently, a long-faced, wiry young woman in a thick navy cotton shirt and muted grey *monpe* work pants entered the living room, bowed to Sonju, turned around and left the room.

Miss Im said, "I should have warned you. She doesn't talk much but is one talented cook."

The three of them soon ran out of things to say. They exchanged a few glances and faint smiles. To break the awkward silence, Sonju said, "You asked what happened to me. When I told my mother about the childhood friend I wanted to marry, she quickly arranged a marriage to a man far from Seoul." Rolling her invisible thinking-stone in her hand, she said, "I had an affair with that friend, and my marriage ended in divorce a year ago. My family disowned me. I am not to see my daughter until she is eighteen." Here, her voice wavered. She took a deep breath and continued, "I moved in with my childhood friend, but he died suddenly in November." She couldn't understand her impulse to offer this clumsy confession that gushed out like creek water after a storm. She closed her mouth tightly so no more words would leak out.

The heavy, thick quiet that followed lasted a while.

"Where are you staying now?" Lady Cho finally asked.

"I am renting a small house in Ahyun Dong. You said on the train that you are working women. I thought I might get some ideas from you about what women do in a circumstance like mine."

"Thirteen years ago, I didn't know what to do with myself either," Lady Cho said. "You will find something to do. In the meantime, you are welcome to visit us."

Miss Im's eyes darted from Lady Cho to Sonju and back.

"Now, I will tell you what we do." Lady Cho's eyes rested on Sonju's for a brief moment. "This is an exclusive club for influential men to come together with other powerful men to share information and to make connections while dining together. Sometimes large business deals are made, and contracts are awarded as a result."

Sonju must have looked bewildered because Lady Cho

smiled before she said, "Quite a few of them have been coming here so long that they are our friends."

"I never knew things like that existed," Sonju said and wondered if she should be at this place at all, a men's club. She glanced at Lady Cho and Miss Im. They were so proper and well-spoken and gracious in every way.

Lady Cho, exuding confidence, said, "It is not that mysterious or unique. It has been in existence for centuries for a certain class of men. Our clients come here for lunch or dinner."

"Or both," Miss Im said. "I make sure that they are served food and drink according to their habits and preferences. Lady Cho and I sometimes engage in conversations with our clients when appropriate."

Well-poised women coming into contact with men, conversing with men, serving liquor to men—Sonju needed time to grasp what she just heard.

Lady Cho spoke again, "Let me show you the room. Among ourselves, we call it 'The Back Room.' It's where the clients dine."

Sonju and Lady Cho walked along a wide corridor, where sculpture pieces on pedestals were displayed against one wall opposite a glass wall. Through those windows a Japanese garden could be seen. It contained three large bonsai pines, four rocks that looked as though suspended at the very moment they tumbled down, and several creeping junipers that hugged the ground here and there. It evoked contemplation and timelessness.

Sonju pointed at another glass wall to the back, perpendicular to the one she was looking out from. "Is that The Back Room?"

"Yes," Lady Cho replied. "The garden view is slightly different from there because you see two solid walls—the fence and the front quarters."

At the end of the corridor, they came to a huge room, where six tall ink-and-brush scrolls hung on one wall, and below them lay two inconspicuous writing tables. In the center of the room sat a series of long wooden tables. Sonju was captivated by the elegance and beauty of the room so well captured in stark simplicity.

"I feel like I have come upon a secret place. It is so intimate and peaceful." She asked, "What is your business called?"

"I didn't name it. Our clients started calling it Cho's Hall and then just The Hall. Unlike most women in Korea, we actually earn our own living."

Sonju caught a touch of defensiveness in Lady Cho's tone. Even so, there was an air of authority as well as sincerity in this handsome woman. She had a presence—her eyes steady, posture erect, her movements assured, and her voice firm—much like her mother, Sonju thought, but more approachable.

Lady Cho came closer to Sonju and said in a warm voice, "We have all known desperate moments and difficulty being alone in the world. You are one of us."

As Sonju considered those words, her view of the world as a disapproving, unforgiving force slid away. On the way home, buoyant glee danced in her chest.

Not to overdo her welcome, Sonju waited seven days before visiting The Hall again. Miss Im greeted her. She looked like a university student in a pink cashmere sweater, navy calf-length plaid wool skirt, and a chin-length bob haircut that framed her peach-shaped face. While serving tea, she said, "I am glad you came. Hopefully, we will see you often?"

Sonju dipped her head. "Thank you. I would like that." After a few sips, she didn't know what to talk about, so she let her eyes travel to the paintings on the wall—a few Impressionistic, some Post-Impressionistic, others more modern with angry colors and thick angular lines—similar to the early twentieth century Western paintings she had seen in the art books she and Kungu had studied together.

Miss Im must have followed Sonju's eyes. "Lady Cho is an art lover. She has many artist friends."

"Are these the works of her friends?"

"Yes. We have an art exhibit here once a year. Of course, you will come, won't you?"

"I would love to."

Lady Cho walked in from the back, and before Sonju could greet her, Miss Im said, "I told Lady Yu about the art exhibit. She agreed to come to the next one."

In Miss Im's excited speech, Sonju detected an almost imperceptible inflection of a province far south with those rough rushed consonants. Sonju said, "My former brother-in-law used to collect celadon pieces of the Koryo period. Once in a while, he took out a piece from the attic and looked at it for a long time before returning it, out of reach of the children." She recalled his slow smile as he carefully turned the vase. "I think a common space exists in the souls of art lovers where they pause and take joy in what they see. They seem to look at life on a different plane. I want to learn how to be in that world."

Lady Cho's eyes brightened. "I will introduce you to my artist friends."

After the visit, her feet light at the excitement of being welcomed by women she could call friends, Sonju walked to the curbside, and hailed a taxi home instead of walking to a bus stop.

Back at home, Sonju opened the bureau drawer in her bedroom. She bent down, sniffed Kungu's white oxford shirt, stroked the two thinking-stones, his and hers, sitting on top of it, and whispered, "It's been a good day for me, Kungu. I have friends. Those women I met on the train I told you about? I visited them again." She then took out stationery from the bottom drawer and wrote to her friend, Misu.

With the letter in her hand, she took the narrow street to the nearby post office where two of her classmates recognized her at the same time she saw them. Sonju almost stopped like some prey animal caught by surprise. One classmate wore a crooked smile upon seeing Sonju and whispered to her friend. They stepped aside as though avoiding filth. Sonju bit her lip and continued to the post office to drop the letter and returned to an empty house. In her room, she leaned on the wall and closed her eyes, and told herself that she must bear the consequences of her choice.

Since Kungu's passing, her life had not been organized by her thoughts. It had been more about getting through the long days, being acutely aware of the sun rising and setting with many hours in between. It took so long to get a day done. Often, she spent nights wide-eyed, hugging a pillow. Another spring was coming. She had known a different spring.

When she visited the women at The Hall again the following Sunday, the conversation flowed the way it did among close friends—mundane, pleasant, assuring. In the middle of a conversation, they heard someone pound on the gate shouting, "Open the door."

Yunghee rose and stepped into the courtyard toward the gate but stopped in the midway and ran back saying she was scared. Loud yelling and insistent pounding persisted. The cook went to the gate and unlocked it. A young man on wooden crutches hobbled into the courtyard, one leg on the ground and the stump of the other hanging. He was wearing ragged torn clothes with one pant leg rolled up to the stump. He yelled at the cook, "What are you staring at?" He thrust his face out and bared his teeth like an animal before an attack. "Give me money!"

"Have the man come to the living room," Lady Cho said loudly enough for the man to hear. Yunghee and Gija ran to the kitchen. Miss Im and Sonju moved close to the wall beside a bronze statue.

The man carried with him the odor of something rotten.

Lady Cho took one look at him and said, "Sit down." The man obliged, moving his crutches and setting them aside before lowering himself clumsily to the floor. Lady Cho scrutinized him. "Why are you yelling instead of talking?"

"Because I'm angry."

"What are you angry about?"

Striking his chest with his hand, he leaned forward as if pleading. "Look at me." He struck his chest again and with

174

frustration in his voice said, "I was a day worker on farms then I lost my leg in the war. How can I work? I came to Seoul to beg for money, but people treat me like a dog, sometimes worse. So, I scare people into giving me money. This house looked like a rich person's house with that tall fence wrapping around a big property." He grinned as if he was proud of himself for picking The Hall.

Sonju stared at the man's crutches and thought some men suffered more damage by the war than an amputated leg. If it weren't for the war, she would be still with Kungu.

Lady Cho spoke, "I will give you money. Any time you are hungry, you can come here, but you are not to make such a commotion next time. You still have two hands. Think about what you can do to make a living. I will think about it too."

The man bowed repeatedly, rubbing his thighs. "I'm sorry. I'm not a bad person. The war, my leg ... I became an angry person. When I'm alone, I think about the way I used to be."

In the quiet of her home, Sonju pictured that angry maimed man before the war when he might have laughed, played, and loved. Her former husband and his brother didn't go to war. The maimed man's body odor seemed a condemnation of all the smug people.

The next time Sonju was at The Hall, she asked about the man. Miss Im said, "He came the following day and ate enough to last until the next day. Lady Cho bought him an outfit, had him bathe in the public bath, and even sent him to a barbershop. A day later, one of our clients put him to work. He told Lady Cho the one-legged man sits on a stool and shines shoes and sleeps in the janitor's room in his office building."

"I am glad," Sonju said and thought about Kungu. "He has a chance to rebuild his life. Some were not that lucky."

Lady Cho's Offer, 1953

Her daughter's fourth birthday fell on a Saturday. Sonju took out Jinju's tiny dress from the bottom drawer of the bureau. Not a hint of Jinju's scent remained on it, but she was reminded of Jinju's chatter like water rolling in a brook and her laughter the sound of marbles hitting the floor. She could see Jinju throw her head back with outstretched arms in happiness.

When she returned the dress to the drawer, her eyes rested on the thin envelope at the bottom. She hadn't looked at her daughter's photographs since the last day in Maari. She wouldn't today, either. She didn't want to cry anymore.

In late April, Lady Cho asked if she could introduce Sonju to her clients. Sonju's heart tumbled for a split second at the thought of meeting a group of men who were not her family, but she said yes, then quickly regretted it. She desperately wished to talk to Kungu.

The following Monday at The Hall, she changed into a traditional Korean dress she brought with her, and while waiting to be introduced, she flicked invisible lint off her sleeve, scratched her nape for no reason, held the ends of the sashes of her dress, and even tried a smile. Her heart began to drum softly. She took a deep breath.

When the men started arriving for dinner, Lady Cho stood next to Sonju and introduced her to each man, "This is my friend Lady Yu. We went to the same school."

Some said, "Ah, Ewha alumna." But others simply bowed. Of the men who came, four were assemblymen, one doctor, nine businessmen, six government officials, and one Yunsei University professor. While the men drank American liquor and ate rich snack food, they asked each other's opinions about various businesses and government regulations, and shared news about people who were not present.

Lady Cho walked around and at times sat near a client to

exchange small talk before moving on to another client. Sonju stayed close to Lady Cho and responded briefly when men asked polite questions. In the meantime, Miss Im was standing at one end of the long table scanning the clients as an elaborate dinner was served.

Men were passing alcohol from one to another, and after several rounds, their gestures and expression became more animated and their language less meticulous and deliberate. Discussions turned passionate at times and conversations more revealing as the evening wore on. Assemblyman Kim stood out among them. He smiled and laughed along but mostly observed others and spoke only a few words. He looked to be one of the youngest at the table but when he spoke, everyone's head turned to him.

At about a quarter to nine, the men started leaving. Some asked Sonju if they would see her again. Sonju just bowed.

Lady Cho asked Sonju to remain with her. After the room had cleared out, she said, "It went well, don't you think?"

Sonju replied that she thought it did.

Lady Cho went on to describe each client and added, "They come here because they value what this place provides—the very best connections they can find. Not one of them would be ashamed to say to anyone, not even to their wives, that they frequent The Hall."

When the clients saw Sonju again a few days later, they were again courteous. Their conversations revealed a world she hadn't even imagined. One man spoke about going to Washington D.C. for a conference. Another man asked him, "When did you learn to speak English?" A third man said, "When you get there, please be sure to visit my son in California. He is in medical school. He had to start over because in America, unlike here, you enter a medical school after completing a baccalaureate degree." "Be sure to see the Grand Canyon and Niagara Falls." "In Sequoia Park, there are trees so tall that to take the pictures of them I had to lie on the ground to get the entirety of the trees."

They talked on and on like intimate, old friends—something Sonju was envious of. Their conversations also made her realize how small, transient, and directionless her life was at the moment and became even more anxious about what her days would be like in the years to come.

One Sunday in mid-May, Sonju visited Lady Cho at her traditional Korean house that looked new. Lady Cho said her old house was destroyed during the war and she had it rebuilt. They entered an inner chamber, and a maid brought a tray of green tea. After tea and small talk, Lady Cho said, "I took notice of your interactions with my clients and their reactions. I would like you to consider working with us. I will pay you enough that when I close The Hall, you will be financially comfortable."

Sonju, though shocked at the idea of working at The Hall, looked down and was quiet for a moment and told herself this would mean the end of her money worries. She asked, "What does the job entail?"

"I would want you to come at nine in the morning to coordinate the kitchen staff before they start cooking," Lady Cho said. "You and Miss Im will be our eyes and ears to help serve our clients the best way possible. You would make sure everything is in order before lunch starts at eleven. Watch what Miss Im does."

"What are your expectations of me regarding the clients?"

"In the morning and in between lunch and dinner, I expect you to read the newspapers, books on art, architecture, literature, philosophy, history, business, and economics. I have books in the bureau in the living room. I will buy more when we need them."

"Will the clients ask me questions? I don't know much about the subjects you mentioned."

"You can say you don't know. At times, you may facilitate the conversation. They like women's sensibilities. These are enlightened men and most of them have traveled to America and Europe. They will not harass you for sex. They can go somewhere else for that." Lady Cho swiped her hand lightly, and added, "They sign a contract when they join."

After telling Lady Cho she would give her decision by

Saturday, Sonju hurried home wishing Kungu were sitting across from her. "A job offer! I can earn money on my own," she would say to him, but upon returning home only to find her house empty and mute, she asked him, "Why did you die?" She secretly criticized him for leaving her, for giving up, but in defense of him, she considered how it would have been for him to live, questioning his conscience, agonizing over his guilt, and eventually coming to loathe himself. Then what would have been left of him and between them?

"Kungu, I'll have to take this offer," she told him in her head. Without an income, she would run out of money in two or three years. By twenty-nine, she would be destitute. But, coming in contact with men in a private social club ... She would be shunned by society for the appearance of it regardless of what Lady Cho said it was or was not.

Waffling back and forth for several days, she told her maid, "I was offered a job by Lady Cho at The Hall. It's an exclusive men's club. The job involves serving men food and drink." She added, "It isn't what it sounds."

"You don't have to convince me," the maid said. "You're worried about what people might think, but what are they to you? They're not paying for your food. Besides, you need people to talk to."

That Saturday afternoon, Lady Cho gathered the women in the living room to announce Sonju's employment. Everyone smiled and chattered. After the excitement died down, Lady Cho said, "One more announcement. I want to help people in the arts, so I plan to close The Hall in ten years, at which time you will still be of marrying age and able to bear children. I hope you will have enough savings to retire by then."

Each one was quiet for a few minutes. Miss Im said she would send less money to her family. Yunghee said she had been saving money. The cook said she had already planned to retire by then. "I can live on very little," Gija said.

Other than the cook, who had a husband and a son, no one talked about what they were going to do after The Hall closed.

Miss Im, Yunghee, and Gija would no longer live in The Hall. Sonju thought she would like to buy a house as soon as possible. In ten years, Jinju would be fourteen, and four more years after that, she would be able to see her daughter.

The following Monday, Lady Cho announced to the seated clients, "I am so happy to announce that my friend Lady Yu has agreed to work with us." One client after another rose briefly to welcome Sonju.

By the end of two weeks at The Hall, Sonju became sufficiently accustomed to the daily routine—arrive at work by nine, read newspapers and books, adjust the day's lunch and dinner menu with Miss Im, count the liquor bottles, and make a purchase list. She inspected the dishes, bowls, and glasses to make sure they were spotless, tidied up the front and back rooms, checked her hair, and changed into a Korean dress thirty minutes before the clients arrived for lunch and dinner. She greeted each of the clients by name and title, walked softly, led them to the back room, took their jackets and hung them in the closet. Then she seated them in their preferred spots, used both hands to serve food and drinks, was vigilant to their needs, and spoke only when spoken to and in complete sentences.

Three weeks into her employment, one client, a business-man, lingered behind after lunch. He approached Sonju and proposed without hesitancy or shame that she meet him some-where outside The Hall privately. Shocked, then flustered, Sonju looked him in the eye and said, "You are terribly mistaken. I am not what you think." She quickly turned and hurried through the corridor and went directly to the women's bedroom in the front. Miss Im came in, and Sonju told her what had happened in the back room. "Do I look that naïve and easy?" she asked, to which Miss Im angrily said, "Absolutely not. He is relatively new and doesn't come here regularly. Lady Cho will hear about this."

Soon after Lady Cho returned to The Hall from the class reunion she'd been attending and learned about what happened, she became visibly upset. "We have never had this happen." She took Sonju's hand. "I am so sorry. He will not come back." Her face was still flushed.

Sonju eventually got over the incident. It helped that all the clients continued to be deferential to her and that she could depend on the women of The Hall for support.

One afternoon during a break, Sonju found Gija sitting on the wide window ledge by the kitchen, reading *The Brothers Karamazov*. Sonju went to the back room and asked Lady Cho, "Gija is reading *The Brothers Karamazov*. Should she be doing kitchen work?"

"She loves to cook. Her relative said she went to school off and on because she was passed around from one relative to another but is nonetheless an avid reader. She is nineteen years old, same age as Yunghee."

Gija might have liked more schooling, Sonju thought. What made her so guarded though? It seemed nothing of herself got out and nothing of others got in. One day, Sonju needed to buy some hand soap for The Hall and Gija wanted to get more books. After getting the soap, they walked into a neighborhood book exchange, a hole-in-the-wall shop manned by an emaciated-looking middle-aged man, undoubtedly a book lover. He seemed to know what Gija had already read and pulled out two books for her. Gija thanked the man and smiled, a rare sight to see.

Sonju received her first pay after working at The Hall for a month. When she found Miss Im alone in the back room, she asked, "How can Lady Cho pay us so well?"

"Our clients pay a membership fee when they join and monthly dues whether they come or not. And they pay for food and drinks separately. I doubt that Lady Cho pays herself much more than she pays us."

"That seems unusual. What's her story?"

"She probably has one but hasn't told any of us." After a short pause Miss Im said in a quiet voice, "I'm glad to have you as a friend."

"Thank you. I need a friend."

Miss Im dropped her eyes after a glance at Sonju. "I'm sure you have wondered how I came to work here." Sonju waited watching Miss Im's beautiful, slightly out-turned lower lip. Miss Im said, "The year before the war, my husband turned me out because I couldn't bear a child. I was married three years. I heard he has remarried since then and has a child."

"Did you go to your family?"

"I couldn't go home. My father drove my family into poverty with his drinking. It's hard to imagine, but he was once a professor at a university."

Miss Im looked so vulnerable at that moment that Sonju wanted to enfold her as a mother would a hurt child, but that would be inappropriate. This was not America. While they both gazed out at the Japanese garden, Sonju felt angry that women were too easily dismissed and discarded. Kungu told her once that his mother had told him that a woman must have money of her own. She herself had told Second Sister that if she were born low, she would have worked until her nails wore out to have her own money so that she could live the way she wanted to. She now believed firmly that for many women financial independence was the way to be free. She decided to discuss with the women at The Hall about the importance of having money of their own. They had ten years to save.

Sonju had planted impatiens in the garden along the side fence in the spring. Looking at the profusion of blossoms through the living room window, she thought of Jinju showing off her nails stained red with the impatiens petals. Those flowers reminded her of Maari, and she missed its people, the Second House family and Buddha Ears. She wondered if her reading group was still continuing. She hoped it did. She then recalled Father-in-Law telling Jinwon he could have a bridge made out of a hundred-meter-long rope by tying it from the chestnut tree to the train station so that she could slide down on it. This imagery of Jinwon riding the rope still made her laugh.

She heard a knock at the gate. It was Misu. "What a nice surprise!" she exclaimed and led her friend to the living room.

During tea, Sonju told her about the job she had recently taken. Misu's face dropped, and after a quiet stare at Sonju, she said, "We don't work outside the home. The poor do." She sighed furrowing her brow. "Working exclusively for men, it doesn't matter what kind of men. Women like us don't do that sort of a thing."

"I am not in a situation like yours. I have to do something to support myself," Sonju said and thought Misu must be thinking first the affair and divorce and now this, so she added, "This job is introducing me to arts, politics, and business, and most of all, to ideas. All this helps me plan how I want to live."

Misu looked away.

"Misu, look at me. There's nothing unseemly going on where I work." She didn't feel it necessary to explain any further than that. She stared at Misu's profile for a time and wasn't sure if she would see her friend again, and not being able to see a reasonable path to change the course, braced for the end of their friendship.

Now and then, a conflict arose among Miss Im, Yunghee, and Gija who not only worked in close proximity to each other all day long, but also lived at The Hall. Sonju understood that twenty-four hours a day of togetherness could be a challenge for anyone. On this particular afternoon, Gija came into the living room with a tray of tea. Miss Im took her cup and said to Gija that the clients again praised the interesting flavors in the food. "I told them you have a gift."

Sonju added, "I am impressed with the beautifully decorated garnishes you make."

Gija turned and walked out.

Miss Im called out in Gija's direction, "'Thank you' would do nicely." That didn't result in any response from Gija. She was not one to have a casual conversation no matter how many times Miss Im tried.

Yunghee, on the other hand, seemed to genuinely want a friend of her own age. After a few cautious glances, Yunghee would talk to Gija only to receive a few barking words. Soon she began to follow Gija around asking questions or offering help. For the most part, Gija kept her emotions in check until one day she seemed to have had enough. She abruptly turned to Yunghee, thrusting her upper body forward and pulling her arms back, snarled at Yunghee. "Something's terribly wrong with you. I get disgusted with your sentimentality and your uncensored curiosity. Must you splatter yourself all over the place?" Drawing her arms toward her chest, she spat out emphatically, "Gather yourself." Her eyes sparked fire and her long face narrowed even more.

Yunghee's eyes jumped up before she burst out crying. Sobbing, she said, "I just wanted to get to know you. I can be a good friend. Why do you have to be so mean?"

Sonju gently pulled Yunghee away and said, "Don't talk to Gija for a while. Talk to me and Miss Im instead."

As soon as Yunghee sat in the living room, Miss Im cajoled her. "Tell Lady Yu what you told me before. I know your father dragged your mother by the hair to the bedroom and beat her up and you hid under the house. You heard your mother scream and scream, then moan." Here Miss Im side glanced at Sonju with a sly little smile.

Miss Im had a mean streak in her, and Sonju didn't like it, but fortunately, Yunghee didn't catch Miss Im's loaded smile and said, "Yes, I thought my father had killed my mother. I thought he might come after me next. Then they were quiet for a while, so I crawled out from under the house and saw my mother come out of the room all bruised. But she was smiling. Not long after that, my father left us for good. I was glad he was gone, but my mother cried for days."

Sonju asked, "How old were you?"

"Seven."

Sonju had noticed that Yunghee often startled as if an old ghost had grabbed her, then after a moment, she would laugh at her own reaction. Yunghee was still that innocent, bewildered child of seven sometimes. She was lucky to be working with all of them, Sonju told herself and thought about Misu.

By the time Sonju had visited Seoul to care for her mother in the fall of 1951, the majority of the residents of Seoul had already returned from evacuation and had resumed their daily lives among the ruins—rebuilding, going to work, going to school, visiting friends and relatives, and buying things at shops and markets.

In July, three years and one month after the war broke out in 1950, the Korean Armistice Agreement was signed by the UN delegation and North Korea establishing the Demilitarized Zone at the 38th parallel and ending all hostilities between the two Koreas. What had the war accomplished at such a high cost in deaths and destruction on both sides? Sonju had read that the devastation was much worse in North Korea as a result of the Allied Forces' use of bombs there. The nation was still divided at the same parallel line as before the war, and had much to recover from, and the war didn't even end. If not for the war, Kungu wouldn't have ended his life. He would have been free of the fog and the memory of the war. She might actually have been working toward something fulfilling rather than just surviving. One solace for Kungu—he would have been happy to learn that the displaced and the very poor were being helped with foreign aid. One solace for her—she was building her life anew with new friendships and with growing savings. She was on the way to becoming an independent woman, and her lifelong desire to bring about changes in the nation still stirred in her head. In the meantime, her focus was her daughter.

On the first Saturday in August, her mother and sister presented themselves at the gate again. "How did you find me?" Sonju asked and led them to the living room.

Her sister said, "We went to your old house and learned you had moved, so I asked Misu. She told me about your loss. I'm so sorry."

Her mother sighed. "All for nothing."

Why did her mother have to rile her up? "It was NOT for nothing. My life is not yours to judge." She sounded aggressive even to her own ears.

Her sister's eyes widened, but her mother didn't flinch. "How are you managing?" she asked.

Now Sonju was going to hurt her mother. "My former father-in-law gave me money when he found out you didn't want me. Kungu and I had savings in my name." Then, knowing that her mother would be shocked, Sonju added, "I work at an exclusive men's club."

Her mother sucked in air. Her sister made a quick "Oh."

"Why?" her mother asked with exasperation in her voice and on her face. "You were well brought up."

"Why?" Sonju laughed. "Why?" She laughed again.

"Let's go," her mother said to her younger daughter, and they left.

Why must her encounters with her mother end the same way each time? she asked herself. Why couldn't she be more like her sister—compliant, yielding, and forgiving? Throughout her childhood, she had treated her sister with indifference, and in one way or another, let her sister know that she lacked a sense of her own person. Yet her sister had not once balked at her. Sonju knew her shortcomings and didn't like what she had done to her mother. All her life, she felt as though she was on the verge of losing herself to her mother every time she had to face her. Her instinct had always been to fight back. After she failed to win the fight over her marriage, regrets had sapped her life for five years, and undoing that mistake meant her daughter had to grow up without her mother. She didn't know when or how she would be free of her anger.

The next day at The Hall, Sonju was still thinking about her mother's visit. Miss Im was fanning furiously to thwart the mid-August heat when she asked Sonju, "Why don't you kidnap your daughter? No one from Maari knows where you are."

They were not even talking about Jinju, so the question

was unexpected. The idea was absurd, of course. No stranger could walk in that village too long without being questioned. Her in-laws would find her anyway. That evening, however, she searched all corners of her mind to find a way to see Jinju. The express train didn't stop at Maari, it being a country stop, which meant she wouldn't encounter any of the village people.

The following Sunday, she arrived at the train station too early and had to wait an hour before she boarded the train. When the train neared Maari, she looked out the fast-moving window, craning her neck forward, first catching sight of Second House at the top of the steep rise. Emotion rushed forward. Then she caught sight of the chestnut tree, and she saw two young boys hanging on its branches. Jinju was nowhere to be seen.

Every Monday Miss Im asked, "Did you see Jinju?"

"I see a few village people sometimes," was Sonju's usual answer.

Sonju skipped her train ride on the first Sunday of October to help with Lady Cho's annual art exhibit. Before the guests started coming, Miss Im told her that Lady Cho was known to have a keen eye for promising artists and had promoted several artists already who became renowned, and that reputation helped her succeed in attracting collectors and investors to her art exhibits.

Many of the invited guests were new faces to Sonju but most of them seemed to know each other. One young artist blushed when she told him she liked his work. By the end of the exhibit, nine pieces by seven artists were sold. The shy artist's work was one of them. The possibility of one day seeing his paintings in the National Museum was terribly exciting to her, and she could understand why Lady Cho wanted to promote them. Sonju said to herself that perhaps she could do something similar one day.

Confessions

At her empty house, Sonju flipped the calendar to the next page and stood looking at the number eleven, the month Kungu died. She slowly rolled her thumb in her palm. She didn't know when she stopped carrying her thinking-stone. It must have been sometime after he died.

On the morning of the first anniversary of his death, she opened the bureau drawer, touched the two thinking-stones with her fingertips. After closing the drawer, she walked over to the living room and stood in front of the glass door. A few mottled ginkgo leaves flew down into the courtyard near the water pump and swept back and forth then became wedged in the drain. She went out, picked them up, rinsed the dirt off the leaves, then placed them under a little stone in the garden.

As soon as she arrived at The Hall, she went to the back room and found Lady Cho and said, "A year ago today, Kungu died. I just wanted to be with someone for a few minutes." She told Lady Cho about three childhood friends who swore life-long friendship on the thinking-stones and how she lost Misu's friendship. "I envy you," Sonju said. "You are well connected and have friends and places to go to."

A subdued smile passed over Lady Cho's face. "I haven't told anyone here because …" Lady Cho pointed and said, "Let's sit over there."

They sat side by side facing the Japanese garden where a small flock of sparrows were busy hopping and pecking between and on top of the rocks. Trees and shrubs in the garden stayed green all year around as if time never passed.

Lady Cho said, "The idea of marriage never appealed to me. I said so to my parents, but they would not hear of it. On my wedding night, I refused to consummate and kept on refusing day after day. On the twentieth day, he hanged himself."

Sonju gasped inaudibly.

Her countenance solemn and dark, Lady Cho continued, "His parents discovered his diary. They sent me back to my parents before the funeral. My parents begged his family for forgiveness, but it never came. Nothing is bigger than a person's life, and I caused a man to hang himself, for which I am forever guilty." After a few seconds, she continued, "My mother said, 'You have to pray to every god there is for forgiveness.' For my repentance and absolution, she took me to a Buddhist temple, a Protestant church, and a Catholic church. My family donated large sums of money to each." She was quiet for a moment. "I told my parents I wanted to live alone, and they bought a house for me to live in as a widow. My maid came with me."

Lady Cho brushed at an invisible speck of dust on her shirt. "Suddenly on my own for the first time, I didn't know what to do, but I wanted to end my parents' financial support. I am not a good artist, but I love art. I frequented art galleries and befriended artists. With their help, I started inviting their wealthy patrons to private exhibits at my home. I did very well and needed a larger place, so I bought this property. At the urging of my artist friends, I added the back room to start this club."

Even though she had told her maid no one else would know, Sonju told Lady Cho about Kungu's suicide. They stayed still for a long while facing the unchanging garden, and quietly mourned together the deaths of two young men. Having shared the part of their lives they preferred hidden, Sonju felt that a special bond formed between them that morning.

Before parting, Lady Cho said, "You and I and the women here, we are all equal in shame and suffering. We need to be kind to each other."

It was true what Lady Cho said about the women of The Hall. Sonju had known about the cook's situation at home— her long-unemployed, women-chasing husband and her adolescent son who blamed her for his father's frequent absence. Each of the women was wounded or damaged in some way—Miss Im's childhood poverty and shame at her father's alcoholism, and her having been discarded by her husband for infertility.

Yunghee witnessed her father's cruelty and hadn't known safety while growing up. And Gija, a young woman of talent and intellect—she was passed around from one relative to another like an unwanted baggage. Gija herself wouldn't tell, but someone had betrayed her, and she had been deeply hurt by it.

Sonju had not been as generous to the women as she could have been with her time. Gija, Yunghee, and Miss Im lived at The Hall and didn't have friends or relatives to visit with. All they had was each other and the sameness of their daily routine.

From that week onward, Sonju remained at The Hall on some Saturdays and spent time with the women, sitting on a warmed floor chatting, knitting, listening to songs on the radio and singing along and forgetting the cold outside. In the spring, they went to Changduck Palace for the Cherry Blossom Festival at night and were intoxicated by the fragrance of the spring blossoms under the magic of lantern lights. In the summer, they glued photographs of American actresses in a scrapbook, listened to the radio dramas and ate melons. In the fall, they walked on the carpet of fallen leaves among the trees and looked up to find leaves of brilliant yellow, orange, and red still hanging. And in the winter, they went to Kyungbok Palace and threw snowballs at each other on the palace grounds, laughing and ignoring the glances of the proper people.

In spite of those Saturday activities, the women at The Hall knew that Sonju's Sunday train rides were disappointing, and that it was difficult for her not to see her daughter for such a long time. Fourteen years. She might have told them once that it felt like a sentence to her. And fear started whispering that she might gradually forget her daughter's face, or that Jinju had changed so much that she might not recognize her daughter even if she saw her. She had to see her daughter.

In early April, she passed small and large train stations along the way and greening fields in between, and when the familiar juniper fence on high plateau came into view, she leaned toward the window. Under the old chestnut tree were two young, animated boys talking to a girl sitting in a tree. Jinju! Jinju! She almost jumped up from her seat. She half-laughed and half-cried. Her child, much grown in two years, was sitting on the branch dangling her legs. Jinju was turning out to be a sturdy little girl. After the train passed, for the rest of the ride, she walked the aisle up and down smiling, unable to calm down and sit.

Sonju didn't see her daughter again. In the fall, she strolled in the Secret Palace with the women of The Hall; after a deep snow, they were back at Kyungbok Palace for a snowball fight; on New Year's Day, they welcomed 1955 and ate rice cake soup for good luck and on the Lunar New Year's Day they ate rice cake soup again just to make sure the luck stuck.

Then spring came with clear, cloudless, blue skies that opened up suddenly and delivered days so perfect that it made Sonju's heart lift like a bird taking flight. When crisp cool breezes passed, she could smell the starched-shirt freshness.

On one such brilliant day, she took a bus to downtown as soon as the clients left after Saturday lunch. People were everywhere. Buses honked. Taxis tooted. Her steps sprang. There, near the Ducksu Palace gates stood Kungu wearing a white cotton oxford shirt with a navy jacket draped on his left arm. He was waiting for her. She rushed toward him and reached out to lay her hand on his arm. The man turned. She stepped back aghast. "I thought … My apologies." She turned and ran, panicked, huffing in fast bursts. Her dry tongue and throat cracked. Pain stabbed her lungs and threatened to shut them down. She didn't remember paying the taxi driver, but upon reaching home, she dropped to the living room floor and buried her face in her hands and sobbed.

What had happened to her to lose her mind like that? She recalled the time when she found Second Sister slumped on a street in the dark night driven mad by relentless gun shots and explosions. Alarmed, she bolted up. She summoned the time she and Jinju played "I can see" game on her last day in Maari. Jinju's smile, smell, voice, gestures. She wished she could have kept her daughter's chatter and laughter in a jar tightly covered so that she could hear it every time she missed her. She missed the village. She missed the smell of burning straw and the taste of the country food. She missed the people, even the cows. Most of all, she missed her daughter. After this trail of imagery and sentiments, she had forgotten about the incident at Ducksu Palace. Now it didn't seem so tragic when occasionally the memory of it returned.

She was tending her garden when the mailman delivered a letter. She wiped her hands on a towel to open it. Her sister wrote that their father, not expecting to recover, had insisted that his son marry while he was still living. He didn't want his son to be at a disadvantage of being a fatherless man with a widowed mother. The wedding was arranged in a hurry to a woman from a house of equal class. It didn't bother Sonju that she was excluded from the wedding. She wouldn't have expected an invitation and would not have gone even if she were invited.

In July, three months after her brother's wedding, Sonju's father passed away, which marked the second time she lost her father. After the funeral, her sister came to visit without her mother. Fidgeting and shifting, with pauses in between, she said, "Our brother doesn't want any contact from you because Mother grieves so much."

Her eyes steady, her back straight, Sonju said, "There's no need for him to worry. Tell him I'll abide by his decision. He is now the head of the household."

Her sister studied Sonju and finding no agitation, seemed relieved

"What did he die of?" Sonju asked.

"As he was dying, the doctor told Mother he had a stomach cancer."

Sonju was relieved. It didn't matter if her family had blamed her for her father's illness before the doctor's words. It mattered to her that she hadn't caused her father's death.

In April of the following year, Lady Cho gathered the women in the living room and said, "People are moving to Seoul in large numbers for job opportunities and better education. I am advised to invest in real estate. You may want to consider buying a house or a piece of land yourselves. I will buy some land south of the Han River just in case the North invades us again. The land is much cheaper there as it's mostly farmland."

After Lady Cho had gone home, Miss Im pulled Sonju to the back room. "I bet it was Assemblyman Kim who advised Lady Cho on real estate investment. He is a close friend of hers."

"Will you buy a house?" Sonju asked.

"No, I want to stay here. I don't want to live alone, and this place is free. Would you buy one?"

Sonju had been thinking about a house for her and Jinju to live in. So, after three years of working at The Hall, she bought a house in her own name in the West Gate District—near work. She loved the simple lines and sunny interior of the house, and imagined her daughter happily moving about from one room to another.

1956 May 25

My Daughter Jinju,

I bought a house near my work. It is a Japanese-built home, not like your grandfather's. It is much, much smaller than your grandfather's house, but it has an indoor bathroom, which I like very much. I wish you were here with me. You would have had such fun dancing, singing, or playing princess on the raised wooden platform in one of the rooms that a Japanese family used as a place for private worship.

An artist friend of mine painted a portrait of you from the photograph when you were two years old. He said it is exactly the same size as Leonardo da Vinci's Mona Lisa. You would like it. It's hanging in my bedroom. I look at you and say good night before I go to sleep.

English Lesson, 1957

Through the window of the train, Sonju saw a spread of golden stalks, frozen fields, and then rice seedlings planted in rows. She saw Jinju on a chestnut tree in 1954 when she was five and hadn't seen her for three years since. She once saw her former mother-in-law waddling down the slope, swinging the same hefty hips. She wanted to run to her and hold those thin veiny hands and talk to her again and tell her she was sorry.

On a June day, Miss Im was flipping through a copy of *Life* magazine and asked Sonju, "Have you noticed our clients use more English words and phrases now? I need to study English, so I don't come across as ignorant. I have forgotten much of what I learned at school other than the alphabet."

They bought a conversational English book and tried to translate *Life* magazine articles using dictionaries. Unlike learning the Japanese language, English didn't come easily to them.

"Why do English letters have so many different sounds when the alphabet has only twenty-six letters?" Miss Im complained. "We should thank King Sejong the Great for having our alphabet developed. It's so easy to learn to read and write. And consistent."

When they were learning nouns, Miss Im questioned why it was necessary to add an s to make a plural. "Two apples. It already said two. Why bother with an s after apple?"

About irregular verbs, she said, "English is so irrational. Wouldn't it be better for all the English-speaking people to agree to add *ed*, like *goed* or *eated* for a past tense instead of *went* and *ate*?"

"That's a good idea," Sonju said. "To whom do we make such recommendations?"

Miss Im threw a mean side glance at her.

Hearing Miss Im tell the clients about studying English with Lady Yu, Professor Shin said, "I can ask my American colleague and friend to teach you American English if you want."

The following Saturday, the American presented himself and returned an awkward, unaccustomed bow to Sonju and Miss Im.

Before entering the living room, Miss Im pointed at his shoes, and he took them off. He was taller than any of their clients and had a foreign smell that was hard to describe. He looked exotic with light brown hair, blue eyes, and long lashes that curled up. His eyes were so transparent that Sonju could almost see the inner workings behind that blue. This was the first time she had seen a Westerner that close.

The American said his name was Roger Williamson, and upon seeing the apprehensive look on Miss Im and Sonju's faces, repeated slowly this time. He then wrote it on a piece of paper.

Miss Im and Sonju read his name together, "Rho...jehru Wee...ree ahmu sohnu."

He corrected their pronunciation a few times until Miss Im, laying her right hand on her chest, said, "My name is Im Nari."

She had practiced it before Mr. Williamson arrived. Then she added, "Nari, American way."

Mr. Williamson nodded and smiled. "Pleased to meet you, Nari."

Sonju showed him the *Life* magazine articles and the English/Korean dictionary. She pointed to the words and went over the lines with her finger, nodding and looking into his eyes to see if he understood what she was trying to convey.

After the American left, Miss Im said, "Each of his shoes would hold at least one *doi* of rice," which caused the women to laugh.

He came every Saturday afternoon, even during the monsoon.

During the occupation, the Japanese had taught British English with a Japanese accent, and undoing the hardened memories of a tongue was a great challenge for Sonju and Miss Im. While learning to pronounce words in American English, they laughed at every mistake they made, which made for a lot of laughs. Mista Weereeahmusohnu seemed used to Koreans' easy laughs and laughed along with them.

After four months of weekly study and practice, Sonju and Miss Im understood English well enough to ask Mr. Williamson why he came to Korea. They asked him to write the spelling of the words they didn't know so they could look them up. Eventually, they understood the gist of what he told them: He was in the United States Army stationed in Japan after the Japanese emperor unconditionally surrendered. There he befriended a Meiji University professor, a Korean expatriate who had studied in Japan for many years. Through that professor, he learned that almost all Korean diaspora in Japan were denied Japanese citizenship as well as social and health benefits. As a result, many worked in menial jobs. This knowledge led to his interest in Korean people. He took his current job after receiving a doctoral degree in political science focusing on the Japanese occupation of Korea.

"Now we call you doctor," Sonju said.

Miss Im said, "Please tell us about your family. Are you oldest son?"

"I am the only son. I have an older sister and a younger sister."

"America is big, yes?" Miss Im asked. "Where in America, do you come?"

"California."

"Oh, California. West," Sonju said. "What do Americans eat?"

"We eat meat, chicken, fish, and vegetables."

"We too," Sonju said.

"Yes, but cooked differently," Dr. Williamson said. "I will take you both to an American restaurant and show you."

The next time he came, he brought three sets of silverware and napkins. After Sonju and Miss Im watched him use forks and knives, they practiced. When Sonju was cutting bulgogi with a knife and fork, one piece flew off the dish and smacked Miss Im on her cheek and fell onto her napkin. Sonju giggled covering her mouth watching Miss Im recover from the sudden slap then laugh while wiping the brown marinade off her cheek with her napkin.

The following Saturday evening, Sonju and Miss Im met Dr. Williamson at the Eighth Army Headquarters in Yongsan. While Dr. Williamson was talking to a soldier in the booth, Sonju looked around trying not to appear to gawk at the Americans, most of them in uniform, a few in civilian clothes. A man and a woman were walking leisurely, their arms around each other's waists, just as she had seen in the magazine pictures. Ah, the Americans, the objects of her envy.

At the restaurant, Dr. Williamson explained each dish on the menu to Sonju and Miss Im. When their food arrived, Sonju watched and followed him, and with a polite smile planted on her face, tried to disguise the small nervous tremors in her fingers.

Afterwards, in the taxi, Miss Im said, "Don't you think it's barbaric to butcher the slab of meat and eat it with miniature farming tools? I think cutting the food before cooking and using a spoon and chopsticks is a lot more civilized."

"The dessert was too sweet for my taste," Sonju said.

"What was that? One whole unpeeled potato plopped on the plate?"

On the fifth anniversary of Kungu's death, the wind howled and wailed like an angry child, whipping fallen leaves all around. Every year, Lady Cho remembered the date and sat with Sonju quietly in the back room looking out at the enclosed garden. Sonju had written to Misu when she moved to her house and Misu wrote that she would visit one day, but Sonju hadn't seen her.

In December, Sonju detected a new softness in the teacher's voice, an eagerness to please Miss Im when correcting her English, and adoration in his eyes when she spoke.

Lady Cho said to Miss Im, "I have the impression that Doctor Williamson is quite taken with you."

Miss Im casually replied with a lilt and a smile, "Oh, in that case, it would be one-sided."

The women at The Hall regarded the man's ardor with

excited interest. He was a Westerner after all. The first week in March, nine months after the English lessons began, Miss Im had agreed to a Sunday date with him. On Monday, Sonju asked Miss Im how her date went, but Miss Im was not telling. At least she was smiling.

After several more dates, Miss Im started spending more time alone in the bedroom. Then one Saturday afternoon in July, Miss Im pulled Sonju into the room and insisted on going somewhere. She had something to tell Sonju. In spite of pelting monsoon rain, they went to a tearoom nearby. While waiting for tea, Miss Im said, "Last Sunday, Dr. Williamson told me he loves me. I told him I don't love him."

"How did he respond?" Sonju asked.

"He said he will wait however long it takes for me to fall in love with him." Then she asked, "How do you know when this thing ... love ... happens?"

"When you think about him all the time and want to be with him all the time and start imagining the future with him. That's how it was with me," Sonju said.

Miss Im's eyes drifted a bit before she said, "When I'm out alone with Roger, even though I don't act or dress anything like a prostitute, people automatically take me as one and give me these loathing looks." She mimicked the look of disgust. "I don't like it. I don't like it at all. I hate it."

Those were strong feelings, but Sonju knew Miss Im. Miss Im was an intense person. She cooled down fast, too. Sonju cocked her head. "Roger?"

"Yes, that's his name, remember?" she said with a petulant tone.

Sonju said, "People stare because he is an American, because he is different from us."

Since then, every time Miss Im found Sonju alone, she talked about Roger. Constantly. And about the different mannerisms, ideas, and expressions she saw in Roger that she called "Americanness."

Sonju was in the back room reading when Miss Im said, "Roger is very attentive. He asks me what I prefer. He stands behind me instead of in front of me. He is thirty-six, five years older than we are. Don't you think it's strange that he has not married yet? So, I asked him if his parents pressure him to come home and get married and he said he is a grown man and what he does with his life is not up to them."

Sonju envied Roger his freedom to dictate his own life, more so because his words seemed so casually uttered as if that freedom was a given and natural. "What do you think about that?" she asked.

"It's so different." Miss Im tilted her head slightly to the side, raised her hand and combed her hair in a slow sweep. "Before him, I thought, who would have me, a barren woman who was once married. I told him everything. He wasn't bothered by it."

Something akin to tender sadness filled Sonju's heart. Under all that bravado, her friend was a fragile woman, unsure of herself. She took Miss Im's hand. "You are full of life and beautiful. Why shouldn't he be attracted to you?"

"Thank you," Miss Im said with an uncharacteristically shy smile.

For over a year since, Miss Im was the source of entertainment for the women at The Hall with the stories of what Roger said or did or what she learned about America. Sonju could tell Miss Im was becoming more comfortable with American ways, even the food she had been so critical about only two years ago.

One day, Miss Im blurted out unprompted, "Roger kissed me." She must not have noticed the shocked looks on the women, because she went on, "What a strange custom. I didn't know what to do with his tongue in my mouth. Don't you think that's strange?" When Miss Im looked at Sonju and the women, their laughter bubbled out of their covered mouths as if they were about to explode. "Never mind," she said. "Go on and laugh." They did, and Miss Im huffed and went into the bedroom.

When Dr. Williamson came to teach English that Saturday, Yunghee and Gija came out of the kitchen, giggling. Miss Im glared at them until they fled back to the kitchen, choking with giggles. Miss Im said no more about Roger.

Revolution and Coup, 1960, 1961

On the front page of the newspaper was a photograph of a fragment of grenade sticking out of a skull. The article revealed that on the previous day, 1960 April 11th, the bloated body of the high school student who had been missing since March 15, the day of the protest, had been found in the harbor in Masan by a fisherman. His skull was split by a tear gas grenade thrown at close range by the police during the riot.

Sonju was still haunted by the murdered bodies she had seen during the war, but something about this image of a brutalized head provoked a primal horror. Perhaps it was the head peeled to the bone still holding the grenade to tell a story.

Guessing by her absence in the living room during their reading time, Miss Im must have read the news already. She had gone to high school in Masan and was already furious about the earlier report of police shooting when violence erupted during a protest against the rigged presidential election. According to the report, there had been about a thousand protesters including many high school students.

After she collected herself, Sonju went to the back room. Lady Cho looked up from the newspaper. Sonju nodded and went toward the window. Standing there she studied all the pock marks and protrusions on the centuries-worn rocks in the garden. Then she felt Lady Cho's presence next to her and heard her say, "This is strictly between you and me. This is not going to end well."

On the 19th, the weather was perfect as expected in April with the bright sun and the temperature just so. Sonju arrived at The Hall earlier than usual to have breakfast with the women in celebration of Yunghee's birthday. Miss Im was practicing "Happy birthday to you" in English. Sonju picked some azalea blossoms from the front garden for the table. After breakfast, while Yunghee sat beaming in her new dress, Lady Cho presented a white cake with pink decorations. Miss Im sang. After tea and cake, the cook and Gija returned to the kitchen.

When the telephone rang, Lady Cho rose to answer it. "Ah, Assemblyman Kim. How are you? We are all here to celebrate Yunghee's birthday. What …?" Lady Cho gasped. After a long pause, she said, "Yes. Thank you for calling." Lady Cho hung up the telephone and turned to Sonju, Miss Im, and Yunghee. "There is a student uprising nationwide. Assemblyman Kim advised us not to leave The Hall today."

"My maid …" Sonju had no way of contacting her.

Yunghee cried, "Oh, what does this mean?" She covered her cheeks with her hands, her eyes darting from Lady Cho to Sonju, to Miss Im.

The cook scuttled into the living room. "What happened?"

Gija followed, took one look at Yunghee and asked, "What is it this time, Yunghee?"

Lady Cho said, "There is a massive uprising going on right now. Assemblyman Kim told me yesterday that Korea University students protested in front of the National Assembly and that I would read about it in the morning."

Sonju grabbed the morning paper. "Yesterday the students protested police brutality and demanded new elections. But today …"

They heard the repeated popping sounds of gunshots. Everyone froze.

Yunghee's voice trembled. "It can't be. No one has guns. It's against the law."

Gija waved off Yunghee and pointed to outside. "I see smoke going up over there."

Some distance beyond the fence, dark and light grey smoke was rising.

"I'm going up to the roof to look." Gija left the room. The cook followed her out. "I'll hold the ladder."

Sonju turned on the radio. Lady Cho, Miss Im, and Yunghee crowded around. They heard screams, the angry shouts of a mob, the staccato sounds of guns. Rapid, breathless words of the radio announcer poured like storm water: tens of thousands of university and high school students demanding the president's resignation, the protest growing, bodies lying on the street, wounded students being carried away. Yunghee startled at the gunshot noises coming over the radio, shut her eyes, and grabbed Sonju's hand. Lady Cho turned off the radio.

Gija returned to the room with the cook and said, "Smoke is coming from the police station."

The cook clasped her hands and squeezed. "My son may be one of the protesters."

Everyone quieted down. The sounds of gunshots were moving into the distance.

With the gate securely locked, they stayed the night at The Hall, each restless on the *yo*.

The next morning there were no bus noises, no taxis honking, no street vendors yelling out their wares.

"I'm going to see what's going on." Gija unlocked the gate, and after peeking, she stepped out and closed the gate behind her.

Yunghee paced in the courtyard waiting for Gija.

About fifteen minutes later, Gija returned. "The streets are empty except for soldiers in full gear standing by sandbags piled high every so many meters along the street."

Martial law was declared. Of over 100,000 protesters, 180 were killed and thousands wounded.

The morning papers arrived late. They showed photographs of bloody students in and on top of taxis, medical students hovering over the wounded on the roof of a taxi, their white medical gowns blowing.

After breakfast, the cook left to go home. Lady Cho stayed.

Sonju was worried about the maid. She stepped out of the gate and found the streets eerily quiet. Buses ran nearly empty. The taxi driver told Sonju, "We transported the dead and the wounded all day. When it got dark, people were trying to go home after being trapped in buildings and shops for hours avoiding the mayhem."

When Sonju unlocked the gate, the maid came running and let out a sigh and said, "I'm glad you're home."

"I was safe, but how did you get home yesterday?" Sonju asked walking to the living room with the maid.

"I didn't know anything was happening. I left here, and as I turned the corner before the bus stop, I saw a line of police shoulder to shoulder running up with guns raised. I dashed into a store. Almost bumped into the owner. He let me stay there until the police cleared out of the area. This morning, I didn't find you here, so I've been waiting for you."

"Maybe I should have a telephone installed."

"To call *me?* No, it's too expensive. Even stores don't have telephones," the maid said.

Touched by the maid's concern for her finances, Sonju smiled and said, "Promise me then, you will stay at your home or stay here if something like this happens again."

Not knowing when the clients would return, Lady Cho, Sonju, and the cook arrived at The Hall every morning as before. The women ate, talked, and played cards to while away the time. Miss Im took off all the buttons on her cardigan and re-sewed them back on. She said it took her mind off what was happening outside. She mumbled something about Roger.

The son of the Vice President killed his family and shot himself. President Rhee resigned one week after the uprising after twelve years of dictatorship, and on the following day, he exiled himself to Hawaii. The first republic collapsed.

Two weeks after the uprising, Assemblyman Kim, Professor Shin, and Chairman Park returned to The Hall. Within a few days, other businessmen, politicians, and government officials came back as well. All the women knew some of their clients would not return.

In the ensuing months, newspapers articles gave Sonju the feeling that she was living in a nation on the brink of collapse again. Following the overthrow of the first republic by the student protesters, an interim administration ruled for a short period until an election was held in July and the second republic was established. Under the new republic came more freedom, but also came the purging of a large number of government officials and military and police officers for corruption. Dissatisfied with the government's lack of progress in meeting their demands, the students continued to demonstrate in the midst of political and economic instability.

When the cook returned from the market, she complained, "Grocery prices have gone up again."

"It's not just groceries." Yunghee pointed at her cream-colored shoes. "I paid double what I used to pay." She bent down to rub a thin black mark off of one shoe and said, "I want the demonstrations to stop. They make me nervous."

Another year began with no sign of stability under the new republic. People were so hopeful after the revolution the year before, but now with resignation, they watched the government getting steadily weaker.

In the biting cold, Sonju visited the middle schools starting with the best schools—Kyunggi, Ewha, Sookmyung, and Changduck. At each school, she joined the crowds of parents at bulletin boards near the school gates where the names of students who had passed the entrance examinations were posted. She didn't find her daughter's name anywhere. She tried the second-tier schools, then the third. Jinju must be living in another city with her father. In that case, it was useless to ride the train now. But where was her daughter?

When the next Sunday came, she dressed to go to the train station almost by habit. Slowly she took off her scarf, gloves, and coat, and let out a sigh that sounded more like a moan.

On May 16th, Sonju woke up and heard a report on the radio that tanks had crossed the Han River Bridge toward Seoul early that morning and that the military had taken all three branches of the government.

A *coup d'état*, this government takeover by the people with guns—just the thought of it made her heart pound with fear and powerlessness. It had been only a year and a month since the April Revolution. As tragic and horrible as it was, the revolution was driven by the will of the masses not by the will of the guns.

This bloodless coup ended the democratically elected but incompetent government of the Second Republic. The military declared martial law, which lasted until May 27th, and in June, established the Korea Central Intelligence Agency. Under the leadership of a two-star general, Park Chung-hee, freedom of expression and the right to assemble were drastically curtailed.

The oppression was more severe under the military regime than under Syngman Rhee. Sonju could tell by observing The Hall's clients during the succeeding weeks and months. They didn't speak of the *coup d'état*, of the generals, of arrests and imprisonments, of the dismantling of civilian institutions, or of the purging of government employees by the tens of thousands. They didn't mention those who no longer came to The Hall. They had been victims of purging. Most of the key positions in the government were held by generals now, and it appeared that the military regime would be in power for a long time.

No one had to point out that The Hall was not as robust as it had been since the April Revolution the year before, but the situation worsened after the coup. Yet in spite of significant decline in membership, Sonju's pay was the same as before, and Miss Im didn't mention her pay being cut.

In September, Lady Cho purchased a large tract of land south of the Han River and hired an architect to design the gallery and its satellite structures. The women talked more about The Hall's closing in two years. Gija had owned a small house for two to three years now and had been renting it out while she lived at The Hall. Sonju had acquired a few more properties since she bought her house. Miss Im and Yunghee preferred to hold onto their cash savings.

In January, Assemblyman Kim's wife died in her sleep, and he stopped coming to The Hall during his mourning period. In his long absence, Lady Cho didn't seem her usual engaged and optimistic self, not because of what she said or did, but because of small things she did during small moments that were hard to define. It made Sonju realize how much Lady Cho relied on Assemblyman Kim's friendship to feel grounded.

A month after his wife's death, Assemblyman Kim with his mourner's armband over his coat sleeve was looking at the exterior walls of the exhibit and reception halls when Sonju and Lady Cho arrived.

"This is a big project," he said to them as they approached. "This opens in April, and you will close The Hall a year after that. Things are moving fast."

"We will be ready, but where will you go after The Hall closes?"

He smiled. "I am hoping to come here to see the two of you."

The two of us? More likely Lady Cho, Sonju mused.

"Come as often as you like." Lady Cho smiled back. "You will be fine. You have survived the political turmoil without compromising yourself."

"I am fortunate that I represent the citizens in Seoul. The majority of them are well informed and they agree with me." He looked up at the sky briefly. "When I was studying law, I wanted to fight the rules the Japanese imposed on us. That's how I got into politics."

Encouraged by what he revealed about himself, Sonju said, "When I was young, I thought equality between men and women was possible. Now I don't know when that will happen."

"Society has to be ready for a change," he said. "It will happen."

When? We are muzzled under this administration that started with guns, she wanted to say but didn't.

The gallery was to be completed in two months when the young architect, educated and trained in America, who was overseeing the whole project, recommended Western furnishings for the cottage.

"Where and how can I get Western furniture?" Lady Cho asked, then after a moment's pause, said, "I know a person who might be able to help me with that."

The next day, Lady Cho and Sonju were in the back room flipping through the pages of a Sears catalogue Lady Cho had borrowed from a black marketeer who borrowed it from the Korean wife of an American working for the US Army.

"We have to pay three times the catalogue price," Lady Cho said, looking at the photographs of furniture and showing them to Sonju.

"Lady Cho, I would like to order a few pieces for my home. Can it be done?" Sonju had been frugal with her money. Now that she was getting close to seeing Jinju, she wanted a bed, a couch, and a table with four chairs. She would be frivolous, just this once. She'd had two small tables made by a local carpenter, one for the lamp and the other for a tea tray. She eyed the room to decide where the couch and the dining table would go. She could see how they would change the look of her living room in her mind's eye already, and her excitement made her jittery.

Her furniture arrived in mid-March. After each piece of furniture was placed the way she pictured it, she ran her fingers up and down the dark brown fabric of the couch, smiling at the transformed room. Outside the living room window, blades of blue irises and daylilies crowded in the side garden. Soon they would be in full bloom. Her daughter would love this house.

A week before the opening exhibit at the newly constructed gallery, Lady Cho and the women of The Hall took an hour-long bus ride and a ten-minute walk to a wide iron gate. At the far end stood two buildings situated perpendicular to each other, and behind the building, facing them peeked a sharply gabled little cottage half-hidden behind trees and bushes. Lady Cho pointed to the building in front them, where G-62, was imbedded in the center of the façade in small black letters. She said, "That is the gallery, open in 1962. The artists haven't finished hanging their work yet. Follow me."

Inside the double doors, the faintly acrid smell of new paint still lingered. They quickly passed through a small room on the left of the entrance and the large exhibit hall with paintings, prints, and sketches on the wall and sculpture pieces on pedestals. Afterwards, Lady Cho led the women to the cottage.

Miss Im said, "This looks like one of those pictures of the houses on the Alps I've seen in an architecture book."

When the women walked into the cottage and saw a round wooden table with chairs by the window and a couch in the living room, they oohed and ahhhed. Miss Im, Gija, and the cook sat on the couch and Yunghee squeezed in, half-perching on cook's lap. In the bedroom, Gija said, "What a waste of space. The bed takes up so much room. I like the *yo* better. It can be folded and put away to make room for other purposes." Miss Im ignored Gija's remarks and lay on the bed and uttered, "Ahhh."

When they came to the bathroom, Lady Cho said, "This is a toilet. You sit on it, and when you are done, you press the lever here, like this." When a swoosh of water came down, swirled, and got sucked under, Yunghee stepped back.

Gija said, "It's outlandish!"

"I can't imagine sitting in a chair with water right below it instead of squatting over a receptacle," Yunghee said. "It doesn't seem natural to me."

Laughing and chattering about the toilet, the women proceeded to the kitchen.

"Watch this." Lady Cho turned the stove on. Immediately, heat radiated as the coils turned orange-red. Each of them held a hand over the burner and felt the heat. After turning the stove off, they returned to the living room.

Yunghee pranced, stepping in and out of the kitchen. "I like the kitchen best. You don't have to go outside to get to it and no more pressed coal to tend."

"We have more to see. Come." Lady Cho ushered them out of the cottage, past the garden, to the reception hall that looked large enough to hold a hundred people. She pointed to the back. "There is a large kitchen behind that wall."

Afterwards, the women followed Lady Cho through the

breezeway to the gardener's house. A middle-aged gardener and his stocky wife were waiting on the porch. Bowing to the women, he said, "Whatever you need, please come by."

The G-62 opened on April 15th. The attendees, in addition to the artists, were art collectors, art professors, art students, and most of The Hall's clients. Sonju saw several art students hanging around the shy artist, the one who had done Jinju's portrait. He was becoming more recognized in the art circle.

Soon after the G-62 tour, Yunghee started wearing her hair severely parted to one side. Above her exposed ear, a fake diamond sparkled garishly at the end of the hairpin. She donned a variety of outfits every day that yelled out excitement and hopefulness—frilly blouses, tight pencil skirts—all worn just to go to a market nearby.

A few days later, during the break between lunch and dinner, Sonju came from the back room, and saw Yunghee through the open door to the bedroom standing in front of the mirror trying on one outfit after another. Finally, Yunghee seemed to have settled on her favorite pink nylon blouse with a ruffled front closure that accentuated her already ample bosom and a striped, muted grey pencil skirt of some synthetic fiber. She then sprayed perfume on herself, the flowery scent too artificial and obvious even from the living room. Sonju was glad Miss Im wasn't around to make disparaging remarks at Yunghee.

"How do I look?" she asked Sonju.

"You look like spring," Sonju said and watched Yunghee's smile stretch.

Hearing Gija come in, Yunghee pranced out from the bedroom, twirled and smiled, the smell of her perfume rising like disturbed dust. She came up to Gija and said, "Let's go to the market. The cook needs some vegetables."

Fanning her nose with her hand, Gija said, "I'm not going to be seen in public with you. Look at you. And you embarrass me with your outlandish flirting."

Yunghee went to the market alone, all giggly, bubbly, bouncy. No cutting remarks seemed to trouble Yunghee.

Not long after that, Yunghee started talking about a neighborhood barber she had met. When she had the women as an audience, she imitated the way he spoke, acted out his quick movements and gestures. She talked about his ironed pants and starched shirt. "He looks at himself every time he passes a window and pats his pomaded hair." She giggled.

Miss Im did her thing. "You two would make a perfect couple. Only, you would need two mirrors, one for you and one for him."

Sonju winced, but Yunghee smiled. She was like a plant that somehow managed to push through a crack in a rock, eager and hopeful. Sonju admired that quality in her.

Miss Im's Wedding, 1962

The kitchen staff was tidying the front room and Lady Cho and Sonju were reviewing the menu when Miss Im sauntered in from the bedroom and announced, "I have something to tell you." Her eyes glinted as everyone turned to hear her. "I accepted Roger's proposal."

Miss Im in America, Sonju thought, though it was not unexpected, America was so far away. She couldn't bear to lose yet another friend.

Lady Cho put aside the menu and the shopping list. "How exciting! When is the wedding?"

"June third. Roger took a teaching position at a university in Texas. He starts in August."

Yunghee cocked her head. "You're actually going to marry an American?"

"*The* American." Gija corrected Yunghee, then turned to Miss Im. "You are one brave woman."

The cook said, "I like our American. He likes my cooking."

Miss Im turned to Sonju. "You haven't said anything."

"I'm happy for you and Roger, but you're going to leave behind everything familiar," she said, but inside, she was already mourning the loss of a friend to a land far away. She recalled her former mother-in-law's fear of losing her youngest son and his family and being forgotten.

"How difficult can life be in America?" Miss Im replied with certainty in her voice. "I've gone through worse things."

Sonju reconsidered her sentiment. "You're right. Knowing you, you'll do fine."

"Yes, she will do fine," Lady Cho said hastily.

Two weeks later, a young woman delivered Miss Im's wedding dress of white silk with lace trim around the neckline and at the end of the sleeves. Miss Im carried it to the bedroom, held the dress up to herself and posed in front of the mirror.

Yunghee scanned Miss Im. "You make a beautiful bride and the dress ..."

"So tasteful," Sonju said. "You did a good job designing it. It's perfect."

Miss Im swirled a half circle to face Sonju and Yunghee, then turned again to the mirror to admire herself.

Then a week later, Sonju heard Miss Im sobbing in the bedroom. "Miss Im, what's wrong? I'm coming in." Upon opening the door, Sonju found Miss Im sitting next to her wedding dress, wiping her tears with a handkerchief. "What happened?" Sonju asked.

Her voice nasal from crying, Miss Im said, "I received a letter from my brother. No one in my family will attend my wedding because I'm marrying an American."

"Did you tell them he teaches at a university as your father did?"

"Yes, but my brother wrote that the family will be shamed if anyone finds out about my marriage because people will think I prostituted myself," she said sobbing, her face flushed under her glistening wet cheeks. Then, she jutted her chin out. "It's not as though my family has a great reputation to uphold. My father is a pathetic drunk."

Sonju knew what that pain was like. "We will be at your wedding to celebrate your marriage to Roger. It will be wonderful," Sonju said, cupping Miss Im's hand.

On the 24th of May, Miss Im and Roger registered their marriage at the city hall, and the next morning, petitioned for her visa at the American Embassy.

On the wedding day on the front lawn of G-62, Sonju gazed at the blue sky and the outlines of the acacia trees, then looked down below and all around. The scent of freshly cut grass hovered just above the ground. The leaves on the trees shimmered. Flowers were blooming in the gardens; butterflies were flitting about. All was well in the world. She passed the chairs in rows, the seated guests, and the white tent. At the entrance of the gallery, Gija, dressed in a simple white blouse and a navy skirt for the occasion, sat at a table recording the gifts received. When she saw Sonju, she pointed to the side room.

Upon entering, Sonju nodded to Miss Im. "Everything is ready. It's time to dress."

She and Yunghee helped Miss Im get into her wedding dress. After checking the veil, Sonju stepped back to look at the bride, and there, in the middle of the room, she saw an ethereal figure in white. "Oh, look at you! I can't even describe what I see." Sonju stood there quite lost.

"Who is here?" Miss Im asked, her voice uneven.

Sonju realized Miss Im might have hoped one of her family members still might show up. She hid her sadness and tried to sound excited. "Our former clients and some wives, artists, about ten Americans, and some I don't know. I guess they are Roger's friends. Lady Cho is greeting them."

Sonju and Yunghee straightened the train of the wedding dress and followed Miss Im to the door. When the wedding march started, Miss Im grabbed a white bouquet and walked out alone, small tremors in her fingers visible in spite of her assured stride. Professor Shin presided at the wedding. Roger stood beaming. Cameras clicked. Miss Im cried and smiled.

When the ceremony was over and the last guest had left after the reception, Miss Im hooked her arm through Sonju's. While walking to the cottage where Roger was waiting, Sonju said, "A lot of things will be possible for you. Take advantage of them." As she said this, Sonju thought of all the things she thought she was willing to fight hard for. It was good that Miss Im would have a chance to accomplish whatever she wanted to in the land where women were free to do so.

Eleven days later, the women of The Hall saw the newlyweds off at the airport. How strange that one person's absence seemed like the ending of something. Sonju then recalled Miss Im and Yunghee saying their time at The Hall with the women had been their happiest. Now Miss Im was embarking on different happiness with Roger and his family.

That night, Sonju sat up in her bed. Jinju looked at her from the portrait on the wall. "Where are you, my daughter?"

"So quiet. Why doesn't anybody talk?" Yunghee said out loud as she went from the kitchen to the front garden, to the gate, and back to the kitchen. For two weeks, Yunghee wandered around like a lost dog. Gija moped. The cook stayed in the kitchen not saying much. Lady Cho remained in the back room. Sonju read newspapers and checked the clock in the living room for the third time. Only seven minutes had passed since she last checked but it felt more like thirty.

Miss Im had been gone three weeks when Sonju heard Yunghee shriek, "A letter from America!" Yunghee shook the letter, running up into the living room to Sonju.

Everyone sat in a circle while Sonju read Miss Im's letter. She wrote that when she arrived at Los Angeles Airport with Roger, she was nauseous from the mixed smell of cheese and all kinds of perfume emanating from the people walking by. After she met Roger's family in Los Angeles, they drove to Texas in their newly purchased car.

"Three days to get from California to Texas?" Gija commented. "How big America must be!"

Yunghee put in, "I can't believe Texas is seven times larger than South Korea. Texas is just one province in America, right?"

Sonju said, "I think it's called a state, but the idea is the same. There are fifty of them. I think Texas is one of the largest."

"And cacti as tall as buildings. What does a desert look like anyway?" Gija mumbled.

A week later, they received another letter from Miss Im. She and Roger were looking for a house or an apartment to rent near the campus.

Then another letter, in which Miss Im said everything was large—not only the people, but the highways, the stores, even the trucks. She wrote about not eating kimchi because of the smell and lamented about the Americans' anxieties regarding body odor.

Ten days later, they received yet another letter. So frequent. Maybe things were not as well as Miss Im had implied in her letters. Sonju tore open the envelope.

1962 July 16

Dear all,

I received Lady Yu's letter. I miss you too, especially when I look around and am reminded that I am a foreigner. I'll get used to it.

Americans have many strange customs. My neighbor was washing his car. He tapped it gingerly, and said, "This is my Betsy. I have had her since college. Isn't she a beauty?" I was very confused. I didn't know who he was talking about. I knew his wife's name was Emily. I asked, "Who is Betsy?" After Roger and my neighbor had a laugh, Roger explained that Betsy is the name the neighbor gave to the car. "But why? It doesn't look like a woman to me." They laughed again.

Americans like to name things. When I first came to America, Roger taught me about the coins. Here, it's not enough to say one-cent coin, five-cent coin, ten-cent coin, twenty-five-cent coin, fifty-cent coin. They have to name each. One-cent coin is called a penny, five cent a nickel, ten cent a dime, twenty-five-cent a quarter, and the fifty-cent coin a half dollar, like you don't know fifty cents is a half of a dollar. To add more to my confusion, the five-cent coin is bigger than the ten-cent coin. When I went shopping alone the other day, the coins gave me a genuine headache. Why don't they stamp a big number on each coin like we do in Korea? I couldn't tell which was which, so I just poured all the coins I had into my palm and had the cashier take whatever coins she needed.

They also use ounces, pounds, feet, miles, and gallons. Isn't the metric system much simpler? Many Americans are not good with simple math. I see people actually counting with their fingers. In spite of all that, I think I will love this country.
Im Nari

Lady Cho smiled. "Miss Im hasn't lost her touch."

Yunghee had a far-away look. "How strange the customs are in the land across the ocean where Miss Im lives now." Sonju loved Yunghee for her innocence and wide-eyed wonder.

Another letter from Miss Im. Again, everyone sat in a circle as Sonju read.

1962 July 22

Dear all,

My life is full of new experiences. A neighbor with a little baby in her arms knocked on the door. Roger was away to meet his colleagues. I was so afraid I would make a fool of myself with my poor English that I never opened the door fully. I mumbled something through a thin opening. She left. When I told Roger about it later, he told me the neighbor was trying to be friendly.

Then some days later, two Jehovah's Witnesses knocked on the door. They gave me books with strange pictures and wanted to come in to talk to me. I told them I was a Buddhist, thinking this would make them leave but they said they still would like to come in and talk about Jehovah's Witness. They would not leave. So, I told them I don't understand English and started making gestures instead of talking. They finally left.

"I can picture Miss Im acting a fool," the cook said, chuckling.

I am bombarded with new things. I feel insecure about not speaking English well and not knowing the ways of America. I just want people to leave me alone. Someday, I'll be comfortable living in my husband's country.
Im Nari

Yunghee's Marriage, 1963

Miss Im's leaving had Sonju thinking more and more about the women of The Hall. Sonju had depended on them, and they had stood by her. Soon, The Hall would close and they would scatter. She would be alone again like the time after Kungu's death.

She had not visited his grave again since that cold December day almost ten years earlier. The thought of him in a box under the ground was too removed from her image of him alive. It disturbed her. Over the years, she came to conclude that being truthful to one's conscience was the essence of being human and that Kungu had to do what he did. She had told herself many times that she must be at peace with it and she had been for the most part. Yet recently, the old ghost of his death returned with undefined unease tinged with whispered fear. She was becoming more impatient too as the time for the reunification with her daughter neared, and that didn't make any sense at all.

Saturday, before leaving The Hall, Sonju told Lady Cho, "I will be going to the cottage tomorrow. It will be good to see you there."

Lady Cho nodded.

Sonju quickened her steps, crossed the grounds of G-62, and passed by the gardener and his wife who were moving flowerpots around their front porch. They bowed and waved at her. Sonju waved back.

When she reached the cottage, the door swung open, and Lady Cho stepped out. Closing the door behind her, she said, "Let's enjoy this beautiful weather. Let's take a stroll." Under the flawless September sky, they walked the grounds side by side.

Sonju said, "Even though I miss her daily, it was best that Miss Im married Roger. She can leave her past behind and lead a less stifled life in America." And here she was, she thought, getting all impatient and nervous at the same time waiting and waiting some more to see her daughter.

Lady Cho nodded and said, "Roger is a good, dependable man."

They walked on quietly, passing the scraggly blackberry bushes and patches of yellowing *kusa* grass that came to Sonju's shoulders. Along the street side, long gone was the dizzying fragrance of the acacia flowers that used to dangle from the branches and the unrelenting shrill song of the cicadas. Everything that was once robust was working its way to an end.

They followed the property line, and before turning the corner in the direction of the cottage, Sonju said, "Have you noticed how dirty Seoul has become, or is it just my perception?" Sonju frowned. "Last Sunday, I went to a market along the Chonggechon stream. Ugh, the stench and refuse in the water. I felt sorry for the poor merchants and laborers working there, breathing those fumes. And," her voice jumped an octave unintentionally, "that isn't all. Downtown, I passed a young boy of maybe twelve or thirteen, hustling in English, asking every foreigner passing by 'You wanna pretty gul, boy?' The boy said it aloud with no hint of embarrassment and laughed if a foreigner ignored him. What happens to a boy like that?"

Sonju couldn't stop talking. "Did I tell you what happened the time Yunghee and I went to a movie a few months ago? After the movie, we were walking toward the restaurant I used to go to with my friend Misu, you know, the famous one in the Chinese ghetto. The cobblestone back alley that led to it was saturated with urine. A drunk staggered toward us, swearing. We quickly veered away and came to a narrow, shabby dark street where we ran into a vagrant crumpled in a heap sleeping with scant fabric barely covering him. Young hoodlums laughed at us until we ran out to a large avenue.

"Then," she swallowed. "All those photographs and articles in the newspaper. Ramshackle houses sliding down a bare hill, and those tin and cardboard houses under the Han River Bridge being swept away by the swollen river. This happens year after year. This city is such a harsh place for the poor."

One year, she and Miss Im had packed a large boxful of bento boxes and took them under the bridge to hand out to those people. Every time the people opened their mouths to thank them, a sour stench rose from their empty stomachs. The next day, they were at the same spots just as hungry as before. Sonju and Miss Im both stopped going. They didn't have to talk about not going. It was hopeless.

She halted her steps. "And I can't do anything about it. It's too much. It's just too much." A sudden sob rose from deep inside her. More and more sobs came stabbing her chest on the way out. When her sobbing tapered, she was depleted. She leaned on Lady Cho' shoulder, Lady Cho gently patted her back. After her tears had dried, she looked up at the sky and saw a white cloud that drifted, carrying its filaments across the expanse of blue space.

When she returned home that afternoon, she wrote:

1962 September 23

My daughter,

> *I wish I were in Maari with you. I want to thank your grandparents. They were good to me until the day I left.*
>
> *When I left Maari, you were soon to be three years old. I can't wait to see you. It is hard for me for some reason to wait out the last four and a half years. I feel powerless about this separation more now than the past nine years. I wonder, too, how I am going to explain myself to you when the moment comes. I guess I start by admitting my many flaws. Some of my decisions made other people suffer, especially you.*
>
> *I used to be certain about things, but things seem less obvious and less certain to me as I get older. Still, I try to have some clear ideas about myself and the world around me. Jinju, leaving you is my greatest sorrow. I beg you to forgive*

me for the years you had to grow up without a mother.
I love you.

Sonju re-read the letter, opened the bureau drawer, and placed it in the box. Next to it were nine boxes that held over five hundred and twenty letters she had written. She stared at the stack wondering if her daughter would ever forgive her.

Sonju was alone reading the newspaper in the back room when Yunghee came and sat next to her. She smiled a tentative smile and folded her hands before she said, "Lady Yu, the barber wants to marry me."

"Do you want to marry him?"

"He is twenty-five, four years younger than I am. He is handsome and clever. Why does he want to marry me?"

"I can give you a long list of reasons why a man would want to marry you, but whatever decision you make, you are never alone."

"I know." Yunghee fidgeted, then a smile bloomed like a morning flower opening its petals. "His dream is to have his own barber shop. He said he will teach me to cut hair so we can work side by side."

The following day, Yunghee told Sonju, "I asked Lady Cho to find my replacement. She told me she wasn't going to look for one, so I decided to stay until the business closes next year even if I get married before that."

On Sonju's advice, Yunghee bought a small house south of the Han River before she married the barber. Her wedding was a small affair at G-62 with just the new couple, Lady Cho, Gija, the cook, Sonju, Assemblyman Kim and Professor Shin present. Yunghee, in her white Western wedding dress with lace trim much like Miss Im's, beamed at her new husband while he, in a tight fitting shiny grey Western suit and with shiny hair, bowed to the guests.

After the wedding, Gija said, "Lady Yu, it's Lady Cho, you, and me who aren't paired. It's a strange feeling to be left out."

Sonju wondered what was in that wistful expression from this person who normally kept her emotions in check. She said, "But you said you'll never marry. Are you changing your mind? It's all right if you do. You'll not lose face."

Gija shook her head once. "I'm sticking with my original plan. Do you plan to marry?"

"I am waiting for my daughter."

"What about Lady Cho?"

"I don't know," Sonju said and hooked her arm in Gija's and was surprised that there was no resistance. "Today, I feel like sleeping at The Hall, just you and me."

Shortly after her wedding, Yunghee told Sonju she discussed with Lady Cho about her husband's desire to open a high-end barber shop near the National Assembly building. "Lady Cho told me Chairman Bae owns a building near the Assembly and she will ask him."

Every day, after her husband's barbershop opened, Yunghee repeated to anyone who would listen what her husband had told her—who came to the barbershop, what his clients said in praise of his skill, and how busy he was. After some time, instead of her usual cursory nodding, Gija hurried to the kitchen as soon as Yunghee smiled and opened her mouth. She went to another room if Yunghee followed her. After several days, Yunghee gave up.

Miss Im's letters arrived about once a month now. In her latest letter, she wrote that she and Roger bought a house and she received her driver's license. She missed the fall colors and the snow.

Four months into her marriage, Yunghee was often seen staring at the wall, pacing in circles, mumbling, and wringing her hands. She took to bursting out for no discernable reason. Then one day, Sonju saw Yunghee standing in a quiet corner in the courtyard with her head down. Sonju walked up to her. "Something has been bothering you...."

Instantly, tears poured out from Yunghee's eyes. She wiped the wetness with the back of her hand, and with the look of a defeated, discouraged child said, "My husband kept putting off teaching me how to cut hair. Now he says it's better for the business if he hires younger, more beautiful women." Her face crumpled. "Sometimes he doesn't come home. I haven't seen him for four days."

Sonju held Yunghee's wet hand. "Have you talked to Lady Cho? Maybe she can find out what's going on."

Two days later, after the clients had left, Lady Cho came to Sonju. "I need you at the back room." She didn't speak until they passed the long corridor and reached the back room. "I inquired about Yunghee's husband. His business is booming, but he owes a great deal of money in unpaid rent and bills in addition to personal loans. He is indulging in gambling, women, and alcohol. He hasn't come to work and has been in hiding to avoid the creditors."

"When will you tell Yunghee?"

"I will talk to her alone. You can wait here until you hear her scream," Lady Cho said. Shortly, Yunghee's howl reached the back room. Sonju rushed to the living room. Gija and the cook had already come in from the kitchen and stood watching Yunghee cry while Lady Cho sat by her, holding her hand.

Yunghee, her face red and wet, her lips twitching, said aloud, "That son of a dog. All the money on girls and gambling instead of paying bills. I'm ruined. That idiot, that bastard." She cried again, calling her husband more names until her voice grew hoarse. Her cry trailed into a trickle. Then she took a deep breath and started all over again.

Gija stood staring at Yunghee with her arms crossed and said, "This is not helping your situation. What are you going to do?" Yunghee shook her head and cried harder.

Sonju sat down, rested her hand on Yunghee's arm. "Yunghee, Gija is right. I think you have to do something quickly before things get worse."

Yunghee stopped crying, her eyes blinking, and with sudden keen concentration, asked, "What do you mean, get worse?"

Gija said, "Your husband's creditors may take the things in the shop that you paid for."

Lady Cho and the cook nodded.

Early the next morning, Yunghee and Gija and two hired men cleared out the contents of the shop and packed them into the storage room off the kitchen. Yunghee shut down the barbershop. She sold what she could at less than half of what she had paid and divorced her husband of four months.

For several days afterwards, Yunghee cursed the barber under her breath, sniveling and wiping her tears. Sonju knew, no matter how kind everyone had been, Yunghee was alone in her pain. She told Yunghee, "I don't have any wise words to say that will make you feel better other than all of us have already survived our pasts and we have each other."

When Yunghee's whimpering and verbal reviling eased, Gija said, "Why don't you rent out your house just as I have done and move back to The Hall? You can save some money."

"But I have to move again when The Hall closes, which is soon."

"You can move in with me."

All heads turned to Gija at the same time. Life still had a way of surprising Sonju. Who would have thought, of all people, *Gija* would be the one to live with Yunghee?

Yunghee kept staring at Gija, her eyes wide, mouth half-open.

Lady Cho grinned. "This is the first time I have ever seen Yunghee lost for words."

Yunghee moved back to The Hall, but nothing changed between her and Gija as far as Sonju could tell. Gija still shot back at Yunghee with sharp retorts.

Gija had said that she preferred the company of her books over men, and after seeing Yunghee's marriage fall apart so quickly, she said, "I can handle a lot of things in life but I can't handle betrayal by men. All that emotional turmoil. Who needs it?" Gija must have been wounded by a man or more than one man, Sonju thought. She said, "Not all men are like that."

After that debacle, the women were glad when Yunghee announced, "Everyone, a letter from Miss Im. Come to the living room."

1963 March 12

Dear all,

I'm sorry to learn about what you had to go through, Yunghee. If I were there, I would have gouged out his eyes for you.

I often think about what you said, Lady Yu, how much you had wanted to go to university and to accomplish something. I am lucky to live in America where one can go to college at any age. This year, I plan to take some courses and eventually I will have a career. My poor English worries me, but it will get better.

I still find Americans interesting. They are very polite people. They say "Thank you" for every little thing. They're very good at standing in line too. I like this country so far.

I miss all of you. You are my family.
Im Nari

"Oh, the things I had wanted!" Sonju placed her hand over her heart. "This letter brightened my day."

Lady Cho smiled. "Lady Yu, there is still time for you to do something for yourself."

After The Hall, 1963

Six days before The Hall closed, Yunghee and Gija took their belongings to Gija's house. Yunghee kept thanking Gija, to which Gija finally said, "That's enough. Stop."

Tuesday, Wednesday, Thursday. The days galloped by. Friday was a sleepless night. Saturday, Sonju greeted the clients for the last time at The Hall. After all the clients had left, Gija said, "You take parting very hard, Lady Yu."

"What do you mean?"

"You could hardly talk when you were saying farewell to the clients."

"Every parting reminds me …" Sonju waved her hand to dispel the memories.

In the afternoon of June 1, 1963, The Hall closed. The cook's voice broke a little when she said, "I won't see you often, but you take care of yourselves."

Gija said, "I don't want to get sentimental. I'll see all of you again."

"We will get together," Lady Cho said.

"I'm going to miss you, Lady Yu," Yunghee said. Stealing a glance at Gija, she added, "Who am I going to talk to about my silly problems?"

"I'll have a telephone installed. It's affordable now. You can visit me any time," Sonju said.

After the kitchen staff left for their homes and Lady Cho for the realtor's office, Sonju went from room to room in The Hall. Without paintings, sculptures, or furniture, the walls were plain pale beige surfaces, the rooms empty rectangular spaces. With no sound of women talking, no clanking of pots from the kitchen, no men's voices, no laughter, no cheers, The Hall was a soulless void, much like Kungu's house after she packed the last box.

Pausing at the courtyard garden, she touched the serrated

edges of the low-hanging green maple leaves, recalling the cook watering the plants and Yunghee pinning a flower in her hair. She closed the gate behind her and stood for a moment before she turned to go home.

When she arrived, her maid opened the gate before she turned the key. "What a nice surprise. I didn't expect you at this hour," Sonju said.

"I wanted to be here when you came home today. How did your last day go?"

"It's a farewell again."

The maid followed Sonju to the living room. "After the master died, I worried about you. You had no one to be kind to you then. I haven't met the women you worked with but if I had, I would have thanked them for being family to you."

Sonju tried a smile, but only managed to hold back a tear. "But you are still with me," she said and thought, how could she be so lucky as to have this deeply caring, loyal woman? The maid lowered her eyes and rubbed her hands, then said, "I have prepared dinner for you. It's in the kitchen. I will see you Monday." Within minutes of her maid leaving, Sonju heard someone knocking at the gate. It couldn't be the maid returning, she thought. She wouldn't knock. She had a key.

It was Lady Cho. Entering the courtyard, she said, "I met your maid. She asked me if I was Lady Cho. She said you had told her how I looked, then thanked me for being family to you."

Sonju nodded and said, "Without her, I wouldn't have gotten through after Kungu's death."

"Then I should thank her."

"You look tired," Sonju said. "Make yourself comfortable. I'll make some tea."

Sonju returned with a tray and poured the tea. "How did it go at the real estate office?"

"I expected some last-minute haggling, but the buyer paid the full asking price for The Hall."

"That's good." Sonju took a sip.

They talked about Gija and Yunghee: now that they were no longer working, what would they do with their time and energy and how would they get along in Gija's small house, how fortunate it was for them to have constant companionship even with occasional conflicts they would surely have. Between sips, they both gazed down for long stretches of time. The idea that they wouldn't see each other daily sank in.

The same must have happened to Lady Cho too. Before leaving, she said, "You and I, we will see each other often." Sonju nodded several times like a child.

On Monday, after finishing her work, the maid said, "This is very difficult for me to bring up." She crossed her hands and looked away, then looking back at Sonju, said, "I planned to work for you as long as my health was good, but my son wants me to quit before he gets married in July. He says it doesn't look right for me to work at my age when he can provide for me. We'll move to Chungju for his job and have the wedding there."

Another loss, Sonju thought, and reached out and covered the maid's hand with hers. "I'm happy for you and your son. I understand that you will need time to prepare for the move and for the wedding. But would I be too demanding if I asked you to give me two weeks?"

"Not at all. Why two weeks?"

"I have been thinking about removing the tall fence and replacing it with a much lower one. I'll do away with the gate, so visitors can come directly to the house. I'll have the workers lay flat stones for the walkway and landscape the rest. I have seen a picture of a garden in an American magazine." Sonju gestured with her arms, laying out the garden, pointing here and there, listing names of shrubs and plants. "I would like you to be with me until the workers finish."

"Of course. But will you feel safe without a gate?"

"In addition to the front door lock, I will add a locking door at the entrance to the living room. I will be fine."

For the next two weeks, workers labored from morning till evening. They planted climbing roses along the low fence, and in the garden, evergreen shrubs, flowering plants, and ground-hugging junipers.

On the maid's last day, Sonju gave her an envelope of money to help pay for her son's wedding. She asked, "Do you want anything of your master's?"

The maid thanked Sonju and put the envelope in her purse. "I would like his teacup. May I? I'll drink tea from his cup and think about him."

"Then you're the person to have it."

Sonju took her maid's hands, feeling the rough, bulging joints of her fingers, thinking back to the days following Kungu's death. The maid turned her hands and squeezed Sonju's. "You take good care of yourself."

"Ah, the cup." Sonju retrieved the cup and the matching saucer from the kitchen and went to her bedroom to wrap the gift.

Handing the gift to the maid, she said, "Thank you for keeping the promise about your master. You've been ... I'm about to cry, so I'm going to turn around and go to my room." Her sobs broke loose before she reached her room. She heard the maid's sniffles fading. Then came the click of the front door.

After she dried her eyes, she thought of the first time she met the unsmiling maid and how warm their hearts had grown for each other over the years. For that she was grateful.

Misu came to see her the following Saturday. It had been so long since Sonju saw her friend that she had given up on their friendship. She wondered why this visit now.

Misu said with a nonchalant air as if they had seen each other only a week before, "No gate. Do you feel safe?"

"I feel quite safe. I don't have to go to the gate to open it every time someone comes."

"That's a maid's job."

"I don't have one. Don't need one." Sonju expected an argument, but Misu must have finally accepted that Sonju would do what she pleased. Misu instead talked about her children, her husband, then casually inserted, "Our classmates asked about you."

She didn't ask Misu how she responded. Misu had never asked about her work at The Hall, but it didn't matter. Sonju said, "The business closed as planned. I'm not a working woman any longer."

Misu had an immediate response, "Oh, good." Then she corrected, "I mean ... you're financially well placed?"

"Yes, I'll be all right."

"I want you to know, you are my best friend."

It was interesting that Misu felt it necessary to reassure her, Sonju mused. She still didn't know why Misu came to see her after all this time, but she let that thought go because it didn't matter any longer.

After a long summer hibernation, Sonju and Lady Cho roamed the streets for two weeks as though to make up for the lost time. They shopped, visited art galleries in search of promising artists, went to movies, museums, and bookstores. They frequented the South Gate Market where the whole strata of humanity bustled in an exuberant mix of colors, noises, smells, and dialects.

Eyeing the merchandise stacked high in each stall, Sonju paused at the memory of the Japanese occupation, the war between the North and the South, the revolution, and the ongoing nervousness of the nation's mood under the strong-armed military regime disguised as a civilian government. In spite of those difficult events, this resilient country had survived as it must.

●

It had been nineteen years since Japan's surrender, ending the Second World War and the colonial occupation of Korea. From the streets, Sonju could see the wheels of progress turning with Korean manufactured taxis and chauffeur-driven cars here and there. Tall buildings were going up; more hotels were built. Manufactured goods, factory woven underwear, ready-to-wear clothes, textiles of every color and design were sold at shops and markets. An increasing number of men and women wore Western style clothing. People craved products from Japan and America if they could afford them. Everywhere, the fingers of America's reach were visible not only militarily but also in everyday life in Korea. Even though the current regime was oppressive, it was beginning to deliver on its commitment to lift the nation out of poverty and transform it into a developed country.

1964 September 20

My daughter Jinju,
   I miss you so much. I don't know where you live now, but I wish you lived here in Seoul.
   I walked the streets in Myungdong the other day and a familiar smell hit me. I knew right away what it was. A merchant was selling roasted grasshoppers and sparrows. It reminded me of the time your aunt cooked sparrows right there in the inner court, a snack your aunt and your boy cousin enjoyed. Lady Cho said people in Seoul eat grasshoppers as health food, for more energy. Sparrow meat is considered a delicacy here too. To me, it is a piece of Maari.
   I often think about my time in Maari. My experiences there taught me many things about people and life in general, which I didn't fully appreciate at the time. I am comforted that you are with good people who show you they love you, but what do I do with the smell of roasted grasshoppers that still lingers in my mind?
   I wish I were with you. I miss you and Maari, the place you were born.

Sonju was on the way to a coffeehouse in Myungdong to meet Lady Cho. The mottled leaves were dropping, each with a resigned sigh. Street vendors in their stalls were roasting peanuts, chestnuts, and dried squid. Passing by, Sonju took a whiff of the aroma and thought of Kungu and of their last night together after he had peeled roasted chestnuts for her. He had said I love you. Sadness no longer accompanied her thoughts of him, even on the twelfth anniversary day of his passing. She still talked to him sometimes, told him she was fine.

After coffee, Sonju and Lady Cho walked a short distance to the art gallery they frequented. They went toward the mid-section of the gallery where the owner usually sat in a chair.

Under the soft artificial light, Sonju saw a woman sitting across from the owner. When he saw her and Lady Cho, he rose from his chair. "Hello, it is good to see you again," he said and moved a few steps to the side. "Please meet Artist Ilchon. Of course, you know her. She is so famous." He bent slightly toward the artist. "Lady Cho owns a gallery outside the city." Turning to Sonju, he said, "And Lady Yu is her friend."

The artist nodded without rising to greet them.

"A pleasure to meet you in person," Lady Cho said in her usual confident voice.

The owner went to the back and returned with two more chairs.

Sonju sat across from the artist, lost for words, unable to take her eyes off of the woman in her layered Western clothes, each layer a different color and different pattern, her long hair streaming down almost to her waist, thick makeup, a cigarette between her index and middle fingers.

Staring at Sonju, the artist brought the cigarette slowly to her mouth, then turning her head slightly to the side, blew out the smoke. Staring back at Sonju, she said, "You have an interesting face."

Sonju had heard that before, but it was different hearing it from the artist. She touched her blushing cheek, then tucked a lock of hair behind her ear. "I ... thank you."

As the artist took another draw from her cigarette, her cheeks sank. Slowly she rose, blew out the smoke, nodded once to Sonju and Lady Cho and walked toward the door, her ankle-length multi-colored, multi-layered attire flowing and trailing.

Sonju and Lady Cho exchanged looks and watched the owner follow the artist. They heard him say, "I would be honored if I could see your new works."

The door closed and the gallery owner returned. He said, "The first time you meet her, you are taken aback. But she is an artist. She lives art."

"She is a colorful person, and not timid," Lady Cho said. "She is perhaps my age?"

"She is older than she looks," he replied. "She is from a good family but left home to dedicate her life to art. She told me she sewed for women and often slept in a closet at some woman's house. She painted whenever and wherever she could. One day an art professor saw one of her paintings and bought it. She became his lover. He died a few years back."

Sonju had seen her paintings in a museum, bold colors and thick flowy lines, much like her attire. She had assumed the artist was a man, based on the name. If she had known about the woman twenty years earlier—a woman from a reputable family who defied convention to live her own life—she might have summoned all her courage and done the same to be with Kungu.

It was mid-December already. With her red wool scarf over her black coat collar and her gloved hands in her pockets, Sonju weaved among the crowded streets. Bing Crosby's Christmas carols blared out of stores decorated with garish red paper streamers. Pedestrians packed the streets in Myungdong. Taxis and buses honked while snaking through the traffic. Sonju saw a young couple walking arm in arm. She entered Shinsege Department Store and squeezed through the crowd. Two women, perhaps a mother and daughter, were chatting, going through the records of carols by American singers. With envy, she watched them. In 1967, three Christmases from now, she would be able to do the same with Jinju. Happiness filled her heart.

By the time she walked every street in the city center, she felt like she had accomplished something without accomplishing anything. At her last stop, a flower shop, she bought an armful. Flowers in winter! She went straight home and arranged them in a large glass vase and thought about Jinju, her daughter who loved flowers.

The following day, after a telephone call from Lady Cho, Sonju met her at a small, quiet Japanese restaurant in her neighborhood.

"I am going straight to G-62 from here," Lady Cho said, dipping a piece of tuna in sauce. "We need to see Assemblyman Kim more often. I think he misses The Hall."

"Me, too," Sonju said.

Lady Cho took the last piece of sashimi on her plate. After she swallowed, she said, "By the way, I received an odd call from the gallery owner. The artist we met painted your portrait and wants to use your full name as its title."

"My portrait? From her memory? With my name on it without showing it to me?"

"Don't worry. It won't look anything like you. She paints Modern Abstract." Lady Cho grabbed her purse. "So how do I answer him?"

"Let's look at the portrait first."

Three days later, Sonju saw the painting. It did look like her, even with thick lines and swaths of yellow and lavender paint across her face. She didn't know what to make of her portrait. Not a sad or happy face, but a face that looked to be holding something back.

"Do I look like that? I mean … my expression." Sonju stared at the portrait.

"Sometimes. You have that enigmatic look."

When Sonju asked the gallery owner where the artist was, he said, "She doesn't want to explain her work but insisted that a woman must announce her name proudly in public. There will be a three-page spread of her work in the *Today's Art*, and this will be one of them."

Sonju liked the artist's attitude. "My name is Yu Sonju," she announced.

On the first day of spring, Sonju was strolling the halls of the museum in Ducksu Palace when she came across two of her classmates. One of them said, "I saw your portrait in *Today's Art* by Artist Ilchon. I showed it to my husband. 'She is my classmate,' I told him. I told everyone." The other classmate nodded.

Sonju forced a courteous smile and thanked them, then left the museum before they could engage her in further conversation.

Sonju hadn't been at G-62 half an hour when she saw Assemblyman Kim walking toward the cottage.

She opened the door. "Is Lady Cho meeting you here? She isn't here yet, but please do come in."

"She didn't answer the telephone at her home, so I thought she might be here. Chairman Park's wife passed away this morning."

Sonju lowered herself in a chair. "Even though she had been sick for a long time, the news still shocks me. Please sit."

He sat in a chair across from her.

Sonju asked, "How did Chairman Park sound?"

"Sad and lost." After a brief look out the window, he said, "I don't remember feeling lost when my wife died. I wonder if that is a character defect."

She realized she parted her lips a little, surprised that he was sharing his private thoughts with her with such ease, almost like talking to himself.

"Do you mean to say you might be too rational, perhaps too unfeeling?" Sonju was thinking about herself when she said this.

He nodded a few times and fixed his gaze on the lawn out the window. "I accepted my marriage as what it was, an arranged marriage. I tried to make the best of it." He swept his forehead with his hand as if he were brushing up loose hair. "I think my wife believed she had lived a good life. I was never unfaithful to her, that is not to say I wasn't tempted."

He was not known to talk much but sounded as though he wanted to, so she listened as he continued.

"My wife was a good woman. She trusted me completely. But she never knew me. I admit that the only reason she didn't know me was because I didn't let her. But then I wondered, would she have understood me better if I did?" He chortled and said, "She often told others she knew me like the lines on her palm. She knew my habits and preferences on some things, but if she had read my inner thoughts and desires, she would have found me a stranger. She never questioned anything about life, didn't have a passion for anything, didn't try to change anything. She just lived with a constant babble about meaningless things."

Sonju had never heard him speak this way. Every client at The Hall knew that even though childless, Chairman Park and his wife had something special between them which not even her long illness could spoil. Listening to the assemblyman, however, she sensed that he grieved the absence of that special something in his marriage. How strange that his thoughts and ideas seemed to flow in the same direction as hers. But then, she could be assuming too much.

She asked, "Did you come to The Hall every day because you were not able to connect with your wife?"

He smiled, and this time, he did look at her. "The Hall filled my needs to some degree. I cherish Lady Cho's friendship. We have known each other a long time."

"She is so wise, isn't she? Sometimes I think she knows me better than I know myself. She was more than an employer to me."

"She thinks very highly of you and has never thought of you as an employee. She was excited when you agreed to work at The Hall. She said you are special, and I agree."

The Snow, 1965

All the way home from the cottage and for weeks afterwards, Sonju thought about what the Assemblyman said. Like him, her life hadn't turned out the way she had envisioned. There had been many things she didn't get right. Society didn't owe her the change she wanted at the pace she wanted, her mother didn't owe her fidelity at the expense of the family's reputation, her husband didn't owe her the expectations she had held for him.

She urgently and wholeheartedly wanted to make peace with her mother. But what would she do with her anger and bitterness then? They energized her. They were convenient. This sudden insight jolted her with an uncomfortable sensation in her chest and in her belly. She felt lost and unmoored. She took a few deep breaths and looked out to the garden. The lilies were blooming. She dialed Lady Cho's number.

In an hour, Lady Cho arrived. Cool spring air followed her in. Sonju placed tea and pastries on the table in front of the couch. Lady Cho picked up a cream-filled puff pastry, and after a slow bite, said, "I haven't talked to Chairman Park since his wife's funeral. I wonder how he is doing."

Sonju said, "There were so many people around him, yet he looked so lonely that day."

"Assemblyman Kim and Professor Shin haven't heard from him either."

Sonju could understand Chairman Park's grief. She still missed Kungu. There was a long moment of silence. After a sip of tea, Sonju said, "I have been thinking ..." She ran her fingers over the folds of her skirt. "I have been wrong about many things."

"Like what?"

"The way I saw things. My mother's attitudes and convictions were probably typical for a woman of her time and of her class. She is a formidable, forceful woman. I saw her as always trying to force her will on me. I fought it, but when I failed, the feeling of my powerlessness made me angry and rebellious. I never felt she cared for me deeply, but she must have because she kept showing up even after my bitter words. I want to reconcile but there is so much anger in me. She took a big breath and let it out slowly. "It's a flaw in me."

"I have my own," Lady Cho said and paused briefly. "After all these years, my mother still frequents the temple to pray for forgiveness for my sin. She sighs when she sees me and starts rolling her prayer beads. My mother feels she has to repent for me because in her eyes I haven't. And there is the club."

"Yes, there is the club." Sonju took another sip of lukewarm tea. She picked up a pastry and chewed on it slowly. Lady Cho did the same. Sonju spoke again, "During the war, I made a vow that I would have no regrets, but I live with so many now. I have asked myself over the years if I had made a different choice then, might I have been better off, and the answer has been always no." She looked at Lady Cho. "I am contradicting myself. My thoughts are all muddled. I don't live with clarity."

"I don't know if anyone does. Most of us just march along, sometimes in confusion, sometimes with clarity, but most of the time without thinking."

"Does striving for clarity lead to a better life?" Sonju asked.

"I don't know. Perhaps you become more aware. I should think about those matters too."

"You seem sound and solid to me."

Lady Cho grinned. "And you seem very agreeable to me, no hint of rebellion."

After a soft laughter, Sonju said, "I have lost the restraint that my mother worked so hard to instill in me. If I were her good daughter, I would have revealed none of the things I have told you over the years. In a way, it is liberating."

"You should be able to let it out sometimes. I am glad you do that with me."

Sonju said, "It's sad that I wasted so much energy obsessing about my mother. I would have been a better person if I hadn't and could have accomplished something instead. I see you lead people and help them achieve their goals. Artist Kang is where he is now because of your encouragement and promotion of his art."

"But that's what I love to do."

Over the next few weeks, Sonju thought about what specific things she could do. She could write about her own experience and about solutions to what she saw as a hindrance to women's advancement. She started writing. Even to her ears, what she wrote sounded amateurish. She read more articles and books to study how authors articulate their ideas. She filled her journal, but none of them were good enough to submit for publication.

Lady Cho and Sonju didn't have to worry about Yunghee and Gija idling in boredom. They had talked about owning a restaurant for some time and had been searching for one for sale since February. They found it near the Yungdeungpo Train Station south of the Han River. The restaurant could only hold fourteen small tables, but they expected a quick turnover of customers because of its proximity to the train station. In April, the restaurant opened with Assemblyman Kim, Professor Shin, a few other former clients, a few artists, and Lady Cho's friends filling the place.

While Lady Cho walked around conversing with the guests in that tight place, Sonju was helping Gija and Yunghee in the kitchen and serving. Once in a while, she felt Assemblyman Kim's eyes on her.

Several weeks later, Lady Cho called Sonju to tell her, "Gija called. She said the restaurant has been packed since the opening. She thinks people come because they saw chauffeur-driven cars parked there on the opening day and assumed the food must be excellent."

In July, Gija called to tell Sonju she still couldn't stand Yunghee's laughter and chattiness, but said she was learning to tolerate her because a lot of men frequented the restaurant to flirt with Yunghee. Gija was annoyed that Yunghee actually enjoyed the attention from men.

Then in the fall, Gija called to say that the business kept her so busy that she didn't notice the time passing until she saw the yellow ginkgo leaves on the streets. She moved onto the topic of Yunghee—the usual complaints.

Sonju listened. Those two adversaries found a way to not only live together but also run a business together. That could be an excellent material for an article.

Those bright yellow leaves that Gija had mentioned had been swept away a month ago. Now the brooding grey sky had dropped to the ground. The lashing wind pushed against Sonju and slowed her steps, but she didn't mind. With her head covered with a woolen scarf, the collar of her coat up to her chin, she was well-protected.

She arrived at Myungdong, the fashion Mecca at the center of Seoul, where the soul of the city throbbed. This place energized her and made her happy. She almost hopped up to the second floor of a granite building and walked into the familiar tearoom. Lady Cho was waiting by the window. Sonju sat next to her, and they exchanged news about Gija and Yunghee when Assemblyman Kim and Professor Shin walked in together. As soon as they took off their coats and gloves and settled down, Lady Cho asked, "Do you have news about Chairman Park?"

A waitress came by. After they ordered tea, the assemblyman said, "I hear that he buries himself in work."

"I hear the same," the professor said. "Perhaps it's best to leave it up to him to decide when he is ready for social gatherings."

Lady Cho put down the cup on the table. "It has been eight months since his wife died. I am worried about him."

Professor Shin told Lady Cho, "I promise we will have a drink with him once in a while." They talked about Chairman Park's reaction to the death of his long-ailing, childless wife. After a meandering talk about his utter helplessness without his wife, Professor Shin said, "I hope my wife outlives me." Then he turned his head toward the assemblyman and said, "Unlike my friend here, I don't know if I can manage a life alone."

The assemblyman ignored his friend, ordered another cup for everyone. "Do you remember Chairman Lee? I heard he has emigrated to Brazil. He told very few people about it."

"I haven't seen him since the fall of Syngman Rhee's government." Lady Cho looked at the two men over the rim of her cup. "Did he go there for undeveloped free land?"

Professor Shin said, "To start a new life. I heard it had been hard for him since the revolution. His children were taunted."

Professor Shin scanned other people in the room before he said in a hushed voice, "Remember, he accumulated great wealth on that government contract President Syngman Rhee granted."

It was risky to be too close to great power and great wealth. Sonju leaned in and said almost in a whisper, "The people in the news … an imprisoned newspaper executive, a judge on house arrest, and who knows who else."

They changed the topic. There were too many ears close by.

After they finished the second cup of tea, Lady Cho pulled out her leather gloves from her purse. They rose to leave. Sonju looked out the window at the sky. "We are supposed to have heavy snow sometime today. I think I will go to the cottage today." She turned to Lady Cho. "Do you want to go with me?"

"No, I am meeting with an artist tomorrow morning and I don't think I can make it back to Seoul in time."

Sonju went home to pack a few things for an overnight stay at the cottage. By the time she arrived at the gate of G-62, it started to snow. Midway to the cottage, she took off her gloves, put them in her coat pocket, and walked with her arms out with a wide smile. The snowflakes grew larger. The fluffy white flowers landed lightly on her upturned face, even into her mouth and on her bare palms. The melted snow dribbled down under her collar. Wiping her face and shaking the snow off her coat, she looked up once more at the steadily falling snow before walking to the cottage.

She hung her coat in the bedroom closet, then made tea. She had packed two books with the intention of finishing them. Instead, wrapping the warm cup in her hands, she sat at the table and looked out the window watching the snow dance toward the tree branches and to the ground covering everything layer upon layer. The snow was still falling when she went to bed.

Upon waking the next morning, Sonju hurried to the living room window. The snow had stopped overnight. A blinding white blanket lay under an immense expanse of blue sky. Ten meters away, a wild rabbit hopped. Nearby, a bird shrilled. After showering, Sonju returned to the window. Staring out, she reminisced about winters in Maari and the round heaps of snow covering the sauce jars on a raised platform near the rise and Jinju poking holes in them with her finger and giggling.

A man in a long black coat with a grey scarf around his neck was walking toward the cottage. He waved at her. Two staggered rows of hollow footprints on the pristine white surface followed Assemblyman Kim. A gush of cold air entered with him.

"Hello! What brings you here?" Sonju said, closing the door.

"I wanted to come yesterday, but I thought it unwise."

Yesterday. A man and a woman alone in the late hours. Scandalous. Sonju pressed her lips.

He took off his coat, hung it on a hook near the door, and sat in a chair by the table. Sonju seated herself across from him and saw his eyes fixed on the view outside. She could sit right there looking out the window, she thought, and talk about the snow until he left. "Isn't the view almost divine?" she asked.

He turned his head to her with a smile. "Yes. I am glad to share it with you." He smiled.

His response sounded a bit personal, and she felt uncomfortable. The muscles tensed in Sonju's shoulders and neck.

He said, "Last year, I was here at the first snow. It does something to me."

"It does me too," she almost said, but she had no intention of encouraging him, so she said, "I forgot to eat. Would you like some breakfast? Tea?" Without waiting for an answer, she went to the kitchen. She rubbed her neck and rolled her shoulders and waited for the water to boil, hoping he would make this visit short. She returned with a tray of tea and heated rice cakes, and thinking she was rude not to respond to his remarks, said, "I am in awe of the snow this morning."

"It is a good day to stay in, drink tea, and enjoy the beautiful view outside," he said.

It sounded as though he meant to stay a while, and she couldn't come up with an idea to end his visit. It didn't feel right to her that they should be alone in a room. She drizzled honey over the cakes hoping he didn't notice her trying to keep her hands steady.

They chewed slowly with an awkward silence and awkward smiles. One minute seemed like ten. He knew better than to be alone with a woman, seemingly without a reason, she was telling herself. The long silence continued. She couldn't stand it but didn't know what to talk about either. She ended up saying, "Miss Im is studying in college to become a professional accountant. I began to write essays on women. I sent a few out to the newspapers but none were printed." It occurred to her then that all of the women of The Hall were engaged in something fulfilling to them. Distracted by this thought she smiled and began to feel at ease.

He said he would look for her essays in the papers because he was interested in what she had to say. The conversation turned to the news about the people they both knew, and eventually they ran out of safe topics to talk about. He left at about ten. He never told her why he came. She didn't ask.

On the way home in the afternoon, she thought her writing needed something, a pivot, and more substance. It was what he said that triggered such thought. Since Kungu, Assemblyman Kim was the first man to take her seriously.

Losses

Warm rays of the sun poured onto her face when Sonju awoke. In a week, Jinju would turn seventeen. Her daughter was born during the best time of the year. How excited she was seeing 1966 in a large print on a calendar on New Year's Day. She had just one more year to wait. Her mood rose and stirred like a canary in the spring season. She walked around the living room, then looked out the window at the garden several times. Still, her body didn't want to settle down. A stroll under the sunlight, the spring breeze, the smell of spring air, perhaps a new outfit, she thought.

She got off the bus at the Ducksu Palace stop and walked, looking at the trees with new leaves over the stone fence and along the sidewalk and noticed the cobblestones were a few shades lighter under the bright sun. She went past the city hall, then to Myungdong. It seemed half the people in the city had the same idea. At Midopa Department Store, she came upon a black-and-white houndstooth suit of European import with black trim on the collar and the sleeves. Her heart dropped when she turned over the price tag. She would rather spend the money on her daughter.

She left the store and walked along the street lined with boutique shops. The photographs of Twiggy on the fashion magazine covers were on display windows, and young women in short skirts and black fishnet stockings walked by. Sonju heard her high-heeled shoes click-clacking on the hard pavement as the hem of her skirt touched her knees. The smell of imported coffee wafted from a coffee shop. It was fashionable nowadays to drink coffee instead of tea.

"Little Auntie!"

Sonju froze. She turned. It was Jinwon from Maari. They grabbed each other's hands at the same time.

"Little Auntie, I thought it was you. How are you doing?" Jinwon's eyes gleamed and her cheeks lifted in a smile.

"I'm fine. Look at you." Sonju glanced up and down at Jinwon as if to see how tall the child had grown. She was thirty-nine, so Jinwon must be thirty-two now. Jinwon wore a plain poplin dress in periwinkle blue but no makeup. There was no glimpse of the girl who had desired a shimmering blue velvet skirt. She led Jinwon toward the wall of a stone building away from the briskly walking pedestrians. "What are you doing in Seoul?"

"I'm visiting a friend. This is my yearly vacation. I left my three children with my mother-in-law. My children want something from Myungdong every time I come to Seoul. So lucky I spotted you. You're with him?"

Take a breath, Jinwon, she was tempted to say. "No. He died in 1952."

"Oh." Jinwon's eyes and mouth drooped. "I'm so sorry." After a short pause, she asked, "What do you do now?"

"Not much, but I used to work for a businesswoman." She asked, "How is Jinju? She will turn seventeen next week."

Jinwon briefly planted her intense eyes on Sonju, then hooked her arm in Sonju's. "Where do you live, Little Auntie? Can we go to your house now?"

"Of course." Sonju laughed a little. Jinwon hadn't changed a bit. "Let's take a taxi."

Jinwon sat in the back seat with her and was unusually quiet for a while, even her body. She then said, "I thought of you often. I can't believe it's been fourteen years since I last saw you."

"Yes." She stroked Jinwon's hand, which was no longer smooth at the joints. She said, "Second House family is close to my heart." She wanted to ask about Jinju again but seeing Jinwon's eyes following the views outside, she thought she would wait. Jinwon was on vacation and there was a lot to take in all around her.

Passing Sonju's front garden, Jinwon flashed a smile, that same delighted smile of her youth. "I knew you would do things differently." When she stepped into the living room, she said, "American furniture. It suits you, Little Auntie." She made a full rotation, scanning the room. She walked to the sofa. "You still get *Life* magazines."

"Sit down at the table. Let me get you some tea." Sonju went to the kitchen to boil water. Jinwon spoke across the living room, "You know, Little Uncle and his wife live in Seoul. I should go see them before I return home. To be honest though, I dread it."

So, her daughter had been living in Seoul. But Jinju's name was not on any of the bulletin boards of the middle schools, and three years later, of the high schools. Jinwon had said what … Oh, about dreading the visit with Little Uncle and his wife.

Sonju transferred the tea to the table and tried not to look shaken. "Why would you dread seeing them?" she asked.

"His wife. Him. I don't …" Jinwon's head made a quick turn to the side, her old habit when she was disgusted with something.

Sonju decided to leave that topic alone. Sitting in her chair across from Jinwon, she said, "Now, please tell me. How is my daughter?" She took a sip and put the cup down.

Sudden tears filled Jinwon's eyes. "Oh, Little Auntie."

Sonju grabbed Jinwon's hand and whispered, "What happened to Jinju?"

"Jinju fell ill some months after you left."

Sonju squeezed Jinwon's hand and shook. The cups rattled. "What happened to my daughter?"

Jinwon held both cups to steady them with her free hand and took an audible deep breath. "She died in April the year after you left." She said in a meek voice, "I'm sorry you didn't know."

"What did you say? My Jinju died? No!" Something crashed with a terrible dissonance and was all jumbled inside of Sonju. She was confused and couldn't grasp what Jinwon said. "I waited for fourteen years. Did you say Jinju is dead? No." She shook her head, her hair flying. Then her thinking became clear. "She is *not* dead. I *saw* her from the train. I saw her on the chestnut tree. She was five. She can't be dead at four."

"Little Auntie, you must have seen Jinjin. She liked to play on that tree. It couldn't have been Jinju."

"No, no." Sonju sprang from the chair and ran to the bedroom. She returned with boxes of letters to Jinju, threw them on the floor. She brought out more boxes. Letters spilled out of the boxes. "Look. I wrote all these letters to her. Waiting for her."

Jinwon tripped getting out of her chair in a hurry, knelt on the floor, and gathered the letters and the boxes. She stacked them neatly as if that would undo the moment.

"For *eight years*," Sonju ran with her words. "I rode an express rail every Sunday to get a glimpse of her. She *cannot* be dead. I don't believe it! I waited. I waited." She let out a long mournful cry as she folded her body down and wept. "I have waited for fourteen years," she said. Please hear me, she pleaded to the world, to someone, anyone.

Jinwon covered her face with her hands and cried. They sobbed together until they were exhausted. Then they looked at each other. Jinwon's face was red and wet, but her eyes were soft. Jinwon, the child who was never seen crying even after her mother left her.

"Little Auntie, we took good care of Jinju. Second Auntie and Grandmother took her to the doctor every day," Jinwon said, but Sonju didn't want to hear the details. Not now, not tomorrow, not ever. Something was sucked out of her body. She went limp.

"Would you like to lie down, Little Auntie?"

"Yes. Please take me to my bed."

Jinwon helped her rise, put an arm around her waist, and guided her to the bed. She then brought one of the dining chairs and sat next to Sonju. Sonju closed her eyes. She didn't want to see anything, didn't want to hear anything, didn't want to talk. There was nothing to say. She lost Kungu. She lost her family. She lost Misu, even Miss Im, and the unborn baby she left behind on the rise in front of the veranda at Second House. And now Jinju. Everyone she had cared deeply about had been taken away from her. Actually, her loss had begun long ago when she found out that her mother would never love her the way other mothers loved their children. When she started school, she understood that her own country was lost to Japan, and later lost to the great powers of the world and couldn't dictate its own fate, and freedom of speech was lost under Syngman Rhee's reign and the current oppressive regime. Her mind had thus roamed, and she thought she must have been born in the wrong decade and to the wrong family.

When she opened her eyes, her daughter was watching her from the portrait on the wall. Oh, Jinju, why did you die? I did not hold you when you were sick. I am so sorry. She turned her head away. "Jinwon, would you take down Jinju's portrait and store it in the bottom drawer?" Jinwon took it down, then hesitated. "I can't bear to look at it," Sonju said. Jinwon quickly put it away and sat back in the chair.

Sonju glanced at Jinwon. That pointed chin, so much like Jinju's. "Can you stay with me? I don't think I should be alone tonight."

"Yes, Little Auntie. I'll call my friend and tell her not to wait for me." There was the muffled voice of Jinwon's whispered words into the telephone. She pattered back into the room and seated herself in the chair.

Sonju kept staring at the ceiling, saying to herself she should call Lady Cho. Silence—Five minutes, maybe ten. With a sluggish turn of her head toward Jinwon, she said, "Tell me how Jina is doing. She was a sensitive child."

Jinwon cleared her throat. "Second Uncle's family moved to Seoul three years ago, just in time for Jina to start college. She studies fine arts."

"Fine arts." Keep on talking, don't think, she told herself. "Tell me what your husband is like. How did you meet him?"

"My husband came to visit his friend, a new teacher in Maari. I was introduced to him." Jinwon leaned in. "Little Auntie, do you want anything? Water, tea?"

"No, thank you. So, you married a man you chose as you used to say you would."

247

"Yes. It was much easier than expected. When I told my family that I wanted to marry him, they didn't even argue. I think, after you left, my grandparents learned something. My grandmother told me an arranged marriage isn't for everyone. That shocked me."

Sonju saw the image of her former mother-in-law in her hobby room saying what Sonju told her was like a new adventure to her. She must have been quiet for a good length of time. "Little Auntie?" Jinwon was looking at her with her head cocked. "Ah, yes, your grandmother," Sonju said, "She can be open-minded. Tell me about your husband's family."

"They own a bookstore in Yesun. Can you imagine me married into a family of book lovers? I still don't read if I can help it."

Sonju half-smiled. "And your children? How old are they?"

"They're nine, seven, and four. Their grandparents spoil them. My husband is an only child."

"How about Second Auntie? How did she manage to join her husband?"

"Second Uncle was promoted to president of a bank in a small village some distance from Maari two years after you left, he wrote a letter to his parents that he was sick and needed his wife to take care of him. Grandmother was rattled." Jinwon smiled. "You know how my grandmother is. She was terrified of losing another son. She told Second Auntie to pack up and go to her husband immediately. Second Auntie left in two days taking the two little ones. She had another baby after you left, a girl again. She left the two older ones to save face for the family, so it didn't look like abandoning the aging parents. Jina and Chuljin cried when their mother left, especially Jina. She cried for her mother every day."

The image of Jinju crying every day for her sent tight, squeezing pain to Sonju's belly. She drew her knees up to her stomach and held her breath until the pain eased.

Jinwon asked, "Is something wrong?"

"No, I am fine. Continue."

"Grandfather passed away in 1958. Second Auntie was there to take care of him when his illness turned serious."

"Your grandfather was very kind to me," Sonju said.

Jinwon looked away. "It's not the same without him."

"What kind of wildflowers bloom on the rise in front of the veranda?" Sonju often imagined flowers blooming on the rise where her unformed child was buried.

Jinwon cocked her head for a moment. "I have no idea. I've never paid attention." She walked over to the window and looked out to the garden. "Jina talks about you. She says she remembers everything about you."

"Would she see me?" Sonju asked.

"I'll ask."

That evening, Sonju called Lady Cho with the news of Jinju. Within half an hour, there was a knock on the door. Sonju sat up in her bed hearing Lady Cho say, "You must be the niece. Thank you for being here with your aunt."

Lady Cho came into the bedroom and sat in the chair next to the bed. Without words, she held Sonju's hand and occasionally pressed it to her cheek. They didn't talk about Jinju. What could they say?

Sonju looked at Jinwon standing near the chair then at Lady Cho. "My niece is spending the night with me."

"I am glad. I will stay a little longer and come back in the morning."

After Lady Cho arrived the next morning, Jinwon left, casting a worried look at Sonju.

Lady Cho sat on the couch next to Sonju and leaned in to sweep Sonju's curly hair off her forehead. "I called Gija and Yunghee. One of them will come."

"Thank you. I didn't sleep well last night. I am going to try to sleep now." Sonju went to her bed. Lady Cho followed. Sonju looked up at Lady Cho as a child would at her mother. "Can you stay here with me?" she asked and was confused by her neediness.

"Of course," Lady Cho said. Sonju fell asleep feeling Lady

Cho's fingers combing her hair. In her dream, Sonju frantically looked for her children, a brood of them, in a vast empty field of wildflowers. But even in her dream, she knew she had only one child. She said, "I see you ..." repeating the game she and her daughter played the day before she left Maari. Upon waking, she saw Lady Cho. "Is Jinju really dead? Jinwon told me ... but did you see Jinwon?"

"Yes, she was here. You saw her leave."

Then it was not a dream. Jinju was really dead. Her daughter was not coming to her. What would she live for now? She went through the images she had of Jinju growing up to age seventeen. At the beginning, a little miracle with downy hair all over her body with all ten fingers and toes, a three-year old examining a flower, a first grader with her bangs almost touching her eyebrows. A ten-year-old playing hopscotch wearing a white blouse with an embroidered rounded collar and short navy skirt. An adolescent girl carrying a heavy school bag, walking and talking with friends to and from school in a dark navy uniform with her hair pinned on the side. A serious high school girl poring over her books. Her daughter didn't even live to age five. She fell asleep again.

She woke up and found Gija sitting next to her bed. "How long have you been here? You should have awakened me."

"Not long. Maybe an hour. Lady Cho said you needed sleep."

"I'm lucky to have you as family. We are family, aren't we?"

"We are family, Lady Yu."

Sonju wept, stopped, looked away, and wept again. She pulled up an edge of the blanket to dry the tears that ran down to her neck.

At midday, Lady Cho returned and told Gija, "I am here to relieve you. You must be busy at the restaurant."

Gija rose to leave. "Lady Yu, I brought you some food. It's in the kitchen. Don't forget to eat. I'll be back."

Sonju got out of the bed and thanked Gija. She rested her head on Lady Cho's shoulder, and said, "I feel empty, but why am I so heavy?" Lady Cho led her back to her bed.

She heard the telephone ring and also a delivery man several times. She thought she had a dream, but Lady Cho told her their former clients sent flowers and that Assemblyman Kim, Chairman Park, and Professor Shin called.

A thought flashed. Sonju bolted up. She was feverish with rage. "He has known for fourteen years and didn't tell me! Why? Why?" she cried.

Lady Cho asked with an alarmed voice, "Who? Your former husband?"

"Yes. I'm the *mother!* All those years waiting not knowing. Must he be that cruel?" Sonju covered her eyes with her arm and wept.

"I will stay with you tonight," Lady Cho said.

The following morning, Sonju insisted that she was not a patient and that Lady Cho should go home. When she was alone, she moved around not knowing what she was doing, or sat on the couch for hours looking out into the garden. During her dream, she said to Jinju, "I thought you died." But her daughter just smiled. She had once heard that in dreams, dead people don't talk.

For two weeks, the women visited daily to check on Sonju. Lady Cho said there were letters from Jinwon. Sonju battled with the vexing thought: if her husband's family had contacted her when Jinju was sick, she could have taken her to the best doctors and best hospitals in Seoul and her daughter might have lived. If she were informed of Jinju's death fourteen years ago, she might have made different life choices. She was ordered not to contact her daughter and she honored that, but not one of them contacted her when Jinju became seriously ill and died. They could have contacted her parents but none of them did. Her anger burned white.

She stared at the letters she had written to Jinju for a while. Jinwon had stacked them neatly on the floor against the wall. She knelt down and tied the fourteen birthday cards with a ribbon, put the letters in the boxes, wrapped them in a scarf, and returned them to the bureau drawer. She took her daughter's portrait, wrapped it in another scarf, and placed it on top of the letters, then Jinju's dress next to it. Afterwards, she went and opened the door to the spare room, and facing the raised alcove, imagined again Jinju performing ballet standing on her toes, arms up above her head, and spinning with a big smile, looking at her. She quietly closed the door behind her. She didn't want to enter that room.

Transformation

Sonju sat at the table and put three letters from Jinwon in order by date, then put them back down. She looked around. The room was mute as death. She dropped a pencil on the floor to hear the sound of it moving. When it stopped, she picked up the first letter.

1966 March 21

Dear Little Auntie,

I hope this finds you in a better state. I was so worried about you. I still am. I am so sorry. I assumed Little Uncle had notified you.

After I left your house, I went to visit him in his office at the Interior Ministry. I told him about you. He just listened. I am very disappointed in him.

I returned home sooner than I planned and went to Maari to visit Jinju's grave. I told her about you, about how much you missed her and loved her. I told her she shouldn't have died. I find that sometimes it helps to think the dead hear you. I used to talk to my father in my head even though I didn't have any memory of him.

I will write you again soon.

Jinwon

1966 March 26

Dear Little Auntie,

I think about you often. I remember the day you left Maari. Jina looked all over the house for you. It was Monday morning. Nobody told her where you were, so her mother finally told her that you left early in the morning for Seoul and you were not coming back. She asked, "Why? What about Jinju?" and her mother said you weren't coming back. She cried and refused to go to school the rest of the week. After you left, she slept with Jinju every night until Jinju became very ill. After Jinju died, she placed wildflowers on her grave every time we visited the burial mountain. Much later, I told her you left because you loved another man.

As soon as I returned home from Seoul, I wrote to her that I am in touch with you. She wrote back immediately and asked if you were happy after you left. She included two photographs of Jinju for you to keep. Those were taken after you left. In them, you can see signs of illness on Jinju's face.

I hope these photographs will be of some comfort to you.

Jinwon

There was no mention of how Jinju reacted to her absence. It must have been bad. Sonju grabbed her stomach and hunched over. When the knot eased, she straightened up and opened the soft rice paper wrapping. Two small photos, one of Jinju alone and the other with her cousins. Her daughter looked so tiny, much smaller than she remembered. She kept looking at the photographs until they blurred.

1966 March 29

Dear Little Auntie,

Jina wrote again to tell me how many fond memories she has of you. She talked about your red lipstick, and the time you let her stain your nails and Jinju's red with impatiens petals. She said the stain lasted for months until the last color was gone from the tips of your nails. You were the only adult that had red nails, she wrote.

Jina regrets she can't see you. Little Uncle's wife put everyone in the clan on notice that they are to have no contact with you. She thinks her husband still has feelings for you.

She had a hysterectomy two years ago, leaving her childless. She must think that makes her position weak in the eyes of the family. No one wants to anger her because of his position in the government and they may need him to secure jobs for their children. Little Uncle pacifies his temperamental wife to avoid scenes. His wife complains to everyone around her that he sleeps with easy women. Second Auntie told me he did the same when he was married to you.

How do you spend your days? I hope you are not too lonely.

Jinwon

Sonju used to feel a lump of ache in her chest for the harm she had done to her former husband, to his public image that he placed such importance on, and to his image of himself—unfit as a man, as a husband, and as a lover. She had no such remorse now. He achieved success in his career and was now sitting smugly in his high place, thinking he got even with her. She didn't care if she was wrong about this.

It was a balmy day in mid-April when Sonju walked into the roomy, upscale office. Age wore well on him. He even looked dignified. He looked up from his desk with a shocked expression. She sat across from him and calmly laid fourteen letters on his desk, one letter for each year. He shifted in his chair. Sonju started reading. She heard him clear his throat and say, "I ..." She put her hand up. He stopped.

After the reading was done, she collected the letters one at a time. She looked at him with her rage-filled eyes and said, "Sitting in this spacious office, you may think you have achieved the success you wanted. I'm here to tell you that you were an endless disappointment to me in every way—as a husband, as a lover, and more importantly as a person. Now I hear your current wife dominates you and rants publicly about your personal failings."

His expression froze. Something passed over his face. He then said, "I lost everything when I lost Jinju. I didn't know what I would say to you."

She slowly rose from the chair and left. He deserved her every word, and she was satisfied. By the time she arrived home though, guilt set in for cutting down an already broken man so harshly.

Lady Cho was determined to keep Sonju busy. They had a late lunch at Gija and Yunghee's restaurant two, three times a week. They met Professor Shin and Assemblyman Kim weekly at a coffee shop. They went to the South Gate Market and the East Gate Market to get lost in the myriad of odors and noises and colors. With all these activities Sonju slept well at night. Even she thought she was doing well.

Then ...

1966 May 13

Dear Little Auntie,
A quick note to let you know that Little Uncle got into a bad traffic accident on the way home after work. He was inebriated at the time of the accident. He is said to take medications for constant pain and is not expected to return to his job. This changes a lot of things in the family.

Sonju didn't bother to read the next line. She paced the room, then halted as if struck by Jinju's ghost when she saw the door she hadn't opened since March. Leaning on the door, she wept begging for her daughter's forgiveness for disappointing her, telling her she knew she loved her father. Sonju took Jinwon's letter outside with a match and watched it burn to ash.

She tried to focus on something beautiful and gentle. She gardened. This summer, her climbing roses were studded with blooms and covered the entire fence in bright pink. Since the start of the garden three years before, she had watched every plant and shrub grow and fill the garden a little more each year. Many neighbors and passersby made comments. She weeded and pruned, and when done, came inside to remove the black dirt from under her nails, only to repeat it a few days later. In the flowers and bees and butterflies and ladybugs, she saw Jinju.

There came three knocks on the door. It was her sister. Entering the house, she said, "Oh, the garden is so pretty. I like the way you lowered the fence. And no gate."

"Thank you." Sonju said, forcing a smile.

Sitting on the couch, her sister said, "I can't stay long. You understand, three boys and a husband."

"How are they and Mother?"

"Mother is the same. My children are growing fast. The oldest one is in college and the second one is preparing for a college entrance examination. My husband expanded his practice and has three doctors working under him."

"I'm glad things are going well for you," Sonju said. Should she tell her sister about her daughter? What would be the point of telling? She didn't want pity, but she didn't want her family to think she was still waiting for Jinju either. After reconsidering, she said, "I recently learned that Jinju died the year after I left Maari."

Instantly, her sister's eyes welled up with tears. She pulled out a handkerchief from her purse, and dabbing her eyes, said, "I don't know what to say." She sniffled. "I feel bad the way ..." She clutched the handkerchief. "I should have stood up for you when our parents disowned you, but I didn't have the courage to go against the family's wishes."

"I should've been the one to stand up for Kungu, but I failed," Sonju said. "After I married, I always had a feeling that I would not be welcomed home for many years. So, when Mother and Father disowned me, it wasn't a surprise." She saw sadness in her sister's face. "I'm fine now. I learned that I can overcome difficulties no matter how devastating."

After her sister left, she felt saddened that her family had not met Kungu or Jinju. If she had brought her daughter to her family, they would have known her as a living person. Jinju had once lived. Kungu had once lived. They mattered because they had once lived.

The next day, her sister returned with their mother. Her mother looked at Sonju, sighed and said, "Why is your fate so harsh?"

"It is not fate, Mother." Sonju said it with such sharpness that she looked down briefly in shame. She had said to herself before that she wanted to reconcile with her mother.

Her sister gently tugged her mother's skirt. Her mother waved off her daughter's hand. "Since you no longer work at such a job, maybe one day your brother and his family will see you."

Sonju's stomach churned. She reminded herself not to react to her mother. She took a deep breath and said calmly, "There was once a time when I hoped you would say, 'Enough time has passed. Why don't you visit home?' But it didn't come, not after Kungu died, not even when Father was dying. I wanted to apologize to him for bringing shame to our family."

Her mother's face fell. Suddenly, she looked old. Wringing her hands, her sister glanced at her mother, then at Sonju.

"Mother," Sonju softened her voice. "For a long time, I resented you for separating me from Kungu. I even blamed you every time my marriage turned sour. I know you thought it best for me and the family, but just as you could not imagine my life being different from yours, I could not imagine unquestioningly following your conventions."

"You would have had an easier life if you did."

"But I didn't want your life," she said.

Thick silence descended between them like an early morning fog in the valley. After a few muted words among them, her sister and mother rose, looking sad as they left. Who knew her mother's decision not to allow Sonju marry Kungu would set the stage for such a disruption in the whole family? Some might say that if only she had stayed in the marriage, she alone would have suffered. Was sacrificing one for the comfort of many a valid ethical argument?

She sank down on the couch and shut her eyes. She saw her mother's lavender jade hairpin, the symbol of her humiliation and lost prestige. She understood her mother's own dream to relive her life through her daughters. She herself had once had such a dream for Jinju. Their dreams for the next generation were the results of their own desires being denied, and in her case, her mother was the one who did the denying. Catching herself teetering on anger, she shifted her thoughts to her mother's hairpin that always elicited in her tender feelings toward her mother, and so it went, running circles in her head.

She still saw Jinju at every age that she had imagined. It made her happy. She watched the fall flowers come up in her garden. She didn't catch the first snow of the year at the cottage. Spring lilies came up again. Soon the roses trailed over the fence and drew admiring people. Some children snatched a few.

Jinwon continued to write. In early March, she had written how difficult it was to see her grandmother all alone playing cards by herself. Her grandmother didn't weave any longer, but after the spring thaw, she visited Big House Lady who was in ill health.

Four months later, Sonju received another letter.

1967 July 1

Dear Little Auntie,

Big House Lady passed away in June. I am worried about my grandmother. She doesn't look well. She looks like she is waiting to die, especially with Big House Lady gone.

I go to Maari with a heavy heart. There aren't many clan men left there. With both my grandfather and Big House Master gone, the farm needs young clan men to replace them, but their professions keep them in Seoul. Maari has become a place of old people, especially of widows. It has become just another village the young have abandoned.

The soil is no longer fertile. Now they use chemical fertil-

izers. Second Uncle has a hard time finding seasonal work-
ers. The village young leave for city life where they can make
more money in factories. Some leave for Vietnam to fight the
communists in the pay of the American government. They
send home good money, I hear. With all these changes, you
can see now only a hint of the clan's old wealth and pride.

Second Auntie told me the farm has become a financial
burden to them. She wants to sell a portion of the farmland
to invest in real estate in Seoul, but her husband won't hear
of it. He tells her it's his ancestors' land to be passed down to
the next generation, not his. He is a romantic.

I hope you are doing well.

Jinwon

Who would have guessed that Jinwon would be the keeper of
the Second House Family's soul? Yet here she was, the only one
to mourn the death of the old glory. Sonju felt sorrow about
her former mother-in-law, the once forceful matriarch who was
made powerless by the changing tide of the nation. She put
away the letter. With rapid industrialization, farmland was no
longer the wellspring of wealth. People were more agile and mo-
bile seeking financial advancement. In the midst of so much
change, the administration's oppression to stem the protests of
the disaffected was becoming ever harsher.

Then in October came a short letter from Jinwon. Her
grandmother had passed away calling her father's name. Sonju
sat quietly for a while before she stepped out to the side garden.
She knelt in front of the white chrysanthemums and stroked each
floret that curled like a spoon as she had stroked the hands of
her mother-in-law whom she had grown to love like a mother.

Sonju didn't have to comb through the newspapers. It was
quite evident that Seoul was changing at an accelerated pace.
She saw more and more shiny things and conveniences all
lined up in the shops every time she walked out of her house.
More luxury goods were pouring in from Japan, Europe, and

America. More factories were being built. Textile export was increasing. Office spaces were filled with small businesses of all kinds. There were more office workers, more students, more merchants. There were bigger crowds on the streets and in the marketplaces. Buses were packed during rush hours. Newspapers reported that an influx of people from rural areas and small towns converging into Seoul looking for jobs contributed to the rapid population expansion. Real estate boomed. Housing shortages placed homeownership out of reach for many working families, and the rich got richer. The government-backed *chaebols* with their conglomerates possessed a larger and larger share of national wealth.

People now might wear better clothes, might have electric fans and electric irons, and even televisions, but they could not speak freely about anything related to the government. University students concerned about expanding the Korean government's relations with Japan continued to protest even at the risk of imprisonment. "Never trust the Japanese. Remember what they did to us," people young and old said. Many were born after the Japanese occupation had ended and hadn't experienced what Sonju and others had, but to most Koreans, distrust and animosity toward Japan were a national inheritance, a collective attitude, and they aimed to remember that wounded national pride.

Mother's Letter, 1968

On a misty day in April the following year, Sonju received a telegram from her sister that her mother had a stroke and passed away. She took the news calmly. Her mother was dead. She could bear the loss. She became aware of silence in the house. Death always brought silence. Then, without warning, a deluge of feelings came. She wept until she was emptied out.

A week later, her sister came with a mourner's bow on her hair and handed her a sealed envelope with Sonju's name on it. "I found it among Mother's things."

Sonju put it aside and asked, "Did Mother die peacefully?"

"She was unconscious when our sister-in-law found her. She never woke up."

Sonju nodded.

Her sister said, "After Father passed away, I visited Mother twice a month. The last time I was there, she received news that her sister passed away after a short illness. I didn't know we had an aunt, did you?"

"When I was fifteen, I met her at our grandfather's birthday gathering." Poor Aunt, Sonju thought. She had wanted to be in touch with her aunt, but doing so had seemed a betrayal to her mother.

"You never told me," her sister said.

"Mother hadn't, so I felt that it wasn't up to me to tell."

Her sister dropped it, but said, "Mother was distraught at the news. She didn't weep, but she looked lost. I have never seen her that way, so it was surprising to me. Then she did something odd. She took off her jade hair pin and replaced it with an onyx pin."

After her sister left, Sonju took out the two thinking-stones from the bureau and started rolling them. She had lost too many people. She was only forty-one.

It was evening when she opened her mother's letter.

1968, April 2

Dear Sonju,

*After my sister's passing, I have examined my own deci-
sions made over the years. It would have been better for you
and for all of us if your father and I had allowed you to marry the man you wanted. But I could not be the person who
yielded to this changing social order that eroded our family's
esteem and honor even though losing this battle was inevita-
ble. I am at peace with your own fight for your future. My
hope is that you won't judge me too harshly after I am gone.*

Her mother who had always brought on a trembling of her fingers and a hardening of her jaw, her mother always upright in
her posture and certain of her position—she would no longer
knock on her door to find out how her shamed daughter was
getting along in life.

Sonju had been angry at her mother ever since she could
remember. Now she felt only sorrow that things couldn't be
otherwise. She recalled what Second Sister had said after her
father died, that she felt like an orphan. As much angst as existed
between her and her mother, there was something between them
beyond their filial connection. She tried to form this something
into words—their deep conviction that originated from the same
starting point, which was the desire to be in a certain place in
the world. She now believed she was her mother's closest and
best understood child, and suddenly, she felt lost like an orphan.

Sonju had been writing. Some things were for her to keep, not
for others to read. When she thought her writing was good
enough, she sent out fourteen essays to the newspapers, and
only two made it to print. Others—about domestic violence,
divorce, women's custody and property rights—must have been
too radical for 1968 Korea.

She hadn't forgotten about her idea of doing something

good for the country in her own way and didn't think writing alone was enough.

An idea came when her realtor telephoned her. He had helped her purchase and sell a dozen properties over the years. He said that there was an eager buyer for the corner commercial lot she had owned since 1960, the year of the April Revolution. After eight years, its value had appreciated enough for her to buy a building with multiple stores. It would provide a steady income. She and the realtor looked at properties all throughout the monsoon rain and August heat. In September, Sonju completed a transaction for the purchase of a two-story building that had three storefronts on the first floor and an English Language academy with three classrooms on the second, each with a solid profit history.

She had the stamped contract in her purse. When she pushed the glass door open into the stationery shop, little bells jangled above her head. "Please come in," a neatly dressed middle-aged man said, standing between the aisles.

Two young girls were chatting and studying colorful ballpoint pens in one aisle, and in the other, a young woman was looking at greeting cards. Seeing that the stationer was busy, Sonju introduced herself, pulled out a piece of paper from her purse, and wrote her contact information. He took it with both hands and bowed.

At the next shop, a plain-looking woman in her late-twenties was checking the bottles and small boxes on the shelves in one of the glass cabinets behind the counter. On the side wall hung her diploma from Ewha Womans University.

When Sonju introduced herself, the pharmacist bowed. "Ah, the new owner. I didn't expect a woman."

Sonju smiled. "I am happy to see a woman pharmacist."

A customer came in. Sonju gave the pharmacist her contact information and went to the next door. Tall bookshelves covered three walls and there was a long table in the center with books piled high. Several high school boys were thumbing through textbook supplements. A small woman finished rearranging books on one shelf and came toward Sonju smiling. "May I help you?"

"I love the smell of ink and paper. I came to introduce

myself. I am Yu Sonju, the new owner of the building. I see that you named the store *Camus*."

"Yes, I read *The Stranger* in college and was deeply affected by it."

The bookstore owner looked to be in her early thirties. Perhaps she had a husband and a couple of children. Sonju bought two books for Gija.

She walked upstairs at the end of the building. Adult English conversation classes were in session. She went to a small office tucked between two classrooms and met the academy owner and a secretary. All three classrooms seemed full. Sonju was aware that with the increased international trading, a person able to communicate in English could secure a decent position in a reputable corporation.

From the street, she glanced back toward the pharmacy and the bookstore. Change for women was coming to the nation without her screaming for it.

She barely got out of her suit and changed into a dress when Lady Cho rang the bell. "Come in. I just came home. The building is mine as of today."

Lady Cho seated herself on the couch. "That is a good buy. You will do well with it."

"I met the tenants. The pharmacist and the bookstore owner are women. When I heard the English lessons going on in the classrooms upstairs, I thought of Roger teaching Miss Im and me English. I met the stationer too. He had long, lean hands with clean nails."

Lady Cho chuckled. "Clean nails."

"I noticed them." She didn't mention that his hands looked much like Kungu's.

"Have you noticed Assemblyman Kim's interest in you?" Lady Cho asked seemingly off-handedly.

Surprised at the question, Sonju's heart stuttered a bit. She wished she hadn't heard this because she still remembered her discomfort at being with him alone at the cottage. She said, "I always thought the two of you had special feelings for each other, which makes perfect sense."

"We are friends. Nothing more."

Sonju's insides squirmed. Warmth began to crawl up to her face. "He knows I was once married."

"So was he."

"Let me make some tea." Sonju went to the kitchen touching her face to cool it down and tried to come up with another topic they could talk about. She returned with tea, and with enthusiasm, said, "The cook's son has found work. She called me." No one knew about his arrest for leading a student protest. The cook told Lady Cho and Sonju only after he was released. She said she hadn't wanted anyone to know because she heard that KCIA agents conducted surveillance on people affiliated with a suspect. He left the prison with two disadvantages in life—termination from his university and a permanent criminal record.

"I am glad," Lady Cho said. "The sad part is that he was finally turning himself around."

Sonju said. "The cook was so proud to have a son soon to graduate from college." He had already served the country by completing his compulsory military service after his sophomore year in college.

Lady Cho said, "He is still young. There are a lot of things he can do."

Lady Cho always focused on what a person was able to do. Sonju, on the other hand, complained all the time. She couldn't help it. "I am glad students keep protesting," she said. Sonju considered those students the nation's guardians. They watched the government. President Park's push for rapid industrialization had improved the economy, but they were not living in democracy. Sonju then hoped that the topic of Assemblyman Kim's interest in her would never arise again.

That she had at times caught the assemblyman's eyes on her was one thing, but being told that he was interested in her was quite another. Now she would look at him differently every time she saw him, and that changed things already in her mind.

Even now on the way to G-62, her head swaying side to side and bobbing up and down at every bump and dip the bus met on the road, she regarded the assemblyman's purported interest in her with mild annoyance and discomfort.

When she reached the cottage, she dropped off her overnight bag and walked the gallery ground, stepping on the fallen leaves, and once in a while, breaking dead twigs off shrubs. She stopped to look up at the flat grey November sky, and afterwards, made four more rounds before she returned to the cottage and lay down on the couch.

From somewhere nearby came a series of high-pitched barks. The noise woke Sonju from her nap. She rose and looked out. In the back lawn, a dog she hadn't seen before was barking, looking up into the midair where two birds were shrieking in a fight. The gardener's wife shouted, "Stop, you silly boy." The dog kept on barking, his head and mouth shaking in great agitation. She yelled again, this time louder, "Stop that barking! Come here!" The dog tucked his tail, put his head down, and walked slowly toward his owner.

Below the branches, Sonju saw a figure walk across the lawn toward the cottage. Was Lady Cho to meet the assemblyman here? If she had known, she wouldn't have come. It would be so awkward to be alone with him in the same room after being told about his interest in her. She hesitated before opening the door.

"Please come in. Is Lady Cho meeting you here?"

He looked confused, then said, "No. I didn't talk to her. I took a chance of seeing you here."

Now her heart tumbled and didn't know where to go. "So … you guessed right then." She didn't like the way her words came out—a bit brusque.

"I would like some tea if it's not an imposition on you," he said, moving closer to the table.

"Not at all. I was going to have some myself. Please sit." Sonju went to the kitchen. Her hands forgot what to do. She stared down at them and squeezed a few times.

When she came to the table with tea, she could tell by the

look of the nervous smile flickering around his mouth that he was trying to appear at ease.

She gave him a quick, thin smile and sat down across from him and picked up a cup, avoiding his eyes, uncomfortably conscious of his firm presence. After a sip, she slowly lifted her eyes.

He put down his cup after a few sips, looked at her, and said, "I don't know how to say this." He shifted ever so slightly in his chair. "We have known each other for a long time." He paused and touched the rim of his saucer. "I respect you and I am very fond of you. This might be premature, but I came to see if there is any chance at all ... for us."

Sonju remained still, but not one part of her mind was calm. She could almost hear the drumbeat in her heart. She held her breath, one, two, three, four ...

He chuckled. "I am quite clumsy at this. Why is it that I can talk to the President and foreign dignitaries without being nervous, yet I have a hard time saying this to you?" He took another sip, watching her.

She said, "I think of you as a former client, a good friend, a confidant, even."

"Now you know where I stand. That is a good start, don't you think?"

She stalled. When words eventually reached her mouth, they poured out all wrong. "I left my husband for another man, a childhood friend." Why did she say that? He didn't have to know about Kungu. What a relief it was then that he showed not a flinch, not a frown, no lifting of eyes.

He said, "I was married to a woman I didn't have feelings for. For the first time in my life, I find myself quite taken." She stayed still. "Can I see you from time to time alone?" he asked.

She considered his request. Her life had its own rhythm, pace and flavor that pleased her. If she agreed to a courtship, she wondered how much would it change her life especially because of who he was, a public person. She said, "My life is good now. I am afraid to disturb it."

"I don't intend to change you."

As she had told Lady Cho not long ago, there were still things she had to figure out about herself, so she said, "I am not yet certain of myself, so how can I include you in my life?"

"Sometimes, you come to know yourself through others."

Sonju mulled over his words, but unease clung like wet cloth on her skin. "There will be a scandal because of me," she said.

"Let them talk."

His words reminded her of what her maid had said when she was unsure about taking the job at The Hall: "What are they to you?"

Before she was to see him again, Sonju paced in her house. This was a bad idea, she kept thinking, even on the bus to the cottage.

Seeing him approach the door, she swallowed a big breath and let it out in one long exhale before she faced him at the door.

He hung his coat on the hook near the door and waited by the table for her to sit. They drank tea. He was fifty-two, eleven years older than she. Gentle creases extended from his nose toward the outer corners of his mouth. At his temples, some hair was greying. She had known him for over fifteen years, but hadn't noticed before how likable a face he had.

She smiled. He smiled back in awkward silence. She pushed her cup aside. "How do we ... start?" she asked, her voice halting and weak.

After he did the same with his cup, he said, "We talk."

A short nervous laugh escaped from Sonju. Clasping her hands under the table, she said, "This is how I start. When I was young, I knew a boy," she stopped here, suddenly overcome with a certain sentiment. She resumed, "Together we were to chart a modern life as equal partners. My ideas were big then, perhaps much too big for me and for the time. I now lead a small, unencumbered life, which pleases me." She looked at him with a faint smile. "I want to hear about yours."

"I have always tried to do my best in everything I do.

Throughout my marriage, I tried hard not to hurt my wife. I spent a lot of time away from home. That was how I was able to tolerate my marriage. My wife took my absence as a part of my job and never complained. In the process though, I lost something valuable. I don't think my children know me. I don't think I know them. I regret that."

His honesty and openness eased her mind. She loosened her shoulders and hands. "My mother forced me into an arranged marriage." She took a sip of tea. "My former husband and I believed in very different things. It was wrong of me to have an affair, but I never regretted it. The man suddenly died less than a year after I joined him. Six months later, I started working at The Hall."

All through December and January, they talked. She learned about his three married children. She talked about the dreams she had had for her daughter. Warm feelings toward him started welling up in her. As their courtship progressed, she worried that he would be talked about because of her, and his children would be affected by it. How would he explain her to his family, colleagues, friends?

Coming into Her Own, 1969

Sonju was at a coffee shop in Myungdong. Lady Cho had news. "Professor Shin told me Chairman Park left for Europe for a month-long tour."

"I think a change of scenery is good for him," Sonju said.

A group of young men and women came and took the empty seats behind Lady Cho. They seemed to be college students. The girls were lovely in their wool miniskirts and boots. They were an animated bunch, chatting away and laughing. A few of their words jumped out.

Sonju smiled in their direction and then at Lady Cho. "I wrote to Jinju once that there are things beyond Korea, that there are things to see and to experience." Her voice was high and light like the college students' when she said, "Let's go to America and Europe one day."

"Yes, let's. We will visit Miss Im and Roger. We will see how American she is now." Lady Cho laughed, then turned serious. "On the phone, you said you had something to discuss."

Sonju took a sip of coffee. "The income from my building has been stable. I am now ready to set up a scholarship for motivated girls who can't afford to go to college."

"I always knew you would do something."

"I haven't figured out how to set it up. I want to remain anonymous. Do you have any idea how I should go about selecting the students? I can do two a year, so that will be eight a year all together once I get it going for a four-year university education."

"Hmm. Let me think ... I can help, but Assemblyman Kim would be a better person to help you with that. A request from him will be taken more seriously by the schools."

Sonju hadn't wanted to rely on him, but he would be taken more seriously not only because of his position but also because of his gender.

The following week, Sonju told him about her plan. "The recipients will not know me. I prefer not to be involved in the selection process. I need your help."

"What type of students would you consider?" he asked.

"Highly motivated, public-minded girls, those who will be able to help many others. At some point, I want an art student in honor of Artist Ilchon."

In February, a month before the first semester began, the assemblyman told Sonju, "I met with students that the schools have recommended. I chose two. One wanted to be an attorney, the other a writer. I told them that their benefactor is a woman. I hope you don't mind. I thought it was important for them to know."

Things were good. The cook had been in relatively good health and her son recently started a metals-recycling business. Yunghee almost married three times in the last two years. She took the last breakup hard even though she was the one doing the breaking up. Gija still bought books from used bookstores and still sported simply cut clothes in muted colors. Miss Im wrote about her seasonal melancholy of missing cherry blossoms, fall colors, and winter snow. She became a certified public accountant.

On the first day of spring, Sonju's sister came to visit with a box of French pastries from a bakery. Her sister kept her life separate from Sonju's and Sonju did the same, not expecting to visit her sister's family or meet her friends. Even though their conversations had become more relaxed, especially after their mother's death, they never talked long. Her sister took a sip of coffee and said her two younger sons in college have to serve in the military very soon. "I'm working on getting them to serve with the American troops. It's known to be much more humane. And they can learn to speak English."

Sonju thought about the cook's son who struggled in high school without the benefit of private tutors like her sister's boys, and he completed his military duty in the regular Army.

Sonju asked without thinking, "So, what does it take to get

those coveted posts for your sons? Bribe someone?" Her sister stirred her coffee with a spoon. Sonju didn't mean to be cynical about her overly privileged sister. Perhaps she did, because she made the situation even worse by saying, "I was thinking about all those young men in regular Army who don't have connections or money to bribe, not about bribery being illegal." She winced at her own words. She watched her sister drink coffee quietly with her eyes down. She decided to try another option. "I'm getting married in May."

Her sister's eyes opened wide with a big smile. She put down the cup. "Who is he?"

"Assemblyman Kim Yungsik. I have known him for many years."

There was a spark in her sister's eyes. "I have voted for him! And now he'll be my brother-in-law! I'm so happy for you."

A few days later, her brother called. "Sister, how are you? It's been a long time since I saw you. You should come and meet my wife and children."

A sickening feeling shot up all the way to Sonju's head and then settled down in her stomach. She shut her eyes and pulled her brows tight. She needed a moment of stillness.

"Sister, Sister? Are you there?"

"... Yes. You have children."

"Four. They are anxious to meet you."

"As you said, much time has passed. I'm content with the way things are. Let that be." She hung up before he said another word.

It wouldn't be just her brother. There would be many—those who used to know her and others who would know her—they would see her as a path to the assemblyman. Would she come to regret her decision to marry him? The image of him, his surprising innocence for a worldly man in his fifties, his willingness to love a woman with all he had to give—Could she give him up? She had been the happiest when she loved without holding back, and she loved this man. Was she strong enough not to lose herself as an assemblyman's wife? Could she withstand the public's criticism of her past? Because during her days with Kungu, she cowered in fear of criticism. And during her days at The Hall, she hid herself from others.

After much thought, she realized she didn't have to give him up. It was her life. The power not to let others dictate her life was always hers. At that moment of clarity, she felt a sudden surge of happiness and vigor. Forgetting thirst and hunger and hardly moving away from the table, she wrote until she finished an essay. She titled it *Six Letters to a Daughter* and sent it to all five newspapers. Two weeks later, one company contacted her and asked her if she would change the title to *Letters to a Daughter*. If the readers' responses were strong, it could turn into a series. Sonju immediately called Lady Cho to share the news. Imbedded in the subsequent *Letters* were many of the same ideas in her rejected essays.

She hummed. Sometimes while dusting the furniture or washing the dishes, she hummed "best roads and bridges, roads and bridges" over and over, picturing Jinju clapping her hands and reciting, "best roads and bridges, roads and bridges."

A whiff of April air blew in through the open door of her living room that faced the side garden. Sonju was listening to the flock of birds in loud arguments outside and didn't hear the first knock on the front door.

"It's me." Misu called out.

Sonju stiffened for a moment. She would be nice, she told herself, and ran to the door. "Misu! What a surprise! I haven't seen you in such a long time. Come in."

Misu sat on the couch. "I saw your sister the other day. She told me your mother had passed away. I heard about your daughter too. I am sorry that you had to suffer so much."

Sonju smiled. "Who would I have become without having suffered? I don't remember ever having wanted an easy life." She pointed to a pitcher of barley tea on the table. "Tea?"

Misu nodded without taking her eyes off of Sonju. "I

read your essays in the paper. Sometimes I think about the three of us in that church garden and what you and Kungu had talked about."

"Me too."

Sonju missed Kungu and all that he had stood for. She told him Misu had come to visit. She told him she was fine with all the choices she had made in her life. Some were good, some were bad, and many were misguided. That was simply how she did her living, she told him.

Sonju put her hair up, put on a cream-colored wool suit, and went to a national museum in Kyungbok Palace. Walking towards her, Assemblyman Kim gave her a nod.

It was their very first time alone together in public. She walked by his side, not three steps behind him. She wasn't his shadow. A few people recognized him and stared at them, which caused her to say to herself, Let them talk, what are they to me? They are not important in my life. After all, she wasn't born to be approved of by others.

He turned and looked at her after they walked beyond the ogling people and asked, "How are you doing with people's stares?"

"I'm fine. I have words lovingly given to keep me steady."

He smiled. "We will be in public places more. I am looking forward to presenting myself to people as the husband of an essayist. By the way, my sons said they couldn't wait to see us married. My daughter may take more time."

"We have the rest of our lives."

Acknowledgments

I am fortunate to work with Kim Davis, the Director of Madville Publishing. After reading my manuscript, she emailed me with the heading, I read straight through. I appreciate her collaboration and her instinct to deeply care about the authors she represents. Thank you, Kim Davis.

I express gratitude to my book-loving friends and the members of my critique groups who lent their support in the writing of this novel.

My special thanks go to Kathryn Berck, Kenneth Bennight, and Barbara Lazar. Published authors themselves, they offered unsparing criticism that helped me grow as a writer. I learned so much from them.

Jean Jackson, Susan Chandler, Valory Pierce, Trudy Barnum, Maria Martinez, Janet Alyn, Jane Dreyfus, Jim Murray, the late John Friedland, and Yogendra Thami, I thank you for sharing the journey with me in our common pursuit of better storytelling.

Stewart Smith, Barbara Stover, Janice and Albert Clayton, June McManus, Carolyn and Richard Wiggins, Ann Marie Rehner, Mary McCormick, Felice Seifert, Sharon Rauch, Janina Kuzma, and Kathleen Kraft, my gratitude goes to each of you for reading my manuscript and offering feedback.

Separate thanks go to Sharon Marr who read my first draft with great enthusiasm as if it were her own. She offered ideas to improve the story, a few of which I incorporated in this novel. She read it again at a later stage and sent me a 9-page report with additional suggestions.

I am grateful to Fran Vetters. I turned to her for a second reading when the manuscript was close to being finalized.

I want to thank Reggie Scott Young, a poet, a writer, and an educator, for advising me and encouraging me when I was struggling to elevate my writing.

This novel wouldn't be what it came to be without the help of my daughter, Suanne Chang-Ponce. Throughout the process of completing this novel, she offered thoroughly honest, fearless criticism, and creative ideas. Thank you, Suanne.

My sister in Korea, Chang Soon-Jee, helped me with her memories of wartime experiences. Also, with unwavering support for my determination to write are my son, Dennis J. Bilbe, Jr. and my husband, Bernard Rauch.

I am very fortunate to have received support from each of you who took part in bringing *Sonju* to fruition.

About the Author

Wondra Chang was born in South Korea and has lived in the U.S. since 1970. Her writing discipline began at age ten, writing five short stories a day under the tutelage of a writing teacher. She won first place in a province-wide in-person writing competition. She studied journalism at Ewha Womans University in Seoul, Korea. She currently lives in San Antonio, Texas, with her husband, Bernard Rauch.

Readers' Guide

1. What was your expectation as a reader after you read the first page?

2. How would you describe Sonju?

3. What characters stood out for you and why?

4. Anger plays a big role in Sonju's life. Her anger began with the humiliation of succumbing to her mother and to the occupiers. How do these early experiences shape her thinking?

5. Sonju's views of places and people change over time. Discuss why this is important to the story.

6. There are two suicides in this book. How does Sonju justify Kungu's suicide and how does Lady Cho deal with her guilt about her husband's suicide?

7. What aspects of the human cost of war does Sonju worry about most even before she reconnects with Kungu?

8. How did Sonju come to understand that she was her mother's best understood child? How are Sonju and her mother similar to each other? How are they different?

9. What images and actions happen repeatedly?

10. Sonju is furious about her former husband's silence about her daughter's death. She thinks she could have made different life choices if she had known about it earlier. How would her life have been different? In what ways, does the waiting for her daughter sustain her sense of purpose and give her pleasure during the fourteen-year waiting period?

11. After she learns about her daughter's death, she puts away

the reminders of her daughter (the portrait, the photographs, the letters), but later she feels happy recalling the images she created of her daughter growing up to age seventeen. Discuss Sonju's particular way of dealing with the loss of a loved one and if this is helpful for others as well.

12. Sonju has strong views about class, poverty, and women's place in society. Those issues still remain today even in developed countries. Share your views.

13. Can Koreans' attitude toward the Japanese in the book be generally inferred to the pathos of other groups of people who have been historically oppressed?

14. This book is partly a story of loss, betrayal, and resilience. Sonju says to her childhood friend, Misu, "Who would I have become without having suffered? I don't remember ever having wanted an easy life." What are your thoughts about what she says?

15. The theme of *Sonju* is that of personal freedom internally attained versus externally given. Is either possible without the other? If so, how and if not, why?

16. Sonju's journey in life parallels that of her nation to some degree. How are they similar and different?

17. In the book, Sonju talks to Kungu even after his death. Toward the end of the book, she tells him that *she was fine with all the choices she made in her life. Some were good, some were bad, and many were misguided. That was simply how she did her living.* What do you think about her statement?

18. The book opens in 1946 when Sonju is 19 and ends in 1968 when she is forty-one. How does she change as a person and how does she remain the same? Do you think that is how we evolve over time?

CPSIA information can be obtained
at www.ICGtesting.com
Printed in the USA
LVHW030442220821
695831LV00002B/176

9 781948 692588